Praise for

"*Her Husband's Harlot* is a pleasing, out of the ordinary read."
--*Dear Author*

"Erotic historical romance isn't as plentiful as many would think, but here you have a very well-written example of this genre. It's entertaining and fun and a darn good read."--*The Book Binge*

"I devoured this book in a couple of hours! .... If you love a story with a heroine who is a wallflower with a backbone of steel or a damaged hero then you will love this one too."--5 star review from *LoveRomancePassion.com* on *Her Wanton Wager*

"I found this to be an exceptional novel. I recommend it to anyone who wants to get lost in a good book, because I certainly was."--A Top Pick from *NightOwlReviews.com*

"I thoroughly enjoyed this story. Grace Callaway is a remarkable writer."--*LoveRomancePassion.com* on *Her Prodigal Passion*

"The depth of the characters was wonderful and I was immediately cheering for both of them."--*Buried Under Romance*

"Grace Callaway is one of my favorite authors because of her fearlessness in writing love scenes that truly get the blood pumping."--*Juicy Reviews*

Books by Grace Callaway

HEART OF ENQUIRY
The Widow Vanishes
The Duke Who Knew Too Much
M is for Marquess
The Lady Who Came in from the Cold
The Viscount Always Knocks Twice
Never Say Never to an Earl
The Gentleman Who Loved Me (Summer 2017)

MAYHEM IN MAYFAIR
Her Husband's Harlot
Her Wanton Wager
Her Protector's Pleasure
Her Prodigal Passion

CHRONICLES OF ABIGAIL JONES
Abigail Jones
Abigail Jones and the Asylum of Secrets (2017)

Her Wanton WAGER

GRACE CALLAWAY

NATIONAL BESTSELLING AUTHOR

Her Wanton Wager is a work of fiction. Names, characters, places, and incidents are the products of the author's imagination and are used fictitiously. Any resemblance to actual events, locales, or persons, living or dead, is entirely coincidental.

Published in the United States

Cover design: © Seductive Musings Designs
Images: © Period Images

Printed in the United States of America

Acknowledgements

As ever, I owe a debt of gratitude to all of you who have encouraged and supported my work. Tina, I couldn't have done this without you—and even if I could, it wouldn't have been half as fun. You rock, girl. Virna, thank you for sharing your keen writer's mind and generous spirit.

Diane, you continue to amaze me with your astuteness and wisdom; both my writing and I have gained so much from knowing you.

To my family, who shows unbelievable grace in living with a writer. Thanks for not only putting up with me, but cheering me on. To my guys: Brendan, buddy, you make me so proud each and every day. Brian, your love is my inspiration. Without you, there'd be no happy ending—and a lot of typos, since you do double duty as husband and editor par excellence.

And to my readers: your support has made all the difference. Writing can be a lonely journey unless it is shared. Thank you for being part of my adventure.

Prologue

SHROUDED IN FOG, still as death upon the dark water, the ship lay in wait.

As dawn's chill seeped through the boy's thin rags, he fought off a shiver and kept the snarl fixed upon his face. Inside, he was trembling worse than a leaf. *Whatever happens, show no fear. Be brave. Look strong.* Ten years in the stews had taught him what happened to the weak. Once, he'd been foolish enough to hope for mercy, and now he was paying the price.

"Step lively now, or you'll feel the lash of this 'ere whip!"

The guard's warning prodded him to fall in line with the other convicts. He stumbled up the gangplank to the ship, irons clanking heavily against his ankles. He kept his head down; he couldn't look at the looming hell that was his future. The hulk's fetid breath wafted over him, and his insides lurched. Misery—he knew it by stench. Had lived and breathed it in the flash house he'd called home.

"Move on," the guard shouted.

Heart thudding, the boy realized he'd reached the ship's entrance. His feet wouldn't move; for some reason, he couldn't make them.

"What 'ave we 'ere? A troublemaker?" A hand wrenched him up by the scruff, and the boy found himself staring into the guard's cruel eyes. "Well, 'ere on the hulks there's a place for guttersnipe like you—to the Tiger's Den!"

The boy struggled, lashing out futilely with his arms and legs while the other prisoners roared with laughter. The guard dragged him aboard the ship and to a trapdoor crisscrossed with chains. Releasing the padlock, the man shoved him toward the gaping hold.

"No!" Despite his earlier vow to be brave, the plea was wrung from the boy's lips. He couldn't return to the darkness, he couldn't. "Please, sir, have mercy—"

With a rough thrust, the guard sent him down the steps into the shadows. Frantically, the boy tried to climb back up toward the door, but the square of light disappeared with a slam. The chains clanked, sealing him in. Trapping him in the stinking black bowels. Memories of darkness spiraled around him: the ash-choked stacks, the master's chamber. A sob wedged in his throat.

"What's this? Fresh meat to feed the tigers, eh?"

A match rasped, and the shadows below parted to a horror dream. Monsters emerged from the cramped pit below, gathering at the base of the steps, hunger gleaming in the slits of their eyes. Dizzy with panic, the boy banged his fists against the door. "Let me out. Please let me out—"

A hand grabbed his elbow, and he screamed, kicking out blindly as he was dragged down the steps. A slap snapped his head back. Rust exploded in his mouth.

"Shut up, you l'il bugger." His captor had a snake-like face and oozing, blistered lips. "Else I'll tear your tongue out an' eat it for supper, you 'ear me?"

A low voice cut in. "Leave off the boy, Sykes."

"Or else what?" Through a haze of horror, the boy felt Sykes' fingernails biting into his arm. "I got to the pretty brat first, so shove off."

A figure separated from the shadows. A huge man, bearded and menacing. "Let 'im go," he said in tones rumbling as thunder, "and I'll spare your neck."

Sykes hissed, and the boy saw something flash in his hand. "Get out o' my way before I gut you like a fish."

"'Ave it your way, then." The man made a beckoning movement.

Blade raised, Sykes went at him. The man dodged the first swipe easily. Paralyzed, the boy watched as the two grappled while the other convicts formed a ring around them, chanting for blood. Sykes gave a wild swing, and the crowd roared when the blade nicked his opponent in the arm. The bearded man sidestepped the next attack, turning so quickly that Sykes plunged off balance. He caught Sykes's arm and wrenched it; the knife clattered to the ground.

"Don't 'urt me. The boy's all y-yours. Swear it on my mother's grave," Sykes whimpered, his face contorted with pain.

"Get out o' my sight," the other man said with quiet menace, "before I change my mind."

With a shove, he released Sykes, who clambered away. Grumbling at the lack of bloodshed, the other prisoners disbanded into the shadows. The boy shrank back as the man approached. All he could see was the thicket of whiskers, and he remembered another man. Another hell.

"You alright, lad?"

Blinking, breathing fast, the boy could not find his voice.

"You ain't daft, are you? You won't last long, if you are." The man's lip curled in disgust. "Sykes's not the only one in 'ere with a taste for—"

At that moment, the boy caught a flicker of movement behind the broad shoulders. Words burst out of him on instinct. "Behind you!"

The man pivoted. Two brutes faced him this time. Quick as lightning, the man reached to his boot. Steel glinted in his hand.

"Now I've a thirst for blood," he snarled. "One at a time

or both at once?"

A blur of silver, the thump of bodies colliding. When the brawl was over, both challengers lay gurgling upon the dirt. Even in the dimness, the boy could see the dark pool spreading beneath them. Breathing heavily, the bearded man rose to his feet. The other criminals cheered as he spat on the ground, the blade dripping in his hand.

The boy froze as another night took hold of him. As another knife flashed in his memory, a terrifying and beautiful arc in the darkness. The master falling, gushing from the chest. And all he'd felt was relief. Relief and trembling hope as he'd begged Nicholas Morgan, the boy holding the knife that had freed them both, *Don't leave me here. I'm scared. Take me with you, Morgan, please.*

"This'll hurt, lad."

The voice jerked the boy back. Past and present melded into one as he stared up at the predator who'd cornered him. The bearded man, not the treacherous Nicholas Morgan who'd knocked him senseless and left him to burn alongside the master's corpse. 'Twas Morgan's crimes that had landed him in this hell—*everything was Morgan's fault.* Anger rushed through the boy, a current so powerful that it walled off fear. As the knife drew near, he made a silent vow.

I will survive. One day, I'll be strong. Then I'll make them all pay.

The blade flashed. A cry sounded in his ears, and the inescapable darkness swallowed him whole.

Chapter One

It began as a day like any other for Miss Priscilla Farnham. Faced with the scintillating choice between marmalade or strawberry jam for her toast, she stared out the window of her cozy breakfast parlor and wished for something—anything—to happen.

—from *The Perils of Priscilla*, an abandoned manuscript by P. R. Fines

EVEN SENSIBLE YOUNG ladies had cause to question their judgment on occasion. As she could not claim prudence as a personal virtue, Miss Persephone Rose Fines perhaps experienced bouts of uncertainty more than most—and the present moment proved a case in point. She approached the squalid tenement with wary steps. Through the gauzy veil tied to her bonnet (at least she'd taken the precaution of disguising herself), she assessed the pair of men loitering near the doorway. Her nape prickled as they barricaded her way to the stairwell.

"Lost, dove?" One of the ruffians leered at her. "Be glad to lend a hand."

"I've got more than a hand for ye," the other brute said. He made an indecent motion with his hips, causing his comrade to snicker. "One taste o' Spitalfields sport an' it'll spoil ye for the rest."

Though her pulse thudded, Percy drew her shoulders

back. *Don't be a faint-hearted ninny. Think of Paul—of everything at stake. Prove yourself worthy of being a Fines.*

Summoning up her courage, she said in brisk tones. "Step aside, if you please. I am expected upstairs, and if I don't arrive on time, my brother shall come looking for me." She paused before adding, "My very *large* brother who happens to be an excellent shot."

The louts grumbled, exchanging glances. Apparently she'd read them correctly as mongrels with bark but no bite, for they shuffled aside and let her pass. Relief filled her as she ascended the rickety stairway, the steps creaking beneath her kid boots as they had the first time her father had brought her and her brother here all those years ago.

Do not be afraid, children, Papa had said. *You must see with open eyes where your own father came from. This is the world I escaped through sweat and perseverance; now you understand why I want better for both of you.*

Sorrow darted like quicksilver through her heart. Four years had passed since her Papa's death, and she still missed him so. As she passed the floors of cramped quarters and wailing babes, she could hear his voice in her head: *If we Fineses were to have a fancy family motto, it'd be this: we never give up, and we always stick together.* Mama would have a fit of hysterics if she knew of Percy's current mission, but surely Papa would approve.

At the top floor, Percy followed her memory to the door at the end of the corridor. She blew out a breath and knocked on the peeling wood. When no reply emerged, she turned the knob; hinges squealed as the door swung open.

"Hello?" she called out in a hushed voice. "Paul, are you there? 'Tis me, Percy."

She entered the dingy room, biting her lip at the squalor. 'Twas a far cry from her family's well-appointed townhouse in Bloomsbury. Windowless and dark, this place reeked of old grease and fresh spirits. The furnishings consisted of a scarred table and a pair of chairs. A straw pallet lay in the far corner. She went over and, crouching, brushed her fingers over the wool greatcoat that looked to serve as a makeshift blanket.

Heat burned behind her eyes. Last year, her brother had suffered a disappointment in love when the lady he fancied had married another. Though Paul had forbidden any further talk of the matter, hiding his pain behind a debonair façade, she knew the loss of Rosalind Drummond had cut him deeply. His behavior had become more and more reckless, with the gaming and drinking and Lord knew what else (actually, she could hazard a good guess at his other activities—her brother was a rake, after all). Everyone in the family had been worried about him, but no one had guessed the extent of his profligacy.

Steps sounded behind her. She spun around to face the figure emerging through the doorway. With a shock, she saw the masculine face, familiar yet utterly changed. Bloating had distorted her brother's handsome features. His golden locks lay matted upon his pale forehead, and scruffy bristle covered his jaw. His shirt collar hung open with no cravat in sight.

For an instant, bleary eyes, blue as hers, widened. Then her brother took measured steps to the table and deposited the bottle he held in his hands.

Gin, she saw with a stab of worry.

His gaze fell short of meeting hers. "I see you remembered the place. I wasn't sure you would."

"The note you sent wasn't all that helpful," she said around the lump in her throat. "But I guessed straightaway that you had come here."

"I had to keep things cryptic. In the event that my message fell into the wrong hands." He sighed, looking at her now. "As you'll recall, I also instructed you not to find me."

Her chest tightened, but she replied in a light voice, "You blasted sapskull, when have I ever obeyed your instructions?"

Unable to hold back any longer, she ran toward him and threw her arms around his neck. Her voice muffled against his shirt, she said, "What on earth has happened? Tell me everything, Paul."

He hesitated before his arms circled her in a brief but fierce hug. Then he set her aside and said in his usual mocking tone, "I'm afraid 'tis a dreary parable, sis. And, predictably, I'm the moral of the tale."

Percy sat across the grimy table from her older sibling, trying to digest what he had just told her. Despite the four year age difference, the two of them had always enjoyed a close connection. Some had even mistaken them for twins due to their shared coloring of golden hair and clear azure eyes. At the moment, however, Percy felt as if she was facing a stranger. This disheveled creature bore no resemblance to her rakishly elegant brother, nor would her brother ever utter such an appalling piece of news.

"I don't understand," she repeated. "What do you mean you *lost* the company?"

Instead of answering, Paul poured himself a drink and shrugged. It was meant as a casual gesture, yet she could see the rigid set of his shoulders.

"If I must be precise, 'twas a game of faro," he said. "I'd lost all my blunt that night, and in a foolhardy attempt to regain it, I wagered the only thing I had left. Unfortunately, I chose the losing card and, ergo, Gavin Hunt, illustrious owner of The Underworld, now holds my vowels promising him my shares of Fines & Co."

Percy's mind reeled. Though a gentleman gaming away his fortune was commonplace, she could not believe her own flesh and blood would do such a thing. "You risked all that

Papa worked for on a game of cards? Have you gone mad?" she cried. "How could you be so dashed reckless?"

Dark emotion flickered in Paul's eyes, the muscles of his neck cording with tension. He downed the contents of his glass and poured another shot. Before Percy had time to regret her accusatory tone, he retaliated with his trademark wit.

"Strange that you of all people should ask that question, sis. As I recollect, I am not the only Fines with a propensity for wild behavior." He paused, letting the barb strike home. "Considering your own less than sterling record, I'd venture to say recklessness runs in the blood."

Percy flushed; she couldn't deny that she'd had a few escapades in the past. In the middling class circle of her youth, her behavior had been described as "lively" and "spirited". Thanks to her family's friendship with the new Marquess and Marchioness of Harteford, however, she now frequented the higher echelons of society, and the *ton* was proving less accepting of unorthodox conduct.

Thinking of her dismal first Season, she winced. Her tendencies to speak her mind and act on impulse had planted her in the field of wallflowers at every fashionable ball. Only the Hartefords' patronage had saved her from complete social failure. This Season, however, she was determined to redeem herself and prove her worth. Papa's dying wish had been for her to make a brilliant match, and she intended to fulfill both his dream—and her own.

For as luck would have it, she'd found her heart's desire at long last. Charles Effington Mansfield, Viscount Portland, was handsome, titled, and a *poet*: ergo, perfect in every respect. Even Mama approved of him (and she and her mother rarely agreed upon anything). To win his affections, Percy had vowed to reform her hoydenish ways. No more getting into scrapes. No more silly notions of writing a novel. No more unconventional *anything* ... today's activities being a minor exception.

"That was the old me," she informed her brother, "and I've turned over a new leaf. I'm a paragon of virtue these days."

"Is that what you call it?" One golden brow lifted. "Correct me if I'm mistaken, but aren't you the chit who nearly burned down old Southbridge's Finishing School?"

Percy's cheeks flamed. "That was ages ago and *not* my fault. Mrs. Southbridge put me in charge of decorations and told me to do as I wished. I thought fireworks would give the graduation ceremony a bit of dash."

"As in guests *dashing* for their lives," her sibling said with a snicker.

Drawing a deep breath, she told herself not to get drawn into one of her brother's infamous bantering matches. "This is not about my behavior, Paul, so stick to the matter at hand," she said. "I still do not understand how you could have risked the company."

"How? Why, with a flick of the wrist," he drawled. "When one stops to think, 'tis ironic, really. Papa retained this cesspit of a building to remind us of his origins and how far he'd come up in the world. How many times did we hear, *Hard work, children, that's the key to success?*"

She frowned. "You ought to show respect for Papa and all he accomplished. I see no irony in his dedication and fortitude."

"I'm getting to that. Our father devoted his life to amassing a shipping empire to the detriment of everything else ... including us."

Bittersweet longing bubbled in Percy's breast, the same feeling she'd had as a girl waiting for Papa to come home. She'd had a habit of posting herself at the front window, her latest story clutched in hand. By night's end, the unread pages would invariably end up crumpled. Mama would scold Percy for getting ink on herself and send her upstairs to wash up for bed.

Percy pushed aside the memories. "Papa did everything *for* us, don't you see? He had to make sacrifices in order to give our family a future."

"Which I managed to squander. In mere minutes." Her brother tipped his head to one side. "So it begs the question: in the end, what is more powerful, perseverance... or prodigality?"

"What is the matter with you?" she said in bewildered tones. "Losing your inheritance is no laughing matter. We must think of a solution immediately. Have you written to Nicholas—"

"No, and I won't have you doing so either." Despite the fact that his eyes were bloodshot, Paul managed a steely look. "I want your word, Percy. You're not to tell a soul about my losses. The last thing I want you to do is interrupt Nicholas on the first vacation he's ever taken, and if Mama were to learn of this..." His mouth flattened. "She'd expire on the spot."

Percy chewed on her lower lip. Nicholas Morgan, also known as the Marquess of Harteford, was the co-owner of Fines & Company Shipping. He was practically an older brother to Paul and Percy, and after Papa's death, he'd become the unofficial head of the family. Recently, Nicholas had taken his wife Helena and their twins abroad for a vacation, and he'd invited Mama to join them. To Percy's surprise, her mother, who'd never set foot outside of London, had agreed to go. Now Mama and the Hartefords were God-knows-where on the Continent; it might take weeks for a post to reach them.

"Your word," her brother repeated. "You're not to betray my secrets, Percy."

Not wishing to alienate her brother, she gave a reluctant nod. "What about summoning the magistrate... or Nick's acquaintance at The Thames River Police. Mr. Kent, wasn't it?"

"What can they do? I gave Hunt my promissory note; he has the right to call it in. Alerting the authorities will only draw attention and lead Hunt straight to me."

"Perhaps Mr. Hunt can be persuaded to relinquish your debt. If you were too in your cups to know what you were doing—"

Her brother gave a harsh laugh. "That's what the hells count on, sis. Pleading with Hunt? Useless as trying to draw blood from a stone. Believe me, I've seen him put babes to work at his club. Children slaving away to pay off their parents' debts, no doubt."

"Why, that is *despicable*." Her outrage found a target. What kind of man was this Gavin Hunt? How could he take such advantage of innocents? "He sounds like an utter villain!"

"He is a cold-hearted bastard," Paul agreed. "Unfortunately, he's also a man of his word. 'Tis practically gospel that Hunt always follows through and collects on his debts."

She frowned as her brother poured himself another drink. His fourth, by her accounting. "Don't you think you've had enough? 'Tis the middle of the afternoon, for heaven's sake."

"Then it appears I am behind schedule. I make it a habit to be thoroughly foxed by lunch." He gave the gin bottle a shake. "In point of fact, this rot-gut usually *is* my lunch."

How could he make light of matters at a time like this? In desperation, she reached over and placed a hand on his arm. "You need a clear head, Paul! How will we come up with a plan to deal with the situation otherwise?"

"Clarity is overrated." Plucking off her hand, he drained his glass. "Besides, I already have a plan. You're looking at it."

Her brow furrowed. "At what, exactly?"

"This." He gestured grandly to the room. "My secret

rendezvous. I am in hiding, don't you know. So long as Hunt cannot locate me, he cannot get my deed to the shares."

Percy rolled her eyes. "*That* is your plan? You'll have to face the problem eventually. How long can you possibly hide?"

"For as long as it takes. I'm rather good at it." He leaned back in his chair and nearly fell off it. "Told the cronies I was off on The Tour, so I shan't be missed for months."

"Dash it all, Paul—"

"Manners, manners, Percy. Don't argue with your elders. 'Tishn't... 'tisn't seemly," he said. "What would your Lord Perfect say?"

She scowled at Paul's derisive nickname for Lord Charles. For some reason, her brother found it amusing to poke fun at the viscount. "I've told you before—don't call him that. And we've only chatted a handful of times, so he isn't mine."

Not yet, she added silently.

As if reading her thoughts, her brother gave her a snide look. "Oh, you'll have him. Madcap, ain't you, but pretty as could stare... not to mention stubborn as a bull. A merchant's daughter who'll bring a title up to scratch." A bitter note entered his voice. "Papa would be so proud of his li'l poppet."

"Never mind that. We must discuss next steps—"

But her brother had risen from the table, knocking the now empty gin bottle onto its side, where it rolled hollowly back and forth. He stumbled over to the pallet and collapsed upon the straw. Percy followed and, kneeling, looked down at her sibling with a mixture of aggravation and concern. She smoothed back a blond forelock.

"Least one of us will make him proud." He rolled onto his side, away from her. But not before she caught the wet shimmer upon his lashes. "Leave me be, Percy. 'Tis done. *I'm* done."

Her heart ached at the naked misery of his tone. Paul had

profligate tendencies, true, but she knew him to be a gentleman of character. A noble brother who'd protected her time and again. They'd already lost Papa; she would not lose another member of her family.

Softly, she said, "Remember the time we went boating in Hyde Park?" When she received no reply, she went on. "I insisted I could paddle as well as you."

A pause.

"Only eight years old and already a hellion. Told you to be careful but you wouldn't listen," he mumbled.

Her lips curved. "I never did. So when I tumbled over..."

"Tried to grab you... fell in as well..."

"We both received a soaking before you got us to shore. Then you shouldered the blame, though it got you the tongue lashing of your life and your allowance revoked for months." Her chest tightened. "My big brother. You've always looked after me, haven't you?"

A faint snore came in response. Seeing his closed eyes and the even rhythm of his breathing, she pulled the greatcoat over his sleeping form.

We Fineses never give up—especially not on each other.

"Now it's my turn," she whispered, "and I won't let you down."

Chapter Two

THE LIGHT OF morning filtered through the office windows. Despite being occupied at his desk, Gavin Hunt noted the way the rays radiated across the sitting area, gleaming off the mahogany furniture and gilt accents. He liked light. Craved it, for all the years he'd gone without. Even with his current success, he still conducted most of his business in the dark. Above the marble fireplace, the gold ormolu clock chimed the hour as eleven, the pleasant sound obscured by the chamber's other occupant, who was bent over the short end of his desk.

"That's it, Hunt, plow me 'arder." Panting, Evangeline Harper looked back at him over her bare shoulder. Brassy curls framed her sharp, feline face, and she tugged suggestively at the rope that bound her wrists at the small of her back. "You know I like it rough. I want to feel ev'ry monstrous inch o' your prick."

"Then take more of it," he said and obliged her with a deep thrust.

Her spine arched in ecstasy, the hills of her buttocks jiggling as he pounded into her. At one time, these games they played had excited him; at the present moment, however, he almost wished she hadn't shown up unannounced and randy for a tumble. Though his body was going through the motions, his mind resisted participating. It had been doing that a lot lately; 'twas as if he'd lost interest in all his vices.

God help him, even fucking had become routine.

Evangeline moaned, pushing back against him. On the blotter beside her writhing form, his lucky dice rattled in their cup. Two sixes, face up.

Gripping her hips, he pumped harder. Mayhap he'd just been working too hard. As owner of The Underworld, the most notorious gaming hell in Covent Garden, he existed in a savage, cutthroat world. Two months prior, a fellow proprietor had wound up dangling from a tree. The cove's tongue had been cut out, his hands and feet missing. No culprit had been found, but everyone in the stews knew one of the rival houses had done the deed. Besides The Underworld, there were four other prominent establishments. All of them were run by men powerful and ruthless enough to kill.

After the last customer had left this morning, Gavin had planned on meeting with Hugh Stewart, his mentor and trusted overseer of the club. They had much to discuss due to a recent attack on patrons of The Underworld. But then Evangeline had shown up, flashing a big smile and equally sizeable tits. Gavin had thought a fast, hard plowing might do him good before settling down to business as usual.

"Don't stop, I'm close, I'm going to spend so 'ard—" she wailed.

The dice continued to jump in rhythm to their coupling. Moaning, Evangeline gyrated her cunt against the wooden edge as he fucked her. If her hands were free, he was certain she'd be frigging herself with abandon. She was as efficient about her pleasure as he was about his. Her eyes were closed, her thoughts concealed. For the two of them, sex was always this way: an activity done together yet separately. Like him, Evangeline had come from the rookery, and they shared a survivor's philosophy.

Be in control. See to your own interests. Reward loyalty... and punish betrayal.

At the thought of betrayal, a muscle ticked in his jaw. The small movement caused a twinge along the right side of his face. The scar that ran from cheek to chin was the memento of a man who'd survived hell—and who now ruled it. The popularity of his establishment had brought him wealth and connections; he now possessed the power to pursue the one goal that had sustained him through his darkest hours.

He'd lived for the promise of vengeance, and it would soon be his.

That got his juices up. Holding her steady, he shoved his cock harder, deeper, each thrust an assertion of dominance. Control. *All those who owe me will pay.* Scarlet dimmed his vision.

"Mary's tits, I'm comin'..." she cried.

Release boiled up his shaft, and he, too, spent himself with a shudder.

After a moment, he untied her, and they each set about tidying themselves. By the time he'd rid himself of the French letter and fastened his trousers, she was fully dressed. A habit of her profession, he supposed, though he knew she styled herself as an actress these days. Not that it mattered to him. Like a cat, Evangeline landed on her feet, and he respected that.

"Will you stay for coffee?" he asked.

She smiled. Some of her paint had worn off, revealing the thin outline of her lips. "Cor, what would we talk about, Hunt? The bleedin' weather? Nay, I think we've done our business together an' done it well. Best be on my way now."

"Before you go, I have something for you," he said.

Opening one of the desk drawers, he removed a filigree locket. A lordling had wept as he'd handed over the family heirloom. All Gavin had cared about was that the piece would fetch a pretty price. While he had no use for sentiment, he did believe in fair exchanges. He dangled the necklace in front of

Evangeline.

"Oooh, that's pretty," she cooed. Slipping the chain over her head, she wiggled her shoulders until the locket slid into the deep crevice between her breasts. "How does it look?"

"Like it's found an enviable home," he said.

She laughed and gave him a saucy wink. "'Til the next time, eh?"

After she departed, he rang for coffee and returned to his desk. Knowing the troublesome business that awaited him, he couldn't summon the wherewithal to search out Stewart. Instead, he picked up the pair of dice, tossing them from hand to hand. He felt on edge, sated yet somehow empty. He was stifling a yawn when the knock sounded. The coffee, about bloody time. When the footman scurried in, a harried look on his face and no silver pot in hand, Gavin scowled.

"S-sorry to trouble you, sir," the servant stammered. "There's a gent 'ere, askin' for you. Says it's urgent."

"Who is it?"

"Gave the name Fines, sir," the footman said.

Paul Fines. Gavin sat up straighter in his chair. "Young toff, dressed to the nines?"

"Sounds like 'im, sir."

"Send him in," Gavin commanded.

He let the dice fall onto the desk, smiling with grim satisfaction as they rolled up sixes. For months, he had bided his time, waiting for the opportunity to take Paul Fines down. The fool had already been barreling down a path of self-destruction, and a game of faro had delivered the finishing blow. Yet instead of fetching the deeds to Fines & Company as he'd promised, the blasted cull had reneged and done a flit. Gavin's men had been searching for Fines for days.

With Fines' shares, Gavin could gain control of Nicholas Morgan's company and set the wheels of vengeance in motion. Because of Morgan, Gavin had spent ten years in the hulks for a crime he did not commit. The ever-present tide of darkness rose within him; he held it off with a familiar barricade of rage. Anger had given him the power and will to survive, and it would help him see justice done.

With simmering anticipation, Gavin watched as the door opened and a figure entered the room. He registered the slight build, the way the overly large green cutaway coat flapped around slender legs. The brim of a hat curved low over short brown curls. The fellow looked up, and Gavin felt an odd jolt in his gut.

The eyes that met his were wide and thickly lashed and the color... he'd never seen eyes so blue. Vivid and pure, the shade of a summer sky in a painting. Befuddled, he took stock of the rest of the face: fine contours, pert nose, and a bushy mustache that overshadowed the small, neat features. A stranger—and definitely not Paul Fines.

"Who the bloody hell are you?" Gavin demanded.

The youth seemed to hesitate on the threshold. Then he straightened his shoulders and came toward the desk, each step infused with coltish energy. He stopped on the other side of the polished mahogany; his head tipped to the left as he perused Gavin, his gaze catching on the scar. Gavin expected the usual averting of the eyes, signs of fear or disgust, yet the clear blue orbs did not waver in their bold assessment.

Devil take it, he was being sized up. In his own bloody office and by a cheeky chap not half his size.

"Thank you for seeing me, Mr. Hunt." Despite the soft and rather musical voice, there was no mistaking the other's determined manner. "My apologies for calling uninvited. I had no choice, you see—"

"Piss on the song and dance. I want to know who you are and why you lied about being Paul Fines."

The oversized patch of hair trembled upon the lad's upper lip. Not with fear, as one would rightly expect, but with...

indignation? "I did not lie, sir. My name *is* Fines."

Gavin's eyes narrowed. "Who is Paul Fines to you?"

"He is my brother." The little chin went up. "And I have come on his behalf."

Did the greenhorn take him for a fool? Beneath the desk, Gavin's hands curled into fists. He'd made it his business to know the ins and outs of his enemy's adopted family. Jeremiah Fines, the patriarch and founder of Fines & Company Shipping, was dead four years. He'd left a widow, Anna, and two children. The heir and eldest was Paul Fines, and he had no brother. Just a spoiled hellion of a younger...

Bloody fucking hell. It can't be.

Gavin pushed to his feet. At the sound of the skidding chair, Fines gave a start, hands flying instinctively to his chest. Those fingers, Gavin saw, were slim and dainty and tipped by neat, oval fingernails.

"I'll have your name," Gavin said, his jaw clenched.

A cough, followed by a gruff reply. "It is Percy, sir."

I'll be damned.

He rounded the desk. "Percy... short for Percival, I assume?" he inquired in silky tones.

"Everyone, um, calls me Percy. You may call me Fines, if you like."

"Well then, *Percy*," he said deliberately, noting the flush creep up those milky cheeks, "what is it that I can do for you today?"

"I have come to discuss my brother's vowels. To negotiate their release, in point of fact."

Gavin had to give the chit credit for her brazenness. For he had no doubt that *Percy* was none other than Paul Fines' younger sister, Persephone. God's teeth, she had a bigger pair of bollocks than most men. Brutes twice her size quaked before him and would sell their own mothers before they dared to deceive him. Yet here she was, masquerading in that ridiculous get-up and demanding to negotiate with him?

In most cases, he'd have quashed such impudence immediately. But this reckless hoyden... he did not know whether he admired her ingenuity or wanted to throttle her for it. While he made up his mind, he saw no harm in teaching her a little lesson.

"Something tells me I'll want a drink for this discussion." He felt her wary gaze follow him as he went to the liquor cabinet and filled two glasses. Returning, he held one out to her.

Taking it cautiously, she sniffed the beverage. Her nose wrinkled. "What is this?"

"Whiskey, of course. The beverage of choice amongst gentlemen." He raised a brow. "Surely you've had it."

Her lush, sable lashes swept up; he was once again struck by the radiance of her gaze. Bright as bloody sunshine upon a lake. With eyes like that, did she truly think that she could pass for a gent?

"Of course I've had whiskey. 'Tis my favorite, as a matter of fact," she said stoutly.

She was also a terrible liar, he observed; if she turned any redder, she'd be mistaken for an apple. Indeed, her cheeks had just the right curve to make a man want to take a bite. He found himself wondering what she looked like without the mustache and wig. Without the gentleman's clothes, as well. Or any clothes, for that matter.

Hmm, interesting direction his thoughts were taking.

"Bottoms up," he said, raising his glass.

Squaring small shoulders, she took a breath... and downed the drink in a gulp. The result was predictable though no less delightful for it. Her eyes watered, and she began to sputter.

"Like it?" he said.

"It's d-delicious," she choked out. "The b-best I've ever tasted."

"Have another, then." He made to take her glass.

She yanked it out of reach. "No! I mean, thank you, I've had quite enough." She cleared her throat. "I wish to discuss the matter of Paul's debt now, if you please."

He waved her into one of the chairs facing his desk. He remained standing, leaning casually against the mahogany edge. "Discuss away."

She sat, and he had to firm his lips at the way she crossed her Hessians primly at the ankle. "My brother is a gentleman of good character," she began. "This has all been a terrible mistake. That night, when he got lured into your den of vice, he'd had too much to drink..."

Christ, the mercy approach. His eyeballs twitched upward. Given her show of resourcefulness thus far, he'd hoped for something a might more original.

"Gentleman or not, your brother knew exactly what he was doing when he wagered against the house," he said. "You are familiar with the expression, *one reaps what one sows*?"

She frowned at him, the hairs of her fake moustache bristling like a porcupine. His fingers itched to rip off that despicable strip. To get a clear look at her once and for all.

"And there are no exceptions to that?" she asked. "Mr. Hunt, can you not find it in your heart to show a little mercy?"

"In a word? No."

"Then at least give my brother time to pay off what he owes you."

"He's had his time." Gavin studied the nails of one hand. "Now he owes me his shares of the company."

"But the company is our Papa's legacy. All that he worked for... and all that we have left of him." Her voice hitched. "Please, sir, you cannot ask Paul to sign it over to you."

The pleading expression in her azure eyes would melt any heart—any heart not made of stone. As it was, even he felt a slight and foreign twinge in the vicinity of his chest.

"Surely we can come up with an alternative?" she said.

"Can we?" He gave her a considering look.

Taking a breath, she said, "I'm assuming you've heard of the Marquess of Harteford?"

"I've heard of Harteford." Though his insides roiled, he kept his voice even. "So?"

"Nicholas—Lord Harteford, I mean—happens to be a dear friend of my family. In fact, he's practically a Fines. When Nick was just a young man, Papa mentored him in the business and later the two became partners. After Papa passed away, Nick tried to persuade Paul into taking over the helm, but my brother hasn't any interest in the company... except for his share of the profits, of course. So Nick runs things and gives Paul a share of the dividends."

"This Nick of yours sounds like a right upstanding gent."

Apparently immune to sarcasm, she gave an enthusiastic nod. "He is the very epitome of a gentleman and truly like an older brother to us. In fact, he's bailed Paul out of trouble numerous times. And if you agree to release my brother today, Nick might be persuaded to pay you,"—she inserted a dramatic pause—"... *with interest.*"

He regarded her silently, gears turning in his head. His original plan for vengeance was simple: destroy everything Morgan held dear. He could, of course, simply off the bugger, but what fun would that be? No, Morgan was going to suffer as he had. Gavin had identified his foe's two areas of vulnerability: Morgan's company and family. With Fines' majority shares in hand, Gavin planned to execute the first part of his revenge by tearing Morgan's life's work apart piece by piece.

Next, Gavin had intended to get to Morgan's wife, the marchioness. Seduction, mayhap, though the scheme would have its challenges since Morgan's marriage was apparently a love match. Even so, women were fickle, unreliable creatures;

Gavin had resolved to find the chinks in Lady Harteford's armor. Now, however, he had a better, easier plan. Here was his enemy's sister—clearly in heart, if not in blood—dangling like a ripe peach in front of him. The opportunity was almost too perfect. He could ruin the little hoyden while Morgan frolicked on vacation, helpless to intervene. Powerless, as Gavin had once been. The notion drove his pulse faster.

Who'll be holding the knife then, Morgan? Whose throat will be exposed? When you plead with me, I'll show you the same mercy you once showed me.

Despite his simmering rage, Gavin perused his quarry with cold detachment. If the rest of Percy was anything like her eyes, seducing her would be no hardship.

With a touch of nervousness, she said, "There's one small problem. Not even a problem, really—more of a temporary snag. You see, at present Nick is travelling on the Continent. However, I'll write him immediately, and I'm certain when he receives my message—"

"Then your precious Nick is not here, is he?" Aye, this new stratagem was falling neatly into place. "Nor is his money."

"Not at the moment," she said. "But he will be. And the Marquess of Harteford is not a man one would wish to make an enemy—"

Fury breached Gavin's wall of control. "You think I'm afraid of that bloody bastard?"

"I never said—"

"I'll take what's owed to me, and I'll take it now." Pushing up from the desk, he stalked toward her. Threatening him, was she? And with Nicholas Morgan of all people—toting the backstabbing bugger like he was some sort of hero. By God, the reckless chit needed a lesson.

She jumped to her feet, backing away from him. She held her hands out as if she could ward him off. His blood fired.

Nothing roused him more than a chase.

"Now, there's no need to get hasty," she said, her eyes wide. She'd forgotten to disguise her voice, her tones rising to the level of a squeak. "We can always negotiate further."

Three more steps, and he'd have her against the wall. "I'm done negotiating," he said.

"But—oof."

Her hat toppled off. Before it hit the carpet, he had his hands planted on the scarlet damask on either side of her head. Trapped, she stared up at him, long lashes rapidly aflutter.

"Done with your games, too," he added, reaching for the mustache.

He peeled it off in one swift motion.

"Ouch," she yelped.

"That's better," he said.

Better than he'd even expected. With that nasty strip of hair removed, her features blossomed before him. Softly rounded cheeks tapered to a piquant little chin. Lips, rosy and full, parted on a breath, and he noted the bottom one had an inviting divot at its center. Unable to help himself, he traced his thumb over the reddened area where the mustache had been. Soft as down.

"Wh-what are you doing?" she stammered.

"Seeing who I'm dealing with. Now let's have a look at what's under here."

He plucked off the wig... and the discovery slammed into him like a blow to the gut.

Sunshine tumbled down. Wavy locks ranging from pale to deep gold spilled into his hand, falling in tangled streamers to her waist. With her dark lashes and brows, he'd expected a brunette... not this. His fingers closed reflexively around a shining tress; it slipped like satin against the roughness of his palm. God's teeth, he'd always had a liking for blondes and more so for the rare natural ones. And Miss Persephone Fines appeared to be completely natural.

"So you knew all along?"

Her breathless voice drew him back. Distracted him from the cockstand burgeoning in his trousers. With deliberate insolence, he tucked the strand of hair behind her ear, his knuckles grazing the tender shell. Satisfaction flooded him when she trembled in response to his touch.

"There's little I don't know, you naughty minx," he said. "The sooner you understand that, the better things will go for you."

Her eyes rounded, and she grew even pinker. Aye, seducing the impetuous little goddess would be a simple matter. Almost too easy. He didn't know which would be the sweeter, having her or his revenge. In this instance, however, he wouldn't have to choose.

By the time he was done with Percy Fines, he'd have his cake and eat it too.

Chapter Three

Separated from her party, Miss Priscilla Farnham came upon a fork in the road. The path on the right was clear and unhindered and likely the way back to the picnic. The other path was dark and cast with shadows, winding deeper into the mysterious forest.

"Oh dear," the intrepid miss said. "I wonder which way I should go?"

—from *The Perils of Priscilla*, a shelved manuscript by P. R. Fines

PERCY WAS HAVING trouble breathing and not just due to the strip of linen binding her bosoms beneath the waistcoat. Sweat trickled beneath her cravat as she stared up at the villain who controlled her brother's fate and who now held her captive. His brawny arms emanated a barely restrained power as he caged her; her heart beat a rapid staccato as his heavy-lidded eyes perused her, the crimson scar pulled taut along the right side of his face.

After her meeting with Paul the other day, she'd concluded that the best plan of action was to confront Gavin Hunt. Clearly, her brother was in no shape to do so, and with no one else around, it fell to her to step in. To defend her brother's future and her family's legacy as any self-respecting heroine would. Yet as she looked up at the beast breathing upon her, she acknowledged with a tiny *frisson* of unease that attempting this feat on her own had been a tad, well, imprudent.

But she could hardly have invited her ladies companion along, could she? First off, Lady Tottenham—known to intimates as Tottie—was recuperating from last night's excesses at supper; at this hour, Tottie could scarcely handle a hair of the dog, let alone negotiations with an infamous scoundrel. No, it was better that the dear remained blissfully unaware of Percy's whereabouts.

Percy reminded herself that she'd never been a shrinking violet, and here was the opportunity to prove her mettle. Steeling her spine, she said, "Please release me, sir. There is no reason why we cannot talk things over in a civilized fashion."

Hunt ignored her request. He continued to finger a strand of her hair, and the gesture affected her strangely. Her blood grew hot, her chest tight. The tips of her breasts stiffened, chafing against the linen. As he continued his bold appraisal of her, she saw that his irises were the brown-black of coffee and embedded with flecks of copper, giving the impression of a burnished gleam. With his thick, tawny brown hair and hard-edged features, Hunt possessed a distinctively wolfish mien.

"Go ahead and talk," he said.

How could she, with the dratted man standing so close? His scent, woodsy and uncompromisingly masculine, curled in her nostrils, and the proximity of his tall, muscled form set loose a swarm of butterflies in her belly. Nerves, that must be it. She was simply unused to gentlemen contemplating her as one might a tasty snack.

Not that Hunt was a gentleman. Oh, he made efforts to carry himself off as such. His ink-black jacket and grey trousers were exquisitely tailored, molding to his long, virile lines. Above the dusky plum waistcoat, his cravat held a perfect knot. Even his accent was polished and not the Cockney she'd expected, making her wonder about his origins.

What does that matter, you ninny? Perhaps he didn't grow up in the stews or he's had elocution lessons... who cares? Beneath that civilized veneer lies a predator. Beware.

"I am very sorry to have misled you," she said, clearing her throat. "But you must understand I only did so out of necessity. Having a reputation to consider, I could hardly walk in here as myself."

"How prudent of you."

Flushing, she said, "Would you mind taking a step back, sir? It is difficult to converse when you are standing so close."

His hard mouth curled in a mocking manner, but he did as she asked.

"Thank you. As I was saying, I did not mean to deceive you. Given my brother's dire situation, I had to resort to desperate means."

"Talked to him lately, have you?"

Though Hunt said the words casually, she sensed his keen interest. His ears might as well have pricked. Well, she was no feather-wit. If he thought she'd betray Paul's location, he was sorely mistaken. She held herself to her full height which, unfortunately, brought her only eye level to his chest. She had to tip her head back to gaze beyond the broad span of his shoulders and past the granite edge of his jaw to meet his eyes.

"Even if I had, Mr. Hunt, I would not tell you. I know that you are after him for the deed to his shares," she said. "So long as you cannot find him, my brother remains safe."

Hunt's gaze darkened. "A coward can only hide so long, Miss Fines. If I am forced to hunt your brother down like a dog, I will do so. I do not treat kindly those who betray me."

He paused, no doubt to let his threat sink in. Her gaze flitted from the damaged side of his face to the massive, large-knuckled hands bearing countless marks of violence. What manner of a man was Hunt? What was he capable of? Up until this point, the only villains she'd encountered were those who populated horrid novels. 'Twas fitting that Hunt's club was named The Underworld for she fancied he possessed the cruel, merciless demeanor of Hades.

On second thought, given her own namesake, 'twas a mythology better left untapped. As she thought of the Hades and Persephone of legend, a shiver passed over her. She slid an uneasy glance at Hunt; even he wouldn't go so far as to cart her off and ravish her... would he?

"There must be something that can sway you. I have an allowance," she said in a rush, "and jewels. It would not cover the debt, of course, but perhaps it might buy a little time—"

"This is not a lending institution, nor a jar in which to toss a few shillings now and again." He cast a pointed glance around the room. "Do I look like I need your paltry baubles?"

She could not deny he was a man of obvious means; the abundance of gilt, marble, and mahogany screamed wealth— if not precisely good taste.

"I suppose you've plenty in that arena," she said with a sinking feeling. Dash it, negotiations were going nowhere... was she bungling things up yet again? She could practically hear Mama's exasperated voice: *For heaven's sake*, think *before you act, Persephone.*

"Why the dejected look? You seem like an enterprising sort, Miss Fines. I am sure between the two of us we can come to an agreeable solution," Hunt said.

To her surprise, he bowed and waved her toward the sitting area. After a moment's hesitation, she scurried past him to the seats clustered around a coffee table and perched on the edge of a settee. Instead of taking the adjacent chair as any gentleman would, however, the blighter sat down next to her. He took up his cushion and some of hers, pulling her toward his center of gravity. She had to cling to the arm of the settee to prevent from tumbling onto his lap.

Seeming oblivious to her predicament, he leaned back and stretched out his long legs. "That's more comfortable, isn't it? Now back to the matter at hand. Since money has no appeal to me, perhaps there is something else you might care to offer."

"Such as?" she said guardedly.

"A service you could render, perhaps. A way to get into my good graces so I might consider leniency toward your brother."

Eyes narrowing, she said, "What kind of service?"

He raked her over with a slow glance. "Your charming company would suffice."

"My... *company*?" When he confirmed her suspicions by waggling his brows, she jumped to her feet and backed away, cheeks aflame. "You must be touched in the upper works! There is no way on earth I'd consent to... to..."

"Warm my bed?" he suggested, following her step for step. "Do the buttock jig with me?"

No one had ever spoken to her in such a fashion before. Shock temporarily divested her of speech. All she could do was scramble away from him, her lungs burning.

"I assure you it's no hardship to share my bed. So I've been told." The immodest scoundrel continued to stalk her through the sitting area. "Something tells me you and I would suit very well in that regard."

"You insult my honor, sir," she said furiously. "If I were a man, I would call you out!"

"Good thing you're not a man, then. For more reasons than one." The bounder had the gall to flash straight, white teeth. "And 'twas a compliment, Miss Fines, not an insult. Typically I would not bother with an inexperienced virgin such as yourself. But I have the feeling that you would be worth the trouble... and then some."

His masculine appraisal sent a quiver all the way down to her toes. No one had ever looked at her with this level of... intensity. A strange thrum entered her blood. Was this how a deer felt when cornered by a wolf? All instincts screamed run, and yet her limbs remained frozen.

She shook herself out of the daze. Blast it, what was this effect Hunt had on her? Perhaps he possessed Mesmeric skills, which would only be fitting for a villain.

"Your tricks are wasted on me," she declared. She'd read enough novels to know how a heroine ought to react. Like arrows of virtue, words flew unerringly from her lips. "I will never succumb to your advances. You might as well know that I have already found my one true love, and nothing could make me betray him."

A copper gleam lit Hunt's gaze. "You do have a flair for drama, do you not Miss Fines?" he drawled. "Those sound like tired lines from an insipid play."

Drat the man. Those were lines from *her* manuscript. In truth, she'd shelved *The Perils of Priscilla* for two reasons: as part of her self-improvement plan, yes, but also because she'd found herself sadly short on inspiration. Her own hum-drum existence provided nothing original or exciting to write about. To have Hunt catch onto that fact riled her.

"The point is," she said through clenched teeth, "my affections are already taken."

"Dear God, what has affection to do with anything?" He sounded genuinely surprised. "We're talking about lust here, not love—if indeed the latter exists. Which I doubt."

She stared at him with jaw slackened. Did he just say the word *lust* in her presence? And what sort of a person did not believe in the existence of love?

"Love does exist," she sputtered.

"In novels," he agreed, "and the minds of feather-brained

females who read them."

Percy held onto the fraying edge of her temper. Barely. "I wouldn't expect a man like you to know anything about love and romance."

"Perhaps not. But I do know human nature."

"You do *not* know me."

"Really." His look turned level, challenging. "Would you care to wager your brother's freedom on that?"

She blinked at him. "I beg your pardon?"

"I am asking whether or not you are willing to back up your righteous convictions by engaging in a little bet," he said. "To sweeten the deal, I'll make the stakes your brother's debt."

Don't listen to him. It must be some sort of trick.

Just to be safe, she scooted behind a coffee table, rattling the bowl of fruit on its surface. An apple wobbled at the top of the pile; if need be, she'd pelt him with it.

She inched closer to the fruit. "Explain yourself. What kind of a bet?"

"A wager of seduction, if you will." He stood on the other side of the coffee table. Scarred and foreboding, all he lacked was a cape and a cackle to make the perfect rogue. "My carnal skills pitted against your notions of love and fidelity. In short, I shall attempt to divest you of your virginity, and we shall see if you can resist."

"That is absurd," she said, "and of course I could resist you, you arrogant ass!"

"Then prove it. If you win, I'll release your brother's vowels. If you lose,"—his nostrils flared—"you will deliver your brother and his deed to me forthwith."

"Do you think I came into the world yesterday?" she retorted. "I am well aware of how a villain's mind works. In this so-called wager, what is to stop you from drugging me or tying me up or resorting to some other dastardly means to claim your victory?"

"My, what a wild imagination you have." His slow smile made her belly quiver like an aspic. "But that wouldn't be sporting, would it? I enjoy a fair challenge, Miss Fines. You have my word that I will not coerce you in any way. Ask anyone: my word is my bond."

Even her brother had said that Hunt was a man of his word. That he never forgot a favor or a debt. Which was precisely what made Paul's position so precarious. She chewed on her lip. There must be some hidden angle to all of this. Something she was missing...

"So you are saying you'd abide by my wishes? That, according to the rules of the wager, you would have to... desist when I tell you to?" she said skeptically.

"*If* you tell me to. Of course, I would have the option of trying to change your mind."

Hah. As if that would happen. "Without force, you say. And if I were to win, you would truly return Paul's vowels?"

Hunt nodded.

"Hypothetically speaking, how would this wager be carried out?" she said. "Clearly, I could not be seen with you. My reputation would be torn to shreds."

Her belly lurched as potential consequences flew through her head. Mama would *murder* her. Lord Charles would never give her another glance. In the eyes of the world, she'd be revealed as wicked and ill-bred—and she'd be ruined forevermore.

"My empire is built on discretion," Hunt said smoothly, "so do not concern yourself on that account. I personally guarantee the privacy of our adventures."

She quelled a quiver at the mention of adventures. Raising her chin, she said, "I have no interest in escapades, sir. How many times would I be subjected to your company?"

"You wound me, Miss Fines." The cad did not look the

least bit affected. "As to the number of visits,"—his gaze fell
to the fruit bowl, and his mouth twitched—"'tis unfortunate
that I am short on pomegranates at the moment."

Her brows climbed at the reference. According to the
Greeks, after kidnapping Persephone, Hades had tricked her
into eating a magical pomegranate. The four seeds she'd
consumed bound her to four months living as his Queen in
The Underworld. The eerie parallel between the tale and the
present situation hadn't escaped Percy, but the fact that Hunt
knew of the myth astonished her.

Her surprise must have shown for he said in dry tones, "In
between extorting chaps and running a den of iniquity, I
occasionally find time to read."

She flushed, feeling unaccountably put in her place. Yet
what did she care what he thought of her? "You have not
answered my question," she said, lifting her chin. "If I am to
consider this wager, I would know the precise terms."

"You are a merchant's daughter, aren't you?" he said.
"Very well. I propose we toss for the period of our
association."

"Toss?"

"Dice, buttercup. You'll roll a pair to determine the
number of *rendezvous*. During the visits, I won't do anything
without your permission. Everything else is fair game."

She turned the proposition this way and that. If he did not
force her, there was no way she could lose. And if she was
lucky in her toss, she would only have to see him twice...

*Are you mad? Haven't you gotten into enough scrapes? Don't
do something you'll regret!*

Her fingernails bit into her sweaty palms. "May I... think
it over?"

After a moment, Hunt said, "I'll give you a week. After
that, the offer becomes void." Before she could feel relief at
the reprieve, he continued, "Just so you know, Miss Fines, if I

have to find your brother, he *will* pay for the inconvenience."

"I—I have to go," she said through dry lips.

He bowed. "Adieu, Miss Fines. Until we meet again."

The very idea set her feet in motion toward the door.

Chapter Four

"So you jus' want me to tail 'er, guv? Nofin' else?"

"That is correct, Alfie." In the empty card salon, Gavin fixed the dirt-streaked urchin with a steely look. "Keep your eyes on Miss Fines—and your hands out of her purse, do you hear me?"

Alfie's expression of innocence was worthy of an angel. With a sprinkling of freckles across the slight bridge of his nose and a wide, gap-toothed grin, the boy looked younger than his thirteen years and as if sugar wouldn't melt in his mouth. "Why, I'm as 'onest as the day is long, guv. Honest-to-God Alfred, that's what they're callin' me these days."

Gavin snorted. Honest-to-God Alfred was one of the most prolific pickpockets in the rookery. At one time, Gavin had thought to reform the boy by hiring him on in the club's kitchens. After a dozen silver spoons and a side of mutton went missing on the first day—followed soon thereafter by Alfie himself—Gavin had reconsidered that idea. Unlike the other street waifs he'd taken in, Alfie had a feral love of freedom that made any kind of routine both unnatural and intolerable.

Now Alfie worked for Gavin on independent assignment, coming and going as he pleased. The boy came when he was in need of coin or lying low from the Charleys. He left as his mood suited him and usually managed to filch a candlestick or two on his way out. Gavin considered it part of the payment for services rendered. No one knew the streets of London as Alfie did.

"You are to report her activities back to me," Gavin said. "I want to know where she went and who she spoke to. If you see a gentleman who looks to be her brother, I want to be apprised." Percy's voice suddenly played in his head. *I have found my one true love and nothing could make me betray him.* Gavin's hands curled in reflex. "Actually, if you see her talking with any gentleman, I want to know. Immediately."

"O' course, guv. You can count on me," Alfie said. "Anyfin' else?"

"No, that is all for now." As the boy started for the door, his tattered rags flapping around his thin body, Gavin sighed. "Hold up."

Alfie turned, cocked his head.

"Find the housekeeper. She'll get you cleaned up and give you a meal before you go."

A sly smile tucked into the boy's cheeks. "Can one o' the 'ouse wenches give me the washin'? The pretty red-headed one wif the big—"

"Alfie," Gavin said in a warning tone.

"Right. The 'ousekeeper it is." The boy scampered off, whistling as he went.

Alone, Gavin watched the dark street from the bow window. He usually savored this slice of peace before Covent Garden filled with the carts of the costermongers, bakers, and other tradesmen with their wares. Today, however, the scene struck him as barren, cold; he had an odd yearning to see the sun break across the cobblestone and the flower stalls blossom into color.

At the sound of footsteps, he dismissed the fanciful notion and turned to see Hugh Stewart stride in. As usual, his mentor's broad, flat features had a disgruntled air, and the greying auburn beard housed a scowl. Built as solidly as a brick house, Stewart's menacing mien had preserved their hides during the years in the hulks and even after their release, when the two of them had scraped by as guards-for-hire in the stews. Now that The Underworld was a success and they'd become nearly respectable, Stewart's looming figure still came in handy, keeping rowdy customers in line.

"How'd we do tonight?" Gavin asked.

Dropping into a chair, Stewart stretched out legs thick as tree trunks. "Broke up three knife fights and five fisticuffs," he rumbled. "Then caught a git cheatin' at the cards and had to give 'im a beatin' myself. And that's to say nothin' 'bout the backbitin' 'twixt the 'ouse wenches."

In sum, business as usual. Gavin poured out whiskey and joined the other man at the table. "What is amiss with the wenches?"

Stewart downed the shot and gave him a sour look. "'Tis the bloody Roman Suite again. They all set their sights on the same toff. Told you, didn't I, that havin' all 'em hen-wits plyin' their trade in one room was bound to lead to trouble."

"The Roman Suite adds to the club's ambiance," Gavin said.

Stewart's broad brow furrowed. "The what?"

"The setting. We're The Underworld after all. What would hell be like without an orgy?"

"Never did get all your fancy words, but if I know one thing, it's that females bring nothin' but trouble." Stewart scratched the back of his neck. "And speakin' on that matter, I 'ave to tell you again, lad: I've got a bad feelin' in my gut 'bout that Fines girl."

"I have the situation well in hand." Gavin savored the slow burn of his drink. The hot tingling was not unlike what he'd felt around Miss Percy Fines... only then the sensations had centered farther south on his anatomy. In fact, just thinking of her—that bright, shining hair, the cheeky attitude—was enough to stir his rod.

"What sort o' female prances around in breeches?"
Stewart said. "And to 'ave the bollocks to demand you give up
what's owed to you?"

"She is brazen, I'll grant you that." In truth, Percy's
contradictions intrigued Gavin. She exuded both girlish
innocence and womanly allure... not to mention a hellion's
spirit. Recalling the way she'd called him an arrogant ass, his
lips twitched.

"Nothin' but trouble, mark my words. Them so-called
ladies'll use their wiles on you, all flutterin' eyelashes an'
swishy silks. Before you know it, *bam*"—Stewart slammed his
fist on the table—"they've hung you out to dry or worse."

His mentor was speaking from experience. Long ago,
Stewart had fancied a well-bred miss who had seemed to
return his affections... until the day her father caught her and
Stewart in flagrante. Then she'd turned on her lover; her
accusations of assault had not only broken Stewart's heart, but
they'd landed him in the prison hulks as well.

"You can't trust a woman, lad, and that's fact."

"Don't worry your head over it," Gavin scoffed. "For
when have I lost mine over any female?"

Stewart's mouth formed a grim line. "There's always a
first time."

"Not for me," Gavin said.

He'd learned his own lesson about females early in life.
His mother had been a clergyman's daughter, and she'd never
let him forget her station, despite the fact she'd had him out
of wedlock. Disowned by her good family, she'd spent the
years thereafter reeking of blue ruin and blaming her bastard
son for her misfortunes. She'd made Gavin mind his p's and
q's and beat him senseless if he dropped so much as a
consonant or made a mistake on his lessons. Up until the day
she'd abandoned him, she'd been a blowsy, sanctimonious

drunk.

Middling class morality—there was nothing he hated more.

Despite his inexplicable attraction to Percy, he couldn't deny she represented the double standards he despised. Headstrong, impulsive, and more than a little hot-blooded by his reckoning, she nonetheless carried herself as if she were a proper young lady. The hypocrisy of her mission annoyed him further: she blamed *him* for her brother's feckless actions. As if he'd held a gun to Paul Fines' head and forced the fool to gamble away the family fortune!

"My only interest in Miss Fines is the role she'll play in my vengeance," he said flatly. *The fact that I want to fuck her senseless doesn't change anything—except make my plans more enjoyable to carry out.* "I am going to ruin her and obtain her brother's shares of the company." He tossed back the rest of the whiskey. "Retribution, Stewart, that's what this is about."

"Nothin' like revenge to warm a fellow's 'eart, eh?"

He smiled wryly at the other's approval. Stewart sounded as proud as if Gavin had just graduated first class from Oxford instead of announcing he meant to seduce a genteel virgin. In a way, Gavin supposed his commitment to righting old wrongs was a rite of passage. In the stews, there was no code more fundamental than an eye for an eye.

Gavin tipped his empty glass over on the table. "Speaking of retribution—is the meeting with the other houses set?"

"Blind Stag next week. Can't say I'm lookin' forward to rubbin' elbows with the bastards."

Several nights ago, cutthroats had held up two customers leaving The Underworld. Not only had the pair been beaten and robbed, but they'd been warned by the masked assailants that all those patronizing Gavin's club could expect the same fate. News of the attack had spread like wildfire, hurting business. It didn't take a genius to surmise that the other

Covent Garden club owners had benefited from Gavin's misfortune. But which of the blighters had instigated the attack?

The most likely players—Robbie Lyon, Warren Kingsley, and the O'Brien brothers—wouldn't blink an eye to do violence. Gavin needed a show of force to stave off future aggression. He'd decided to start by calling a meeting where he would flush out the culprit.

"Have our men track our competitors in the meantime. One of them sneezes, I want to know about it," Gavin said. "And contact Magnus. I need his help locating Paul Fines."

"Don't know why we have to involve that crafty codger," Stewart grumbled.

Though Stewart despised John Magnus, Gavin liked the scoundrel. Magnus was old as the hills, and though his was a fading star, he still did business as a trader of information. Magnus' secrets had proved useful to Gavin in the past. Perhaps because they shared physical deformities—the other man had lost an eye in his youth—Magnus had shown a paternal bent towards Gavin... a fact that seemed to nettle Stewart to no end.

"Call for Magnus," Gavin said firmly. "I want Fines found."

Scowling, Stewart left to attend to the tasks.

Gavin made his way through the gaming rooms, nodding to the staff cleaning up the night's excesses. When he'd first laid eyes on the place years ago, it had been a dilapidated shack with rotting beams and tumble-down walls. He'd seen its potential at once. It had taken his life savings—earned through a combination of violence and investment—to buy the place.

Pausing to gaze around the brilliant circular marble foyer, he didn't doubt that his risky venture had paid off. Three premier stories of the tried-and-true triumvirate of depravity—gaming, drink, and whores—and all of it belonged to him. Normally, this fact brought a charge of satisfaction. Today, however, he felt... weary.

He continued to an alcove in the hallway. Running his fingers along the wall, he released a hidden mechanism, and a panel swung open. He'd had this private corridor built so that he could survey the entire house at his discretion. The passageway snaked behind the walls of every room on every floor. From the card parlors to the wenches' quarters, he monitored all that passed in his domain. Some might call his a controlling nature—and they'd be right on the money.

Power was everything; he'd never be without it again.

He followed the corridor all the way to his private wing at the back of the building. Sunlight hit him as he entered his suite; the series of spacious chambers had large windows overlooking a vibrant gated garden. His own personal oasis. Yawning, he headed to the bedchamber. He waved off his valet, and not bothering to draw the curtains, stripped off his clothes and climbed naked into the postered bed.

Despite his fatigue, the moment his head hit the pillow, his mind leapt awake. The cursed habit of too many years spent in the rookery, where vigilance had been the key to survival. Where between one eye blink and the next, a man could get himself gutted if he let his guard down. Gavin lay there, surrounded by the smell of fresh linens and sunshine, staring up at the embroidered bed hangings. And instead of sleep came the unbidden memories of his past.

He'd been a boy not yet ten when his mother deserted him. Alone in the world, he'd faced the chilling prospect of the workhouse when a sweep named Grimes had come along and offered him an apprenticeship. Relieved at the prospect of learning a trade, of joining a coterie of boys his own age, Gavin had gone along.

What a bloody fool I was.

He'd soon learned that his new master cleaned more than chimneys—Grimes had used his sweeps to rob some of the finest homes in the City. The bastard had a predilection for violence... and also for young boys. The knowledge had come too late; Grimes had kept his apprentices caged like slaves. The first time Gavin had been summoned to the master's chamber, he had feared the worst.

He'd not been the only boy sent for that night. Nicholas Morgan, one of the older boys, had been there too; Grimes' depravity had known no bounds. Helpless fear had twisted Gavin's empty belly as he'd crossed the creaky threshold toward the master, whose eyes had glowed a sinister orange in the firelight. But then matters had taken a different turn. A knife had flashed in Morgan's hand and landed in Grimes' chest.

The bastard had deserved the blade in the heart; Gavin wished he'd put it there himself. Morgan's sin had not been killing Grimes, but what he'd done afterward. Gavin could still feel the sharp steel, wet with blood, pressed against his own throat.

One word o' this to anyone, an' I'll gut you like a pig, you understand?

Dazed, he could only stare into Morgan's hard eyes.

Answer me, you filthy git! The blade bit into his throat, and he felt a sticky trickle—his blood or Grimes', he didn't know. *Your silence or I'll end your miserable life right now. Don't think I won't do it.*

A whimper sprang from his throat. He heard his own voice, words tattered by sobs. *Don't leave me here. I'm scared. Take me with you, please...*

Shame simmered as Gavin recalled how he'd begged Morgan to take him out of that place. Instead of showing mercy, Morgan had knocked him senseless. When he'd come to, flames had consumed the room. A lamp lay shattered by the curtains. Morgan had wanted to burn all the evidence, had left him to die … only he hadn't. Gavin had suffered a worse fate. He'd escaped the fire only to be caught and found guilty of arson. No one had listened to his cries of innocence; no one had cared that he was a child, alone and afraid. The only silver lining had been the ruling of insufficient evidence for murder, else he'd have swung from the gallows for certain.

Instead, they'd tossed him into the prison hulks along with the most hardened and depraved of criminals. Ten years he'd spent in that rotting hell for another man's sins. Had it not been for Stewart, Gavin might not have survived. His scar burned at the memory—he tamped down the dark swell of emotion. Stewart had protected him and taught him the skills to protect himself. The practice of ruthless violence had kept him alive. He'd endured perdition, knowing that one day he would exact his pound of flesh.

Morgan had caused Gavin's suffering; Morgan would pay. With his company... and his family.

Despite her innocence and fresh beauty, Percy Fines was a creature of strong passions. Gavin had no doubt that she would accept his wager—out of loyalty to her brother, yes, but also out of curiosity. Desire. He hadn't mistaken the flicker in her eyes at the word *adventure*. Nor the way her bosom had risen and fallen when he'd come near, those pillowy lips of hers parting with each breath. Though she might not recognize the welcoming signs of her own body, he did.

He exhaled, his blood heating at the welcome diversion. Without realizing it, he'd begun to stroke his cock. The shaft stiffened in his fist as he closed his eyes and imagined taking Percy here, in this very bed. Pinning her wrists above her head, he'd strip away the layers until she could hide from him no more. No disguises, not even a shred of clothing between them.

Her tits would be medium-sized and full, a perfect fit for

his palms. If her lips were any indication, the nipples would be pert and dusky pink. He could picture Percy's blue eyes widening as he fondled her, tweaking the buds between finger and thumb. Her mixture of naiveté and wantonness inflamed him. He would taste one saucy nipple, suckling one peak then the other, until she began to squirm and buck against his hold.

Disobedient chit. She would need to be taken firmly in hand, and by God, he was the man for the job. Nothing stirred his blood like control, and the notion of harnessing Percy's wild yet innocent spirit, of training her to his pleasure, aroused his darkest desires. He knew that once she surrendered, she would do so completely. 'Twas not in her nature to hold anything back. The tempestuous little vixen would give him everything he wanted.

The notion made his rod pulse in his fist. He imagined turning her over his knee. Tracing the elegant dip of her spine and palming the contours of her soft, quivering arse.

You've been a naughty girl, he said.

I haven't. She looked back at him, her hair a glorious tumble. *I only did what I had to.*

Impertinent chit. Even in his fantasy, she gave him lip.

You'll have to be punished for playing your tricks on me, he said.

His first slap made her gasp. Not out of pain—he hadn't spanked her hard—but indignation. Before she could speak, he delivered another swat to her bottom. His cock throbbed to see her flesh bear his mark, to hear her gasps melt into breathy sighs. She began to wriggle against his lap, telling him without words what she wanted. He parted her trembling thighs, and his breath caught at the sight of her quim. Soft and fluffy blond. Perfectly untouched.

He ran his middle finger along the seam of Percy's pristine pussy, and she sighed with pleasure. Virginity held no special appeal for him (he preferred bed partners who knew what they were doing), yet the thought of being the first man—the only man—to diddle Percy's dewy slit sent heat rushing up his shaft. Wetness oozed from the bulging crown, slicking his palm. He frigged himself harder, his breath driving in and out in harsh rushes.

Please, oh please… take me now, Gavin…

Rolling her onto her back, he spread her white thighs, exposing her pink crease with his thumbs. He buried his tongue deep. He could hear her cries as he licked her. He savored the sweetness of her desire, the intoxicating wildness of her response as she arched her hungering cunny to his mouth, whimpering his name. The pressure mounted in his bollocks. He replaced his lips with his cock, running the head along her drenched sex.

Beg me to take you, sweet. Ask for my cock. Ask to be fucked for the first time.

Her eyes heavy-lidded and bright, she whispered, *Please put your cock inside me, Gavin.*

With a wild groan, he thrust inside. She was tight as a glove, lush and wet, the perfect hole for his prick. He took her slowly at first, then harder and deeper as she pleaded for more. His lungs burning, he slung her sleek legs over his shoulders and gave it to her. His hips slammed again and again. *Take it, take what only I can give you.* His muscles tensed as she screamed, her pussy milking him as she spent, dragging him with her… The climax ripped through him. His shout echoed off the walls as hot seed shot between his fingers.

He fell back against the pillows, panting, confounded by the power of his release. *What is it about that bloody chit?* Before he could ponder further, fatigue began to spread outward in languorous waves. His eyes and limbs grew heavy. Sleep beckoned, and too spent to resist, he finally followed.

Chapter Five

"It's not my fault, Mama," Miss Priscilla Farnham *protested.*
"I don't look for trouble. It finds me."

—from *The Perils of Priscilla*, a stalled manuscript by
P. R. Fines

THE DANK AIR of the catacombs filled her nostrils as she struggled against the chains. The villain standing in the shadows gave a wicked, cackling laugh.

"'Tis no use. You cannot escape me," he said.

"Let me go!" She strove to free her wrists from where they were shackled above her head. The stony wall abraded her back through the thin linen—goodness gracious, why was she clad only in her unmentionables? "And give me back my clothes, you cad!"

"You won't need those anymore. Not for what I intend, my dear." In the light of the single torch, his eyes reflected a sinister gleam. She tried to make out his face, yet it remained shrouded by the dark. All she could see of him was his hulking, powerful form.

"You'd better release me before my beloved arrives." She glared at him, the effect ruined by the errant blond strand that fell in her eye. Blowing at the irritating piece of hair, she said, "He is a prince. And he will lop off your head and skewer it to the parapet if you harm me."

"Bloodthirsty wench, aren't you? I like that."

His dark voice made her insides quiver in an odd manner. "You won't like it when he runs a sword through you," she retorted.

The villain laughed. Suddenly, he reached up and doused the only light. Pure darkness enveloped the cavern. Her cry for help echoed off the rocky walls.

"You and I both know the prince isn't what you need. You're no princess to sit idly eating bonbons all day."

"As a matter of fact, I love bonbons—"

She broke off in a gasp as the villain's lips skimmed the curve of her ear. Shocks danced along the delicate shell, and before she could regain her senses, he nipped the tender lobe.

"You're a wicked girl, meant for wicked things," he murmured.

"I am *not*—"

His mouth cut off her arguments. She strained against her confinement, and yet she could not get away from the relentless kiss. Disoriented, she tried to focus on the prince, her rescue... yet sensations unfurled within her. Sinful... *exciting*. Panting, she tried to shut out the feelings, the exquisite chafing of her skin against her chemise. The tips of her breasts turned taut and throbbing. Liquid heat pooled between her thighs.

With her last ounce of willpower, she tore her lips free. "Let me go," she whispered.

"But my sweet," the deep voice said, "there is nothing holding you here."

She yanked against her bondage. To her shock, her hands fell free. No chains at all...

"*Nothing but your own desire,*" he rasped.

His eyes glowed a subterranean gold, and his scar was a flash of scarlet—

Percy woke on a gasp. Heart thumping, she blinked at the

sight of the familiar yellow striped walls, the cluttered rosewood desk, the canopied bed. Her bedchamber. As she sat up against the pillows of the window seat, a book fell from her lap and thudded to the carpet. *The Castle of Otranto.* She must have fallen asleep reading. Her skin tingled all over. Her cheeks burned with sudden panic.

Dear God, did I have a wicked dream... about Gavin Hunt?

She was honest enough to admit that naughty dreams were not exactly uncommon for her. In the past year, certain impulses had been plaguing her with increasing frequency and intensity. The more she tried to ignore the sensations, the worse things got. A few times, in the middle of the night, she'd awakened burning with such a feverish need that she'd discovered an unspeakable... solution.

Shame and confusion tightening her chest, Percy went to the washstand to splash her hot cheeks. As she reached for a towel, her gaze snagged on the portrait above her dresser. Papa had arranged for the four of them to be painted when she'd been a mere babe-in-arms. Looking at her family's content, beaming faces—including her own cherubic one—she experienced a fierce yearning to somehow go back. To that simpler time when they'd all been so happy.

Before Papa had gotten wrapped up with the company. Before Mama had found fault with everything that Percy did. Before Paul had decided to ruin himself and Percy had to consider taking on an indecent wager to help him—

Oh, no. Get the notion out of your head. You are not *going to accept Hunt's bet.*

She'd learned from her past mistakes. She was no longer a silly hoyden to be tempted by Hunt's machinations. Why, the reason she'd dreamed of him was likely because he'd unsettled her nerves. Any miss would be disquieted by a villain proposing to deflower her, wouldn't she? Besides, dreams didn't mean anything. Feeling a bit better, she resolved to forget about Hunt and the wager and to focus her attention on finding another way to rescue Paul.

A knock took her from her thoughts. "Good mornin', miss." Violet, the cheery-cheeked housemaid, poked her head in. "Thought I'd see if you was ready to get dressed for the picnic."

The picnic. Stifling a groan, she said, "Yes, Violet. Thank you."

Percy was not looking forward to the gathering of her old classmates from Mrs. Southbridge's. Though she liked the other girls well enough, their attitude toward *her* had noticeably cooled since she started mixing in higher circles. She sighed. At least her bosom friend Charity Sparkler would be there. She'd already apprised Charity of Paul's situation— the two girls had shared secrets since their school days—and Charity had promised to put her sensible mind toward a solution.

Fitzwell, the long-time canine member of the household, trotted in behind Violet. He wore a scowl, which Percy didn't take too seriously. He was a pug, after all. When she bent to pet him, however, he walked past her, his snout high in the air. He circled thrice in front of the fireplace and plopped down, presenting her with a pair of cold, fawn-colored shoulders.

"What's the matter, old boy?" Percy said in surprise.

Violet hung the ensemble on the dressing screen and waved Percy over to the full-length looking glass. "With Mrs. Fines travelling, 'e was already in the doldrums," the maid said as she helped Percy dress. "Now with Lisbett gone as well, 'e's been in a downright snit."

Lisbett, the Fines' loyal housekeeper, had been called away unexpectedly to attend an ill relative. Knowing the burden this put on the small household staff, Percy said sympathetically, "Any news when she'll return?"

"Lisbett writes she'll 'ave to stay in Dorset at least a fortnight to care for 'er sister. Hold your breath now." Percy obeyed, and Violet gave a deft tug on the corset strings. "She 'opes that you're doing well, miss, and worries about you being left to your own devices."

"I'm not alone. I've got Lady Tottenham to look after me."

Violet gave her a speaking glance in the mirror, and Percy hid a grin. No one had known of Tottie's tendency to tipple when she'd been hired on to chaperone Percy during Mama's absence. Now with everyone out of the house and Tottie proving rather true to her name, Percy was having a heretofore unknown taste of freedom. Which she didn't mind a bit.

"'Er ladyship's still abed. Rang twice for 'er tonic already. *Tonic.*" With a grunt, Violet worked on the buttons along the back of the ivory muslin. "Where I come from, they've got other names for it."

"Is there anything I can do to help?" Percy asked.

Violet finished tying the lavender sash below the bodice. She aimed a glance at the hearth, where the pug continued to lay with his head upon his paws. In a low voice, she said, "Do you think you could take 'im with you to the picnic? The beast's drivin' us mad below stairs. Last night, Cook nearly carved 'im up after 'e stole a suet puddin' from under 'er nose."

"Poor little chap. He misses Mama so," Percy murmured.

"We all do." Violet sighed, picking up a hairbrush. "Can't think why the missus had to take a trip when she hadn't for all these years."

Percy swallowed, feeling the tug of shame as well as that of the brush. She had a pretty good inkling why Mama had needed a vacation: to get away from *her*. Since Papa's passing, she and her remaining parent had been at logger-heads over everything. No matter what she did, she could not please her mother. The failure of last Season must have been the last straw. Her throat thickened.

As she watched Violet tame her unruly tresses, she blew out a breath. Firmed her chin.

I'll make Mama proud this time around. I'll win Viscount Portland and the ton's approval. And I'll find a way to free Paul from Hunt's clutches, if it's the last thing I do.

Percy and Charity made their way up the picturesque knoll away from the rest of their group. As usual, White Conduit Fields teemed with middling class folk escaping the confines of Town. The pastoral grounds offered rolling green hills and paved walks as well as tea rooms overlooking colorful gardens. Cheerful shouts rose from the cricket grounds, where matches played endlessly. Ahead of the two girls, Fitzwell jogged along the grassy ridge, stopping now and again to sniff at a wildflower.

"They hate me," Percy said in despair.

"No, they don't." With her severe, ash-brown topknot and straight brows, Charity projected a somber demeanor. Yet up close, her moss-colored eyes shone with sympathy, dominating her small, angular face. "The girls just don't know how to treat you now that you're no longer one of them."

"Have I grown horns? Sprouted another head?" From the way the others had subtly avoided her or grown quiet when she came near, Percy had felt like some unwanted, alien creature. "I'm still *me*, aren't I?"

"Yes, but now you circulate amongst the *ton*. For many of our sort, your situation would be considered a dream come true," Charity said matter-of-factly.

"A nightmare more the like," Percy wailed. "Now I don't fit in *anywhere*."

At least before she'd had a place with her former classmates whose families had also gained their wealth through trade or other professions. Girls like them occupied *terra nova* as far as society was concerned: no one knew what to make of them. Rich and privileged, they had difficulty finding suitable matches within the working class. At the same time, their origins in "shop" prevented them from marrying up.

"Fitting in hasn't exactly been your forte, has it?" Charity said mildly. "Why the concern over it now?"

Given that Charity had stood by her through her countless antics at Mrs. Southbridge's, Percy did not fault the other's honesty. In fact, she admired her friend's steady, sensible temperament—and wished some of it might rub off on her.

"Because Mama thinks I'm a wicked girl. She's… ashamed of me," Percy whispered.

"Pish posh. Mrs. Fines only wants the best for you. Indeed, you should count yourself lucky to have a mama to give you guidance."

Charity's wistful tone reminded Percy that her friend had grown up without a mother, Mrs. Sparkler having succumbed to a difficult childbirth. Feeling even more wretched due to her own relatively minor complaint, Percy mumbled, "Well, when I win Viscount Portland's affections, I'll show everyone. And I shan't be a snob about it, either. I'll invite all the other girls to my wedding."

"An invitation that will no doubt turn them green with envy."

Percy aimed a rueful look at her friend. "I suppose that would be small of me?"

"Human of you," Charity said. Linking a slender arm through Percy's, she asked, "How are things progressing with his lordship, by the by?"

The image of Lord Charles' rich auburn curls and dreamy grey eyes rose in her mind's eye, accompanied by an effervescent feeling in her breast. Out of nowhere, another visage popped into her head. Her giddiness gave way to alarm at the flash of harsh, scarred features.

"Percy, dear, are you alright?"

She jerked her attention back to her friend. "Yes. I'm fine."

"And what about Portland?" Charity said, giving her an odd look.

"As you know, I've had other matters to deal with." Percy pressed her hands to her cheeks. "Dear God, why am I even bothered by those silly chits when Paul is in danger? It's been three days since I saw Hunt. Time is running out,"—Percy bit her lip—"and I still don't know what to do."

"I've thought it over. I believe there is only one proper course of action," Charity said.

"Yes?" Percy said hopefully.

"You must write your mama and the Marquess of Harteford. Once they know about Mr. Fines' situation, I am certain they will return home with due haste and take care of the matter."

Percy frowned. "I already told you. I promised my brother I wouldn't tell the family. He doesn't want word getting out of his troubles."

"You haven't much choice," her friend pointed out. "You already tried taking matters into your own hands, and look how that turned out. You are lucky that nothing worse happened."

Sometimes Charity could be a bit *too* sensible. Which was why Percy hadn't consulted her prior to meeting Hunt—she'd known her friend would disapprove.

"I knew what I was doing," she said, kicking at a rock in her path. "I could have handled Hunt. In fact, I have half a mind to take the wager—"

"Oh no, you don't." Charity braced her hands on her thin hips. Beneath the brim of her plain bonnet, her brows lowered, and she gave Percy a stern look. "That is precisely the kind of thinking that led to all those scrapes at Mrs. Southbridge's. Remember the time you snuck out of class to see the gypsy caravan, and I had to make all those excuses for you?"

"It was a once in a lifetime opportunity to have my fortune told," Percy protested. "Besides, I didn't miss anything important. 'Twas just an etiquette class."

The irony struck them both at once. Exchanging a look, they chuckled.

"Now that you've set your cap for Viscount Portland, I thought you meant to reform your ways," Charity said, her lips still twitching. "Ruining yourself is hardly the way to win his affection."

"You're right, of course." Percy sighed. "Writing the family *is* the wisest option."

"If all goes smoothly, they'll be back in a few weeks," the other said in encouraging tones. "'Tis best for you to wait and carry on as usual so you don't compromise your brother's situation."

Waiting was one of Percy's *least* favorite activities. "How am I supposed to attend parties and the like knowing that Paul might be in danger? What if Hunt searches him out?"

Worry pinched the other girl's waifish features. For years, Percy had suspected that her chum nursed a secret *tendre* for Paul—but Charity, being Charity, would never admit to such a thing. And much as Percy loved them both, she could not imagine a pair more opposite than her dashing, feckless brother and her unassuming, responsible friend.

"I doubt Mr. Hunt would think to look for your brother at his current location."

"But Paul will have to remain in hiding. By himself and in that horrid place. I daren't visit him again for fear of leading the fox to the chicken coop."

"You think Mr. Hunt is monitoring your movements?" Charity said, sounding aghast.

"I wouldn't put it past the man." With a shiver, Percy recalled his parting threat. "I wish I could at least bring Paul some supplies. Foodstuffs, shaving implements, that sort of thing."

After a moment, Charity said, "I could do it. Mr. Hunt doesn't know about me."

"You? But Paul is in *Spitalfields.* Your papa would never allow it."

Charity's father owned an exclusive jewelry shop frequented by King George IV himself—a fact that garnered prestige, if not the prompt paying of accounts. The only thing Mr. Sparkler guarded more zealously than his business was his only child. Though Charity spent most of her time working at the store, she never complained about the long hours or her parent's strict rules.

"I wouldn't tell my father," Charity said, causing Percy's brows to climb. "I could say I was going to worship. The groom and my maid are sweet on each other, so they'd be happy to wait outside while I go inside the church. They won't even notice I'm gone. I could leave by the back door and hire a hackney—"

So much for her *rubbing off on* me. "Goodness, I am a bad influence on you, aren't I?" Percy said. "But I wouldn't want you to risk—"

"I want to do this. *Please* let me do this."

Percy blinked at Charity's fierce tone and the resolute set of her slim shoulders, as if she were ready to march into battle. "Um, if you are absolutely certain..."

"I am," the other said with a vehement nod.

"You'd have to be very cautious," Percy warned. "To make sure no one is following you."

"I will take every precaution. Just tell me what to do, and I will do it."

Percy studied her friend. "My brother is deuced lucky, and he doesn't even know it."

A flush stole over Charity's pale cheeks.

"All right, then," Percy continued briskly. "I liked your plan about the switch up at the church. I have a few additional suggestions, however..."

Chapter Six

Hᴀɴᴅs ꜱᴛᴇᴇᴘʟᴇᴅ, Gᴀᴠɪɴ sat at his desk as John Magnus gave the report. Leaning heavily on his cane, the old man looked out with one rheumy eye; the other was covered by a black patch. As usual, Magnus' wild grey mane was uncombed and his garb patched and tattered, lending him a disheveled air.

"You've searched everywhere?" Gavin said, frowning.

"The likely places a gent like Fines would hide. I'll start on the less likely." Magnus paused, stroking his straggly beard. "It'd help if you told me why you want the cove."

"I told you. He owes me money."

"With the coin you're paying me to find him, his debt must be worth its weight in gold. You're certain there are no other details you can give me?" Magnus said shrewdly.

Gavin's policy was to give the least amount of information necessary. In this instance, however, he needed to unearth Fines soon. To his surprise and displeasure, three days had passed, and Percy had not yet returned to take him up on the wager. Well, he meant to have her one way or another; what he required was leverage, and her brother was the ticket.

Mulling it over, he said grudgingly, "Fines is connected to the Marquess of Harteford. Perhaps he is hiding at one of Harteford's properties—though I've had those checked."

"Harteford, eh? Powerful man. Wouldn't want to tangle with him myself," Magnus said, his eye widening.

"You're not tangling with him," Gavin said. "Your job is to find Fines. Besides, you needn't worry—the marquess is touring the Continent."

Gavin had kept tabs on his enemy. Morgan must feel free as a lark flitting about French *châteaux* and Italian vineyards with his precious family. Well, the bugger had better enjoy his days of freedom because they were coming to an end.

Magnus scratched his head. "As you wish, then. Perhaps Harteford has other holdings you're not aware of. I'll make the inquiries." The wizened man hobbled to the doorway. "And Hunt?"

Gavin raised a brow.

"Heard you'll be meeting with the Covent Garden bunch soon. None of my business, but they're a bloodthirsty lot." Magnus gave him a concerned look. "Keep your friends close, your enemies closer, I always say."

"I'll keep that in mind."

After Magnus departed, Gavin found his thoughts returning to Percy. He'd been so confident that she would come to him. If he felt the bite of disappointment, he told himself it was due to the fact that she'd put a dent in his plans. His revenge just wouldn't be as... complete without Percy. Well, he was no namby-pamby to sit by and bemoan the lack of results. Nothing in his life had come without a struggle; why expect anything different in dealing with a little hellion? Drumming his fingers against his desk, he began to strategize.

The following day, Gavin looked out the window of Plimpton's Haberdashery, careful to stay out of view. The little shop was part of the newly opened Burlington Arcade, a shopping mecca next to Bond Street. Beneath the graceful arched roof, stores such as this one offered all manner of high-end goods, from exotic blooms to specially blended scents. 'Twas just the sort of place for a privileged miss to spend her morning. Feral anticipation unfurled in his belly when he spotted Percy and her maid in the distance.

Right on time. As usual, Alfie's information proved spot on.

"They're coming," Gavin said. "Take your place, Plimpton."

The famed haberdasher, who happened to be a client of The Underworld, mopped at his balding pate. "If I do this, Mr. Hunt... the slate's wiped clean? I won't owe you anything?"

Not until you gamble the shirt off your back again. "Yes," Gavin said.

With a shaky nod, Plimpton took his place at the front counter. Gavin strode to the back; concealed by a velvet curtain, he could view all that transpired in the little shop.

Minutes later, a tinkling bell announced Percy's arrival. His blood stirred at seeing her dressed as a lady for the first time. By God, she was... stunning. Her feminine appeal struck him like a blast of sunshine after the rain. Shiny curls peeped from beneath her bonnet, and her cheeks glowed fresh and dewy. Her high-waisted white frock clung to her lithe figure, and he'd been right about her breasts: though covered by a modest bit of frill, those twin beauties were high and rounded and had a tempting bounce to them when she walked.

Hell's teeth, he was developing a cockstand just looking at her.

"Good day, sir. I hope you can help me—I'm in desperate need of a pair of gloves," Percy said, dimpling.

Damnit, even her voice makes me hard.

"You've c-come to the right place, miss," Plimpton stammered. "I have a fine selection, if you'd care to have a look?"

As the shop owner placed his wares upon the counter, the bell rang again. Gavin's lips twitched at the sight of Alfie dressed like a proper young lad. Sporting a child-sized jacket, waistcoat, and breeches, the urchin could pass for the son of a well-to-do family. As Percy's maid helped Percy try on a glove, Alfie ambled toward them. The boy reached out—with a notable lack of his trademark finesse—and snagged the maid's purse.

The woman spun around. "Why you thieving pup!" she sputtered. "Give that back!"

Alfie dangled his prize. "Come an' get it," he said and dashed out the door.

With a cry of "Stay put, Miss Percy!" the maid took off after Alfie.

Plimpton's gaze darted to the back curtain and back to Percy. As rehearsed, he said in a loud voice, "I'd best go lend a hand, miss. Wait here. I'll, er, lock up to keep you safe until I return."

Before Percy could utter a word, the haberdasher scrambled out of the shop, securing the door behind him.

"What on earth?" Percy muttered as she stared after the retreating figure.

With stealthy steps, Gavin made his way over. He tapped her on the shoulder. She whirled around; to her credit, she didn't scream or—God forbid—faint. As usual, Persephone Fines was proving no typical female.

"*You*," she said.

He bowed. "Good day, Miss Fines. Enjoying your shopping?"

Against the white satin lining of her bonnet, Percy's eyes were even bluer than he remembered. Her glorious gaze narrowed. "That boy was no thief. You set this up, didn't you?"

"I wanted a moment alone with you," Gavin said.

"Why?"

His lips quirked; he liked the way she cut to the chase.

"I didn't wish for you to forget me or my wager," he said.

"If only I could be so fortunate." She tipped her chin up. "I am, however, doing my best to put the incident behind me."

"Come, Miss Fines, surely you've at least considered the wager? Had a moment's curiosity about the adventures you and I might share?"

A flush tinged the curve of her cheeks. Her pearly teeth sank into her dimpled lower lip, a tell-tale sign of nerves. *Aha. You have thought about me, you shameless vixen.* Satisfaction expanded his chest; he'd *known* the animal attraction between them was mutual.

"Or," he said deliberately, "perhaps you're afraid to take me on?"

"I am *not* afraid of you," she retorted.

The fact pleased him. He chucked her beneath the chin—aye, her skin was even softer than he'd imagined—and she gasped in indignation. "Brazen little chit," he murmured.

"Keep your paws off me." She swatted his hand away. "I am not *brazen*. I'm a proper miss, and I want nothing to do with you, you worthless scoundrel."

Some of his amusement faded. "You're lying," he said.

"I am *not*. You… you disgust me!"

His jaw ticked as another's voice shrilled in his head. *One day you'll find me gone, you worthless guttersnipe. Rid of you and happier for it. Who'd blame me for wanting to be free of a stupid, disgusting brat like you?* His mother had made good on her threats, too. One day, he'd returned to their miserable hovel to find her and all their earthly belongings gone.

"You want me, you little baggage, and you know it," he ground out.

"I would *never* want someone like you."

Red filtered his vision. Before he could think, he had her

pressed up against the display case. Her breasts heaved an inch away from his waistcoat. Her skirts skimmed his thighs. Her little tongue darted out, wetting her lips. Lust and anger mixed, driving his breath out in harsh rushes.

"Think you're too good for the likes of me?" he sneered.

Her eyes wide, she said, "Are you mad? You're planning to destroy my brother—of course I don't want anything to do with you! *Let me go, you oaf.*"

She shoved at him; his hands clenched the counter on either side of her. Even as her words sank through his haze of rage, he knew it was too late. Her clean, citrusy scent blossomed inside him, her ripe mouth beckoning. Hunger clawed at his gut. *Just one taste...*

He bent toward her.

Crack. The force of her slap snapped his head to the side.

Jaw throbbing, he stared at her rosy features. Her eyes shot sparks at him. Stunned by his loss of control, he muttered, "I suppose I deserved that."

"You'll get more if you don't let me go," she warned.

What the bloody hell is the matter with you? Get a hold of yourself. Don't scare her away, you sod. He released his grip on the counter and raked his hands through his hair. Immediately, she scooted out of his reach.

"You *cad.*" Her hand fluttered to her bosom; the half-buttoned glove flapped open, and the glimpse of her slender wrist was more erotic than a roomful of naked wenches. "You'll stoop to anything to get your way, won't you?"

He was hardly the epitome of morality. Yet he'd never forced himself on an innocent. The fact that he'd come close to losing his head battered at his pride. To add to the humiliation, now he had to wonder if he'd imagined the magnetism between them. A figment of his own lustful fantasies? He could have sworn that she'd felt something too...

Don't be an idiot. Take command of the situation. Turn it to your advantage.

"As you claimed, you have no trouble resisting my advances," he drawled.

"Of course I don't!"

"Then why not agree to the wager and win your brother's freedom?"

"You need ask?" she said in incredulous tones. "I cannot trust you, sir, and today's incident only proves that fact."

"I stopped, didn't I?"

"Only after I slapped you!"

"Do you honestly believe that a slap could deter me from what I wanted?" He cast a pointed look around the shop. "We are standing here alone. The two of us in a locked room with no key in sight."

A furrow appeared between her fine, curving brows.

"I ceased because I gave you my word, Miss Fines," he said. "To my mind, today's event demonstrated that you *can* trust me."

"That's just... ridiculous." Yet she didn't sound quite so convicted as she had before.

"Think of it. If you had agreed to the wager, you could have chalked up this meeting as a victory," he said, shrugging.

She bit her lip.

Now dangle the bait, Hunt.

He approached her, catching her hand before she could pull away. Deftly, he began to fasten up her glove. She quivered as his fingers brushed the supple underside of her arm; her breasts rose on a shaky breath. And if that didn't tell him enough, she swayed subtly toward him like a flower to the sun.

He released her and took a deliberate step back. "I think it isn't me in whom you lack trust, Miss Fines, but yourself."

She frowned. "That's absurd."

"Is it?" He lifted a brow. "The truth is you're afraid you'll succumb to my charm."

"Your *charm*? Hah. I have another term for that."

"In fact," he said, tapping his chin, "you probably couldn't even handle a kiss from me."

Her eyes narrowed. "I'm not an idiot, Mr. Hunt. I know what you're doing."

"Then you'd see this is a simple test. To decide which one of us is right." He paused. "Unless one of us is a... coward?"

Her brows came together. Aye, he had her mark, alright. Miss Persephone Fines possessed a competitive streak—'twas not in her nature to back down.

After a few seconds, she said between her teeth, "'Tis to be one kiss only. No... touching or anything else of the sort. And it ends when I say it ends."

"Agreed."

"And after this, I want your word that you'll leave me alone. You'll stop pestering me about this idiotic wager."

Clever girl. But he wouldn't have to pester her. He planned to hook her curiosity with a single kiss; after this, she would come to *him*.

"Again, agreed." He gave her a meaningful look. "Shall we?"

In answer, she shut her eyes and pushed out her lips.

Adorable as that gesture was, this time he would not lose control. It was no easy feat to seduce a woman with a mere kiss and one that involved no touching—and, he guessed, no tongue—at that. To lure a skittish miss without scaring her off. But he was up to the task.

He lowered his mouth to hers. At the contact, he felt a tremble of awareness pass through her and, damn, if he didn't feel a jolt himself. Her lips were as soft and full as they looked; she tasted of honey and lemon drops and a unique tart-sweetness that was hers alone. Flames ignited from their single point of connection, spreading through his veins. He could feel her responding to the fire, too. On a tremulous sigh, her lips parted, and if he wanted to, he could slip inside, show her the kiss that burned in his dreams...

He lifted his head. Managed to master his breath and the hot swell of desire.

Her eyelashes fluttered open to reveal dazed, sapphire eyes.

"That was edifying, to say the least," he murmured. "Thank you."

"I—I don't know what..." She took a stumbling step backward.

He made her a leg. "I bid you good day, Miss Fines." Reaching to his pocket, he withdrew a key and went to unlock the door.

"You had the key all along?" she burst out from behind him.

He bowed to her again. Stepping out into the arcade, he realized he was smiling. Because though the stakes were high and Percy was more worthy an opponent than he'd first suspected, he could not deny the simple truth.

Bloody hell, he enjoyed the games they played.

Chapter Seven

Miss Farnham gazed at the giant cake upon the table. She'd sworn to abstain from sweets. Yet bursting with marzipan and jeweled fruits, the kingly confection seemed to call to her in a seductive whisper.

"You know you want me..."

—from *The Perils of Priscilla*, a manuscript that ought to be finished by P. R. Fines

TWO NIGHTS LATER, Percy stood poised at the top of the staircase leading down into the bustling ballroom. A bittersweet pang struck her.

If only Papa could be here. If only he could see me now.

Given his origins, Papa had always dreamed of hobnobbing with high society, and she was certain he'd be tickled at Lady Stanhope's overblown event. Indulging in her latest craze for antiquities, the hostess had decked out the ballroom of her grand Mayfair townhouse in the Egyptian mode. A pair of plaster sphinxes greeted guests at the stairwell, and giant palms in golden urns surrounded the dance floor. Overhead, colorful streamers of Pharaoh blue were festooned between glittering chandeliers.

Descending the steps, Percy managed to find a quiet spot next to a pair of upright sarcophagi. She'd taken Charity's advice and sent a letter off to Mama and Nick; now she was at one of the premier events of the Season, trying to act as if things were normal. Trying not to think about Paul—or the fact that Hunt's proposition expired on the morrow.

The memory of the haberdashery gripped her. She still couldn't believe Hunt had gone to such lengths to see her. He'd eyed her with such *hungry* intent. And then the kiss... Her pulse quickened. She'd been kissed twice before, by friends of her brother's. The pecks had been sweet and harmless. On the surface, her kiss with Hunt had been equally innocent, yet she'd felt something... new. Different. Unbidden, his darkly masculine flavor permeated her senses, a hot promise rushing through her blood. That strange throbbing began deep inside again, the flutter of wings beating for release...

Stop it! You're not a wicked girl. You slapped Hunt, put him in his place. The only reason you allowed the kiss was to get rid of him. And now you have.

Heart thudding, she told herself she'd never succumb to a villain's temptations. She was only interested in a prince. In Lord Charles. Scanning the room, she spotted her beloved conversing with a circle of Corinthians. Her heart calmed at the sight of him. With his dark auburn curls coiffed *à la Titus* and his slim form showcased in black and white, he embodied elegance. They'd exchanged a brief greeting earlier in the evening, and he'd requested the favor of a dance later on.

As *if* he'd had to ask. She'd come for the sole purpose of furthering their acquaintance, and he was the very thing she needed to get her mind off that bounder Hunt. If she was lucky, she and Lord Charles might even have a waltz. In fact, she ought to find Tottie, whose permission would be required for the dance. She hadn't seen her chaperone for ages and hoped the dear was not lying sauced beneath a table somewhere. Before she could start her search, high, cultured accents drifted from behind her.

"Fine party, what," said a gentleman's voice. "Plenty of

prime quality here tonight."

"I'd say it's not so much prime as overdone," a female drawled in reply. "Lydia's done up the place like a stage... and not Theatre Royal, either. Our hostess has a taste for Haymarket."

Another lady giggled in response.

Now Percy knew it was impolite to listen in on another's conversation (Mama always said that eavesdroppers deserved what they overheard), yet she couldn't help but peek through the narrow space between the sarcophagi. She saw the three speakers consisted of a rail-thin redhead with a haughty expression, a plump blonde dressed in debutante's white, and a gentleman whose curled, windswept coiffure likely required more time to style than Percy's own simple coronet.

"Lady Eleanor, surely you are not implying that the Stanhope soiree is in poor taste?" The gentleman raised thin eyebrows.

"I don't bother to imply anything, Lord Carlton. I simply say it as it is." The redheaded Eleanor sniffed. "One need only have eyes to see that the guest list is hardly *crème de la crème*."

With a *frisson* of unease, Percy knew she should stop spying on the trio. Instead, she leaned closer to the gap.

"You are absolutely right as usual, my lady," the blonde said in a simpering voice. "Why, I do believe I saw a barrister by the punch table."

"That is not the worst of it. The place has been overrun by Cits. Did you not see who Lord Gregory was dancing with earlier?"

The blonde's face scrunched in thought. "Miss Appleby?"

"No, sister dear, Lady Eleanor is referring to the chit in yellow," the gentleman said in a snide tone. "Dear me, what is her name... it's ridiculous, Aphrodite or something..."

Percy's cheeks grew hot as she looked down at her pale jonquil skirts.

"She smells of shop," Lady Eleanor said. "And she's no less common this Season than she was the last. Do you recall what she told Lord Overton last year?"

The blonde giggled. "How could I forget? He gave such an amusing account of it. He asked her about her hobbies, and she regaled him with the details of some sordid *novel* she was working on. A novel, imagine that!"

"Common, as I said. The only reason anyone is paying her any attention is that vulgar dowry of hers." Lady Eleanor sneered. "'Tis like waving a red flag in front of maddened bulls."

"Impoverished ones, more like." The gentleman finished off his champagne. "Ain't a title I know of who don't need more blunt, and chits with plump pockets are in shortage this Season. In point of fact, I may have to have a go at our little shop girl turned authoress myself."

"My dear Miss Fines, is that you standing by those atrocious remains?"

At the sound of the musical voice, the gossip halted on the other side of the sarcophagi. Percy spun around. Mortified, she recognized Lady Marianne Draven, a bosom friend of the Marchioness of Harteford. With her moon-bright hair and classically sculpted features, Lady Draven cast all other females in the shade. Tonight, a gauzy silver gown caressed her willowy figure, and a string of emeralds circled her slender neck, the jewels outshone by her striking green eyes. Percy much admired the widowed baroness who was not only beautiful, but also independent and terribly clever.

"Good evening, my lady." How much of the sniping had Lady Draven overheard? Despite the humiliation churning her stomach, Percy managed a proper curtsy. "It's so nice to see a familiar face."

The baroness smiled. "I imagine so, when so many of the unfamiliar ones are less than hospitable." In a voice that delicately carried, she said, "In my opinion, there is a thing more vulgar than your dowry, Miss Fines. Would you like to know what that is?"

Shame and misery stole Percy's words.

"Sour grapes." The edge of Lady Draven's flawless mouth curled with derision. "I, for one, am hardly surprised that the gentlemen tonight would rather enjoy champagne than cut-rate wine... or should I say, whin-*ing*?"

Percy heard a furious gasp from the gap between the stone coffins and instantly felt better.

"I find the air here rather stuffy," Lady Draven continued. "Won't you join me on a circle around the floor?"

"I'd love to." Once they were out of ear-shot of the trio, Percy said in a rush of gratitude, "Thank you for intervening, my lady. Though, I must confess, the situation was in part of my own making. I ought not to have eavesdropped."

"Perhaps not. But Eleanor Worthington and her smug superiority set my teeth on edge."

Lady Draven coolly surveyed the room as they walked; one had the feeling those green eyes missed little. All around, gentlemen hovered like insects, trying to get her attention. Fascinated, Percy made note of how she shooed them away with a glance or a flick of her fan. Percy strove to keep her own pace as sedate and graceful as her companion's. To quash her tendency to rush along or, as Mama described it, *pell-mell, as if all the world's afire.*

"I fear I shan't ever fit in here, my lady," Percy said in glum tones.

"Good God, why bother to try? You've spirit, which I'll take over insipidity any day," Lady Draven said. "By the by, let us drop the tiresome formalities, shall we... Percy?"

"Absolutely, Marianne," Percy said, flattered. "And whilst I do enjoy your company ever so much, I feel I should ask... being seen with me won't bring down your countenance, will it?"

"My dear, you have the wrong impression," the other drawled, waving her feathered fan. Between her long, gloved fingers, diamonds glittered on the sticks. "Between the two of us, I far outrank you in notoriety."

Percy grinned. "In that case, I can only hope *you* don't rub off on *me*."

Marianne's laughter pealed like silver bells. "A minx after my own heart. How delightful. Now tell me—what have you heard from the Hartefords of late?"

"The last letter I received was over a fortnight ago. Helena wrote that they were enjoying Venice immensely, though the twins were driving everyone mad. Apparently, one of them nearly overturned the gondola during a trip through the canals whilst the other got them ejected from a cafe on the Piazza for trying to lure the pigeons in with his tea cakes."

"The little hellions take after their mother it seems."

"Jeremiah and Thomas, like Helena?" Percy said, surprised. "Surely not. She is the most proper lady I know."

"You'd be surprised." Her lips faintly curved, Marianne said, "And you, Percy? How are you faring in your family's absence?"

"Oh, I'm keeping busy..."—*trying to save my brother, kissing a ruthless rogue*—"... with a little of this, little of that." Percy sounded nervous even to her own ears.

Green eyes narrowed. "Indeed. Who is your chaperone tonight? At an event like this, sticklers are everywhere."

"My companion, Lady Tottenham, came with me. But I'm afraid she's gone missing. You haven't perchance seen a short, robust lady with a turban that resembles a giant green macaw perched upon her head?"

"I can't say I have." The other lady's lips twitched. "But with that description, I shall certainly know what to keep an eye out for. Now tell me, how are things progressing with

Portland?"

Percy's cheeks warmed. "How did you know? Did Helena mention something?"

"Not a bit," Marianne said. "But you've been discreetly monitoring his movements throughout our conversation, and he's pretending not to look your way at this very moment."

"Lord Portland's looking at me?" Delighted, Percy stopped in her tracks and craned her neck to get a clearer view of him.

"Lud, Percy, keep walking. That's no way to go about flirting."

Apparently, Marianne was right. The moment Percy caught sight of Lord Charles, he turned away, leaning down to murmur something to an exquisite brunette.

"I asked Helena how to flirt properly, and all she told me was to be myself." Sighing, Percy took up the stroll again. "Easy enough for her to say, seeing as how Nick is madly head over heels and finds anything she says or does utterly ravishing."

"Sickening, isn't it?"

"Beyond. And when one is a lowly merchant's daughter in love with the most sought-after viscount..." Percy gave a dejected shrug. "Let's just say I could use a little help." Just like that, an idea struck her. "Could *you* teach me how to win Lord Portland's affections, Marianne?"

The lady said something under her breath. Something sounding curiously like, *Not again.*

"I beg your pardon?" Percy said.

"Never mind." Marianne sighed. "If I may ask, why this interest in the viscount?"

"Isn't it obvious? He is the most handsome and distinguished man in the room. And he has an artistic sensibility—"

"Allow me to be direct: how well do you know him?"

"Not well. But look at him." Percy risked a peek over at the object of her affections, who was now surrounded by a bevy of debutantes. Blast it. "He is all that any girl could hope for."

"Hmm."

"You do not agree?" Percy said in astonishment. "But Lord Portland is highly regarded. Mama would swoon to have him as a son-in-law, and even Nicholas approves, which is saying something."

"Do you not find Portland a rather staid match for your own disposition?"

Percy made a face. "If that is your polite way of saying I am a hoyden, trust me I've heard it in no uncertain terms from Mama. She says I am too impulsive by far and could use a husband with a firm hand."

"You are a woman, not a child, Percy." Marianne's tone took on an icy quality. "What you'll want is a husband who will respect you as an equal."

"Of course I want that," Percy said earnestly, "but I also know I must reform my ways."

Yet another reason why you should stay away from Hunt!

"I, for one, find your artlessness charming, but"— Marianne's white shoulders lifted in a motion as chic as any Frenchwoman's—"as you wish. I will provide you with guidance. I cannot, however, guarantee the outcome."

Percy wanted to hug her new mentor. "Oh, that would be marvelous. Thank you, Marianne!"

Unable to help herself, she looked back at Lord Charles again. Dash it all, he was bowing over the brunette's hand... A firm grip took hold of Percy's arm. Startled, she turned back to a level emerald gaze.

"Lesson one," Marianne said, "is to rein in your emotions. Your object of interest does not wear his heart on his sleeve nor does he wish it of any lady he chooses to pursue."

"Oh. Right." Drawing her gaze ahead, Percy focused it on the most convenient item, which happened to be a buffet table. "How is this?"

"He may think you're famished, but at least he won't think you're pining over him," Marianne said dryly. "Relax, dearest. Act as if you're having the time of your life."

Percy forced out a chuckle. "How am I doing?"

The other sighed. "We had better call in the reinforcements. Now, here's my advice—flirt with every single one of them, but say yes to only two dances. You'll want to leave the third one free."

"Every single one of who? And why leave the third?"

Instead of answering, Marianne stopped in front of a pair of chairs. In a graceful, sensuous movement, she seated herself in one of them and motioned for Percy to take the other. Marianne fanned herself with white feathers, an inviting smile curving her lips.

Within a minute, they were besieged by gentlemen.

Percy said yes to a cotillion and a reel.

By the time she returned from the second dance, flushed from the exertion as well as the flattering prattle of her partner, she found Marianne surrounded by an impenetrable wall of males.

"I say, Miss Fines, would you care for a turn about the room?" her partner said as the strains of a waltz began to play.

Before she could reply, a grave voice cut in.

"I believe the next dance is saved for me," Lord Charles said.

The following morning found Percy treading back and forth across the parlor. In her current state, she feared she might wear a trail through the flowers and vines of the Wilton carpet. Due to the excitement of the prior evening, she was giddy from lack of sleep to begin with. Then Charity had sent word that she meant to visit Paul this morning and would stop by afterward to report in.

Charity ought to have arrived hours ago. Percy's thoughts whirled with increasing panic.

I should never have allowed Charity to go through with it. What if something has happened to her? Should I go after her... but what if I compromise Paul's location?

The doorbell rang.

Rushing out into the foyer, Percy opened the door before Violet could reach it and yanked Charity inside. "If Lady Tottenham asks," she said to the maid, "Charity and I will be in my room."

"That one? She never asks." Violet snorted and trotted off.

Percy turned to her friend. She'd been so relieved to see Charity that she hadn't noticed the other's disheveled appearance. Now, with growing concern, she saw the wisps of ash brown hair that had escaped Charity's top-knot and the crumpled state of her friend's gown.

"Charity?" she said.

"Let's go upstairs," the other girl said in a tremulous voice. Once the door to the bedchamber was closed, Charity burst out, "Oh Percy, it was *horrible*."

Chapter Eight

LOOKING OUT THE window of his office, Gavin came to a disturbing conclusion: Persephone Fines was driving him mad. He wasn't sleeping, he barely ate—even his work was beginning to suffer. In just two days, he was to meet with the club owners. Was he strategizing on how to manage the cutthroats? Devising an alternative plan in the likely scenario that the meeting blew up in his face?

No. He wasn't. Instead, he was thinking of *her*.

Like a pebble trapped in his boot, thoughts of her poked at him. Constantly. He couldn't get their kiss out of his head; apparently, she didn't have the same trouble. According to his plan—a bleeding fantasy, more like—she would have come to him by now; instead, he'd seen hide nor hair of her since Plimpton's. And the wager expired today. He was *never* indecisive, and yet here he was torn up over what to do concerning the taxing chit.

On the one hand, he wanted to track her down and demand that she agree to the bet—fat lot of good *that* would do. He swiped irritably at the back of his neck. His wiser, rational side advised abandoning this hare-brained proposition altogether; he could find another way to hurt Morgan. Through Morgan's wife, for instance. Before meeting Percy, Gavin had considered the marchioness the best way to tear out Morgan's heart. How had he forgotten about that? How had he gotten so twisted up over Percy that he'd lost all focus?

His hands fisted. He was not a man who lost control. Least of all over a female.

So Percy hadn't come up to scratch? Fine. He had his pride; he wouldn't force her into it. He'd seduce the bloody Marchioness of Harteford instead. His gut clenched in denial. Or he'd arrange for someone else to do it. Whatever. The minute the fucking Hartefords returned from Italy he would set the new plan into play...

Hearing footsteps, Gavin felt his pulse speed up. He willed a golden head to appear... but instead Alfie marched into the office. Gavin's snarl faded when he saw the taller, ganglier boy the urchin had in tow. Dressed in the tattered uniform of the stews, the new lad had brown hair that stood in unruly tufts and ears that would do justice on an elephant. He also sported a fresh, purpling bruise upon his cheek. His left eye had swollen to the size of a walnut.

"Mr. Hunt, this 'ere is Davey." Alfie jerked a thumb at his companion. "'E's 'ad a bit o' a problem wif 'is last employment. Thought you might set 'im up like the others."

"I see." As Gavin came near, he saw the newcomer flinch. Instinct—it never left you. In a grim tone, he said, "How old are you, Davey?"

"I'll be fourteen in the spring, sir." Davey's voice was little more than a whisper. "I'm stronger than I look. I'm a 'ard worker, an' I always get the job done."

"What happened at your last place of employ?"

Davey's gaze fell to the carpet. "I swear I didn't do nothin' wrong," he mumbled.

Knots tightened in Gavin's chest. He knew too well how easily pleas of innocence were ignored. "Have you any family?" he said quietly. "Anyone to take you in?"

Biting his lip, Davey shook his head.

"You may stay here if you like," Gavin said. "You will be

trained to work in the club—housekeeping or the kitchens. As long as you fulfill your duties, you'll have fair wages and room and board."

Davey looked up, and for an instant Gavin saw himself in that thin, battered face. The flicker of hope in the boy's good eye pierced his chest, releasing a spurt of cold rage. Predators on the weak—they deserved to be punished.

"Who did this to you?" he asked.

Fear filled the boy's expression. "I—I can't say, sir."

"Can't or won't?" Before Gavin could press on, he heard a feminine voice outside the office.

"My concerns are urgent, and I must see Mr. Hunt immediately." There was a low, murmured reply, and then the voice said more stridently, "No, I will *not* wait. This is a matter of life or death. Kindly convey my message forthwith, sir."

Percy's bold fire warmed him, melting away some of his tension. *She's come to me at last... not that I was worried. I was right all along about her.* As usual, the cheeky chit knew how to make an entrance. Life or death, indeed—she could have made her living on Drury Lane. A minute later, the harried-looking footman appeared. Before the man could utter a word, Gavin said, "Send her in."

Percy traipsed through the doorway. Her bonnet with its filmy veil obscured her face—the minx did like her disguises—but the rest of her form was nicely outlined by her fashionable lilac dress. She pinned up her veil. Her eyes widened, and before he could utter a greeting, she strode over to Davey. Before Gavin's befuddled gaze, she lifted a gentle hand to the boy's jaw. Moreover, Davey allowed her touch, his expression moonstruck.

"You poor thing," she murmured. "'Tis a shiner, to be sure. Does it hurt dreadfully?"

"N-no, miss," the boy stammered.

She rummaged through her reticule and pulled out a lace-edged handkerchief. The fine scrap would cost more than Davey earned in a year, yet she handed it over to the boy.

"Fill this with ice, if the cook has some. If not, cold water will do. Hold it to the bruise, and the swelling will go down more quickly," she said.

"Yes, miss. Th-thank you." Davey sounded as stunned as Gavin felt.

Percy turned to Gavin then, and his bemusement faded with her next words. "How could you," she hissed. Her eyes spit flames at him. "He's but a boy and not even half your size. You ought to be ashamed of yourself."

For a minute, Gavin could not speak. Blood roared in his ears. Out of nowhere, a voice boomed in his head. *You are hereby found guilty of arson and sentenced to a term of ten years imprisonment.* Helpless rage curled his fists. *I didn't do it.*

"Beggin' your pardon, miss, but I think you've painted the wrong picture." This came from Alfie, who swept a spritely bow.

Percy frowned. "Who are you?"

"Name's Alfie, miss, an' I was the one who brung Davey 'ere today. To see about a job. Mr. Hunt 'ires on us lot—an' by *lot* I mean urchins an' ragamuffins," Alfie explained matter-of-factly. "The gent's a decent sort, you see, even if 'e looks like the devil 'imself."

"Oh." After a strained pause, Percy said to Davey, "Is that true?"

Davey gave a small nod.

She rounded on Gavin. Seething with anger, he readied for another attack. He knew all too well that the way to cover a mistake was to launch another barrage of insult and blame. Attack or be attacked. 'Twas the way of the stinking world.

"I—I'm afraid I owe you an apology, Mr. Hunt," she said. Roses bloomed in her cheeks. "I jumped to conclusions when I oughtn't have. For that, I am truly sorry."

Her contrition took the wind out of his sails. The storm within him came to an abrupt halt; he could only stare at her, bewildered by the intensity of emotion she provoked in him. Why did she have such an effect on him? Why should he give a bloody farthing what she thought? Out of the corner of his eye, he saw Alfie usher Davey out of the room and close the door behind.

"Forget it," he said flatly. "'Tis nothing."

"But it is." Her vibrant eyes held his, the expression in them impossibly sincere. "My accusation was most unfair. Mama is forever lecturing me on being too impulsive, and I fear she has the right of it." Biting her lip, Percy said in humble tones, "Will you accept my apology, Mr. Hunt?"

What could he say to that? He inclined his head gruffly, and she gave him a tremulous smile in return. Beneath her chin, yellow bonnet strings formed a cheerful bow. His fingers itched to undo it. To knock that stupid bonnet off and sink themselves into warm locks of sunshine...

Don't lose control, you fool. Focus. Close the deal.

"Might I inquire to the purpose of the day's visit?" he said in even tones.

The warmth fled from her expression. Her gaze lowered to the vicinity of his cravat. "I think you know why I've come. I wish to discuss your offer. Though," she added hurriedly, "I have some stipulations of my own."

Once again in control of himself, he closed the distance between them. She did not shirk from him, which he took as a good sign. She looked at him with surprise when he held out a chair.

"I am occasionally capable of good manners," he drawled. "As I have a feeling your provisions may take some time, you might as well be comfortable. Shall I ring for tea as well?"

"No, thank you." She took the seat he offered, folding her skirts primly around her. "Here are my terms, Mr. Hunt.

First, I wish to have the details of the wager spelled out—in writing, if you please."

He leaned against the desk, studying her. "I gave you my word, Miss Fines. That should be sufficient."

"Papa always said to get everything in writing. When all is said and done, I want tangible proof of my brother's freedom. That is, your signature clearing him of all debt when I win this bet."

Thought she had it in the bag, did she? Reminding himself that he gained nothing from baiting her at this juncture, he said curtly, "Fine. If you want a contract, you'll get it. What else?"

Eyes narrowing, he watched the play of emotions across her lively features. Percy would be terrible at cards; she had more tells than a leopard had spots. Seeing her gnaw her lower lip, he braced himself for news he wasn't going to like.

"I want your promise that during the wager you will not try to find or harm Paul," she said. "You will not even accept payment from him, should he decide to find you."

"You must be joking."

"I assure you I am not." Her voice was calm, but he noted the rapid rise and fall of her bosom. "Why should I risk agreeing to this bet if you can snare my brother at any time? Why should you get your cake and eat it too?"

Damn, but she was cleverer than he gave her credit for.

"I will still have both you and your brother's company," he said. "When I win the wager."

"*If* you win." Pink blossomed in her cheeks, but her gaze did not waver. "But if you lose, the Fines' debt to you will be dissolved, and you will leave us in peace."

He looked at her stubborn, piquant little face and felt something close to respect. For a female, she possessed strong notions of loyalty. Too bad those bonds tied her to Morgan.

He gave a slow nod. "Agreed."

She released a breath, clearly relieved. "Well, then, there's only one more thing."

He cocked a brow.

"It has to do with the manner of deciding the number of visits. I will toss but only,"—she raised a delicate gloved finger—"*one* of the dice."

His jaw tautened. He was not so much concerned over her proposal itself as he was over her temerity in bargaining with him. She was growing bolder by the minute; if he did not take care, she might begin to think she could run roughshod over him. A pretty thing like her was probably used to getting everything she wanted. Probably had all the gentlemen wrapped around her precious little finger.

"Give me one good reason why I should agree to that in addition to the other concessions I am making," he said.

Her sable lashes angled upward. "Because you happen to be in a magnanimous mood?"

"Try again, Miss Fines."

She chewed on her lip. "Because you are so confident in your own prowess that you believe you could seduce me within six meetings?"

"Better reasoning," he acknowledged, "but still not good enough."

"I don't see why using one die should matter so much," she said in a tone just short of wheedling. "After all, I am agreeing to risk my reputation and my person for the sake of this wager. The least you could do is accommodate this request."

That smile of hers could probably charm birds from their leafy perches and well she knew it. He stroked his chin. "I suppose I might consider it..."

"Excellent. I knew you'd come around," she said, beaming.

"... if you'd grant me a request in return."

Her brow furrowed. "What sort of request?"

"Nothing much. Just a kiss. To seal the bargain, you understand."

"*Another* kiss?" she said with clear dismay.

"Yes, Miss Fines. A gesture of good faith on your part for all the concessions I am making." It was his turn to smile. "Unless you're afraid of kissing me again?"

Chapter Nine

DRAT AND DOUBLE drat. Hunt thought he'd cornered her; she could tell by the arrogant look on his face, the relaxed line of his scar. Why was the man so... befuddling? Earlier, she'd glimpsed a wholly unexpected side of him. A streak of kindness and nobility. He had shown compassion for that unfortunate boy and apparently many others as well. Though she cringed at how she'd maligned Hunt in that instance, the current ruthless set of his features sent a thrill of warning up her spine.

She gave her head a wary shake. "I cannot kiss you."

"Then I'm afraid I cannot agree to your request."

"That is not very gentlemanly, sir."

He lifted a sardonic brow in answer.

She tried to summon a viable alternative, but came up short. After Charity's report on Paul yesterday, Percy had known what needed to be done. Her friend's trembling voice played in her head.

Mr. Fines was not at all as I remember him. He was... out of sorts, t-terribly so. Charity's face had drained of color. *He's tired of hiding, he said, and doesn't give a... a damn about anything anymore. Oh Percy, he said he's going to march over to Mr. Hunt and hand over his inheritance!*

Percy straightened her shoulders. She could not allow her brother to destroy his future and their father's legacy on a drunken whim. She *would* not. And what difference would another kiss make? She'd made it through the other one unscathed, after all. And now she knew what to expect of Hunt. She could manage this.

"One kiss," she said, her nape tingling, "but I get to roll the die first."

He inclined his head and reached to the desk for the die. She came to stand beside him, her gloved hand held out. He dropped the ivory cube into her palm; given the fortunes lost and won by that small piece, its weight felt oddly insignificant.

She cupped her palms together and shook. In her head, she tried to visualize a single black dot. *Please, God, let it be a one...*

"Praying doesn't help." Hunt's mocking voice cut through her focus. "Just so you know."

"Will you kindly stop talking and let me concentrate?"

"That doesn't help either," he said.

Gritting her teeth, she gave the die another shake and let it loose onto the blotter. The cube rolled several times, her heart flipping with each motion. When it teetered on an edge, her breath caught. All air whooshed from her lungs as the die fell.

On *six*.

"Devil take it!" The words burst from her.

"I think he already has, Miss Fines."

Her gaze cut to Hunt, who made no attempt to hide his look of satisfaction. Temper piqued, she said, "I demand to roll again! You interrupted me."

"Tossing more than once was not part of the contract," he said. "I never took you for a welsher, Percy."

Despite her competitive nature, she believed in playing fair. He had the right of it, and it galled her to no end to know it. "I am not a spoilsport," she muttered, crossing her arms over her chest, "but you did interfere with my focus."

"As I said, it would not have made a lick of difference." He smiled, no doubt because everything was going his way. Which irked her further. "Come now, look on the bright side. 'Tis only six meetings. If you hadn't negotiated with me earlier, you'd have rolled both dice and might have wound up having to see me twelve times instead of six."

That much was true. Feeling slightly mollified, she said, "I suppose."

"Now about that kiss..."

Dash it all, she'd rolled a blasted six, and she *still* had to endure another kiss from the man? She heaved a sigh of disgust. "It hardly seems fair, but have at it. Just do it quickly," she added ungraciously. "My chaperone believes I am at a sewing circle and expects me back by two."

"Then by all means, let us get on with the business." His lips quirked. "I'll try not to lose track of time."

Lose track of time? What is he talking about? He must be trying to unnerve me. Well, I won't give him that satisfaction. Once and for all, I'll prove I'm not a wicked girl.

She angled her chin upward. "Just so you know, I am no green chit. You're not the only one who has kissed me, you know."

His brows shot up.

Good. Loftily, she went on, "I am familiar with this particular activity and how it's done. I know for a fact that it never takes more than a minute to accomplish—like the last time."

A choked sound left him. Good again. Now he knew she was no inexperienced ninny. With a twinge, she thought of Lord Charles. The man she ought to be kissing and with whom said gesture would likely be heavenly. But it couldn't be helped; she best handle herself with cool aplomb and get the matter over with.

"I'll, er, do my best not to disappoint," Hunt said.

"Just get on with it." Pursing her lips, she shut her eyes.

And nearly jumped when a warm caress slid along her neck.

"Wh-what are you doing?" she stammered. Her skin tingled where he'd touched her; she'd never known that patch beneath her ear to be sensitive. Yet sparks danced over the surface of her skin.

"Untying your bonnet." His eyes gleamed, the golden flecks in them pronounced against his darkened pupils. "'Tis a grand brim, to be sure, but surely you don't expect me to fit under there with you?"

"Oh. I suppose not." *Do not overreact. Remain calm and collected.* Reaching up, she fumbled with the ribbons; to her consternation, they were hopelessly knotted.

"You're making things worse. Allow me."

Nudging aside her hands, Hunt expertly took hold of the strings. She swallowed as his fingers brushed against her neck, the calloused pads rasping lightly against her skin. A shivering awareness spread over her, raising the fine hairs on her arms and tightening her lower belly. All of her senses chose that moment to come fully awake: Hunt's scent penetrated her nostrils— leather and male spice, familiar yet exotic.

In a rush, the dream of the catacombs came back to her, and she swayed. Suddenly, she remembered she'd forgotten to invoke the no-touching rule. "Mr. Hunt, I—"

He placed a finger to her lips. The brightness of his eyes mesmerized her. "Enough talking. Close your eyes now, Persephone, and take my kiss."

All thought fled as his hands cupped her head, held her in place. She quivered within that strong yet strangely gentle grasp. A breath rushed out, and before she could draw in the next, he kissed her. Firm, warm lips against her own. She tried to think of Lord Charles, to distract herself by recalling his elegantly worded invitation to go for a drive... to Hyde Park... her mind grew blurry. The lulling heat of the mouth moving over hers carried her farther and farther away from the shores of rationality.

She began to float, adrift in sensation. In pure and stunning discovery.

Then the kiss deepened, and a mysterious undercurrent stirred within her. *What on earth is happening?* she wondered foggily. *It wasn't like this last time...* She felt her knees give out, but she didn't fall; instead, she was lifted upon something solid, and all she could do was cling to the warm, hard muscle that was anchoring her and turning her inside out all at once. Her lungs burned, she could not breathe, and when her lips parted to pull in air, he moved inside with bold alacrity.

The caress shocked her. Rocked her.

A single thought flashed in her head: *more.*

He tasted of decadence, of freedom. He probed boldly, and she responded with the ungovernable need rising within her. His tongue slid against hers, and a molten wave washed over her. She moaned and the kiss tangled, growing hotter and hotter. Just when she thought she might die with the pleasure of it, he left her lips to suck her earlobe, to lick his way down her neck.

She was afire; she wanted *more* heat. A whimper lodged in her throat as he cupped her breast, fondling her through the bodice. Beneath the thin layer, her nipples sprouted, and need steamed in her veins. *Touch me there, oh please touch me—*

The bright chime of a clock shot through her sensual daze.

In a single, shocking moment, several facts crashed into her awareness. She was sprawled across a desk, clinging to Gavin Hunt like a limpet to a rock. His tongue was planted firmly in her mouth, while his hand palmed her breast, his thumb strumming lazily across its hardened tip. As she registered this last fact, a shock of pleasure radiated from that wanton bud to the juncture of her thighs. A flush of wetness alerted her to reality.

Dear God. Panic imbued her with sudden strength. She shoved at Hunt's heavy shoulders with all her might. "Let me go!"

He barely budged, but he did lift his head. His thick brown hair lay disheveled over his forehead. The laces of his shirt dangled, hair-dusted muscle visible where his cravat had once been. The buttons of his waistcoat had popped free.

Good heavens... had *she* done all that?

The wicked gleam in his eyes told her the answer and sent a humiliated ripple over her already tumultuous senses. A pulse beat madly in her throat. If he meant to ravish her...

"As you wish," he said and pulled her into sitting position.

She was off the desk like a shot. She yanked her bodice up, her face so hot she was certain the skin would melt from her bones.

"I m-must go," she stammered, edging toward the door. "My companion... 'tis late..."

"About our meetings, Miss Fines."

Meetings? Her feelings were a fracas. Her body tingled in all the places he had touched her... and some where he hadn't. *What has he done to me?*

"Will Friday evenings work for you? I will come for you at, say, ten o'clock?"

She moved her head numbly.

"Excellent." Male satisfaction imbued that single word. Before she knew what he intended, he caught hold of her hand and kissed it. His eyes roved over her with dark possession. "I must say, I am looking forward to the next six weeks."

Not knowing how to respond, she tugged her hand free and dashed out with as much dignity as she could muster.

Chapter Ten

RETURNING TO THE Seven Dials, Gavin felt neither shame nor pride about his origins. The rookery had spewed him from her dirty womb and left him to survive or die. The way he saw it, he'd paid any filial dues he owed in blood, sweat, and misery. He kept his eyes moving, scanning the derelict buildings. Beside him, Stewart was doing the same.

Instinct—it never left you.

"Why do the club owners always insist on meetin' at The Blind Stag? I *hate* the Dials. Nothin' but cadgers and thieves." Stewart scowled. "An' blowsy bunters, to boot."

Following his mentor's gaze, Gavin saw a drunken strumpet in the street up ahead. With a bottle of gin in one hand and a rod in the other, she shouted obscenities at a boy, beating him as he huddled against a wall. A scene straight from Gavin's own childhood. Inside his gloves, Gavin's fists clenched... but he walked on. From his own experience, he knew that interfering would only guarantee the boy double the knocks afterward.

Motherly love, he thought with derision. Nothing hurt more.

Then his glance shifted over to Stewart, and his scar throbbed with another indelible memory. He and his mentor had never spoken of that first night in the hulks. Stewart had done what needed to be done; Gavin had never blamed him for it. After all, some things were best left unsaid, and the two of them had never had any use for sentiment. They were men of action: they worked together, fought together, and watched each other's back.

Then why did he sometimes sense that dark moment hovering between them?

"You alright, lad?"

Stewart's voice yanked him back to the present. His mentor was giving him a strange look. "I'm fine," he said. "Just, er, thinking."

"Not about that chit, I 'ope," the other man said sourly.

In truth, 'twas a fair guess seeing as how thoughts of Percy continued to plague Gavin. She mystified him. One minute, she'd showed uncommon concern for a mere street boy and the next she'd torn up at Gavin for no reason. Then she had apologized, and her sincere acknowledgement of her mistake had floored him.

He couldn't recall the last time anyone had cared to have his forgiveness (and certainly never a female). Nowadays, people feared to cross him at all—and if they did, they either hid the fact or found someone else to blame. In his mother's case, she'd found the most convenient solution of all: she'd blamed *him* for her failures.

Percy's honesty, her obvious concern that she'd misjudged him, had blown through him like a zephyr from some exotic, sun-drenched land. His chest had prickled with warmth, pins and needles awakening a dormant part of him. In that moment, it had seemed that she... cared. About him. Then came their kiss. Christ, the way she'd responded to him, her intoxicating taste and wanton passion—

"Don't like that look on your face, Hunt," Stewart said.

Feeling like an idiot, Gavin coughed in his fist. "I'm, er, reviewing strategy for the meeting. Thinking on how best to approach the other club owners."

"Shoot first and don't get shot," came the laconic reply.

They approached the center of the Dials, where the seven streets collided in a celebration of depravity. Taverns faced each other on all seven apexes, and prostitutes swarmed even at this early hour to ply their trade. Bending their heads, he and Stewart entered through the low doorway of the Blind Stag. The tavern was packed with the usual crowd of riff-raffs, the air ripe with the stench of stale ale, smoke, and unwashed bodies. Pushing their way through the rowdy main room, they went upstairs to the private meeting chambers. Gavin was not surprised to see who'd been the first to arrive.

"Good day, Mr. and Mrs. Kingsley," he said.

He bowed over the bejeweled hand the latter held out as if she were royalty. Which, in a manner, she was. Mavis Kingsley came from powerful criminal stock; her father, Bartholomew Black, was an infamous cutthroat who controlled much of the Seven Dials. Several years ago, Mavis had wed Warren Kingsley, owner of The Palace. Kingsley's club now almost rivaled the success of The Underworld, in no small part due to Mavis' connections.

Gavin exchanged bows with the richly dressed Adonis standing beside her.

"La, Mr. Hunt, such fine manners you have." In contrast to her husband's polished good looks, Mavis had a plain face, sallow and sharp-edged from a chronically frail constitution. Even her opulent gown could not hide the meagerness of her figure. "I was telling Kingsley here that we should have you over for supper soon. All work and no play, as they say."

"How kind of you," Gavin said noncommittally.

"I could arrange for a few eligible ladies to be present as well." Mavis batted sparse eyelashes. "'Tis past time there was a *Mrs.* Hunt, wouldn't you agree, Kingsley?"

"Of course, my dear," her spouse said indulgently. "Marriage makes the man."

On the rare occasion Gavin had thought about wedlock,

he'd pictured his bride as a hard, practical sort... mayhap like Mavis, though he wouldn't suffer being led by the bollocks like Kingsley. His would be a properly submissive wife. Who'd be loyal and content with a partnership based on mutual benefit.

A woman the very opposite of the troublesome Miss Fines.

"A man makes 'imself. 'E can't depend on no one—and 'specially not one in a skirt," Stewart said tersely. "Anyone who says differently is a fool."

Mavis gave a brittle laugh. "Never argue with a bachelor."

"While we have you, Hunt," Kingsley said, "I wanted to express my outrage at what happened to your patrons. Know that you have my full support in getting to the bottom of this."

Utter claptrap, of course. Less business for The Underworld meant more for competitors like The Palace, and they both knew it. Kingsley had always been a tricky, underhanded bastard. Years ago, before his marriage to Mavis, he and Gavin had had a "misunderstanding" over a wench. Gavin had given Kingsley a public drubbing, leaving the man weeping in the dirt like a babe. He was certain Kingsley had never forgiven him for the humiliation.

"That is the purpose of meeting with all the houses today—to discuss how to avoid such incidents in the future," Gavin said evenly.

"But we can't be certain who to trust, can we?" Kingsley made a show of shaking his well-coiffed head. Not a single strand of golden hair fell out of place. "Though it pains me to say it, I've had suspicions for a while now about Lyon—"

"So that's why me ears were burnin'," announced a roguish voice. "Back-bitin' again, are we, Kingsley?"

Robbie Lyon, proprietor of Lyon's Lair, stepped into the room with his typical flourish. Despite his wiry build, the man was a scrapper and one who never pulled his punches. He was like a small mongrel who'd take any opportunity to piss on you, just for the hell of it. Last year, he and Gavin had had a few skirmishes over territorial lines, so he, too, had cause to make trouble for The Underworld.

"Nonsense," Kingsley said, the smile never slipping from his face. "You must be hearing things in your old age."

Lyon bristled from his grey mane to his thick-soled boots. "Care to test out more than my hearin', you lily-livered dandy?"

"Gentlemen, please." Mavis coughed delicately. "A lady is present."

Snorting, Lyon ran the back of his hand under his nose. "Get your mount under control, ma'am, and then we'll get to the business o' meetin'."

As the two men glowered at one another, their guards reached for their steel.

"Not starting the fun without me, are you lads?" said a rich, lilting voice.

All heads turned as the final two members joined the group. Though Patrick and Finian O'Brien shared a mother, their appearances did not betray their relationship. Patrick was as tall as Stewart and twice as wide, with the traditional red Irish coloring; Finian, the younger brother, had the rangy look of a rat with beady brown eyes and a thin mustache.

Bad blood existed between Gavin and both O'Briens. Half dozen years ago, Gavin had outbid Patrick to secure the property for The Underworld, and the latter held a lasting grudge. As for the younger brother, cases of expensive French brandy had once gone missing from Gavin's storeroom and somehow ended up at Finian's club. Gavin wouldn't trust either O'Brien farther than he could toss him.

Kingsley straightened his velvet lapel. "You haven't missed a thing, O'Brien," he said easily. "Lyon and I were just arsing around."

"If that's the case, let's eat," Patrick said. He licked his lips as he looked over at the abundant sideboard. "Ah, no one roasts a joint like the Blind Stag. Been buried to the armpits in fish of late, on account of Mrs. O'Brien's plan to reduce me." He winked at his brother. "Never heard her complaining about my size in the bedchamber, though, eh?"

Mavis Kingsley sniffed and returned to the table, her husband following at her heels.

Minutes later, they were all settled around the long trestle, a mimicry of a genial gathering as each of them was backed by armed guards. Sitting at one end, Gavin could feel Stewart's bristling impatience beside him.

No time like the present.

"Thank you all for coming," Gavin said. "I invited you today to discuss the assault on my customers." A quick scan around the table did not reveal any nervous twitches or flutters; then again, he didn't expect any. He was dealing with a band of seasoned cutthroats, after all. "Not only did they sustain grave injuries, but the smear to my club's reputation cannot be overlooked. Whoever was behind the attack aimed to halt business to The Underworld."

"How terrible." This came from Kingsley, who was seated to Gavin's right. "Have you any idea of the perpetrator? You have the backing of The Palace to set this matter right."

"Maybe 'twas you who set the matter in motion," Lyon said with a sneer.

"Why you uppity little—" Kingsley began.

Mavis cut her spouse off with a hand. "There is no need to point fingers amongst friends, Mr. Lyon." Her smile could slice diamonds. "And we *are* old friends, are we not? As I recall, you are acquainted with my father."

The implied threat in Mavis' words brought a chill over the room. Few would dare cross Bartholomew Black. Those who did wound up strung up by the thumbs—with the rest of their body parts scattered in the Thames. Gavin had never met Black in person, and he planned to keep it that way.

"This hasn't a thing to do with your pa, and you know it," Lyon muttered—but he fell silent after that.

Mavis' eyes honed shrewdly upon Gavin's face. "As my husband was saying, have you any idea who is responsible for this heinous crime?"

"I'd wager Hunt has his pick of enemies." Patrick looked up from the mound of food on his plate. "Who knows how many skeletons he's got rattling in his closet?"

'Twas true that a man couldn't get to where Gavin was without treading on a few toes. He'd made his fair share of enemies in the hulks, for instance; of the few convicts who'd survived, none had the sophistication to carry out such a revenge. Moreover, Gavin couldn't think of anyone from his past who had as much to gain as the bastards in this room.

"There are enough live bodies for me to consider," he said, "without digging up corpses."

"A man who pilfers another's good fortune has what's coming to him." Chucking a rib-bone aside, Patrick O'Brien gave a satisfied belch, causing Mavis to shudder. "No crime in that."

Gavin reined in his temper. "The property was not yours to lose, O'Brien. I outbid you, and The Underworld belongs to me. End of story."

"If it wasn't for you, I'd be rolling in the ready." Behind pads of fat, Patrick's small hazel eyes glinted with malice. "Instead, I had to make do with an inferior club at an inferior location. You owe me, Hunt, and don't think I'll forget it."

"I don't owe you a bloody thing. Look to your own ham-handed management if you want something to blame. Only a fool would do business with moneylenders."

Patrick's fist pounded against the table, rattling the dishes. "You insolent pup, I'll rip your head off."

"I'd like to see you try," Stewart growled.

The armed men in O'Brien's corner leaned forward.

Shoving to his feet, Gavin said, "I'll take on any challenge, and I'll do it man to man. You want a pummeling, O'Brien? Come and get it."

The Irishman's face purpled with rage. The buttons on his waistcoat strained as he tried to get to his feet, but fell back, wheezing. "I'll give... you... a basting... any time..."

"Hush, Patrick. Remember what the physician said." Finian gave a sharp nod to one of his guards, who set about loosening Patrick's neck cloth. "As you can see, Mr. Hunt, my brother is in no shape for violence. We came today to make peace, not war."

Muscles bunching, Gavin looked around the table and read hostility in every gaze. "Hear me now: I will not countenance further aggression against my club." Staring down each cutthroat in turn, he vowed, "All actions against me will be returned ten-fold. If it's blood you want, it's blood you'll get."

Lyon was on his feet in an instant. "Who're you to make threats?" he barked, rolling up his sleeves. "I'll take you down a notch, boy, an' see what tune you're singin' then."

Gavin's blood went from a simmer to a boil. He knew well enough the rules of the stews: fight violence with violence. Reasoning had no place in dealing with these buggers, and he'd never in his life backed down from a fight. Stepping back from the table, he made a come-hither motion with his hand.

Lyon charged at him, knife raised. Gavin sidestepped the attack, shoving his elbow into Lyon's back. With a grunt, Lyon fell forward, smashing against the sideboard, raining food everywhere. But the bastard recovered, rising and coming again, this time feigning the attack so that Gavin had to spin at the last second to avoid being gutted. Acting on pure instinct, Gavin jabbed his elbow up, connecting with the other's windpipe; Lyon grunted, his knife clattering to the floor.

Taking the advantage, Gavin drove Lyon into the wall, pinning his opponent by the neck. As his fingers squeezed the other's throat, the dark power of the hulks washed over him.

"I give... " Lyon choked out. "Let me... go..."

The call of violence rippled through Gavin's blood. His grip tightened, and Lyon's eyes bugged out. Behind him, Gavin heard the squeal of chairs, felt Stewart's towering presence at his back.

"Lad?"

His mentor's voice returned him to the present. *Nothing to be gained from killing Lyon*. With an effort borne of sheer will, he loosened his death-hold. Lyon sank to the ground, gasping like a landed trout.

Pivoting, Gavin faced the audience. This time, he saw fear and grudging respect in their eyes. "Let this be a lesson to all," he said with soft menace. "Cross me, and you'll pay."

Finian reacted first, taking his brother by the arm. "Come, Patrick, let us go. There's nothing to be gained from acting like a bunch of jackals."

With a glare at Gavin, Patrick O'Brien stomped out of the room followed closely by his brother and their men.

"I don't need your bloody help!" This came from Lyon, who shoved away his guards' efforts to assist him. Stumbling to his feet, he bared his teeth. "Mark my word, this isn't the end of it, Hunt."

"I won't have mercy the next time," Gavin said.

Swearing, the wiry figure stalked off with his coterie. Which left Gavin with the Kingsleys.

"What coarse language and in front of a lady. Lyon's nothing but an uncouth brute." Kingsley's face creased with distaste. "You can take a man from the stews but never the stews from the man."

Teetering, Mavis murmured through pale lips, "Kingsley, I think I need to rest now."

"Of course, my dear." Her husband put a solicitous arm around her. "Hunt, I'll drop by soon, and we'll discuss things under more civilized circumstances."

The two departed, leaving Gavin and Stewart to look at each other.

Gavin rubbed his neck. "Went well, don't you think?"

"Got your point across," Stewart said.

Chapter Eleven

The gallant steed pulled up in front of Miss Farnham just as she stumbled out of the bushes. She recognized the rider as Lord Petersby, the object of her secret crush. As she gazed up into the perfection of his face, time seemed to stand still. Lord Petersby's refined voice cut through the passionate swell of violins in her head.

"Is that you, Miss Farnham?" Holding up a quizzing glass, he peered at her. "My dear lady, what has happened to your bonnet? And are those grass stains on your gown?"

Too late, she realized that the journey through the forest had left its mark.

—from *The Perils of Priscilla*, a manuscript sitting upon the desk of P. R. Fines

"Is anything amiss, Miss Fines? You seem preoccupied."

"Oh, um, it's nothing."

With a guilty start, Percy directed her gaze back to Lord Portland. They were strolling along Rotten Row, the most fashionable stretch of Hyde Park. At this time of the afternoon, members of the *ton* crammed the tree-lined path. Some descended from the cluster of gleaming carriages to walk on foot whilst others paraded on horseback; all vied to see and be seen. Percy noticed how passersby—the ladies in particular—slid appreciative glances at her companion.

She couldn't blame them. Lord Charles cut a dashing figure in his crisp china blue cutaway jacket and buff breeches. A polished walking stick swung with elegant indolence from his hand. The sun glinted off the rich auburn hair curling over his ears whilst his boots reflected a mirror's shine; it seemed even dust daren't meddle with such masculine perfection. She ought to have been prancing with joy to be at his side.

Instead, that infernal kiss with Hunt kept interrupting what ought to have been a prime opportunity to advance her acquaintance with the viscount. Her hands balled inside her butter-smooth gloves, and her cheeks grew uncomfortably warm. Why had Hunt affected her so? She was not in love with the bounder. Even if she found him the *teensiest* bit attractive—in a rough, uncouth sort of way—it was no excuse for her actions. She'd acted worse than a trollop.

Her heart thudded as she recalled the sensations he'd elicited in her. So strong... and *intense*. Beyond anything she'd come across in novels—and she'd done *a lot* of reading.

Dash it all, I am not *a wicked girl! Hunt... caught me off guard, was all.*

'Twas true that witnessing him with those children had revealed a hidden side to the man. There was more to him than met the eye. A mystery below the surface—

"I think you have wandered off again, Miss Fines."

Focus! "I am ever so sorry, Lord Portland," she said. *Who cares if Hunt is an enigma? He is your opponent now—and a tricky one at that. Don't forget how he lulled you into a sense of false security with that first kiss. Think how smug he'd be if he knew you were thinking about him instead of your beloved.* Summoning her brightest smile, she added, "It must be the heat. I think it has addled my senses."

Beneath his smart tall hat, Lord Charles' grey eyes warmed. "No need to apologize, Miss Fines. 'Tis only natural and admirable that a lady should have delicate sensibilities.

Indeed, your sensitivity to the clime does you a compliment—would you like me to send for the carriage?"

He looked behind them, where her maid and his groom followed at a proper distance.

"Thank you, but it won't be necessary. I think I can manage for a while longer." *Note to self: do not let on that you have the constitution of an ox.* She lowered her lashes in what she hoped passed for a demure manner. "I have been so looking forward to this, after all."

"How delightful of you to say so," Lord Charles said.

He paused to tip his hat at an acquaintance.

His merest gestures were like poetry. One never felt unsettled around Lord Charles; he was all that was proper and good. Precisely the type of gentleman Papa would have wished for a son-in-law. And utterly unlike that other dratted someone *who intended to ruin her family*. She resolved not to think of Hunt again for the remainder of the outing.

Yet as the viscount led the way down the path, she found herself short on conversation. Just perfect. Most of the time, she couldn't keep her tongue still. Being a chatterbox was practically a family trait; unfortunately, most of that chattering involved bickering or debating inappropriate topics, neither of which was fit for present company. She concentrated on the tips of her half-boots, noticing the layer of fine dirt coating the teal leather.

Think of something clever to say, else he'll think you a graceless Cit ...

"I do so like your hat," she blurted. "It is very fine."

"Thank you," he said. "I should say the same of your ensemble. Madame Rousseau, I believe?"

She looked at him in surprise. "How did you know?"

"I make it a point to know quality." Stopping, he made an elegant leg. "And that you possess in spades, Miss Fines."

His compliment boosted her self-confidence. She was

glad she'd taken great pains with her toilette today, choosing a white sprigged muslin trimmed in sky blue satin. Beneath the high waist, the front of the walking dress parted to reveal a lovely tiered underskirt. A fitted spencer and a fashionable leghorn hat completed the outfit.

"Thank you, sir." She dimpled up at him. "I'm afraid I spent quite some time in front of the looking glass. I didn't wish to be put in the shade by my companion, you see."

He rewarded her with a smile. "Your candor is most refreshing, Miss Fines. If I may return the compliment, I quite enjoyed our waltz last week. You follow beautifully."

With relief, she surmised that he had not noticed her restrained and rather wooden movements during the set. She'd exerted laborious effort to refrain from an unfortunate tendency to lead. As her beleaguered dancing master had put it, *You must accompany your partner like a butterfly, signorina, and flutter softly behind... flutter... flutter... Per* l'amor di dio, *I said flutter, not charge ahead like a Pamplonian bull!*

Luckily, she had pulled it off. *Take that, Signor Dancing Master.*

"And I must return the returned compliment," she said impishly. "You dance divinely, my lord. And I've heard that is only one of your many accomplishments."

"I do try. Being a gentleman, one has so much time on one's hands. I've always said that leisure is wasted, if it is not spent in the pursuit of beauty."

"How romantic, my lord," she said. "You write poetry, do you not?"

"I have tried my hand at verse. In point of fact, a publisher is considering my work," he said. "He likens it to the style of the poet Shelley."

"Oh, I adore Mr. Shelley's poems," she breathed.

Before she could say more, they had to stop for him to greet a giggling lady and her mama. Percy took the moment to discreetly gaze upon Lord Charles. He was perfection. He possessed a noble forehead and nose, the refined lips of an artist... Out of nowhere, the memory of another mouth assailed her. Hard, sensual lips made not for poetry, but for sin. Heat flooded her insides, her nipples prickling beneath her bodice as awareness throbbed in her blood...

"Miss Fines, are you ready to go on?"

"Yes, of course." Her breath not quite steady, she took his arm, still trying to shake the memory of Hunt's kiss. Peeking over at the viscount's flawless, placid visage, she felt the tiniest niggle of uncertainty. *Surely I'd enjoy kissing Lord Charles far more, wouldn't I? Why, if he were to kiss me, surely I'd forget Hunt altogether...*

"Now where were we?" the viscount asked.

She flushed at the direction of her thoughts. "Um, discussing poetry," she said. "Mr. Shelley's, in particular."

"Ah, yes," he replied, his walking stick making an elegant arc. "Which one of his poems do you most admire?"

She slid a look at Lord Portland's fine figure. A man couldn't be *too* perfect... could he? A puckish notion caused her to blurt, "*Love's Philosophy*."

The viscount's brows jumped at the mention of the racy verse. "Indeed."

Knowing she was being an awful flirt and yet unable to help herself, she said, "I find the poem's sentiment affecting. Do you, my lord?"

Though she knew it was not fashionable, she'd always dreamt of a passionate, loving marriage. The kind Papa and Mama had shared and that Nicholas had found with Helena. She'd assumed that beneath Lord Charles' polite breeding lay an ardent soul. Nicholas, after all, could appear quite stoic on the outside, and yet she had caught him stealing kisses from his marchioness when he thought no one was looking.

Percy's breath held. Surely Lord Charles understood

passion. He was a poet—he *had* to.

A tinge of color touched his high cheekbones. "In theory, certainly."

In theory? What on earth does that mean?

Clearing his throat, the viscount consulted his watch fob. "My, it's grown late. It seems we shall have to postpone our conversation to a later time. Shall we return to the carriage?"

The door to the carriage opened, and the urchin clambered in and onto the opposite seat.

"Fill me in, Alfie," Gavin said as he observed the scene beyond the window.

"She an' that carroty-pated git been wearin' their 'eels down for an hour or more. 'Im's a stuffed shirt, if I e'er saw one." The boy snorted. "Walks wif a stick up 'is arse an' bends 'is 'ellos more times than a ha'penny whore."

Gavin released the curtain, bringing the carriage into darkness once more. As usual, Alfie's description was spot on. The boy had got Lord Charles Portland down to the last priggish detail.

"And Miss Fines?" he said. "How would you describe her manner during their exchange?"

Beneath his grimy cap, Alfie's eyes swung heavenward. "Like a moon-struck booby, that's 'ow. Makin' eyes an' spoutin' 'eaps o' rubbish." Fluttering his lashes, the boy mimicked, "Ooh, my lord, you're so 'andsome. I ne'er seen a gent so 'andsome. Why, you're the 'andsomest—"

Gavin held up a hand. "I get the idea, Alfie."

His jaw clenched. He told himself it should come as no great shock that Percy would fancy herself in love with Lord Portland. Half the chits in Town would give their eyeteeth to wed the bloody viscount, and the other half would give much more than that. Aye, Gavin thought with disgust, he understood the workings of the *ton*. Thus, he should not be surprised. Nor should he wish to tear Portland's head off and dismember the rest of the niff-naff limb by limb.

What the devil did Percy see in that bloodless fop?

A title and loads of blunt, that's what, the cynical voice in his head answered. *'Tis what all middling class chits aim for. Percy may honey coat it with talk of romance, but in the end she's no different from the rest of her kind and don't you forget it.*

The anger focused him. While Percy might have delusions of love where Portland was concerned, *Gavin* was the one she'd kissed with unbridled enthusiasm. He could still taste her lips, sweet as spun sugar, melting against his. He could feel her eager hands and the way her soft curves had molded with perfect pliancy to his own hard form, which grew instantly harder at the memory.

Portland wanted her heart? He could have at it. That organ was useless as far as Gavin was concerned; what he meant to have was Percy's delectable body. And his revenge. Raking a hand irritably through his hair, he told himself to stay fixed on the goal. In a nutshell: ruin her, take her brother's shares, and destroy Nicholas Morgan, all in one fell swoop.

"You want me to keep tailin' 'em, guv?"

"No, I have it from here." Gavin flipped the boy a coin. "You go on."

Alfie caught the guinea mid-air and saluted. "Pleasure, sir, an' won't mind if I do. Plenty o' pigeons in the park today, an' all o' 'em ripe for a pluckin'." With a grin, he hopped out of the carriage and melted into the crowd.

Having seen enough of Percy and her beau cavorting in the sunshine, Gavin instructed the driver to proceed home. The route took him through the Covent Garden market, and he stared pensively out into the bustling piazza, formulating his strategy. Coercion would only elicit Percy's rebellious streak, so the way to seduce her was to let her think she was making her own choices. To lay out the lures and let his curious (and more than a little competitive) adversary take the bait.

Having a competitive nature himself, he had to admit he found their games... entertaining. His lips twitched, thinking of the grudging manner in which she'd held her side of the bargain. She hadn't wanted to yield that second kiss, yet when she had, she'd participated with a pure passion that had roused him utterly. With her, the innocent act of touching lips had fueled his lust more than the most debauched acts with other women in the past.

He wondered if Percy had thought about their kisses. Wondered if she—like him—had done more than just think about it. The notion of Percy frigging herself made him hot all over. Of course, proper young misses did not do such things, but a man could dream, couldn't he? By the time he arrived at the club, his trousers had gotten uncomfortably tight again. So he was not especially pleased to see Kingsley's velvet-clad figure at the front steps of The Underworld.

"Hunt, well met." Kingsley waved a greeting.

Gavin buttoned his jacket over his front. Thank God he'd not worn a cutaway today. "To what do I owe the honor?" he said.

"I'm following up on my promise to lend a hand," Kingsley said pleasantly. "The wife's off in Bath for a few weeks so I thought you and I could talk. Man to man, eh?"

"Shall we meet in my office?" Gavin said without enthusiasm.

He led the way up the steps into the circular atrium. Sunlight streamed in from the windows, gleaming off the black marble floors and the crystal tiers of the chandelier. Like spokes of a wheel, six lavish hallways extended outward toward the gaming salons. Industrious servants cleaned and swept; Davey paused in the act of polishing a mirror to bow low.

Gavin noted the envious slant to Kinglsey's gaze. *Let the bastard look. But if he tries to take what's mine, I'll do more than pummel him into the dirt. This time, I'll wring his bloody neck.*

They entered the office, and Gavin waved Kingsley into the chair facing the desk. He poured the man a drink, knowing the other wouldn't touch it. If the tables were reversed, he wouldn't either. Sitting back against studded leather, Gavin eyed his uninvited guest and slowly sipped his whiskey. "What sort of assistance are you offering, Kingsley?"

The Adonis smiled, showing perfect white teeth. "A proposal of mutual benefit. The way I see it, there's only two men deserving of the riches Covent Garden has to offer, and they're both sitting in this room."

"I'm certain the other proprietors would disagree."

"Who—Lyon? The O'Briens?" Kingsley made a scoffing sound. "They're uncouth and uncivilized, not fit for greatness. And the attack on your patrons? I wouldn't put that cowardly action past any of the three."

Or you. "What are you proposing?" Gavin said.

"We join forces, Hunt. Between the two of us, we have more men, more power than the rest combined. I say we use it to put the others out of business. Then we expand our clubs and split the riches." Leaning forward, Kingsley said, "Covent Garden, fifty-fifty between us."

There was truth to Kingsley's words: they *were* the two most successful of the bunch. If they banded together, they could likely run the others out of the area. Or make them disappear, which, Gavin guessed, was what the other would prefer. Though there was no love lost between him and the other club owners, Gavin had no desire to murder the competition. He knew where that path led: carnage begat carnage. And the last thing he wanted was to be sharing a blood-splattered throne with the Judas across the table.

"Why me? If it's more power that you're after, why not band with your father-in-law?" Gavin said. Teamed with Bartholomew Black, Kingsley might become an unstoppable force.

Anger flashed across the other's man features before he tucked it away, leaving nothing but a smooth, unperturbed surface. "I'd like to make a name for myself without the old man's help," he said easily. "Never liked mixing family with business."

So the rumors were true. Gossip had it that Black had never taken a shine to Kingsley, whom he considered a fop. The old man had consented to the marriage only because he could deny his daughter nothing. Mavis was the apple of Black's eye, and any man fool enough to marry her had better keep her happy... or suffer the consequences.

Gavin stood. "I've never liked mixing my business with another's. So I must decline your offer."

"Consider my offer with care, Hunt." Kingsley rose as well, his lips pulled tight. "You're not the only one I can ally with. There are many players in this game, and you'll want to choose the winning team."

"I don't need a team to win. I'll do so on my own." Gavin made a mocking bow.

Kingsley's mouth turned white. He gave a stiff nod and stalked from the room. Gavin continued to sip his whiskey. Magnus' advice floated into his head. *Keep your friends close, your enemies closer...* but too close and they'd slit your throat. In the end, a man was a fool to rely on anyone but himself. Having lived with that reality for as long as he could recall, Gavin wondered why it now left him cold.

Chapter Twelve

AT TEN MINUTES to ten on Friday night, Percy climbed over the window sill. She grabbed onto a sturdy branch of the oak tree outside her bedchamber and descended nimbly into the garden. Looking up, she saw no glow in the windows of the servants' quarters, and Tottie had gone to bed hours ago. No one would miss her. Heart racing, she let herself out the back gate and, pulling her hood closer around her face, hurried through the mist toward the street corner.

Moments later, a gleaming black carriage emerged from the fog, the enormous wheels rolling to a stop in front of her. The door opened, and her breath hitched. Having so recently experienced the refinement of Lord Portland's company, she could only marvel at how primal Hunt seemed in comparison. Moonlight glinted off his burnished eyes, limned the huge and menacing shape of him. He wore unrelieved black, the same color as the brutish four-in-hand stamping at the ground.

"Good evening." His voice was as deep and dark as the netherworld. "I trust you haven't been here long."

He held out a hand, and she had no choice but to take it. Even through the layers of leather, his touch scorched her. She snatched her hand away the instant she was aboard.

"I arrived only moments ago myself," she said, scooting to the farthest corner.

To her relief, he took the opposite seat. His presence seemed to fill the plush velvet and leather interior, his clean, masculine scent curling in her nostrils. In the flickering light of the lamp, his features were rendered in harsh relief, his scar raised by the shadows beneath it. Her lungs stretched to fill themselves as the enormity of the situation suddenly struck her. *I've a date with the devil.* By then, he'd shut the door, and the carriage spun into motion. Percy had the sensation of gliding into dark and uncharted waters.

The River Styx, perhaps.

"A lady who doesn't keep a man waiting," he said. "How unusual."

His mocking tone annoyed her and dispelled some of her nervousness. "When I sign my name to something, I follow through with it," she said tartly. "Where are we headed, Mr. Hunt?"

"I think we're better friends than that. Let us drop the formalities. Agreed... Percy?"

"I repeat, Mr. Hunt, what is our destination this evening?"

"You wound me, Miss Fines." He sighed, not at all convincingly. "The fact of the matter is, where we are going is a surprise, so you will just have to wait."

Dash it. Had waiting turned into some sort of national exercise? If she got a penny for every time... Disgruntled, she lifted the corner of the curtain and peered out at the passing darkness. They were headed down Pall Mall; they could end up anywhere.

She turned to him in exasperation. "Can't you at least give me a hint?"

"I suppose I could," he said. "But I have a better idea."

She gave him a wary look. "What sort of idea?"

"Quid pro quo. I'll tell you the destination if you'll answer a question of mine."

"Which is?"

He studied her with fathomless eyes. "Who is this gent you're infatuated with?"

Blood pulsed in her cheeks. "That is none of your business. And I'm not infatuated—I am in love." She quelled a quiver of uncertainty, raised her chin. "There is a difference."

"Either way, you want to kick up your heels for him, correct?"

"I do not want to... to do that, you vulgar swine!"

"You don't wish to bed your gentleman, then?" Hunt said in innocent tones. "There must be something wrong with him. He's balding, perhaps... or fat as our newly crowned King?"

"He is none of those things! Lord Portland is perfect—" Too late, she realized her error.

"You wouldn't mean *Viscount* Portland?" Hunt let out a low whistle. "For a merchant's daughter, you set your sights high."

Do not let him goad you. Remain calm.

"Can't say I blame you for not wanting to make the two-backed beast with that stick-in-the-mud. Though if I were you, I'd at least give it a try," he said. "You wouldn't want to discover on your wedding night that said stick is not in working order."

She kept her lips pressed together.

"Have you kissed him at least? He isn't as repulsive as all that?"

That did it. "He is not repulsive at all, curse you! And the reason we have not kissed is because he is a gentleman and would never dream of taking such liberties—"

"Good thing I'm not a gentleman, then." The smug tone and the flare in Hunt's eyes made her stomach leap. "I've dreamed of our sweet kiss, Persephone."

She felt words slipping away from her.

"Aye, I've dreamed of that... and more." A dark, wicked look came into his eyes. "Have you?"

She meant to deny it. But he was staring at her mouth with a greedy intensity that drove all thought from her mind. Her lips tingled with remembered heat. The spicy taste of him flooded her senses, and she felt the firm, velvety thrust of his tongue...

"So much for our game." His husky voice broke her reverie. "It seems we've arrived."

She realized the carriage had stopped. Flustered, she reached to the curtain to look outside. A dark river flowed into her vision... the Thames. She saw floating barges filled with people dressed in masks and colorful evening garb, and despite the circumstances, a tide of excitement rushed through her.

"We're taking a boat to Vauxhall?" she exclaimed.

"Indeed." His lips curved. "Been before?"

"Once, on my birthday," she said. "But there was a melee that night, and Mama has not allowed me back since."

"Don't worry," he said, "I will keep you safe."

Who will keep me safe from you?

As if reading her thoughts, a muscle twitched at the side of his mouth, his scar flickering. He lifted the cushion of the seat next him, revealing a hidden compartment. Reaching inside, he withdrew a large, bulging bag and handed it to her.

Curious, she looked inside. "A wig?"

"It's hardly an unfamiliar accessory, is it?"

"I suppose not," she said ruefully.

"There are plenty of feminine whatnots in there— everything you need to disguise your identity and protect your reputation... as promised." He paused, tapped his chin. "The only other thing you'll need is to a pick a name for the night."

"You mean... an assumed identity?"

This was getting better and better.

"We can't go around calling you Miss Fines all night if you wish to safeguard your reputation," he said reasonably.

"Shall I choose the name or will you?"

"What names do you have in mind?" she couldn't help but ask.

"Hmm. Something exotic and bold to match its owner." He gave her a considering look. "Juliette. Or Titania, perhaps."

She had to stifle a grin at his estimation of her. "You know The Bard," she said approvingly. With a hint of mischief, she added, "However, I think I'd rather go as Priscilla, thank you very much. And that will be Miss Farnham to you."

"Priscilla Farnham. It does have a ring to it." Opening the door, he sprung easily to the ground. "I'll leave you to your privacy then."

Bemused, she looked at the closed door. She had to admit—the man had a quicksilver wit. *Not that it matters. You're only here to help Paul.*

Worry gnawed at her as she wondered what her sibling was up to at the moment. Since Hunt had agreed to leave Paul alone, she'd gone to Spitalfields to find her brother, but without success. She'd left him a note, saying that she'd written Nicholas. She'd also stated that she'd negotiated with Hunt and that the latter had agreed to let Nick pay off the debt. 'Twas a half truth and Paul wouldn't like it, but he'd like her actual arrangement with Hunt far less. She couldn't risk him calling Hunt out and getting hurt.

In the meantime, she had to focus on winning the wager. She had a foolproof strategy worked out for the evening: avoid physical contact with the man and remain in full public view. If she stuck to those rules, he wouldn't have any chance of seducing her, would he? As additional reinforcement, she had the magic word at her disposal. Per their *signed* contract, all she had to do was tell him to stop; at the haberdashery, he'd proved a man of his word.

So there was no harm in playing along until then, was

there? Emptying the bag, she sorted through its contents and used them to complete her toilette. When she glimpsed her reflection in the hand-held mirror, a little thrill coursed through her. She couldn't help it: this business of disguises was so much *fun*. She fluffed her new shockingly red coiffure and examined the gaudy gold hoops dangling from her ears. Removing her cloak, she donned the scarlet silk domino she'd found in the bag; its bold color made her feel dashing, like a heroine on the brink of adventure.

Really, what possible harm could it do to enjoy the sights a little? When would be the next time she found herself at Vauxhall at midnight, after all? Surely she could enjoy herself *and* best Hunt at his own game. She tied on the last part of her costume, a lacy black demi-mask, and opened the carriage door. "I am ready, Mr. Hunt."

"That was quick—" Turning from where he'd been contemplating the water, he froze. A strange expression came over his face.

"Is something the matter?" She patted the wig. "Is my hair showing?"

"No. But you look... different."

"That's the idea, isn't it? So I won't be recognized?"

"Right. Of course." He cleared his throat and held out his arm. "Shall we board the barge, Miss Farnham?"

As he watched Percy's rapt expression beneath the famed lights of Vauxhall, Gavin's insides heated with anticipation. *Like taking candy from a babe.* Just as he'd predicted, she couldn't resist the dark excitement of the bustling pleasure garden. Oh, she'd made a show of keeping a safe distance, scooting as far away from him as possible in the supper box for two. Yet beneath the half-mask, her eyes sparkled, her attention riveted upon the operatic duo currently on the stage. It gave him the opportunity to study her.

Christ Almighty, she tempted his self-control in that disguise. The paints emphasized her natural sensuality, bringing out the naughty pout of her lips and the saucy slant of her cheekbones. Her kohl-rimmed eyes appeared even larger, sultry in their frame of black lace. His only regret was that her shining tresses remained hidden beneath the false curls. How he wanted to tear off that offending wig, sink his fingers into her hair and hold her steady for his kiss—

Don't lose focus. Cast out the lures and let her take the bite.

When the opera singers came to an ear-splitting finale, Percy jumped to her feet, clapping wildly. He had to bite back a smile as she whistled with the rest of the audience for an encore. He found her exuberance charming. It also made him wonder if she'd bring that kind of unschooled energy to bed… and his groin flooded with heat.

"Did you enjoy that, Miss Farnham?" he said.

"That was *brilliant.* I have a subscription to the Opera, yet I've never heard anything so sublime." Cheeks flushed, she sat down again, reaching for her arrack punch (strong stuff, and he'd subtly re-filled her cup twice). "Why is it that music sounds so much better outdoors?"

"Because that's not where it's usually played. Things tend to capture our interest when they're unusual." His glance slid over her glowing, vivacious face. "Different from our ordinary experience."

"I can vouch for that. In my experience, ordinary is just another word for boring."

"Have a lot of experience with the ordinary, Miss, ahem, Farnham?"

She wrinkled her nose. "I'm a middling class miss, Mr. Hunt. My entire *life* is ordinary. Tonight excepted, nothing interesting ever happens."

That might explain her theatrical bent. If he had to guess, a spirited chit like Percy didn't do well with boredom and would *invent* excitement if need be. Intrigued, he said, "And by *interesting* you would mean..."

"Something other than endless rounds of calls and visits to the dressmaker?" Shrugging with a blitheness that made him think the punch was beginning to take effect, she said, "Activities more stimulating than the correct serving of the tea?"

He could show her a stimulating activity or two. "I thought chits liked clothes."

"To a *degree*." Percy rolled her eyes.

Sauced or very close, he guessed.

"I'd like to think there's more to life than frocks and fripperies... oh, you wouldn't understand."

"Why not?"

"Because you're a man. You get to dictate your own fate. Whereas we ladies have to listen to everyone else's ideas of what we're supposed to do."

You have no idea how hard I fought to secure my future. Before he could reply, a waltz began to play. Percy's attention flitted to the stage where other guests had gathered, whirling in pairs about the makeshift dance floor. Her shoulders swayed with subtle eroticism to the music.

Enough talking—here was his opening.

He stood and held out a hand. "Dance with me."

She looked up at him, and his lips quirked at how torn she looked. "I'm not certain I should..."

Not quite foxed enough. Then again, he was familiar with that line. A female who *shouldn't* was one who most often *did*.

"It is up to you, of course," he said. "My own legs want for a stretch after all the sitting. Perhaps you'd care for a stroll down one of the walks instead?"

Her lashes fluttered as she made the calculation he

intended. What was more risky—walking with him along one
of the notorious lover's walks or sharing a dance in public?

"I suppose one dance wouldn't hurt," she said.

He bowed to hide his look of triumph. Taking her hand,
he led her into the thick of the dance floor. The heat of bodies
surrounded them as did the mingled scents of heady perfumes.
The night sky blazed with stars as he pulled her close. So close
that her skirts brushed against his thighs. Her eyes rounded,
but it was too late. The mad whirl of the waltz carried them
away.

Being a physical man, Gavin enjoyed dancing. For the
vigor of the activity and also for the way it forecasted how his
partner might be... in bed. If you couldn't find rhythm
together on the dance floor, matters weren't likely to improve
between the sheets. He'd had his fair share of partners—some
of them exceedingly skilled—but he'd never danced with
anyone like Percy.

By God, how the saucy baggage could move.

This being Vauxhall, rules of propriety had flown to the
wind, and Percy seemed to soak up the air of exuberance. She
glowed with a youthful, dazzling energy as she danced; he
could not take his eyes from her. Neither could other men,
and he used his elbows and threatening glares to warn them
off. He swung Percy into another dizzying turn, and her
breathless laugh rippled over his senses. The infectious sound
warmed his chest... and drove the situation down south to
near-disastrous proportions.

He'd never had a partner who could keep up with him this
way, step for step. Whose blood—if the delicious flush upon
her cheeks was any indication—seemed to burn as hot as his.
Her movements matched his in perfect synchrony. To
imagine a carnal pairing, that lithe body arching in rhythm to
his thrusts... his hand tightened on the supple curve of her
spine as he spun her into another turn. Her red silk cape

swished against his erection, and he bit back a groan.

Mayhap her dramatic nature was rubbing off on him because he was sure that he would die if he did not have her tonight. This minute. Wager or no wager. The melody slowed; the song was coming to an end. He had to strike while the iron was hot—and, hell's teeth, at this point *his* iron was on bloody fire.

"Thank you for the dance," he said. It required every ounce of willpower he possessed to release her from his grip. It wouldn't do to scare her off now.

"That was so... exhilarating." A needless statement, seeing as she spoke between fragmented breaths. Her eyes were brighter than the stars and thousand garden lights combined. "It was like flying... like fl-fluttering... like a butterfly." For some reason, she dissolved into giggles. "Oh, how I wish Signor Angiolini could have seen me!"

Gavin subtly pulled her along through the throng of dancers. "Who?"

"My dancing master. According to him, I dance with the delicacy of a bull."

"The man must be daft or blind. Both, actually." Scowling, Gavin looked back at her. "Anyone with eyes can see you dance beautifully."

She grinned. "Thank you, but I know I have a depressing tendency to lead."

"You didn't have that problem with me," he said.

"I didn't, did I?" She sounded bemused.

He'd maneuvered her to the edge of the crowd and could see the maze of shadowed paths up ahead. The Lovers' Walks. There, the thick canopy of giant elms and dense foliage of bushes provided ample opportunity for trysts. Through the haze of lust clouding his brain, he tried to recall his plan for convincing her to plunge into unknown territory with him.

"Do you like fireworks, Miss Farnham?" he said.

"I do not like them. I *adore* them," she said.

"They will be set off soon, and I know a place to view them at their most spectacular."

A little crease appeared between her brows. "And where is that?"

Tread with care. "Up ahead," he said casually. "There is a clearing with fewer lights. That way we can see the fireworks in their full splendor."

The merriment fled her eyes. She angled her head at him. "Surely you don't expect a proper miss to go traipsing into a dark and secluded place with a scoundrel bent on seducing her?"

Damn.

"An *ordinary* miss mightn't." He smiled the devil's smile. "But one never knows what Miss Priscilla Farnham will do."

Chapter Thirteen

Standing at the crossroads, Miss Priscilla Farnham looked from the well-traveled path to the one less taken. A minute ticked by. "Oh, what the hell," she said and gathered up her skirts.

—from *The Perils of Priscilla*, a manuscript-in-waiting by P. R. Fines

P ERCY DIDN'T KNOW what it said about her that she could never resist a challenge. Even as a girl, all her brother had to say was "I dare you," and she'd be off climbing the tallest tree in the park or stealing a pie from Cook. No matter how atrocious the outcome, it seemed she never learned.

Case in point? The present moment.

She looked at the fading lights behind and then to the shadowy darkness ahead. Already she and Hunt had passed by the magnificent Octagon temples, which marked the perimeter of the well-populated area. Now they were trespassing into a far more dangerous realm, one containing the infamous twisting walks and lovers' coves. Overhead, colossal elms waved their leafy arms like ancient magicians casting a spell.

A breeze shivered against her cheek, warm from the dancing and the punch... wait, how many cups had she had? Frowning, she realized she felt ever so slightly tipsy. She needed to regroup for a minute, reinforce the rules.

"Before we go any further, Mr. Hunt, I wish to remind you of our contract," she said.

He didn't break his stride. "I haven't forgotten the bloody thing." He looked this way and that, muttering, "The entrance to the clearing is here somewhere..."

"So if I tell you to cease, you must cease." She cleared her throat. "In whatever you happen to be doing. Correct?"

He shot her a sardonic look. "Haven't I kept my word so far?"

He *had* honored his promises thus far, and the dancing had been sublime. Besides, people were still gathered here along the main walk, couples mostly, giggling and chatting in the manner of lovers. She had a moment's wonder about what it would be like to be here with Lord Charles instead of Hunt—but the notion was so inconceivable that she let it go. Instead, she inhaled the scent of flowering jasmine and wood smoke, gravel crunching under her slippers as she followed her companion. From head to toe, she felt giddy with sensation.

"It's marvelous here," she sighed. "I wish I could come all the time. Do you?"

Hunt was poking around in the bushes, an annoyed expression upon his face. "Do I what?"

"Visit Vauxhall. On a regular basis."

"Not usually." Stopping, he contemplated the gap between two elms. "This is the way to the clearing, I think."

She peered at the trail snaking into the blackness. "Are you certain? It looks rather dark in there. I don't see any indication of a break in the trees."

"I know where I am going," he said with a scowl. "Follow me, else we'll miss the fireworks entirely."

Rolling her eyes at the broad back in front of her, she followed him into the dense maze of hedges. Hunt cleared the way, chopping at the overgrown bushes with a snapped branch. The sounds of the gay crowd faded into the distance, and the ever-deepening dimness took on a surreal quality. The air was sultry against her skin, thickened with the scent of greenery and rich earth. Her heart seemed to beat in rhythm with the whoosh and whack of Hunt's makeshift scythe.

Yet not all adventures ended in success, and after a few minutes it became clear (at least to her) that they were not going to find what they were looking for. By that time, her slippers had accumulated enough pebbles to line a drive, and tendrils of the wig lay pasted against her sweaty forehead.

"Hold up a moment, will you?" Percy said. They'd reached a small opening in the dense brush, what might have once been a lover's nook. The faint moonlight revealed a small bench covered in moss, and she cast herself upon it gladly. She removed one slipper, and gravel showered to the ground. "If you are lost, perhaps we should go back and ask for directions."

"I am not lost." Towering over her, Hunt spoke through his teeth. "I never get lost."

"You and most males," she said.

The dim light glazed the harsh planes of his face. "What did you say?"

"Oh, nothing of import," she said blithely. "No need to get in a lather. Why don't you relax and sit down, have a bit of a chat?"

He remained standing, hands braced on his lean hips, a perfect rendition of a thunderous Hades. Not exactly the type of man one invited for a *tête-à-tête*. For some reason, the notion made her want to giggle.

"What in blazes do you want to chat about?" he demanded.

Dare she ask the question burning in her mind? The punch must have loosened her tongue, for she said, "How did you get your scar?"

Silence greeted her question. After a few heartbeats, she said, "Um, if that is too personal—"

"It was a gift," Hunt said curtly. "From a friend."

"A friend?" Brow furrowing, she tipped her head to the side. "I'm afraid I don't understand."

"I wouldn't expect you to."

When he failed to elaborate, she prodded, "Why would a friend hurt you?"

"Because it was better than the alternative," he said flatly. "Because people hurt one another. Friends, enemies, lovers,"—his eyes flickered, and a strange, answering twist emerged in her belly—"it's just a matter of degree."

"What a horrid, cynical notion," she said.

He shrugged. "'Tis reality. I'd wager you couldn't name one person you've loved who hasn't caused you pain."

She opened her mouth to snap back a reply... and realized in astonishment that she had none forthcoming. She'd never doubted her family's love for her and yet... An ache wriggled into her chest as she thought of Papa. Recalled the countless hours of her childhood spent waiting for him to come home. Longing for his attention, for more than the distracted pat on the head when she showed him her latest painting or poem. She'd so desperately wanted his approval, to be *seen*.

Perhaps to make up for Papa's absences, Mama had been wont to give the children extra attention. A little too much attention, as far as Percy was concerned. For as long as she could remember, she and her mother had been at odds over something—that something usually involving her wayward behavior. Percy knew that Mama meant to improve her hoydenish disposition; for some reason, however, the endless lectures only made her want to rebel *more*. With a stab of remorse, Percy thought of the grief she must have caused her mother over the years; the disappointment that had driven Mama to another Continent.

"Can't do it, can you?" Hunt said with a smirk.

"No one's perfect," she said, swallowing. "What matters is that I know they love me, and I love them. We'd do anything for each other."

"As you say." Hunt sounded bored.

A sudden boom sounded overhead. Relieved for the interruption, she looked upward.

"Do you hear that? Sounds like the fireworks, doesn't it?" As a series of whistles and booms followed, both of them looked up into the thick awning of leaves. She squinted. "Over to the left, I think I saw a bit of a red spark—"

Her words ended in a squeak. In a disoriented flash, she registered his hand covering her mouth and his arm trapping her at the waist. He'd dragged her off the bench, holding her captive against his rigid form. Panic and disbelief collided. After all his promises, he meant to assault her?

She began to struggle with all her might, but his arms confined her like steel bands. His fierce whisper heated her ear. "Be still. There are men afoot. They move like footpads."

Her eyes widened. *Footpads?*

Before she could digest that piece of news, the dark figures emerged from nowhere. Three of them, large and menacing. Something glinted in their hands... She hadn't time to note anything else, for the next instant Hunt shoved her behind him. The force sent her sprawling into the brush.

"Run," he roared.

Shock froze her in place. She couldn't run... couldn't move. Couldn't do anything but watch as the three strangers circled Hunt like dogs a baited bear. One went in, blade raised. Hunt evaded the swipe of the knife and landed a blow to the cutthroat's jaw, knocking the man to the ground. In a swift movement, he reached into his boot, pulled out his own blade. Just in time, for the other two pounced upon him.

Hunt dodged their deadly attacks. He caught one of the

brutes by the arm; there was a sickening crack like a twig being snapped, followed by a loud groan. But the last footpad took the opportunity to attack Hunt from behind.

"Behind you!" The words flew from Percy's lips.

Hunt pivoted in the nick of time. Barely. The blade missed his back but caught the edge of his domino. He cursed and launched himself at his assailant. They exchanged lethal swings of their knives. Hunt was quicker, fiercer; ducking the arc of his opponent's blade, he rammed his fist into the other's midsection, the force loosening the weapon from the man's grip.

Just as Hunt hauled his foe up by the scruff, Percy saw a sudden movement. One of the footpads—felled, she'd thought—grabbed Hunt from behind and collared him by the throat. Hunt gasped for air. His knife fell to the ground as his hands went to grapple with the choking hold.

"I got the bastard," the villain hissed to one of his partners. "Get yer blade an' finish 'im off."

Hunt struggled like a frenzied beast while the other brute rose, steel shining with sinister malice in his hand. *Two against one—the bastards!* Anger dissolved the last of Percy's panic, and, without another thought, she yanked off her slipper and rushed into the fray. She glimpsed the attacker's look of surprise the instant before she let loose the contents of her shoe. Gravel and sand sprayed him directly in the face.

"You bloody bitch!" he yelled, grabbing at his eyes.

Pulse pounding, she turned to Hunt; in the brief moment of distraction, he'd freed himself from his attacker's grip. He and his opponent crashed onto the ground, grappling. As she dashed over, Hunt gained the upper hand. His fist smashed into the other's face. The man groaned and lay limp.

A rustling came from the brush, the sound of rough voices.

"O'er here!" The blinded footpad shouted an alert to his

comrades. "They're gettin' away!"

    Hunt grabbed her hand. "*Run.*"

Chapter Fourteen

HE DRAGGED HER through the winding maze, his eyes scouting the darkness. He sensed that whoever they were, the ruffians were not far off. He had to get Percy to safety.

His lungs burned, his mind racing through the options. The cutthroats had planned their attack well, chasing him and Percy farther and farther away from the populated areas. Here, deep in the heart of Vauxhall's dark gardens, the bastards could slit their throats with none the wiser. Alone, Gavin might consider fighting them off, but he would not risk endangering Percy.

He would have to find some way to evade their pursuers.

He saw a wavering brightness in the distance, and it hit him. The bloody meadow. He'd found it at last. In the next instant, he recalibrated his sense of direction.

He slowed, and Percy rammed into him. "*Oof.*"

"We haven't much time," he said, keeping his voice low. "Give me your wig and domino then lay low until I return."

Eyes huge, she wordlessly removed the red curls and cape and handed them over.

He motioned for her to crouch behind a bush, and then he crept with stealthy speed toward the clearing. He raced along the perimeter until he found a path that led westward through the trees. Tossing the wig upon a bush, he sprinted down the path several paces. He tore a strip from the domino and hung it from a branch. A decoy to throw off their scent.

He circled back to Percy.

"I think I hear them coming," she whispered.

"Follow me and keep low," he whispered back.

He led her eastward through the labyrinth. Now that he knew exactly where they were, they made speedy passage. Before long, he saw the sparkle of garden lights in the distance, and within minutes they were free of the twisting hedges and upon a deserted walk. There was no sign of their pursuers; with any luck, the brutes had fallen for his trick and were headed in the opposite direction.

"Those men..." Percy was standing close enough for him to feel the tremor travel through her. "Why are they after us? Money?"

He didn't think so. They'd been intent on killing him, not taking his purse. But now was not the time to get into specifics. "We're not out of the clear yet. A guard station is up ahead where we can get help. Can you make it?"

"Of course."

They hadn't gone several steps when he noticed her limping. He grabbed her arm, assessed her swiftly. His gaze caught on her right foot, which was missing its slipper; her delicate toes poked out from the tattered stocking. He remembered what she'd done, the reckless bravery of her actions. An unbalanced feeling came over him.

Without a word, he caught her up in his arms.

"That isn't nec—"

"Hush," he said without breaking his stride. "We're almost there."

Minutes later, they arrived at a wood hut no bigger than a horse stall. The door was unlocked, but no one was inside. A lamp had been left burning on the small table, which stood crammed against the wall. Setting Percy down on the wooden surface, Gavin closed the door and bolted it. He drew the curtain over the small window and doused the light.

"The guard is likely out on patrol," he said. "He'll be back soon. How is your foot?"

"It's f-fine."

Just to be sure, he lifted the small appendage. He ran his hands over the slim ankle, the pretty arch. When he satisfied himself that there was no damage, he let out a breath... one he hadn't realized he'd been holding. Releasing her foot gently, he looked up at her. The faint sliver of light from the curtains turned her eyes into luminous pools. At some point during the chase, she'd lost her mask. Her lashes lowered, and he could see the rapid rise and fall of her bosom.

"I... I c-can't believe... that was..." she stammered.

"I know." He found himself running a hand lightly over her hair. Her real hair, softer than silk. The idea that those bastards might have harmed even a single strand of the fine stuff... Angry beyond words, mostly at himself, he gritted out, "Believe me when I say I had no intention of putting you in harm's way. It won't happen again."

She bit her lip, and her shoulders began to shake. She shook her head. "Oh, no, that's not—"

"Not enough?" he said grimly.

He couldn't blame her for wanting to back out of the wager. Bloody hell, he might even owe it to her, seeing as how she'd saved his damned hide. Percy had stuck her neck out for him; no milk-fed miss would do such a thing. Unfortunately, her unexpected actions only fueled his attraction to her, causing a war within him.

Eye for an eye. But I don't want to let her go.

He forced himself to say the words. "If you wish to put an end to our bargain—"

"End it? But Mr. Hunt,"—she raised her eyes to his and they were sparkling, not with tears but... *merriment?*—"that was the most brilliant night of my life!"

"Brilliant?" Mayhap the stress had made her cracked.

He'd seen it happen before.

"I've never dreamed of such adventure. Well, I've dreamed of it, but never have I experienced such life or death drama. I was working on a novel, you see, but I got stuck. After tonight," she said gleefully, "I shall be *swimming* in inspiration."

He didn't understand a damn thing she was saying. But the sight of her safe, of her dancing eyes and dimpled cheeks... without warning, lust returned in a crashing wave. It washed away logic, plans he was supposed to remember. All he could see was the valiant, unspoiled goddess in front of him, her laughing, sensual mouth, and blood roared in his ears.

"Persephone," he said hoarsely.

Her eyes rounded. Before she could speak, he took her mouth in a ravenous kiss.

Hell's teeth, she was so sweet. His eyes closed with the pleasure of it, with the unbearable hunger he felt. She trembled, so he knew she felt it too. The attraction that flared brighter than fireworks between them, that exploded over the frozen, dark terrain within him and showered it with light and warmth. With a groan, he slid his hands in her hair, angling her head to deepen the kiss. Her lips parted naturally beneath his, and then he was inside her again where he belonged. Licking, tasting, staking his claim.

Yet he was not the only one doing the claiming. When she touched her tongue to his, the pleasure of that bold caress tautened every sinew in his body. The muscle between his thighs, in particular, sprang to full attention. Cradling her delicate jaw, he returned her little love play, magnified it. He plunged his tongue deeper and deeper, leaving nothing unexplored. She was his, all of her, and he would allow her to hold nothing back. If the breathy little sounds she made were any indication, she wanted him to take it all.

As he continued to kiss her, he skimmed his hands from

her shoulders to her breasts. God, the feel of her made his blood pound. Though not large, her tits were firm to the squeeze, the perfect shape for his palms. He *had* to see them. Reaching behind her, he fumbled his way through buttons and laces until he could ease her gown off her shoulders. His mouth followed, kissing the curve of her jaw, the fragrant hollow of her neck.

She moaned softly, and he had to agree with the sentiment for there, bobbing in the moonlight, was the most delectable sight he'd ever beheld. Twin beauties, perfectly firm and round. Mouthwatering. He thumbed one saucy, upturned nipple, and she made a hitched sound in her throat.

"By God, you're beautiful." The guttural words escaped him. "The most beautiful goddamned thing I've ever seen."

She licked her lips, and some of the dazed look faded from her eyes. "I don't think—"

"Don't think." He fondled the budded tip until her eyes grew unfocused again. "Just feel," he said huskily. "I won't hurt you, buttercup. I promise. I'll stop anytime you want me to."

Before she could argue further, he put his lips on her. Groaned as the clean sweetness of her skin saturated his senses. Lemon blossoms and soap, the combination feminine and fresh, as unique as she was. Easing her back onto the table, he kissed the smooth curve of her breast, licked in teasing circles toward the tight peak. All the while her sweet sighs urged him on, drove him to a fevered pitch. He drew her nipple into his mouth.

Her gasp tickled his ear and made his rod leap against his smalls. "Do you like that, sweetheart?" he growled.

To help her make up her mind, he did it again. This time, she pressed herself into his kiss, her hands clutching at his shoulders, so he got his answer alright. He took his time playing, going from one quivering mound to the other, lashing and flicking with his tongue. Her eyes were closed, and she was panting, moaning.

By God, I'm going to make her spend just by suckling her tits.

Her passion inflamed him. He gazed upon her, his own chest heaving as if he'd run for miles. With her hair tangling in pale streamers across the table and her breasts wetted from his kisses, she was the wanton of his deepest, most carnal fantasies. His cock throbbed with the imperative to be buried as deep inside her as possible. To take her and make her his.

He reached for her skirt, drawing it upward. Her eyelashes fluttered open.

Already ragged, his breath took another blow from the wonder-struck expression in her eyes. From the passion shining there... and the innocence.

"Mr. Hunt?" she breathed.

Just like that, with a bloody utterance, she erected a part of him he'd long neglected. Not his cock—which was already stiff as a poker and which frankly had never suffered inattention—but his... conscience. Scruples he'd believed decimated by the years in the stews came all of the sudden barging into his head like a nosy fishwife.

She saved your life. She's likely suffering from the aftermath of bloodlust, if not shock. She doesn't know what she's doing.

He stared at his hand, large and dark against the vulnerable curve of her knee... and he almost didn't recognize his own appendage for what it did next. The bloody thing yanked her skirt, not further up as every other part of his body was clamoring for but... back in place.

Goddamnit. He drew a shuddering breath.

Some of the dazzle faded from Percy's eyes. "Mr. Hunt... Gavin?" Her voice quavered this time.

"We had better stop," he said flatly, "before the guard gets back."

Chapter Fifteen

WHEN ALL ELSE failed, a visit to Hatchard's was Percy's panacea for ailments of any kind. Settling her maid on the bench outside the popular bookshop on Piccadilly Street, she entered the premises. The scent of vellum and ink comforted her ruffled senses like a cup of warm milk. One of the clerks standing behind the desk greeted her.

"Good morning, Miss Fines," he said with a little bow. "Is there anything in particular I can help you find today?"

"No thank you," she said. "I am just browsing."

"We recently received some new works you might be interested in," he said with a smile. "A few imitators of the inestimable Mrs. Roche and some of them quite good."

"Marvelous. I'll go take a look."

She headed through the rows of shelves with the familiarity of a mole navigating the hedgerows. This was her home away from home. Whenever she felt any sort of malaise, Hatchard's provided a gateway into another world, one where boredom and the nagging sense of purposelessness could not reach her. Today, however, a new set of feelings plagued her.

Confusion, if she had to name it. Topped by a healthy dollop of panic.

Memories of three nights ago flooded her, causing her breath to quicken. She tried to push away the thoughts as she skirted past the main reading area where gentlemen sat with newspapers before the fire. She made her way through the stacks to the section of novels at the back of the shop.

Scanning the spines, she picked up a new title, *The Castle of No Return*. After a few seconds, when the florid prose failed to distract her, she snapped the book shut.

Blast Gavin Hunt. One night of adventure with him and even the most dramatic, far-fetched plot seemed tedious in comparison.

With a delicious shiver, she recalled his prowess against the cutthroats, the raw fearlessness with which he'd taken on three of them at once. Perhaps all the novel reading had given her a bloodthirsty streak for she had not found his aggression distressing. Far from it. To her mind, he'd battled with the ferocity of a true hero, one who'd never go down without a fight. What did disquiet her, however, were his actions *after* the carnage.

Hunt had literally swept her off her feet. Cradled against his strong chest, she'd never felt more safe or... cared for. She'd caught him holding his breath as he examined her foot. Then he had kissed her, and all further thoughts had melted away, dissolving in the sweet, fierce burning of her blood. Even now, her bosoms ached with the memory of his shocking caresses, the way he'd groaned as he'd suckled her, telling her she was the most beautiful thing in the world...

Then had he stopped. Why?

She'd gone over that question countless times. Hunt had halted of his own accord; though it made her squirm to admit it, the notion of interrupting their embrace had been far from her own mind at that moment. He could have pressed his advantage, tried to take the wager... yet he hadn't. He'd kept her at arm's length until the guard returned and all during the journey home.

The man didn't seem the type to give up what he wanted. Which left her with another interpretation. One that, when coupled with his compassion for street urchins, made her question whether Hunt was the through-and-through scoundrel he made himself out to be. Beneath that hard, embittered exterior, could there be a man capable of compassion... tenderness, even?

How could Hunt be kind toward her and yet so ruthless toward her brother? 'Twas confusing, and that wasn't even accounting for her reactions to the man. Why did she find Hunt utterly compelling? For the last several months, she'd placed Lord Charles' distinguished countenance on the mantel of her fantasies, weaving tales about their happily forever after. Had she misled herself? Had her feelings for Portland been nothing more than infatuation?

She had to admit it: the reality of the viscount's company had fallen short of her expectations. And if she was to be brutally honest, at night when she closed her eyes, it was no longer his flawless visage she saw, but another's.

Scarred, imperfect... and terrifyingly real.

Dash it all, Hunt was her *opponent*. The man who held her family's future ransom. Not only that, but he tapped into a part of her that she desperately wanted to keep at bay. Because of him, she could no longer deny the wicked streak in her nature—but she'd be damned if she gave into those feelings. Thinking of Mama, her throat clogged. She would not bring further shame to those she loved by behaving like some depraved romp.

Lord, she needed someone to talk to, someone experienced in female matters. Charity, dear that she was, would not be of any help in this instance. If only Helena were here... Percy had come to think of the marchioness as an older sister, one in whom she could confide the sort of concerns that she dared not bring up with Mama.

Then the solution hit her. *Of course.* She would go straightaway.

At the rustling of skirts, Percy turned to see a patron approaching. A fair-haired girl, several years younger than she, came over to peer at the shelves. Bright, inquisitive eyes fell upon the book in Percy's hands.

"Excuse me, miss, but when you are finished, might I have a quick look at that novel?" The newcomer blushed. "I'm afraid I've been awaiting its release with bated breath."

Percy handed over the volume. "Please take it." With a bemused smile, she added, "I've read so many others like it that I think I'm ready for something different."

Percy arrived at her destination a half hour later. Rumor had it that Lady Draven had been left a fortune by her late and unmourned husband the baron, and she'd wasted no time in making use of her hard-earned wealth. Located on a stately street in Mayfair, the Draven residence was a lavish Georgian townhouse with gothic styling. Despite the morning sunshine, the property retained a distinctly mysterious air with its crenellated roofline and tracery windows. Percy climbed the short steps to the front entrance, which was recessed beneath a high arch.

A rather brutish-looking fellow answered the door. Claiming that he was the butler, he took Percy's card and left her to wait in the drawing room with a tea tray. She sat on the plush cushion of a curricle chair and admired the exquisite surroundings. Lady Marianne's famed sense of style extended beyond her wardrobe to the decoration of her home. The sea green walls and delicate French furnishings created an ambience of cool, self-assured femininity.

What would it be like to have such confidence in oneself? Percy wondered.

Her hostess entered minutes later. Clad in a dressing gown of peach satin, her silver blond hair flowing to her waist, Lady Marianne looked as radiant as Aphrodite.

"What a delightful surprise," the lady said. She waved away Percy's curtsy and arranged herself upon a chaise longue of emerald velvet. "You'll have to excuse my *dishabille*. I was not expecting company at this hour."

"I know it is rag-mannered of me to barge in on you like this," Percy said in a rush. "I should have sent a note around or at least waited until a more fashionable hour to call—"

"No need between friends." Smiling, Marianne reached over to the tea tray and plucked a ripe strawberry. "Though I am curious at what brings you here at this ungodly hour."

On the carriage ride over, Percy had rehearsed what she planned to say to Marianne. She could not in good conscience reveal Paul's problems, nor could she disclose her arrangement with Hunt. Marianne was a sophisticated lady, but Percy guessed even she had limits. Besides, Marianne was Helena's best friend, and the last thing Percy needed was for the Hartefords to find out about the wager.

It was a tricky business: to ask for advice yet remain discreet at the same time.

"I have a problem," Percy said earnestly. "One I am hoping you can help me with, Marianne. It has to do with... a man."

"Most problems do. This is about Portland?"

"Well, yes... and no."

Marianne's brows climbed. "How intriguing." Finishing her berry, she reclined with languid grace against the rolled squabs. "Do go on."

Percy took a deep breath. "I have been thinking about what you said to me that night at Lady Stanhope's ball. About Lord Portland being too staid for me. Now that I've actually spent time with him,"—she gave a rueful shrug—"I'm wondering if you weren't rather on the mark."

"I usually am," Marianne said.

Yesterday, Percy had gone for another drive with the

viscount; she'd felt ill-at-ease the entire time. 'Twas as if the night at Vauxhall had stripped away her rose-colored spectacles, and she saw unfiltered reality for the first time. Around Lord Charles, she was constantly treading on eggshells, fearful of offending his delicate sensibilities. She'd also discovered that his favorite topic seemed to be... *himself.*

Chewing her lip, she searched for the right question to ask her wise friend. "Marianne, how do you know when you've met the *right* gentleman?"

"Ah, the age old question. I thought that was the way the wind was blowing." The other lady smiled. "Now do you want to hear the socially sanctioned response... or what I believe to be true?"

Percy thought it over. "What is the difference?"

"Shall I tell you both, and you can decide which version you prefer?"

"Yes, please."

"If one is to believe the wisdom of Society, then finding the proper match has everything to do with breeding and money. Attraction can figure into the equation, if one has the luxury. But in the end, the right spouse is undoubtedly the one whose status and pocketbook enhances one's own."

"From that perspective, I suppose there's no arguing that Lord Charles is the right choice," Percy said. Why did the fact make her feel resigned? "He is titled and wealthy, not to mention very handsome. He's everything my papa wanted for me."

"Be that as it may, there is my own view on the matter."

Percy leaned forward.

"It falls simply to this: the right gentleman is the one who values you for who you are. Who sees your flaws and cares not a jot. When you are together, you love not only him," Marianne said, "but yourself."

Silence spun into the golden light of the drawing room.

The hairs prickled on Percy's skin as she contemplated the words. She recalled how alive and free she'd felt dancing with Hunt at Vauxhall. And during their lively back-and-forth bantering matches and their kisses... *Lud.* It hit her like the first icy splash of morning ablutions.

Could she be developing feelings for Hunt? Her sworn adversary?

"Have you ever been in love, Marianne?" she blurted.

There was an uncharacteristic flicker in the other's clear eyes, and Percy immediately regretted the impulsive and altogether intrusive question. "I beg your pardon—"

"Once. Long ago, before my marriage," Marianne said quietly. "I was too young to know what I was doing. Being older and wiser now, I must add a caveat to my answer about love."

"Yes?"

"Choosing the right man—the lover your heart and soul demands—is not without risk. Indeed, it often leads to more pain than simply going along with society's rules." Marianne gave her a level look. "I do not want you to misunderstand my earlier comment. Portland may be a staid choice, but he is also a sensible one. I have a feeling the same cannot be said of your other gentleman, whoever he is."

Percy's cheeks grew hot. There was no point in dissembling before that perceptive emerald gaze. "How did you know?"

"Dearest, it's written all over your face. Besides that, there's only one quick cure I know of for infatuation—and that is the real thing." With a sigh, Marianne sat up and poured tea into the Sèvres cups. "Do you want to tell me who he is?"

"I cannot." Biting her lip, Percy took the offered beverage. "I wish I could. But it's... complicated."

"Affairs of the heart are rarely anything but. I gather your family would not approve?"

Percy shook her head. "They'd murder me if they found out. And I know you and Helena are the best of friends, so I must beg you not to say anything to her. If you tell her, she'll tell Nick because she tells him everything. Then he'll feel honor-bound to tell Mama... let's just say I shall wind up in very hot water indeed."

"If your well-being is at stake, I will not be able to keep such a promise." Marianne sipped her tea. "But in all other circumstances, yes, I can be discreet."

A fair response. Percy mulled it over. "Can we discuss a hypothetical situation in confidence?"

Marianne's lips twitched. "I suppose. Since it is hypothetical."

"What would you do if you found yourself attracted to a gentleman you ought not be attracted to?"

The other's brows lifted. "I am a widow, Percy. What I would do and what you should do are two entirely different matters."

"Widows have all the luck," Percy muttered. Realizing how that sounded, she added hastily, "The loss of one's husband excepted, of course."

"I find the state quite agreeable. With or without the exception."

"What I mean to ask is how does one test the veracity of one's feelings?" At this point, Percy didn't know if she could trust herself to know the difference between fact and fiction. She was starting to realize that she'd spun tales in her head for so long that she'd fallen prey to some of her own fabrications. "I thought I was in love with Lord Portland," she said bleakly, "but now that I've spent time with him I'm not as certain."

Marianne set down her cup. "I wonder if I should be the one giving you advice on love. I am not a paragon when it comes to these matters. And you, dearest, are already far too susceptible to romantic notions."

"Please tell me what you think," Percy begged. "I am utterly at a loss."

"The truth is..." The other hesitated, then sighed. "I've always found the answer is in the kiss. Whether or not the passion is real and whether or not there is the possibility of love."

Dash it. If kissing was the barometer, then she was in trouble for certain. She could not afford to fall in love with her opponent! Paul, the future of Fines and Company, her own self-respect—all of it was dependent on her withstanding Gavin Hunt's seductive wiles. No matter how irresistible his kiss. Or how wicked his caresses.

"Right." She blew out a breath. "So how does one fight off an imprudent attraction?"

"Stay away from him," her hostess said flatly.

"If that is not possible? If I—er, I mean one has no choice but to see him?"

For the first time, a hint of alarm entered Marianne's voice. "Good God, you're not enamored with a footman, are you?"

"Oh no, it's nothing like that," Percy assured her.

"Because I can tell you definitively that the mistress-servant scenario never works out. Except in those dreadful Minerva Press novels—and then only because the footman turns out to be a long-lost prince in disguise." Marianne shuddered. "Now what was the question again?"

"Strategies for fending off an unwanted attachment," Percy said promptly, "when avoidance is not an option."

"Hmm. I suppose if you cannot avoid him, you could make him want to avoid you."

Now why didn't I think of that? "How?" Percy said eagerly.

"The same way one wards off gentlemen in general." Stretching, Marianne gave a delicate yawn. "Males can be so tiresome and never more so when one has to contend with hordes of them."

"I'll have to depend on your expertise in this instance," Percy said with a wry grin.

"It's simple, really. There's an entire list of things ladies do that drive a man mad. In my observations, the masculine temperament cannot tolerate certain female habits, any more than we can stand some of theirs." Marianne snorted. "For example, the typical male inability to listen. Or their need to smoke those nasty cigars."

"Or... the way they balk at asking for directions?" Percy said with dawning insight.

"Precisely. Thus, if the hypothetical suitor is particularly persistent,"—Marianne shrugged—"drive him away with your gender-given talents."

'Twas a brilliant plan. Subtly diabolical. Rummaging through her reticule, Percy withdrew a notebook and said, "Would you mind if I took down a few pointers?"

When one was fighting the devil, one must meet him on his own ground.

Chapter Sixteen

Later that afternoon, Gavin looked up from the club's ledgers as Stewart entered the office and shut the door behind. The big man hadn't bothered to knock, which meant the news was grim. Gavin had asked his mentor to investigate possible culprits of the attack at Vauxhall; in his bones, he knew that had been no random robbery attempt.

"There's a price out on your 'ead, lad," Stewart said.

Gavin digested that piece of information for a moment. "How much am I worth these days?"

"'Tisn't a laughin' matter." His mentor scowled. "A hundred pounds."

Gavin closed the ledger he'd been working on. "For that price, one would think to get a better bargain than those incompetent buggers at Vauxhall. Three of them, and they still couldn't finish the job."

"Didn't count on the fact that you learned to fight from the best," the other man said with a hint of satisfaction. "No half-arsed cutthroat is goin' to take you down." He sat in one of the chairs facing the desk. "But that's neither 'ere nor there. We've got a problem on our 'ands."

"Too much to hope you discovered who's funding the enterprise, I suppose?"

Stewart's bushy brows lowered. "Whoever 'e is, the bastard's covered 'is tracks well. I questioned all my contacts an' no one knows where the rumor o' the bounty started. But ev'ry Tom, Dick, an' 'Arry believes it to be true. You might as well 'ave a bull's-eye painted on your back."

Gavin rubbed his neck as he considered the possible suspects; four came readily enough to mind. "I'd start with Kingsley," he said. "He seemed none too pleased when I turned down his offer to join forces. What do we know about his movements?"

Will, Gavin's head guard, had been keeping an eye on Kingsley.

"Will says Kingsley's a slippery bastard. Apparently, the man visits a public 'ouse e'vry Saturday, and ne'er the same one twice. He chooses places outside o' London that are so packed to the gills that Will couldn't spot 'im inside."

"Wenching, do you think?" Gavin mused. "Mavis would nail his bollocks to the wall if she knew."

"Could be. Could be Kingsley's plottin' in secret for some other reason." Stewart frowned. "Until I get to the bottom o' this, you had best keep your wits about you. Take one o' the men to accompany you if you must step out. But no more midnight jaunts with that chit, lad, not until the matter is settled."

"I'll not hide like a bloody coward," Gavin said coldly.

The idea was unpalatable. And he had no intention of interrupting his *rendezvous* with Percy. Minutes ago, when he'd supposedly been reviewing the club's accounts, he'd in reality been fantasizing about the steamy interlude in the hut. About what would have happened if he had not stopped; if he had, instead, drawn her skirts farther up, baring her sleek thighs, getting ever closer to the sweetest spot of all—

"Goddamn it. I *knew* it. She's bewitched you."

Gavin shook himself free of the image. His mentor was glaring at him. To his chagrin, his cheekbones heated as if he were a schoolboy caught in a prank. "That's nonsense."

"Don't bother lyin' to me. I know you better than the nose

on my own face. That Fines girl 'as got you wrapped 'round 'er finger, an' you're too blind to see it."

"The opposite is true. I am using *her* for my purposes."

The other man snorted. "You tumbled 'er yet?"

"No. Not that it's any of your business." God help him if Stewart found out he'd let the opportunity slip at Vauxhall. In truth, he'd spent a great deal of the last two days trying to figure that out himself. Why had he stopped, when he could have had Percy—her and Morgan's company?

"What's she good for, if not that?" Stewart shook his grizzled head. "This is bad news, son. I ne'er known you to wait pretty on a female, which means one thing: she's got 'er claws in you."

"I've got a thicker hide than that."

"You think that, but you're wrong. Trust me, I know what it's like." The other man speared him with a dark, prophetic gaze. "'Twas the same with Marissa, and we both know 'ow that ended."

With Stewart in irons and tossed into the hulks for assault—aye, Gavin knew the story. But the situation with Percy was different... wasn't it?

"At the beginnin', 'twas like havin' a megrim an' a stomach ache at the same time. Couldn't focus, couldn't eat... all I could think about was the bleedin' wench," Stewart said grimly.

Not so different, then. Damnit.

"An' not jus' the beddin' part neither... though God knows I couldn't get enough o' that. No, I wanted other things with 'er, finer, softer things—" Stewart stopped abruptly, scowling. "Things men like us 'ave no business wantin', not if we value our 'ides. She poisoned me, Marissa did. Made me weak an' then called the dogs in for the kill."

The fact that he'd stopped short of his goal—had that been a sign of weakness? Gavin squelched the uncomfortable

thought. She had saved his life, and he'd owed her was all. Eye
for an eye. Now they were even, and he wouldn't falter again.

"I am in full control of the situation. This is about
vengeance: Morgan left me to burn in Grimes' flash house
and, because of him, I spent years rotting in the hulks. I have
one purpose for Percy Fines," he said, his jaw hardening, "and
it isn't soft or weak."

From the other side of the desk, Stewart gave him a man-
to-man look. "Mean to give it to 'er 'ard, do you lad?"

"Precisely."

His mentor grunted. "See that you do. That's what
wenches are for, after all. Maybe you should tup a few to 'elp
you remember the fact."

A sudden scraping sound cut off Gavin's reply. He tensed,
and his mentor took on the same vigilant posture. They both
waited for the furtive noise again... where had it come from?

Stewart motioned to the door.

"My thanks for the advice." Gavin said the words loudly
as the other man moved with rapid stealth to the entrance.
Gavin removed a pistol from his desk, readying it. Stewart
yanked open the door... and Evangeline stood framed in the
doorway.

Her thin brows arched. "That's some welcome, lover."

Gavin cursed and tossed the weapon back into the drawer.

Stewart, however, gave Evangeline a considering look.
Beneath his beard, his mouth settled into what might have
passed for a smile. "Well, if it ain't a sight for sore eyes. Good
day to you, Miss 'Arper."

Evangeline sauntered in. "And to you, Mr. Stewart." The
randy gleam in her eyes and the low cut of her gown gave an
inkling of her purpose. A bulging reticule swung from her
hand.

Just bloody perfect.

"Was just sayin' to Hunt that 'e's been workin' too 'ard. A

man needs a bit o' distraction now an' again." Stewart aimed a pointed look at Gavin. "'Elps 'im to keep 'is focus."

"Well, it just so 'appens I'm lookin' for a bit o' distraction myself," Evangeline said. With easy familiarity, she perched onto the arm of Gavin's chair, her generous rump pushing into his lap.

"I'll leave you two to your business, then." Whistling, Stewart shut the door behind.

"What's with 'im?" Evangeline jerked her chin at the door. "Usually 'e's grimmer than the reaper, but today 'e's practically dancin' a jig to see me."

"Never mind him." Gavin cleared his throat. "What can I do for you today?"

"'Tisn't so much what you can do for me, love, as what I can do for you," she cooed at the same time that she wriggled fully onto his lap.

The contact with the feminine curves led to an immediate physical response. He'd been dog drawn since the first bloody meeting with Percy. Even frigging himself on a daily basis— fine, *several* times a day—didn't seem to help matters. He couldn't get her out of his head; as a result, he was hard. Constantly.

With deliberate slowness, Evangeline undid the strings to her purse. His throat flexed when he saw what she'd fished out and let dangle from her fingers. A silver chain, with a leather cuff swinging at each end.

"I've a new game for you today, lover." She shimmied against his turgid flesh. "And something tells me you're more than up for it."

When it came to carnality, he and Evangeline were cut from the same torrid cloth. For both of them, pleasure and power were sides of the same coin. His first sexual encounter flashed in his mind's eye. A grimy corner of the hulks, one of the whores brought in by the guards to keep the prisoners from rioting. He had been thirteen and, after three years aboard that stinking ship, had left boyhood far behind. Yet he'd quivered as the moll climbed atop his tense form, her eyes glinting slits in the dark. Her taunting voice returned to him.

First fuck, is it? You ain't much to look at. Let's see if you 'ave what it takes to be a man.

His hands had fisted, pulling his shackles tight as she'd explored him with a touch that was anything but gentle. In the darkness of that despicable place, with the sounds and smells of human degradation all around him, he'd had his first sexual release. Had discovered that chains against flesh could rouse desire as well as pain. It hadn't taken him long to learn that nothing, but nothing, matched the potency of dominating another. Of making an old slattern scream with unaffected bliss as he'd turned the tables and fucked her into submission whilst the other prisoners cheered him on.

Use or be used. Of the two, he knew which option he'd choose.

A hand palmed his groin, and he looked down to see Evangeline kneeling between his thighs. In her leering expression, he saw his past in its sordid entirety, and it made him feel … weary. For the first time, he wondered if a different sort of future was possible. Unbidden, the smell of lemons and soap tickled his imagination. A smile that warmed instead of humiliated. Summer-bright eyes promising a brand of passion that he had never experienced before: one that was pure and unconditional, meant only for him.

Was such a thing possible? Could one taste of sunshine dispel the pleasures of the dark?

"Mmm," Evangeline purred. "I think you're ready to play, lover."

He took hold of her hands. Removed them from his person.

"Not today," he said.

Bloody hell... mayhap not ever again.

Chapter Seventeen

F RIDAY EVENING, GAVIN paced the length of his suite as he awaited Percy's arrival. He'd given into Stewart's relentless nagging about not taking "unnecessary risks" and arranged for her to be brought here for their second meeting. It was for the better. In his own territory, he would not have to contend with outside distractions.

Tonight, he meant to seal the deal and seduce Percy. Days ago, he'd found himself ending things with Evangeline because a meaningless tup no longer appealed. He wanted something else, something more. Something he could only have with Percy. Anticipation simmered as he heard the sound of approaching voices.

Davey came in first. Free of bruises now and looking much like any other adolescent beanpole, the boy held a lumpy bag in hand. Percy followed behind, and though his pulse quickened at the sight of her, Gavin frowned. What was the bloody thing she was wearing on her head? It was a hideous shade of green and resembled a dead animal. A bird, maybe. It hid all of her gorgeous hair and for that reason alone deserved to be incinerated.

"Davey, would you mind putting my things..."—scanning the room, Percy pointed to the chair—"over there, if you please?"

The boy almost tripped over himself in his eagerness to do as she bade. "Anyfin' else, miss?"

"No, thank you," she said. "But I'm so glad we had a chance to chat."

Chat? What on earth had she and an orphan from the gutters to talk about? Besides, the boy was not what one would call a conversationalist. With Gavin, he spoke only when spoken to; when asked about what had happened at his last place of work, he became silent as a clam. Understanding the desire to shut out the past, Gavin had stopped prying about the boy's abuser.

Though perhaps what he ought have done was put Percy in the role of interrogator. From the looks of it, if she asked Davey to jump, the boy would somersault into the air. As Gavin had long suspected, the chit had a disconcerting effect on the males of the species—and apparently age offered no protection against her charm.

"This is for you, Davey. I hope to hear good news the next time I see you," she said brightly.

The boy's eyes grew as large as the coin she handed him. With a moonstruck expression, he stammered, "Th-thank you, miss. I'll not forget your advice."

"That is all for now, Davey," Gavin said shortly. "Close the door behind you."

The boy left, taking Percy's smile with him. Tension filled the room as she took stock of the private chambers and assiduously avoided Gavin's gaze. He'd had the sitting room set up for seduction. Beeswax candles flickered in silver holders; crimson roses bloomed in crystal vases. A cloth-covered table sat ready for an intimate supper for two.

"What were you and Davey talking about?" he said.

"Oh, this and that." Percy wandered over to the table, looked it over. "Mostly I was giving him some pointers on love."

"On love?" Gavin scoffed. "He's a boy, for Christ's sake. He has better things to fill his head with than such nonsense."

"Be that as it may, he has quite the crush on the milkmaid." Percy's cheeks took on an apple-sweet curve. "Her name is Nan. She has red hair and freckles on her nose."

"He's wasting his time on rubbish," Gavin said. "He needs to build himself up, prove himself a man. Hard work and self-discipline—that's the ticket for the boy."

"Is that what you were doing at that tender age?" she asked innocently.

At thirteen, he'd been living in the hulks amongst criminals and vermin. He'd given and received beatings in equal measure. On a good day, he'd escaped the guards' violent whips and had a crust of stale bread in his growling belly. The bad days... he didn't care to remember those.

All because of Morgan. Stay focused.

"Suffice it to say," he said in grim tones, "I was planning for the future, not mooning over some wench. I'll have a word with Davey and set him straight."

Percy came nearer, her eyes searching his face. "Why is it that you have such compassion for children? According to Davey, you've given him food, shelter, the skills of a trade— and he's not the only one. It would seem that you're the benefactor of many an unfortunate orphan."

His cravat seemed to tighten. He didn't like the gentle expression in her gaze. He did not need her pity—anymore than the children did.

"I'm no soft touch, if that's what you're thinking," he said flatly. "Anyone who works for me earns their keep. If they don't, they get tossed out on their arses."

She continued to study him, head tipped to the side. "Tit for tat—that's your philosophy?"

"In my world, it's called justice. Nothing comes for free, and anyone who owes me will pay." Deliberately, he added, "I'd have thought you understood that by now."

Instead of looking put off, she only raised her brows. "I

suppose I am not the only one with a reputation to protect. You have one, too, don't you, Mr. Hunt?"

He liked her astuteness even less than the sympathy. "May I take your, er, bonnet?" he said abruptly.

"It's a turban," she said. "It's supposed to stay on."

Not if he could bloody help it. But he'd pick his battles one at a time.

"Your cloak then," he said, reaching to her shoulders. As he removed the velvet, he had a moment to savor her tremor of awareness before a pungent odor assailed him. Holy hell. His eyes started to water, and his body shook with the sudden force of his sneeze.

"Bless you," she said sweetly.

His nostrils quivered in warning, and he took a step back.

"Oh dear, I hope it isn't my new scent," she said. "The perfumist blended it specially for me. 'Tis essence of lilac and lily-of-the-valley."

No wonder she smelled like a cross between a dowager and a hedge.

His eyes narrowed upon her gown, which furthered her similarity to a prickly old bush. It wasn't as if Percy tended to seductive clothing (more the pity), but tonight her gown eschewed her usual fresh, unaffected style for a look that was... well, frankly, repugnant. The dress matched the sickly shade of the towel upon her head, and rows and rows of frilly things decorated the shapeless monstrosity which covered her from chin to toes.

He wanted to see her lithe, nubile form. He wanted to rip the frock off and fling it into the flames of the fireplace. Most of all, he wanted to know what the minx was up to—though he had a pretty good inkling.

"Took special pains for the evening, did you?" he said.

She smiled, looking pleased with herself. "I didn't want to be caught unprepared again. Vauxhall was a distraction. From here on in, I plan to approach our wager with the utmost prudence."

"A distraction. Is that what you're calling my kiss?"

Satisfaction rose in him as her smile wavered.

"The mayhem overexcited my nerves. A momentary lapse," she muttered. "It won't happen again."

The hell it wouldn't. Whether or not she realized it, she'd just thrown down the gauntlet, and he'd never been one to resist a challenge.

He waved to the seating area adjacent to the supper table. "After you."

Since the wingback chair by the fire was occupied by her large, knobby knitting bag (did she plan to mend a pair of socks this evening?), Percy had no choice but to take a seat on the satinwood sofa. He sat down next to her... and sneezed again. *Damnit.*

"Perhaps you'd be more comfortable at a distance," she suggested.

"I'm fine where I am," he growled.

"Suit yourself."

He forced himself to calm. He looked to the coffee table in front of them, which held a platter of his chef's tantalizing hors d'oeuvres and a bottle of the best vintage. "Would you care for some refreshment before supper?"

"No wine for me, thank you. I prefer to keep my head clear. And I shan't be requiring supper, either."

He scowled, glancing over to the carefully laid out supper table. Apparently it was going the way of his well-laid plans. "Why not?"

"I am on a slimming plan."

"What the bloody hell for?" he said, incredulous. "You're slender as a reed."

Not in all parts, praise God, but the notion of Percy reducing was nothing short of asinine. Equally ridiculous was the way she then proceeded to launch into a lecture of her imaginary flaws. Not only her weight, but the shade of her hair, her insignificant nose, her too-full lips. 'Twas a conversation common enough amongst other females of his acquaintance—and the kind that usually signaled the rapid exit of any self-preserving male.

He'd never pinned Percy for a hen-wit. His jaw tautened.

"Oh, I could go on forever on this subject." She peered guilelessly up at him. "Ladies have ever so much to chatter about, don't they? And I am a lady after all."

Like hell she was. *She* was a vixen, a saucy little romp. Oh, he saw through her act: she was irritating him on purpose—and doing a damn good job of it. If she thought her ploy enough to ward him off, however, she had better think again. He tried to focus on his strategy. It was a bit difficult, given that he was fantasizing about throttling her. That, and kissing her mouth until it lost its mischievous curve. Inclined toward the latter option, he was just leaning toward her when a movement jerked his gaze toward the wingback chair. Had Percy's bag... moved?

What the devil... did it just *bark*?

"It looks like Fitzwell is awake," Percy said cheerfully. "Come on out, old boy."

A fawn-colored head poked out from the bag. After surveying the environs, the beast stepped out fully and gave its squat little body a thorough shake. Pale hair rained over the chair.

Gavin's *favorite* chair.

"With Mama away, Fitzy has been so lonely of late. I thought I'd bring him along to cheer him up. I hope you don't mind," Percy said.

"I don't mind at all." The words slipped through Gavin's clenched teeth. He had no particular fondness for small dogs—and the one currently eyeing him with a hostile, piggish stare only reinforced that fact.

The beast bared its teeth at him; Gavin nearly returned the gesture.

"He's excellent company," Percy said. "After Papa's death, Mama quite depended on—oh no, Fitzy, don't do that!"

Her admonition came too late. The beast sniffed the air; its gaze shot unerringly to the platter of appetizers. Something like a grin spread across the dark muzzle. With a speed that belied its stubby legs, the pug took a flying leap from the chair and onto the coffee table. Snorting joyfully, it buried its face in the perfectly arranged platter.

"Oh dear, I hope you weren't intending to eat that." Percy put on the most pathetic attempt at looking apologetic that he'd ever seen. The edge of her mouth was actually quivering.

The idea came to Gavin in a flash; he had to stifle his own grim smile at its devilish simplicity. Having fun at his expense, was she? Two could play at that game. She thought to use his temper against him... well, he knew a thing or two about her vulnerable areas as well.

"Since it appears the dining portion of the evening will be curtailed," he said, "I propose we move onto the next activity."

She tensed. "What sort of activity?"

"I thought you might like to see the club."

She chewed on her bottom lip, and he couldn't blame her—he wouldn't mind having a nibble at that luscious pink ledge himself. And he would... soon. "I'd like to, but I cannot risk the exposure," she said.

"You won't have to. I'll take you through the secret passageway."

"The... secret passageway?"

She almost breathed the words, her eyes rounding. He bit back a smile. Aye, he knew exactly how to entice his Persephone; hold out the right fruit, and the curious goddess could not resist taking a bite.

"'Tis my own private corridor from which I can monitor The Underworld unseen. I am due for my evening rounds about now." He let his shoulders lift and fall in a casual motion. "If you'd like, you can come along."

"Oh, I really oughtn't." When she shook her head, the turban slipped a little. A golden curl slipped free. "Um, Fitzwell. He needs me here."

A belch came from the direction of the coffee table. Having inhaled all the food, the canine hopped down to the floor. It trotted over to the settee and sniffed the turned mahogany leg.

"Do that and I'll have you stuffed and mounted," Gavin said sharply.

Apparently, the beast was smarter than it looked; with a grunt, it abandoned the furniture and went to flop in front of the fire.

Gavin turned back to Percy. "You did mention that you are an aspiring novelist?"

"Yes. No." A crease appeared between her curving brows. "That is, it was a hobby of mine at one time, but I've given it up."

"Perhaps a tour of a bona fide gaming hell might inspire you to pick up the pen again. But it is up to you." He shrugged. "If you'd rather wait here and spend time with your pet ..."

They both looked at the animal lying comatose on the hearth. At present, Fitzwell's company was about as interesting as watching ink dry on parchment. After a minute, Percy said, "I think Fitzy will be fine for a few minutes on his own. Won't you, little chap?"

The pug rolled onto its back and emitted a snore.

Firelight danced in Percy's eyes. "Off to the secret corridor, then?" she said.

Chapter Eighteen

Percy's heart thudded as the hallway panel swung open, revealing a flickering tunnel. *A genuine secret passageway!* The part of her that was supposed to protest that she shouldn't go in had been abandoned back with Fitzwell. Along with her perfume. Prior to the tour, Hunt had asked that she remove the stuff as his sneezing might compromise the stealth of their mission.

Mission. Stealth. The words tickled her pulse.

"Watch your step," Hunt said as he led the way.

Percy discreetly studied her host as they traversed the shadowy corridor. His broad shoulders nearly brushed the walls, and he had to duck his head at points where the ceiling hung low. In the light of the lamp he held aloft, his hair gleamed like a pelt, causing her palms to prickle. She remembered how those thick locks had slipped between her fingers…

Much like her plan. What had earlier seemed like a brilliant strategy now felt rather foolish. The turban made her scalp itch, and beneath the thick gown, perspiration slickened her skin. She'd used up her supply of inane feminine chatter, too.

"Have you seen a gambling club before?" Hunt looked back at her.

"I haven't, no." The notion rustled a laugh from her throat. "Perhaps you missed this fact, Mr. Hunt, but ladies are never allowed anywhere interesting."

The flickering light threw his face into bold relief, licking over the intriguing hollows and masculine planes. "I find it difficult to believe that normal rules apply to you," he said.

How often had she furtively thought that very thing? According to Charity, that line of reasoning was precisely what landed Percy in scrape after scrape. Under Hunt's watchful gaze, she felt suddenly transparent, exposed despite all the layers she wore.

Stay on guard. Don't let him see your weakness.

"I follow rules. Most of the time," she amended.

"You didn't when we were attacked at Vauxhall. I believe etiquette has it that I was supposed to fend off the ruffians. You were supposed to succumb to your delicate sensibilities. To scream and faint—not jump into the fray."

Now *that* irked her. "So sorry, but fainting has never been one of my fortes," she said tartly. "I will, however, make note. The next time we are accosted by cutthroats I will be certain to stand by and wring my hands whilst they finish you off."

At that, Hunt smiled. A true smile, something that she had not seen from him before. Her heart skipped a beat, and that was before he took her hand and kissed it.

"You did not disappoint—far from. I'll take courage and honesty over propriety any day." The approval in his deep voice turned her blood to honey. "You, Miss Fines, are a rare creature."

Rare—and apparently not in a bad *way.* She was grateful for the darkness that hid her blush. If this was Hunt's version of gallantry... it was *working.* His direct praise made her insides melt like butter on a hot crumpet. He took up the lead again, and as they continued to walk, she became aware of a hum; the sound soon grew into an indecipherable mix of voices and background clatter.

"Here we are." Hunt indicated a series of wooden slats on

the wall. When he pushed one back, two small beams of light penetrated the dark tunnel. "This is one of the gaming rooms. Have a look."

As Percy peered through the viewing hole, her jaw slackened. She didn't know what she'd expected—fire and brimstone perhaps? Instead, multi-tiered chandeliers blazed from the high ceiling, and a fountain of champagne bubbled at the center of the room. Men surrounded the room's many tables, their eyes riveted upon the action on the green baize. Shouts and groans erupted as dice were thrown. Like peacocks, brightly dressed wenches paraded around the room.

The buzz of energy and color flowed into her as she observed the fascinating world. Hunt was right; this was a treasure trove of inspiration for a writer. Her head spun with the sorts of adventures Miss Priscilla Farnham might encounter in such a place. For the first time in ages, her fingers actually itched for a quill.

"Why, the club is magnificent," she said in an awed voice. "All of this is yours?"

"When I bought the place, it was a tumble-down building. Now it's one of the finest clubs in London," he said. "I mean to make it the best."

Seeing the ambition in his dark gaze, she had an intuitive flash of what this place meant to him. Papa had looked that same way when talking about Fines & Company. Fortitude, a drive to succeed—she'd always admired those qualities. For so long, she'd been searching for the purpose of her own existence. She hadn't found it yet, but she suddenly realized one thing: it wasn't Portland.

The truth was oddly relieving. With a smile, she said, "Better than this? Is that possible?"

"Anything is possible if you set your mind to it."

Exactly as Papa would have said.

They continued the tour, each room grander than the one

before.

"How many rooms are there in The Underworld?" she asked after they mounted steps to the first floor. She peered through the viewing hole into the dining chamber. With delight, she saw that clever painted wood fronts made the supper tables appear like small boats and the walls were painted with rolling waves. Supper on the River Styx.

"A dozen, give or take. There is another floor in addition to this one."

"May I see it, please?" She twisted around eagerly.

Hunt's expression turned apologetic. "I'm afraid not."

"Why?"

"Because it isn't suitable. You'll have to take my word for it," he said.

Her brow furrowed. "But I *want* to see—"

"Excuse me." He consulted his pocket watch. "Devil take it, I'm late for the nightly report from my club manager. Stewart hates to be kept waiting."

"Can't I just take a small peek—"

"I'm afraid that's not possible." With a distracted air, he looked at his watch again. "My meeting won't take more than a quarter hour. Do you wish to see the rest of this floor on your own, or shall I summon someone to escort you back to my suite?"

"I'll stay here," she said immediately.

"You're to wait for me *here*, Miss Fines. No wandering about." A muscle twitched oddly beside his mouth. "The club can be a dangerous place, and I won't be here to look after you."

"Please take your time." She kept her voice nonchalant. "No need to worry about me."

Perfect. He's gone.

Taking one last look to make sure there was no sign of Hunt's muscular form, Percy made a gleeful dash for the stairs at the end of the hallway. She could not bear the notion of waiting, twiddling her thumbs whilst a mysterious, forbidden realm lay mere paces away. As she mounted the steps, she told herself she would take a quick look and return before Hunt even knew she had gone. What harm could that possibly do?

The air in the top floor corridor was sultry and swirling with incense. At first glance, the narrow passageway resembled the ones on the other floors. She heard muffled sounds filtered through the walls; though the voices were indecipherable, something about their quality made her hesitate. *You're already here. Just take a quick peek.* With a hand that trembled slightly, she slid back the nearest wooden panel and pressed her cheek against the peephole.

Her breath stuttered.

Oh. My. Goodness.

A Bacchanal. Wickedness beyond imagining.

Against a backdrop of ancient ruins, people in various states of undress frolicked about, drinking, dancing... and *fornicating*. Percy's face blazed with heat. If she had ever wondered what the sexual act entailed, she got all her answers in a single, blinding moment. Before her stunned eyes, a man wearing a mask with horns grabbed a laughing rouged brunette and bent her over a fallen column. His member—so *that* was what a man's part looked like!—poked outward from his thighs like a lance. An apt analogy, for no sooner had he grasped the lady's hips, then he lunged forward... *impaling* her.

At the brunette's keening moan, sweat sprouted upon Percy's brow. She felt her turban slip as the woman looked over her shoulder, moaning to the man heaving between her thighs. *Fuck me 'arder, get your cock good and deep...* The man responded by pumping furiously, his hips slapping her bottom again and again while she screeched, *Yes, luvie, like that! Oh, I'm goin' to come so hard...*

Heart thundering in her ears, Percy's gaze flew to another couple. As the man lounged on a Roman bed, a redheaded woman knelt between his legs, her expression salacious as she stroked his member with her fist. Eyes heavy-lidded, the man twisted his fingers in her hair and pulled her head toward his lap. Percy sucked in a breath as the woman's tongue darted out and licked the flaring dome of his member. The man groaned, pressing her head down more firmly. Red curls bobbed as the fleshy pole disappeared within her lips...

On a nearby couch, a woman was on her knees between *two* men, her frenzied cries blending with hoarse, guttural shouts as they jousted her between them...

Dazed and feverish, Percy stumbled back from the hole. *Dear God, what am I doing? I have to get back downstairs, have to before—*

The hairs suddenly lifted on her skin; even though she'd heard no footsteps, she knew he was there. His presence lived in the rapid tattoo of her heartbeat, the tightening of her nipples against her bodice. She whipped around.

Hunt stood there, watching her. Golden hellfire raged in his eyes.

Her throat squeezed. "I—I was only..."

"Didn't I tell you to wait downstairs?" As large and foreboding as Hades himself, Hunt stalked toward her. Her breath rushed in and out of her lungs as he bent his head and glanced into the viewing hole she'd been looking through. "My, what a naughty girl you've been," he drawled. He shut the panel, muffling the lascivious sounds.

Her cheeks pulsed hotly. "I didn't mean to—"

"Lie to anyone you wish, but not to me. You knew *exactly* what you were doing." In a quick motion, he disposed of her turban; her hair tumbled free. "You're a hot-blooded little baggage, Persephone Fines, and there's no use denying it."

Lips trembling, Percy lowered her head. He was... right. About her. She wasn't the good, proper daughter her parents had wanted—why did Hunt have to be the one to see her for the wicked girl she truly was? She wanted to curl into a ball and die of embarrassment. Heat burned behind her eyes.

A finger tipped her chin up. Eyes of infinite darkness held her.

"Don't be afraid of who you are," he said. "You're perfect, Percy. Passionate and brave, everything a man could want." Before she could understand the relief, the joy rippling through her, his lips were hot upon her neck. "And hell's teeth, how I want you."

Desire sizzled along her nerves. Yet she pushed at his shoulders. "The w-wager," she stammered. "I cannot do this. I can't betray my brother."

"But you want me, don't you Percy?"

She could no longer hide from the truth. She desired Hunt—a man who did not abhor wickedness, but understood it. Understood *her*. She gave a small nod.

Triumph flickered in his gaze. "I'll do what it takes to have you, Percy. Even if it means calling a truce."

"A truce?" A gasp edged from her arched throat when his lips returned to their wanton exploration.

"An armistice, if you will. We will continue our wager, but your maidenhead will be safe with me..."—his grasp tightened on her hair, exposing her further to his touches, his kisses—"until our sixth and final meeting. I give you my word."

His words barely permeated the haze of pleasure. She moaned as a hot lick titillated her ear. She had to think, to resist the desire spinning out inside her. "You won't try to seduce me?"

"I didn't say that. I said I wouldn't put my cock inside you... for the time being."

A tremor shook her at the wicked words, at the sharp nip to her earlobe.

"For the next three meetings, I won't take your virginity. There are many other avenues to bliss, after all. Think of it, Percy," he murmured, "nothing but pleasure between us—and you'll be guaranteed three victories against me to boot."

Three meetings in which she needn't worry about losing the wager or betraying her brother—not that she was worried. Of course, she understood that Gavin was only giving her the skirmishes and delaying the ultimate battle until the final *rendezvous*. Still, to have three encounters in which she could explore the desire burning within her... She moaned as his hands molded her breasts, teasing the tight nipples beneath the fabric. She couldn't take the torture much longer.

"My darling, curious girl," he coaxed, "all you have to say is yes."

Could she do it? Could she put aside everything she knew to be proper and right? The choice came from the part of her that could no longer remain hidden. That *would* not remain suppressed. The answer sprang from her like a bone snapping from stays.

"Yes," she sighed. *Oh, a thousand times yes.*

His mouth found hers, and the kiss surged with hunger, with the giddy joy of reunion. His lips were hot and fierce against hers; their tongues twined, stroked. She could not taste him or feel him enough. She gave in—to him, herself. To the hunger twisting her insides.

Humid air wafted against her skin as the gown fell from her and whispered to the ground. Layers followed, and as the weight dropped from her, she could not be rid of it quickly enough. When she was clad only in her drawers, he backed her against the wall, the wood smooth and cool against her bare shoulders. His hands closed over her breasts, his fingers lightly tweaking the budded centers.

"I love your tits," he growled. "I want to suck these pretty nipples so hard they'll remember my kiss. Do you want me to?"

It was so easy to answer him in the dark.

"Yes, please," she whispered.

A shudder racked through her as he bent his head. He suckled her as he promised—fiercely, without restraint. Her fingers dug into his scalp, wanting to hold onto the exhilarating pleasure as he went from one breast to the other. When she felt the scrape of his teeth, she jerked in surprise. Warmth flooded her lower belly.

"Too much?" he said.

"I—I don't know."

He laughed softly. "Let's find out. Tonight is about your pleasure, my sweet. I want you to tell me what you feel, what you like. This, for instance." His hard thigh wedged boldly between her legs. "What does that make you want to do?"

Oh, it made her want to rub herself against him. To feel that exciting friction she'd furtively discovered in the privacy of her own bed... She bit her lip.

His grin turned wicked. "Naughty girl. I think you *do* know what to do. Go ahead, then," he murmured, his mouth lowering to hers again, "ride me."

As the heady taste of him washed over her senses, she couldn't help but obey. Her arms winding around his neck, she rocked herself shamelessly against the muscled leg. It felt *delicious*. She did it again, and this time her thigh brushed against another sizeable muscle. His man's part. Oh my. He was so hard, so large—*everywhere*.

"Christ, you don't know how good that feels," he groaned against her lips.

Oh, but she did. Nearly naked, crushed against this big, fully clothed male, she was seized by a primal drive. She began to ride him with feverish abandon. He encouraged her with hot words, petting her breasts, making her grow wetter. Through the slit in her drawers, she could feel how she was dampening his trousers, yet she couldn't stop herself. She clung to him, trying to get the pressure right where she needed it...

"I can feel how wet you are, Percy. I *have* to touch you." He replaced his thigh with his hand, and she cried out.

"So goddamn perfect." The words sounded scraped from his throat. Her hips jerked as his fingers found her through the thin lawn, sliding along her slick groove. "You have the sweetest pussy. So soft and lush. Shall I pet it, make it purr?"

His thumb circled the peak of her pleasure, and her legs gave way. He held her upright against the wall, rubbing her, giving her no ground. His scar taut and chest heaving, he stared into her eyes. As if challenging her to deny the pleasure as if she could. He knew exactly how to touch her, his rough words driving her more and more out of control.

"Do you like having your pearl tickled? Do you want me to diddle you harder, faster?"

"Yes," she gasped as fire streaked down her legs. "Oh, yes."

"I'm the only one who touches you this way," he rasped. "Say it."

For goodness' sake, who else would—A whimper escaped her lips when he pulled his hand away. He gave her a stern look. "Say it, Percy, or we stop this instant."

"You." The admission came from her lips, but the recognition was deeper. The past and future faded away. There was only this moment, this man, and a certainty she'd never known before. "Only you," she whispered.

"Good girl." For some reason, his approval aroused her as much as his masterful touch. He watched her face intently, as if she were the only thing in the world that existed. "Work yourself against my finger," he instructed. "Show me how hot and wet you can get."

Delirious with desire, she obeyed. She rode his hand, her secret knot seeking the pressure of his thick digit. Oh, she *was* hot and wet and needful of relief. Broken pleas escaped her as the slick friction coiled ever tighter in her belly. "Oh, please Gavin, help me…"

"You're so damp for me, so perfect." His eyes anchored her as the tempest inside her raged. "You want to come, love?"

"*Yes.*"

"Then spend for me right now." He bent his head and sucked hard on her nipple. His teeth grazed her at the same time that he gave her pearl a sharp flick. She catapulted over the edge, the finish searing through her senses. A cry broke from her lips as spasms rocked her. *Bliss*—as she'd never known existed. As she dissolved into bone-melting ecstasy, she caught his voice above her thundering heartbeat.

You're mine, Percy.

For once, she hadn't the strength to argue.

Chapter Nineteen

Seated before the looking glass, Priscilla studied her reflection. For so long, she'd seen a too-round face, an insignificant nose, and bothersome freckles. Her features had not changed, yet now she smiled... and the pretty girl in the mirror smiled back.

—from *The Perils of Priscilla*, a manuscript-in-progress by P. R. Fines

Scanning the dining lounge of The Temple of the Muses, a bustling book emporium in Finsbury Square, Percy spotted Charity at the far corner by the window. She navigated past the crowded tables, distracted by snippets of gossip along the way. Most centered around His Majesty The King's latest efforts to divorce his wife on the grounds of adultery.

"And do you know what Her Majesty supposedly replied to the accusation?" a patron said to her companion. "That she did indeed commit adultery once—with the husband of *Mrs. Fitzherbert.*"

As the two ladies laughed, Percy's own lips twitched. Though it was improper, she could not help but appreciate the beleaguered queen's wit. Everyone knew that the King had kept Mrs. Fitzherbert as a long-time paramour; not only that, but years earlier he'd married his mistress in an illicit ceremony. *Talk about the pot calling the kettle black.*

Reaching Charity's table, Percy said breathlessly, "Sorry I'm late."

"Not a problem. As you can see, I've ordered for us both," Charity said, nodding to the pot of chocolate and dish of pastries on the table.

"I got held up with Paul," Percy said in a low voice as she took a seat.

Framed by the brim of her dove grey bonnet, Charity's eyes looked even larger than usual. "How is he?"

Inebriated, belligerent, and impossible to reason with. Snagging a biscuit, Percy bit into it with frustration. Paul had been so far gone that he hadn't even questioned her story about Hunt agreeing to release his debt to Nicholas. Instead, he'd pressed her for money. Not knowing what else to do, she'd given him what she had in her reticule.

"Paul is getting worse and worse. I'm certain he's gaming again, and I couldn't convince him to come home with me." Throat tight, Percy added, "This isn't like him. Ever since that blasted Rosalind Drummond, he hasn't been the same."

Charity kept her gaze on the pot as she poured out the chocolate. "Do you think he is still in love with Miss Drummond?"

Percy shrugged helplessly. "I don't know. Whenever I try to ask him about her, he shuts me out. He won't countenance any mention of her name."

"He must still have feelings for her."

Seeing Charity's downcast gaze, Percy reached for the other girl's hand and squeezed it. "Well, Rosalind is married now, so there's no going back," she said. "If only my idiot brother would realize that you—"

"That's neither here nor there." Charity pulled her hand away, straightened her narrow shoulders. "Have the Hartefords and your Mama written back?"

"No, and I sent the missive over three weeks ago. What if

it got lost?"

"It could be that their reply got delayed," Charity said, her brow furrowed. "Perhaps you should write them again."

Percy nodded. She sipped her chocolate, letting the creamy sweetness soothe her.

Looking left and right, Charity leaned over the table and whispered, "In the meanwhile, how did things go at your second meeting with Mr. Hunt?"

Up until this point, Percy hadn't been completely truthful with her friend. She'd omitted all the debauched details, saying only that she'd garnered a victory against Hunt at Vauxhall. Now she set her cup down in its saucer, chewing on her lip.

"It went... well," she hedged.

Charity looked relieved. "Perhaps this wager won't be a disaster after all."

Percy could have let it rest at that—but she realized she was tired of lying. Of hiding who she was. Her last encounter with Gavin had given her a taste of true freedom... and she yearned to live the rest of her life as authentically, as fearlessly, as she had during those moments with him.

Drawing a breath for courage, she said, "Hunt, um, kissed me." Actually, he'd done rather more than that. But she decided to start with the smaller sins and work her way up. "What is more... I liked it."

"What?" Charity gasped.

Percy darted a glance around. Luckily, the other customers were too engrossed in conversations to pay the two of them any mind. "You heard me, Charity. I think... I think I may be falling for Hunt."

"You *cannot* mean that. What about your brother's future?" Charity said in a furious whisper. "Not to mention your own!"

Percy had spent the bulk of the week mulling over the

conundrum. "What if Hunt and I can come to an agreement about Paul?"

"You think Hunt will release you brother because of his feelings for you?"

She didn't know. She did believe, however, that Hunt was not as merciless as he made himself out to be. Giving Charity a brief summary of his work with urchins and the way he'd protected her at Vauxhall, she concluded, "He's a complex man, Charity, and I'm just beginning to understand him. His world is... different from ours. He has survived much, I think, and all on his own merit. Is it any wonder that he wants to collect what is rightfully his?"

Her friend's eyes narrowed. "You cannot be taking Hunt's side against your brother's."

"I am not taking anyone's side. But I know Hunt is not the evil scoundrel everyone says he is." Thinking of his scar, what he had said about people hurting one another, Percy said, "Having fought for everything in his life, is it any surprise that compassion does not come naturally for him?"

"So you'll stand by and let him ruin your brother."

"I didn't say that," Percy protested. "Perhaps with time I can convince him to forgive Paul's debt. Or I'll win the wager and free Paul that way."

Charity shook her head. "As your closest friend, Percy, I must be honest. Your judgment is clouded. Not long ago, you thought you were in love with Portland. Now you think it's Hunt. Hunt, who has the power to destroy your *family*."

Self-doubt gnawed at her. "I didn't say I was in love with Hunt," she said in a small voice. "Just that I *might* be."

"Have you thought about the consequences? Forget for the moment that your brother will be ruined. And that your mama will never recover from this. And that Hunt is wildly inappropriate in every way. Does the man intend to wed you—is he even the marrying kind?"

The cracks in her self-confidence spread. Gavin had never mentioned anything about marriage. She had no idea what he wished for in a wife. With a sinking feeling, she imagined he'd want someone worldly and level-headed... a woman capable of helping him in his world. *But he said I was beautiful. Courageous and honest. Surely that must count for something...*

"We haven't reached that bridge yet," Percy said in faltering tones.

"You may never," Charity said bluntly. "Are you willing to risk the rest of your life over this man?"

"I... I don't know. I need time to figure things out." During the truce with Gavin, surely she could discover what his intentions were. If he cared about her. And if her own feelings for him were true.

"I'd tell you to stay away from him," the other girl sighed, "but I know I'd be wasting my breath."

"I appreciate your advice, Charity. Truly, I do," Percy said, taking her friend's hand.

"Then you'll heed it." Charity returned the squeeze. "And you must also take care to end things well with Portland. Something tells me the viscount is not used to being set aside."

"It's not as if promises were made between us." Abashed at her own capriciousness, Percy fiddled with the handle of her cup. "When I see him at the Lipton's ball on Thursday, however, I shall make matters clear to him."

The longcase clock along the wall began its sonorous toll. "Oh, heavens," Charity muttered. "I'm supposed to be back at the shop by now—there's new inventory arriving today."

"Do you want me to come along, lend a hand?" Percy asked.

"Thank you, but you know how particular Papa is about the shop," Charity said apologetically. "I shall see you soon, I hope?"

After Charity left, Percy decided to clear her mind by

browsing the books. She made her selection and headed to the massive circular counter at the center of the emporium. As she waited for the clerk to ring up her purchase, she studied the dome overhead; it soared three stories high, revealing stacks upon stacks of volumes.

The clerk returned and handed her two wrapped packages.

"There must be a mistake," she said. "I only bought the one book."

The clerk pointed to the bill of sale attached to the second parcel. "Says here it's yours, miss,"—he looked to the lengthy line of customers behind her—"and ready to go."

Bemused, Percy collected her things and stepped to the side. She tore the string and paper off the unfamiliar package, revealing a first-rate edition of Greek mythology. She flipped open the cover, and her heart sped up at the sight of the masculine scrawl.

Meet me in Ancient Rome. -H.

Gavin was not a man driven by impulse. As he looked over the second floor balcony, the bookshop's famed dome rising above him, he told himself he had good reason to search out Percy today. He needed to solidify his position with her, to ensure that she did not have second thoughts about the new terms of the wager.

That's bollocks and you know it. Gavin scowled. He wasn't a man to lie to himself either.

The simple truth was that he wanted to see her again. Had been craving the sight of her since she'd climaxed in his arms four nights ago. Almighty, her passion had been so sweet, so abandoned. His shaft stiffened at the memory of her hot honey coating his fingers...

He'd come to terms with the fact that he could not ruin Percy as he'd initially planned. She was too rare, too fine to use in such a manner. Instead, he wanted to... keep her. To have her passion, her bright laughter all for himself. Then it had struck him: he could have her *and* his vengeance. All he had to do was seduce Percy's heart as well as her body.

He knew her fierce loyalty toward those she loved; if she was in love with him, he could use that to keep her at his side even after he'd won the wager. In fact, he'd realized that by marrying her—a man could do worse than wedding the sweetest, lustiest wench he'd ever met—he could exact a different sort of revenge. How would Morgan like having his only sister claimed by his enemy? Once Percy was Gavin's, he would never let the bastard near her again.

In return for her loyalty, Gavin would see that Percy wanted for nothing. A big house, carriage, fine clothes—he would do better by her than that bloody viscount. All he had to do was convince her of it. That, he assured himself, was why he'd come. And why his pulse thudded at the sight of the jaunty straw bonnet appearing at the top of the steps. Christ, she stole a man's breath. In a yellow-striped frock that clung sweetly to her bosom and swirled around the rest of her lithe figure, Percy looked as fresh and vital as spring itself.

She came toward him, peering anxiously this way and that.

"There's no one near," he told her. He'd chosen Ancient Rome for the privacy it offered.

"What are you doing here?" she said, her eyes wide.

He quirked a brow. "Can't a man shop for books?"

"Oh... of course." Her lashes lowered, and her cheeks turned pink.

A smile tugged at his lips. Obviously, his little minx had thought he'd had other ideas in mind. "And I wanted to see you," he added gravely.

Her azure eyes sparkled up at him. "You did?"

Before he could answer, he heard footsteps coming up the stairs. Taking her hand, he led her quickly into the maze of the stacks, following several twists and turns until they reached a secluded nook. Towering bookshelves surrounded them on three sides.

Leaning against one of them, Percy said breathlessly, "This is rather exciting. I've never had an assignation in a bookstore before."

He flicked a look around the corner. No one about. "Precisely how many assignations have you had?"

"A lady doesn't speak of such things, sir," she said.

The fierce stab of jealousy took him by surprise. "Don't play games with me, Percy," he said shortly. "Is it Portland? Or are you dangling after some other fine lord?"

"I was only teasing. I am not dangling after anyone. Gavin, you're holding me too tightly," she protested.

He hadn't even realized he was gripping her upper arms. He released her, muttering, "And Portland?"

She chewed on her lower lip. "Well, I *did* promise him a dance at a ball this Thursday." Gavin wanted to growl with rage at the idea of that prat dancing with *his* woman. "But after that," she said, sneaking a peek at him, "I shan't encourage him anymore."

"You had better not," he said sternly. "You're mine."

She glanced at him from beneath her lashes. "For the duration of our wager, you mean?"

Forever. But he gave a brusque nod; it wouldn't do to scare her off. He must stick with his plan to win her over one meeting at a time. The armistice had been an inspired move on his part; with her defenses lowered, he could reel her in with the passion she so clearly craved. By their sixth meeting, he would have her, body and soul. A strange yearning twisted inside him—possessiveness, surely. Yet he couldn't recall feeling this possessive over any woman before.

She gave him a smile that seemed… wistful. "I can't stay long. My maid is outside."

"She can wait a few minutes longer." Unable to help himself, he brushed his knuckles against her cheek. "How are you, buttercup?"

"I'm happy to see you," she said, dimpling.

He tweaked a silken curl between finger and thumb. "I meant after the other night."

"The other… *oh*."

She turned bright as roses and fell silent. All of a sudden, he remembered that ladies did not like to be reminded of their peccadilloes. As his mother had told it, she'd been seduced, impregnated, and left with no alternative but to turn to drink. The beatings his mother had given him? *His* fault for being an unlovable, disgusting brat. Her desertion? Nothing more than what he deserved.

Tensing, he wondered if Percy expected him to shoulder the blame for what had happened at the club. If she'd rewritten the events in her head. He told himself he couldn't expect a virgin to admit her own desires—

"The other night… I liked being with you." Still blushing, Percy said softly, "More than *liked*, actually. 'Twas the most wondrous experience, and I am looking forward to more."

Her honesty dispelled the shadows, replaced them with… pride. His chest swelled as did his shaft, which rose and strained toward her. Could someone so fine, so innocent belong to him?

"Do you know how irresistible you are?" he said, his tone husky.

"Irresistible? Me?" she breathed.

Unable to resist her lush lips, he leaned down—at the same instant, a flash of a dark jacket caught his eye. The hairs rose on his neck; his past taught him never to ignore his instincts. He scanned the stacks with an alert gaze. He saw nothing but shelves piled with books. But then, on the far right wall: a shadow. A second later, it *moved*.

Someone was hiding behind the bookshelf. Watching.

He bent as if to nuzzle Percy's ear. "Don't say anything," he whispered. "Someone is watching us. I'm going to get the bastard—*stay here*."

She tensed against him. Gave a slight nod.

In the next moment, he ran straight for the bookshelf shielding the Peeping Tom. The shadow flickered and footsteps sounded. Through the rows of books, he saw snippets of a black jacket moving away from him. The bastard was trying to escape. Rounding the corner, Gavin saw the man run down the empty aisle toward the staircase, and he gave chase. Grabbed the spy's arm just as the other reached the top of the steps.

"What the hell do you want?" Gavin snarled.

The stranger shook loose and threw a punch at him. Gavin dodged the blow and threw one of his own. His fist connected with a crack against the man's jaw. The man lost his balance, and the next instant tumbled down the stairs. A scream erupted; people flocked around the fallen figure. On reflex, Gavin pulled back against the wall, remaining out of view. He didn't need trouble. With his business and his reputation, he was a prime target for the magistrates.

He peered around the corner and saw that his attacker had risen. A good Samaritan offered the man a hand and was knocked to the ground for his trouble. The brute shoved through the crowd to the cries of "Well, I never!" and stumbled out the front door.

Percy came running up the aisle, yellow skirts and reticule flying.

He motioned her to keep out of sight of the stairwell. Once the crowd below cleared, he crossed over to her, led her back into the thick of the stacks.

"Are you alright?" Percy gasped. "Who was that man?"

"I don't know. He got away," Gavin said in disgust. "I thought I told you to stay put."

She looked upward, as if for patience. "What is going on, Gavin? It cannot be a coincidence that you have been attacked twice now."

He could have denied it, but the shrewd expression on her face told him it wouldn't do much good. "It's no coincidence," he said gruffly. "I don't know who is behind it."

"Perhaps this will provide a clue?"

Stunned, he watched as she removed a *dagger* from her reticule. "Where the bloody hell did you get that?"

"Instead of staying put, I searched the area where the man was hiding," she said pertly. She handed the weapon over. "It has an odd stamp on the handle. Some sort of an animal—a bear, perhaps?"

Gavin's blood turned cold. He'd seen that particular emblem before. "Not a bear. A lion."

The mark of Robbie Lyon, to be exact.

Chapter Twenty

Looking at Lord Petersby's flawless countenance in the moonlight, Miss Priscilla Farnham heard herself say the words she never thought she would.

"It's not you, it's me..."

—from *The Perils of Priscilla*, an inspired manuscript by
P. R. Fines

BENEATH THE BLAZING brilliance of hundreds of candles, the quadrille seemed to go on forever. Preoccupied, Percy missed a step and aimed an apologetic smile at her partner. She couldn't stop thinking about Gavin. After giving him the dagger she'd found, she'd pressed him for more information. *Someone wants me dead.* He'd said it in the off-handed manner one might use to request the passing of a salt cellar. Briefly, he'd told her about the competing gaming houses in Covent Garden and how any one of them could be behind the attacks.

Then he'd chucked her under the chin. *Don't worry, buttercup. I can take care of myself.*

She didn't doubt it. Yet if he was in danger, she wanted to help him. After all, she had assisted in warding off the villains at Vauxhall, and she had found the dagger in the bookshop, hadn't she? Apparently, the clue pointed to one of the club owners, a man named Robbie Lyon. Gavin had said he'd be looking into the matter.

If only I could see him tomorrow night as planned.

But she'd had to postpone her weekly meeting with Gavin. As luck would have it, Lisbett had returned, and upon learning of Tottie's *laissez-faire* chaperonage (no doubt from Violet), the housekeeper was keeping an eagle eye on Percy. For the last few days, Percy had made every effort to be on her best behavior so as not to rouse suspicion. She would have to prepare a sterling excuse to be out of the house next Friday night.

At the moment, however, she had another mission to accomplish. 'Twas one she was not looking forward to. As the dance finally came to an end and her beleaguered dancing partner hobbled off, she scanned the sweltering ballroom. She found her target standing by the punch table; as usual, he was surrounded by a gaggle of giggling debutantes. Sighing, she made her way over and entered the fray.

"Good evening, Miss Fines." Bestowing a smile upon her, Lord Portland bowed his pomaded auburn head and made the introductions.

Razor sharp smiles greeted Percy as she curtsied to the titled ladies. She wished she could tell them that she only wanted to borrow the viscount for a few minutes and would bring him right back. After a few minutes of listening to the debs snipe at each other in an attempt to gain Portland's attention, she summoned up her courage and said, "My, it is stuffy in here, isn't it?"

The other women glared at her, their fans beating the air.

Portland made a clearing sound in his throat. "Would you care for a turn in the garden, Miss Fines?"

"If you would be so kind, sir," Percy murmured.

The viscount took his leave of the group, and Percy could feel the daggered glances following them as they exited through the double doors onto the veranda overlooking the dark gardens. Due to a chilly night breeze, they had the space to themselves. Portland led her to a secluded bench in the far corner, hidden from the general view by a row of potted bushes. Percy's throat fluttered with nervousness as she sat and arranged her peach chiffon skirts.

Portland remained standing, one elbow upon the balustrade in a casual yet affected stance. Against the velvety night sky, the moonlight gleaming on his perfectly coiffed curls, he looked more like a storybook prince than ever.

In sum: pretty, flat, and uninteresting.

She flushed with guilt. It wasn't Lord Portland's fault that she'd developed a taste for complexity not found in faerie tales. That she now yearned for the kind found in real life, where heroes might masquerade as villains. And love might take the guise of a scandalous wager.

Inhaling deeply, she told herself that she owed Portland the courtesy of honesty. Though nothing had transpired between them, she didn't want to encourage him any further. He spoke before she did.

"Will your chaperone worry with you gone?" he said.

Unlikely, since Tottie was currently taking a nap in the retiring room. "Lady Tottenham, um, trusts my judgment," Percy said.

Portland cleared his throat. "Well then, Miss Fines, I believe I know why you sought me out this evening."

"You... do?"

"This has been coming for some time now, has it not?" he said. "I will not say I am surprised."

She felt a rush of gratitude for his exquisite manners. He was going to make this easy for her. Viscount Portland was, first and foremost, a gentleman.

"You are very kind, my lord," she said. "I confess this conversation is rather difficult for me. Please believe me when I say I have thought through the matter with care."

"I know you have, my dear. You have brought it up before."

"I have?" She frowned.

"Perhaps it is not gentlemanly of me to remind you," he said indulgently, "but yes, you did. Once before, during our stroll down Rotten Row."

What in blazes is he talking about?

"Clearly the matter is of import to you. And while I cannot say I approve, I feel I can satisfy you this once. With the understanding that this is all just a bit of fun, eh?" he said lightly.

Her head was spinning. "You have lost me."

"The time for coyness has passed." All of the sudden, Portland was leaning over her, blocking the garden from her view. "*See the mountains kiss the high heaven. And the moonbeams kiss the sea?* You naughty little minx, I'll show you what *all these kissings are worth*."

She froze at the rendition of Shelley's impassioned verse. Before she could react, Portland's arms closed around her. His mouth pressed against hers—wet, *disgusting*. Regaining her senses, she shoved at him with both hands. With a surprised grunt, he lost his balance, his arms twin windmills as he fell backward and landed with an ungraceful *thud* upon his posterior.

Percy leapt to her feet, wiping her lips with the back of her glove.

"What the devil did you do that for?" Portland glared at her as he picked himself up from the stone floor. He inspected his jacket, and his expression darkened at the sight of a tiny tear on the sleeve. "This is a new Weston, by God."

Guilt and horror mingled in her. "I am so sorry," she said helplessly. "I didn't know what else to do."

"To *do*, you little baggage? You have been hounding me for weeks for a kiss. You might have sat there and received it properly like a lady."

That stopped her short. "I wouldn't quite say *hound*, my lord. I expressed curiosity about it. One time."

"You are nothing but a tease, Miss Fines," he fumed. "A common, ill-bred trollop."

Percy's cheeks flamed. She supposed she deserved the insult, if only for her stupidity in believing herself in love with this fop.

"I ought to have heeded Mama. In the end, breeding and class always shows itself," he continued in snide tones.

Her guilt dissipated. *The snob.* "That is unkind and unfair, sir."

Portland took a deep breath. Seemed to gather himself. "I must return to the ballroom," he said stiffly, "before my absence is remarked upon."

"We are not quite done, my lord," she said grimly.

His perfect brows shot up. "Never say you want another kiss."

"I never wanted a kiss in the first place." The words emerged through her teeth. To her credit, she managed to filter back the last two words: *you ass.* "What I wanted to say was that I don't think we ought to be spending any more time in each other's company."

"You don't think..." His jaw quite literally dropped. Why hadn't she noticed how weak his chin was before? "*You* are jilting *me?*"

"Well, not exactly." She had not realized a person could look apoplectic in the moonlight. Yet above the pristine cascade of his cravat, the viscount's face had turned an unmistakable shade of crimson. She said in more cautious tones, "I'd say *jilt* was too strong a word. I mean, there was never an understanding between us, was there?"

"You have been casting your wiles at me this *entire* Season, you little Jezebel!"

Her eyes narrowed. "Hold up, my lord. While I may have encouraged you, you have never been clear in your affections to me. You have surrounded yourself with debutantes these months past, and if you had chosen one of them, I would not have a word to say about it."

"Is that what this is about? You are jealous?"

His obtuseness robbed her of speech. What had she ever seen in the arrogant prig?

"One cannot blame you, of course," he said with a condescending smile. "Coming from trade, your options are rather limited. If it consoles you, I did have you on my list of bridal candidates—but near the bottom, I'm afraid. There are many eligible ladies this year, and a man in my position must choose wisely. I hope you understand."

"I do understand." She could restrain herself no longer. "Allow me to assist you in your decision. Take me off your bloody list, you insufferable stuffed shirt!"

She stomped past him and down the steps into the garden. Seething, she headed into the dense maze of bushes. How could she have made such a cake of herself over that self-important prat? *I wish I had never met Portland. I hate him, and I hate the ton!*

"Having an interesting night?"

She jumped around, her hands flying to her bosom. To her shock, Gavin stood there, his black evening attire blending with the shadows. The moonlight glazed his thick hair, turned his eyes to gleaming gold.

"What in heaven's name are you doing here?" she gasped.

"Waiting for you."

She blinked. "You are waiting for me. In Lady Lipton's garden."

He smiled faintly.

"However did you manage to get in?"

He shrugged. An off-handed gesture.

She gave a bewildered laugh. "Alright then. Will I get an answer if I ask you why you've come?" Even in the dimness, she caught the flicker in his gaze. And suddenly she understood. "You came to *spy* on me, didn't you? Because of Portland?"

He didn't bother to deny it. "I wanted to be here in case you needed me. Which you clearly did not." In spite of her indignation, her belly quivered at the appreciation in his deep voice. "You handled him with finesse, buttercup."

For a moment, she teetered toward annoyance... but she blew out a breath. He wasn't the one she was angry at. "What I did was seal my fate," she said with a grimace. "Before the week is out, Lord Portland will have all the tongues wagging. I'll probably be labeled a jilt."

"I doubt it."

She frowned. "Why do you say that?"

"Because the bastard is leveraged up to his eyebrows in bad investments. 'Tis a little known fact," he said when her jaw slackened. "And if he doesn't want it to become common knowledge, he'll keep his mouth shut."

"You're *blackmailing* Portland?"

"Not me personally. But the man he owes happens to owe me a favor." Gavin gave her a satisfied look. "Portland needs his reputation, so he'll stay quiet."

Percy gawked at him. She didn't know whether to be annoyed at his high-handedness or grateful that he'd taken such pains to protect her reputation. "Why would you do such a thing for me?" she managed.

"I protect what's mine," he said.

No poetic flummery, no pretense—just a statement of fact, thrilling in its primal promise. Yearning blossomed within her as she stared up at his strong, scarred face. What would it be like to truly belong to this man? Dare she trust him—and her own feelings?

Another thought hit her. "Is it safe for you to be here like this?"

His large palm cupped her cheek, the graze of his rough skin making her tremble. "I have everything in hand, sweet, and men posted nearby. There's nothing to worry about."

"But what about that Lyon fellow—"

"I've my eye on him." Gavin shrugged, as if the threat to his life was inconsequential. "Trust me, I can take care of myself."

"No man is an island," she said. "You mustn't think yourself invulnerable. Isn't there anything I can do to—"

He put a finger to her lips, halting the flow of words. "There's no need to fret, sweet." The golden flames in his gaze entranced her. "I've dealt with such matters before. Trust me?"

She nodded reluctantly, and he gave her one of his rare smiles. Her heart did a flip.

"Tonight, I don't want to think about such things," he said in a husky tone. "Not when the stars are out and we have this garden all to ourselves. Will you walk with me, Percy?"

Her gaze darted from the arm he offered back to the townhouse glowing in the distance. Once, she'd thought that her future lay in that latter direction. A respectable marriage, a fine house. A lifetime of sensible choices ahead of her. Now, looking into Gavin's burnished eyes, she realized fate had something more compelling in store. Something mysterious—and with no guaranteed happy ending. Was she brave enough to reach for it?

She placed her fingers on his arm, feeling the quiver of iron-hard muscles.

"Yes," she said. "I'll go with you."

Chapter Twenty-One

TALL FLOWERING HEDGES surrounded the winding path, night jasmine perfuming the brisk air. Overhead, stars blazed like diamonds cast across velvet. Triumph filled Gavin as he led Percy deeper into the dark garden. She'd just turned her back on everything she'd thought she wanted—*for him.* The notion made him feel taller than a mountain. He could win her heart; he could have all of her.

Beside him, she ambled along like some gorgeous fairy creature. The moon turned the curls piled atop her head to silver, and her blush-colored gown clung like petals to her slender form. The modest scoop of her neckline showed only the barest hint of a crevice. He wanted to nuzzle her there, to delve beneath that filmy fabric and lick her breasts all over. As his mouth pooled, he saw goose pimples prickling her skin.

Unbuttoning his jacket, he placed it over her shoulders. "There's a gazebo up ahead," he said. "We'll stop there."

She nodded. Kicking at pebbles as they walked along, she slid him a glance. "Why aren't you crowing about Portland? After all, you were right."

"About what?"

"About me being a silly chit who mistook infatuation for love," she said gruffly.

Her candor drew forth a surge of tenderness in him. Never before had he experienced this desire to soothe a woman, to protect her from all ills. "Come now," he said, "'tis not so bad."

"I feel like an idiot," she said.

His lips twitched. "You'll get over it. Blows to the pride don't last long."

She seemed to mull it over. "I suppose you're right. It certainly doesn't hurt anywhere else." Shaking her head, she said, "Why is it that you seem to understand me more than I understand myself?"

Because you're mine. The possessive certainty gripped him, yet he managed to say in calm tones, "I understand ambition. You're too spirited and intelligent to follow the herd. You need to find your own purpose."

She glanced at him. "Like you did?"

"As I did." Perhaps it was the dark or the intoxicating scent of her perfume that drew more out of him. "I wasn't always a successful business owner. There was a time when I barely scraped by, making a hard living in the streets. For years, I worked as,"—he cleared his throat—"a guard-for-hire."

A polite term for a mercenary. But there hadn't been many other options open to a scarred ex-criminal. If nothing else, the hulks had given him a talent for violence.

"No wonder you fight so well," she said. "How did you find that line of work?"

He cast her a swift glance; there was no trace of mockery or disdain in her expression. Could it be that she did not judge him for his past? "I hated it," he said. "But I invested every guinea I earned, and when I had enough, I bought the club."

The years of brutality had paid off; he'd never forget the feeling of walking into his own property for the first time. From that moment on, he'd vowed to dictate his future.

"You remind me of my papa," she said, surprising him yet again. "He came from poverty too and built an empire out of nothing." Her gaze dropped, and her slipper chased away another stone. "Whereas I grew up with every privilege and have done nothing of worth with my life. Sometimes I think I'm not much more than a spoiled miss."

Once, he had thought the same of her. Knowing her now, her courage and loyal heart, her untamed spirit... nothing could be farther from the truth.

"You have had material advantages," he said. "That does not make you spoiled."

She shot him a troubled glance. "Does being headstrong? In the end, the only thing Papa asked of me was to be a good daughter. To have the kind of life he could not, even with his fortune. That was his dream for me—for our family."

It all made sense now. Why Percy would try to be someone other than who she was. She'd tried to hide her true self not because of middling class hypocrisy, as he'd originally assumed, but because of... love. The desire for her family's approval.

"Your father wanted you to have a position in society," Gavin said.

She gave a forlorn nod. "With Nicholas' title, it should have been so easy. I have everything—money, access to the best circles. But I still couldn't do my family proud. Because I am a hoyden who has no business masquerading as a lady."

For once, the mention of Morgan did not affect Gavin. He was too angry with so-called polite society for making this lovely, sensitive girl ever doubt her own worth.

"There's nothing wrong with you," he said roughly.

The path came to a small gazebo. They entered under the sloping roof, and she went to look out at the dark vista. She kept her back to him, her gloved fingers trailing along the railing. "The truth is... they were right. I am *not* a lady."

"That is utter bollocks."

"No, it's true. From the time I was a child, I've been getting into scrapes. I've had more tutors than you could count on both hands, yet I cannot claim a single accomplishment." Her shrug was nearly obscured by his jacket, which dwarfed her and made her look like a little girl in a game of dress-up. "I don't know why I thought I could suddenly transform into a paragon."

"You can do anything you put your mind to." He hated that she thought differently, hated that the world could crush her spirit. Her beautiful exuberance. The need to protect her clawed at his insides. "If you had truly wanted Portland, you would have figured out a way to snare him," he said. "Or any one of those fine prancing bastards."

She swiveled and looked fully at him. Her expression made his breath catch. "But I don't want Portland," she said softly, "or any of those gentlemen. I realize now that I don't give a damn what the *ton* or anyone else thinks. For the first time, I know what *I* want."

Words seemed to stick in his throat. "What is that?"

She came closer to him, her eyes luminous. Captivating. "Adventure and passion, for starters. I've started writing again, you know, and this time I want my life to inspire my work."

Adventure and passion. He swallowed. Aye, he could give her that.

"I want to live without regrets." She stopped in front of him, the tips of her slippers nearly touching his boots. "I want to experience everything I've ever dreamed about and more."

A smile curved her lips, and in that single, awesome moment she transformed before his eyes. From lovely girl to a sultry, bewitching woman. A siren of indescribable power.

"I fear I would shock even you with my true wicked nature," she said.

"Wicked, you say?" He cleared his throat, trying to think. It was difficult, seeing as how all the blood had drained from his brain and gone straight to his cock. "Wickedness is my stock in trade. Trust me, nothing you could say would shock me."

Yet he froze when she lifted one palm then another to his chest. Her light touch burned through his waistcoat. "So you would not be shocked if I said... I desire you, Gavin?" Her bottom lip caught beneath her teeth. In a trembling voice, she confessed, "That I'd want to be with you, even without the wager?"

Arousal knifed through him. White-hot, alarming in its intensity. In spite of loyalty to her brother, she wanted to be with him... He forced himself to inhale and exhale. "Not shocked, no." He ran his knuckles softly along her cheek. "Grateful, definitely."

That caused her to grin. Her eyes sparkled with excitement, with a bold feminine desire that washed heat over his insides. He'd been with lusty women before. He'd fucked women who screamed with pleasure and demanded more. But this was different. He'd never felt *desired* as he did now. As if he was more than just a randy beast, an obliging cock. A handful of gold.

As if Percy wanted *him*. Just... him.

Her hands slipped under his waistcoat, making his heart pound even faster. "Before we go on," she said, "I wish to clarify a few matters. About our bet."

"Yes, buttercup?" he managed.

"I assume you're not willing to forfeit at this point?"

Instantly, suspicion and mistrust mangled inside of him. Instinct whispered in his ear: *Is she trying to manipulate you, use your attraction to her to get what she wants?* Though he told himself Percy was not capable of such underhandedness, his jaw tightened.

"I am not," he said flatly.

"Can you tell me why? It's not only about the money, is it?" Her eyes searched his. "Gavin, I just want to understand..."

He dragged a hand through his hair. Mayhap trust *was* possible for him after all, for he believed her sincere intentions. A small part of him even considered telling her about the past; the wiser and larger remainder balked at the notion. Her ties to Nicholas Morgan were too strong, her bond to Gavin too tenuous. When it came down to choosing, at this juncture he knew where her loyalties would lie. He would not risk losing her or compromising his well-laid plan for revenge.

"I always collect my debts. That will not change," he said.

I do not know how to make it change.

For a minute, she said nothing. Sudden panic gripped him. Would she walk away? Leave him to his own devices? Anger followed swiftly. Like hell she would. He'd never let her go—

"Well, I'm not going to forfeit either," she said, popping a button free on his waistcoat.

Relief and desire spun his head. "So where does that leave us?" he rasped.

She slid another button free. "At a standstill in the matter of my virginity. However, according to the terms of your truce, there is much else to explore. And I want to." Her tremulous smile curled in his chest. "I want to make the most of the next three nights with you, Gavin—"

He didn't let her finish. He couldn't.

With a growl of pure need, he captured her lips. She tasted of nectar and sunshine, everything he'd ever hungered for. And she yielded her sweetness so readily. Her lips parted, her tongue welcoming him inside her warmth. Nothing in his life had come without a struggle, a price. Yet Percy, who had every reason to distrust him, to despise him, was offering him her luscious self. Did she *know* what a gift that was?

He backed her against one of the poles of the gazebo, his

mouth coursing greedily along her neck. With possessive hands, he cupped her breasts, finding the stiff peaks beneath the fabric. "You were made for loving, Percy," he said, "and I'm going to show you just how much."

She gave a little sigh of pleasure. "Like you did the last time?"

"Liked that, did you?"

"Very much so." She smiled up at him shyly. "It felt so wonderful, only... "

Only? His brows raised. "You shuddered in my arms when you came for me."

"Oh no, that part was perfect." Even in the moonlight, he could see roses in her cheeks. "It's just that this time... well, I was wondering..."

"Yes?"

"If I could... return the favor?"

Her earnest request blazed heat straight to his groin. His prick throbbed with the unqualified answer, his balls drawing taut. *Holy hell*, could she. But she was a virgin. Even though he was no gentleman, he'd thought to ease her into the business of lovemaking. To make her comfortable with her own response first before introducing her to—

Her hand feathered across his crotch, and all his good intentions vanished.

"Do you want to touch me, sweet?" he said hoarsely.

Her curls wobbled as she nodded.

Praise God. With hands that shook slightly, he undid the fasteners of his trousers and shoved the layers of fabric past his hips. His cock sprang free, the shaft thick and upright, the flared crown brushing his abdomen. Below the jutting instrument, his stones hung heavy and swollen with seed. He watched her intently, wondering what his little miss thought of his rampant erection.

"Oh." Her eyes were wide and curious. "It's, um, rather

forthright, isn't it?"

Beneath her scrutiny, the randy monster swelled further.

"It gets that way around you, sweetheart," he said wryly.

Despite the desire straining every muscle, he forced himself to wait. To let her decide what she wished to do. When she gently curled her hand around him, his breath hissed between his teeth. The sight of her delicate, satin-covered fingers petting the dark, rearing beast was beyond erotic. She explored him with a torturously light touch, the pressure nowhere near enough, and yet pleasure shot to his toes, hotter than anything he'd experienced before.

"How am I doing?" She sounded as breathless as he felt.

He answered her with a ravenous kiss. "You, my sweet Persephone, are heaven and hell," he whispered against her lips.

Her forefinger dipped against his cock slit, rubbing gently and sending another blast of heat through his veins. "Heaven and hell?" she said. "What does that mean?"

"Let me show you." He drew up her skirts, nudging her thighs open with his own. He found her pussy through her drawers and groaned at the dampness of her flesh. "You're drenched for me already. Does it excite you, touching my cock?"

Biting her lip, she nodded. Her grip on his pulsing rod tightened.

The admission filled him with heady triumph. "That pleases me," he said. "It makes me big and hard and yearn to be inside this sweet part of you." He slid his middle finger down her lush slit, finding her opening. He pushed upward and her virginal muscles gave a little, clamping onto the very tip of his finger. By God, she was tight. His lungs worked harshly as he strove to hold onto his self-control. "I want to bury my cock inside. I want to be as deep inside you as possible... and I can't. That is hell."

"Gavin," she whimpered.

The sound of her voice saying his name burned through his blood like an aphrodisiac. Whether or not she was aware, she'd begun to squeeze his shaft more tightly, pumping him in the instinctual motion.

"Good girl, you know just how to frig me, don't you?" Her lashes gave a sultry sweep at his guttural praise. Simultaneously, he penetrated her quim more deeply. "This is how we're going to find heaven together. What feels good to you feels good for me. When you hold my cock so sweetly, it tells me what you want, doesn't it?"

He saw understanding enter her expressive eyes. The next instant, her satiny fingers began to slide harder, faster against his turgid stalk.

"More," she sighed, devastating him. "I want more."

He drove his finger home, swallowing her cry as he did so. He fucked her slowly at first, then quickened the rhythm as her pussy softened, wept into his palm. He gave her another finger, and she took him eagerly, her plush heat whirling his senses, her grip wild and passionate upon his prick. He pumped himself into her soft hands, her exquisite sex, half-mad with the intensity of his lust. His longing. Pressure mounted in his stones, and he knew he couldn't hold back much longer.

He found the center of her pleasure with his thumb. Her response was instant, her sheath pulsing around his plunging digits, her hips angling to take him deeper.

"Oh Gavin, don't stop, *please*..."

Her sex milked his fingers, so demanding and hungry. *Too much, can't hold on.* "Go over now, Percy," he growled, "with me—"

Her body spasmed, the luscious pull dragging him over the edge. With her beautiful cries in his ears, he shut his eyes against the fierce pleasure, the powerful release boiling up his shaft. He spent with a violence that robbed him of all control. Time slowed as he spewed hotly again and again, bellowing as ecstasy turned him inside out.

When he came to his senses, it was to find Percy gazing at him. Her hair was falling from its pins, and she held a stained glove to her heaving bosom. The stars in her eyes outshone those in the heavens above.

And, finally, he realized the danger he was in.

Nicholas Morgan awoke in a strange bed. He yawned, blinking groggily at his surroundings. Another hotel room. Next to the bed, the large window was open, the curtains stirring in the warm breeze. He saw a field of red tiles lining the rooftops, and it all returned to him. Florence. They'd arrived early this morning. After the exhausting journey, Nurse had bundled the twins off for a nap, and Helena had decided the adults needed a lie down too.

Being an accommodating husband, he'd gone along with his better half. They hadn't gotten much sleep. As it turned out, vacationing made him randy as hell—and that was saying something, given that he couldn't keep his hands off his wife under normal circumstances. He raised himself up on one elbow, gazing down at his marchioness. Curled on her side, Helena dozed as peacefully as a little girl with her chestnut hair tangled and her delicate skin flushed.

Yet despite her innocent looks, his Helena was all woman. The sheet had slipped, revealing one round, plump breast. That ripe curve with its lovely pink crest was too much to resist.

Leaning over, he drew his tongue languidly around the nipple. It stiffened immediately, and he took his time licking, teasing it into a ripe berry. Though Helena's eyes remained closed, she shifted, a sigh escaping her. Enjoying the game, he explored beneath the sheet, his hand skimming over her plush backside before slipping between her thighs.

His heart sped up to find her deliciously, wantonly ready for him again. Positioning himself on his side, he took his turgid member in hand and ran the thick head along her slit. He savored her wetness, the sudden hitch in her breathing. He entered her in a slow, mind-melting thrust. Even as heat engulfed his senses, he told himself to draw out the bliss this go around. But then his naughty marchioness moaned, wriggling her bottom against him, and he had no choice but to give in, plowing her harder, needing to be deeper and deeper—

A series of raps sounded on the door.

Bloody fuck. He nipped his wife's ear. "Ignore it," he whispered.

"We can't just—*ohh.*" She broke off as he nudged higher, finding her favorite spot.

The knocking continued. "Nicholas? Helena? Are you awake? 'Tis me, Anna."

"We'll be, er, just a moment," Helena called out breathlessly.

She wiggled away from him, and he let her go with a grunt. Scrambling from the bed, she donned a dressing gown and tossed him his. He put it on. Grimaced as he looked down at himself. "What the devil am I supposed to do about this?"

Helena's eyes widened at the sight of the tented brocade.

"Here, take this." She shoved a newspaper at him, clearly trying to smother a laugh. "Just, er, hold it in front."

He raised his gaze to the ceiling.

Helena went to the door and ushered in Anna Fines. Nicholas' lust faded when he saw the worry lining the older lady's soft features. Behind her spectacles, Anna's typically serene blue eyes held an apprehensive gleam. The last time he'd seen that particular expression had been when Jeremiah—Anna's husband and Nicholas' mentor—had fallen ill.

"What is the matter, dear?" Helena said, sounding as concerned as he felt.

"I'm so sorry to disturb you, but,"—Anna's lips trembled—"dear heaven, it's the children."

"The twins?" Helena said on a note of alarm.

"No, not your children. *Mine.*" With a shaking hand, Anna held out a letter. "I'm afraid we must depart for London immediately."

Chapter Twenty-Two

GAVIN PLACED HIS newly cleaned pistols upon his desk. They gleamed in readiness. Hearing footsteps in the hallway, he tossed a piece of black velvet over the weapons and rose to his greet his late night visitor.

Magnus shuffled into the study, his cane knocking hollowly against the floor. "Sorry to disturb you at this hour, Hunt."

"You have information for me?" Gavin said without ado.

"Aye. Found that gent of yours," the old man said. "Led me on a merry chase, Fines did. Turns out he's been hiding in Spitalfields."

Gavin had to give it to Percy's brother. Bloody Spitalfields, of all places. Ingenuity—and recklessness—must run in the bloodline.

"If you plan to take the cully, you'd best to do it soon," Magnus continued.

"Why?"

"Fines has gotten himself in debt to Finian O'Brien. As you and I both know, patience isn't one of O'Brien's virtues— from what I hear, he's circling like a shark." Magnus' rheumy eye blinked at Gavin. "You'd better get to Fines while there's any of the cove left."

Bloody fuck. Did Fines *want* to get himself killed? Two annoying facts struck Gavin at the same time. First off, though he now knew where Fines was, he couldn't collect the company shares because of his promise to Percy. Second, he'd probably have to *protect* her feckless fool of a brother because he was quite certain Percy wouldn't want Fines dead.

The irony of the situation dumbfounded him. More disconcerting was the realization of how much Percy's happiness mattered to him. Of how much he wanted her. The memory of her generous passion in the garden warmed his chest, made him ache to be near her. Though the return of her housekeeper had made it more difficult for her to slip out, she'd promised to meet him at the club this Friday.

A few days apart from her felt like bloody weeks.

"Thanks for the warning," he said to Magnus. "I'll attend to matters."

The old man gave him a worried look. "Has the Marquess of Harteford returned from abroad yet? You'll need a plan to deal with him. He considers Fines a brother, and from what I hear the marquess protects his own."

Gavin knew the hourglass was narrowing. According to his sources, Morgan had made an abrupt departure from Florence last week; the marquess would be back in England within a fortnight at most. Before that happened, Gavin must bind Percy to him, body and soul. He had to be certain of her love and loyalty to him; he had to know that she would choose him over Morgan, her family—anyone else. And carrying on with the wager—keeping her close, seducing her more and more with each meeting—was the way to achieve this goal.

"I'll take care of Harteford," Gavin said.

"Do you need my assistance..." Magnus began when the door flung open.

Garbed in a black, many-caped greatcoat, Stewart looked even bigger and more intimidating than usual. He stalked over to Magnus, dwarfing the frail, older man.

"What's your business 'ere, you old goat?" he growled.

"I'm here to help Hunt, same as you," Magnus said in a

calm voice.

"We don't need your help. Hunt's got me to watch 'is back." Stewart's chin jutted up. "Just as I always 'ave—isn't that right, lad?"

Stifling his impatience, Gavin said, "Magnus brought me news of Paul Fines."

"Took your time 'bout it, didn't you?" Stewart said to Magnus. "For the coin you charge, I'd expect be'er service."

"Fines was wilier than most. And I gave Hunt a decent rate... as *I* always do." With dignity, Magnus adjusted the fraying lapels of his jacket and turned pointedly to Gavin. "I'll be on my way. Be in touch if you want my assistance with Harteford."

The instant the door closed behind the old man, Stewart burst out, "I don't like that codger, an' I trust 'im even less. You don't need 'is 'elp with Harteford. You've got me."

Hell's teeth. Gavin was not in the mood for one of his mentor's rants. "My business with Magnus is done," he said brusquely. "Is the carriage ready?"

"Aye. But I still—"

"For God's sake, man, let it lie." At his mentor's sullen expression, Gavin said gruffly, "I know you don't like Magnus, but he's been of use, alright? Now let's stop this shilly-shallying, shall we, and go catch ourselves a cutthroat."

As he watched the hulking bawdy house with its shuttered windows, Gavin said, "What the hell is taking Lyon so long?"

"It ain't stamina, that's for sure," Stewart said from across the dark carriage. Thank God his mentor had recovered from the snit over Magnus—nothing like staking out a brothel to improve the man's mood. "The bastard's a lit cannon—can't 'old 'is liquor or 'is temper," Stewart went on, smirking. "If 'e lasts five minutes with a wench, I'd eat my topper."

Gavin observed the men going in and out of the bawdy house. According to Alfie's reconnaissance, Lyon visited Madame Antoinette's establishment every Thursday from ten to eleven in the evening to indulge in his particular brand of sport. It was one of the rare times Lyon went anywhere unaccompanied and, therefore, the perfect occasion to nab the bastard for questioning.

Percy's parting words in the garden echoed in Gavin's head. *Whatever you do, you will be careful? I couldn't bear it if anything happened to you.* He'd clutched her close, reveling in her sweet concern for him, in all that had passed between them that night. More than sex play. More than he'd known with any woman. Reminded of the conundrum with her brother, Gavin frowned. What the devil was he going to do about Fines?

"It's nearing midnight. Lyon should have come out an hour ago," Stewart said.

Unease stirred, and Gavin set his thoughts aside to focus on the business at hand. "We've waited long enough. We'll have to go in."

In reply, Stewart slid a pistol into his greatcoat pocket.

After paying their entry fees, the two men crossed the threshold of the infamous brothel. Smoke made the air hazy, the rich scent of roses emanating decadence. Candles saturated the main room with a muted glow and cast shadows upon the gilded furnishings done in a vaguely French style. Well-dressed gentlemen mingled with wenches who wore candy-colored wigs, paint … and little else.

"I don't see 'im anywhere," Stewart said. "'E must be upstairs in one o' the rooms."

"*Messieurs, quelle plaisir.*" The silky voice coiled around them like a snake. Gavin turned to see a small, sharp-eyed woman wearing a towering powdered wig and dressed in the costume of Louis XIV's court. Her accent was as authentic as the beauty patch above her hard mouth. "I don't recall seeing you here before. First time?"

Gavin gave a curt nod.

"Bienvenue, je suis Madame Antoinette." She performed a low curtsy, her wide skirts skimming the floor. "Here you will find that *la joie de vivre*,"—she fingered the thin scarlet ribbon around her neck—"is the night's only purpose. Now tell me, *messieurs*, have you a particular fancy in mind?"

Gavin recalled his brief interview with Alfie. Shaking his head, the urchin had said, *That Lyon, 'e's a queer git, alright. Visits a wench by the name o' Polly Whippit*—Alfie had snorted—*and 'er name says it all. Gor, who'd spend blunt on a thing any schoolmistress or fishwife be 'appy to give for free?*

"I'm told you have a girl here by the name of Miss Whippit," Gavin said.

"Mais oui, she is one of my most popular ladies-in-waiting." The bawd's eyes took on a calculating slant. "But I'm afraid she is occupied at present. May I instead recommend another disciple of the art, Mademoiselle Birchim?"

Beside Gavin, Stewart shook his head in disgust.

"I've heard Miss Whippit is the best." Gavin removed a bag of coins, allowing them to clink. He saw the madam's eyes widen. "I want nothing but the best."

"And you shall have it," she said, holding her palm out. He let the bag drop, and the money disappeared in a blink. A smile stretched her lips. "Follow me, *s'il vous plaît*."

She led the way through the main rooms and up a wide curving staircase. On the first floor, they passed by a half-dozen naked wenches posed upon pedestals. A few cooed bawdy suggestions for the evening's entertainment.

Madame Antoinette arched her brows at Stewart. "Perhaps *monsieur* would like companionship as well? You look like you could use a girl—or two." She gestured to a pair of tarts who were giggling and fondling each other's rouged nipples. "Juliette and Monique are twins, you know."

"I'm just 'ere to watch my friend's back," Stewart said with a scowl.

"Like to watch, do you? Well, to each his own," the madam said airily.

Beneath his beard, Stewart's face turned a dull red.

"What about you, *monsieur*?" Madame Antoinette turned to Gavin. "Perhaps you'd like to spice up your visit with a merry ménage?"

Gavin could not help but take note of his reaction—or the lack thereof. Being a hot-blooded man, such depravity might have tempted him once and despite the night's mission. But now, he felt nothing but distaste. The sordid business of paid pleasure soured his stomach; he wondered how he'd ever found satisfaction in it. After tasting a goddess' ambrosia, he could never again drink from the common well.

"I'm here for Miss Whippit," he said shortly. "Let us proceed."

They continued on their path. Gavin thought of cornering Lyon tonight and anticipation unfurled. Once he figured out who wanted him dead and why, he could put an end to the mayhem. Then he could get on with more important matters—namely, how to make Percy his. For the first time, he imagined a tantalizing light at the end of the dark tunnel he'd inhabited most his life. Aye, he'd get his answers tonight, even if he had to beat it out of that whoreson Lyon.

"Here we are," the bawd announced.

They'd reached a pair of doors at the end of the corridor. A pair of columns flanked the entrance and supported a plaster pediment in the manner of a classical shrine. The bawd unlocked the door with a key and bowed with dramatic flourish. "I give you, *messieurs*, The Temple of the Rod."

The high-ceilinged room was supported with columns and painted with frescoes to resemble a holy place of antiquity. The activities currently taking place, however, bore no resemblance to any ancient worship Gavin was aware of. Clad in skimpy tunics and golden sandals, the molls here wielded various instruments of torture: birches, paddles, even the occasional cat-o'-nine-tails. The hiss and snap of leather and wood elicited groans of pleasure from the bound, naked male patrons.

"Blimey, these sods belong in Bedlam," Stewart muttered under his breath. "They can't be right in the upper storey. No sane man would allow such a thing—'tis a bloody disgrace."

Gavin had to agree. His shoulders tensed as a whore with a shiny black whip landed a particularly robust blow. It reminded him all too keenly of the hulks. The punishments meted out for the amusement of the guards and the endless struggle for dominance amongst his fellow inmates. He couldn't fathom yielding control to another, much less finding pleasure in such a thing.

In sexual matters, as with everything else, he would always be the one on top. A scenario flashed in his head... of Percy bound and begging for his touch... Even as his groin tightened, he acknowledged that what he wanted from her transcended ropes and cuffs. Those trappings were mere symbols of his deeper need: to have her complete surrender. To know he didn't need to tie her up for her to stay. To know without a doubt that she belonged entirely and only to him. Forever.

Madame Antoinette approached a brunette who was busily employing a leather crop to the reddened backside of a man bound face-down to a table.

"*Cherie*," the bawd said, "have you seen Mademoiselle Whippit?"

The brunette paused, tapping her chin with the tip of the

crop. "Earlier, she came in with one o' 'er regulars, a ginger-
'aired fellow. They're in one o' the back rooms, I reckon."

"*Merci.* Carry on."

The brunette winked and then said in the high, strident
tones of a schoolmistress, "Now, my naughty Johnny, did you
forget your homework again?"

Pleasured yelps rang behind them as the bawd took them
to the back of the temple and through a curtain. Doors lined
both sides of a hallway; Madame stopped at a closed door on
the right. She placed her ear against the door and then
knocked discreetly. When no answer was forthcoming, she
frowned.

"*Excusez-moi, messieurs,*" she said, fitting her key to the
lock. "Wait here a moment. I shall return shortly."

As the bawd went inside, closing the door behind her,
Stewart said in a low voice, "Wait my arse. I say we go in there
an' take 'im now. We can buy the bawd's silence."

Gavin nodded. He readied to shoulder the door down—
at that instant, a scream rang through the walls. With a quick
glance at one another, he and Stewart knocked the door off its
hinges. They rushed through an antechamber, into the back
and there...

"'Oly Mother o' God," Stewart said.

Gavin had seen plenty of violence in his life; even so, the
scene lurched his stomach. On her knees, the bawd clutched a
pink wig, rocking beside the small figure lying on the floor.
With shorn brown hair and open yet unseeing eyes, Miss
Whippit resembled a pretty doll whose neck had been
snapped in a childish temper. Behind her, spread-eagled upon
a wooden rack, lay a more grotesque end, if death could be
compared.

Robbie Lyon's throat had been sliced, ear to ear. His eyes
bulged from their sockets in an expression of unholy fear.
He'd likely watched as his life had gushed from him, bathing

his wiry nude form and pooling onto the floor beneath. Flies had already begun to gather and feast; Gavin's gaze shot to the open window.

He and Stewart exchanged a grim look. Apparently, they had not been the only ones looking for Lyon. And someone had gotten to him first.

"There's going to be hell to pay," Stewart said softly.

"Aye." Gavin could feel the storm rising.

Chapter Twenty-Three

"LORD ABOVE, MISS Percy, is that any way to tidy up?"

Percy paused in the act of nudging a book beneath her bed with her foot. From across the chamber, Lisbett pinned her with a rheumy yet eagle-eyed gaze. 'Twas a look Percy knew well; after all, she'd grown up under the housekeeper's firm auspices—and Lisbett had been old even back then. Still spry and tough as a soup chicken, the good woman continued to rule the roost and keep the Fineses in line.

"Caught red-handed," Percy said with an affectionate grin.

She retrieved the offending object and went to shelve it in its proper place. 'Twas after supper, and Lady Tottenham was already abed. Lisbett had come up for a bit of a chat, but being the housekeeper, couldn't help but try to bring order to the chaos that was Percy's bedchamber.

"Away but a few weeks and the place goes to pot." Shaking her snowy head, Lisbett carried a basket of fripperies over to the armoire. "I'll have a word with Violet, I will—" She broke off as she stumbled. The bin thumped to the floor, scattering items everywhere.

"Are you alright, dear?" Percy rushed over to steady her. With a stab of worry, she felt the frailness of the bones beneath the black bombazine. As a girl, that shoulder had been invincible and a resting place for all hurts. "You mustn't over do. Sit down and have a rest."

"'Tis my dashed joints." The housekeeper gave a disgruntled sigh as Percy helped her into a chair. "Aging is a petty business, miss, and made tolerable only by its alternative."

"You're not allowed to grow old on me," Percy said lightly.

Lisbett snorted. "You aren't a girl any longer. Soon you'll be married to a fine lord with a home of your own. You'll have no need of old Lisbett and her managing ways."

An odd panic clutched Percy's heart. After all she'd experienced with Gavin, she knew she was no longer the girl she'd been even a few short weeks ago. Her life's course had altered: she was falling for a man more complicated than she'd ever imagined. Who answered every need in her—including some she hadn't even known existed—and who made her want to do the same for him.

Everything was changing; she both feared and anticipated what lay ahead. Could her family accept her choices? Would they support her decisions, whatever the consequences?

She crouched down next to the woman who'd taken care of her all her life. Who'd crooned Gaelic lullabies to put her to sleep and who'd seen her through many a scrape. "I'll always need you, Lisbett. And I shan't be married so soon as you think." With a tremulous smile, she said, "Not to a fine lord, at any rate."

"Is that the direction the wind blows now, my girl?" When Percy gave a small nod, Lisbett peered at her closely. "So in the time I was gone you threw over Lord What's-his-name?"

"I discovered Lord Portland and I were not suited." Percy cringed at the memory. "In fact, he was not at all the man I thought him to be."

"I could have told you that, missy, and spared you the trouble."

"But you never met the viscount," Percy said in surprise.

"Didn't need to. Know you, don't I, like the nose on my own face. You were chattering on like a girl with her head in the clouds,"—Lisbett patted her on the cheek with a wrinkled hand—"not a woman readying herself for marriage."

"Well, I hope the others take the news as well as you do," Percy said. "I fear Mama will be ever so disappointed." Her gaze went to the family portrait on the wall, and a lump formed in her throat. "And Papa... oh, Lisbett, do you think I have let him down?"

"Let Mr. Fines down?" Lisbett said, frowning. "What do you mean?"

"You know how he went on about me marrying a title."

"I knew your father longer than you did, and what he wanted was for his children to be happy," the other said firmly. "And if you ask me, there's more to happiness than a fancy title and a house in Mayfair."

Percy agreed wholeheartedly. With a thrum of hope, she wondered if Lisbett could be convinced of the merits of her plan to live life on her own terms.

"As for your mama, she wants your happiness as well." Lisbett wagged a finger at her. "You've had your share of predicaments, missy, and there's to be no more of that, viscount or no viscount. When Mrs. Fines comes home, you best show her what a proper good girl you can be."

Percy wrinkled her nose at the admonishing tone. No doubt her relationship with Gavin Hunt qualified as a predicament... if not a full-blown disaster. What was she thinking? The housekeeper would never understand her desire to be with Gavin. In fact, Lisbett would probably box her ears. Soundly.

"I'll do my best—" Percy began when a loud thud cut her off. "What on earth was that?"

"It came from down the hall. Mrs. Fines' bedchamber, I

reckon." The other rose, the wrinkles on her brow deepening. "None of the servants would be there this time of night. I best go have a look."

"Why don't I go instead," Percy said.

Lisbett harrumphed. "I'm not so old that I can't make a trip down the hall, missy."

In the end, they both went. Percy took the lead, her lamp flickering in the dim corridor. As they headed toward Mama's suites, the muffled sounds grew louder. Through the closed door of the chamber came the soft whir of drawers opening and closing. Sounds of a furtive search.

The hairs on Percy's nape prickled. "Should we go and alert Jim?" she whispered, referring to the Fines' groom.

"Jim? By the time the old codger takes his creaky bones up the stairs, the thief will have made off with the whole house," Lisbett grumbled. "No, wait here a minute. I know what to do."

A few minutes later, Lisbett returned carrying something in her hands. Percy put down the lamp to take what the housekeeper thrust at her. "Um, a cricket bat?"

"Nicked it from Master Paul's old room," the other replied matter-of-factly. "One for each of us. We can't go in there unarmed, can we?"

Percy straightened her shoulders. "Right. So what is the plan?"

Lisbett's gaze had a maniacal gleam. "We surprise the ruffian and wallop him into submission. Then we tie him up,"—she held up the coil of rope in her other hand—"and send for the constables. No two-bit Billy is going to waltz into our house and get away with it."

"Brilliant idea," Percy said. "I'll go in first."

"Mind you take a swing right away, my girl," the housekeeper said sternly. "Make it a good, solid hit. No hesitation, do you hear me?"

Percy's grip tightened on the wooden bat as she nodded. Leaving the lamp behind, she opened the door and entered stealthily. Mama's sitting room lay in perfect stillness. A faint light came from the connecting bedchamber. Percy navigated her way around the furniture with the ease of a girl who'd spent countless hours playing in the room.

With Lisbett close behind her, she peered around the corner into the other room. Her heart thumped in her ears. *Oh, bloody hell—the blasted burglar.* Moonlight from the parted curtains outlined the dark shape of the villain looming over her mother's dresser. His back was turned to her as he rummaged through her parent's belongings. He held up a brooch, turning it this way and that; Percy recognized the cameo Papa had given Mama for her birthday years ago.

Anger surged through Percy's veins.

Not in my house, you blighter.

She dashed forward. Before the thief could turn around, she swung the bat. It connected with a satisfying whack against his shoulders, knocking him face-first into the mirror above the dresser. Over the roar of blood in her ears, Percy heard the offender curse.

"What the devil—"

Before he could utter another word, Percy hit him again.

"That's the way," Lisbett shouted. The housekeeper delivered a good solid blow of her own. "That'll teach you to trespass upon a decent home."

The thief spun around, arms raised to protect his face, and gasped, "*Ouch.* Devil take it, stop! 'Tis me, Paul!"

Percy halted, the bat raised mid-swing. "Paul?"

"Yes, you bloodthirsty fiends. Oh, hell, I think you broke my nose."

A moment later, a match rasped; Lisbett held up a candle, revealing Paul's sulky features. The bridge of his nose sported a large cut, and blood was leaking from one nostril onto his cravat. One eye was beginning to swell as big as an egg.

"Oh, dear." Percy bit her lip. "What in heaven's name are you doing here?"

"Before we get into explanations, would you mind fetching me a handkerchief? I'm bleeding all over the Aubusson." With a groan, her brother stumbled into the sitting room and collapsed onto the settee. He clutched his head. "Christ Almighty, the world is spinning. You may have done irreparable damage."

Crouching down next to him, Percy dabbed his nose with a piece of linen. "I am ever so sorry. How was I to know it was you?"

"I think your head must have suffered some knocks before tonight, young man." This came from Lisbett, who'd finished lighting the lamps. With her hands planted on her narrow hips, she looked down at Paul. "That can be the only explanation for your behavior. Why are you skulking in your mother's room in the middle of the night?"

Percy saw guilt flash in those eyes so like her own. And she knew.

How much did you lose this time? Helpless frustration and worry warped her insides. As she looked closely at him, she could see his bloodshot eyes, the haggard lines beneath the fresh injuries. She smelled the telltale odor upon his breath, and her throat clenched.

Oh, Paul, when will this end?

"I wasn't skulking." She wasn't fooled by her sibling's nonchalant tone. The more important the topic, the more blasé he became. "Thought the household was asleep, so I didn't bother announcing my visit. As it happens, Mama had promised to have a pocket watch of mine fixed." Paul sat up, straightening his jacket in a righteous motion. "I was looking for it when the two of you came charging in like an army of Hussars."

"Have you forgotten who you're talking to?" The housekeeper snorted. "'My eyes mightn't be what they used to be, but I can still spot a falsehood from a mile away."

"Perhaps it is *you* who has forgotten who you're talking to," Paul retorted.

Lisbett's white brows drew together.

Aghast at her brother's rudeness, Percy said, "You cannot speak to Lisbett in so disrespectful a manner. You must apologize at once, Paul."

"Like hell I will." He stood, tottering as he did so. "I'm not a boy any longer, and she's just a servant in this household, even if she's older than sin." His chin jutted upward. "I am the master of this family now, and I will not be ordered about like some dull-witted child."

The octogenarian began to roll up her sleeves. "If you act like a child, you best expect to be treated like one—"

"Lisbett, may I speak to my brother alone?" Percy gave the housekeeper a pleading look. "There are things I need to discuss with him."

"In private," Paul said in a snide tone.

Lisbett grunted. "I'll be downstairs if you need me, Miss Percy. And you, sir,"—she waved a bat in Paul's direction, and he stumbled back—"just because you've gotten too big for your boots, don't think I can't bring you down a size. Master of the manor, indeed," she muttered as she marched off. "It'd have broken your father's heart to see you acting like a fool."

Percy closed the door and turned to her brother. A stranger, in truth, for the wreck of a gentleman who stood mulishly before her bore no resemblance to Paul.

"How much this time?" she said quietly.

"I don't know what you mean—"

"I'll give you all my jewels. All my pin money. Will that cover it?"

Above the shambles of his cravat, Paul's throat worked.

"Percy, I—"

"This has got to stop." Her words were firm, despite the welling of heat behind her eyes. "You are going to lose everything. Not only your fortune, but your... life." When he remained stubbornly silent, she expelled a breath and said, "No one is worth such a disgrace. Not even Rosalind Drummond. You've had your heart broken—do you think you're the only person to suffer such a fate?"

"Goddamnit, I told you never to mention that name—"

"You leave me no choice. Stop feeling so bloody sorry for yourself and listen," she said.

He shot her a livid glare.

"Rosalind married someone else. There's nothing to be done. Either you get over that fact or,"—she shook her head— "you will destroy any chance you have at happiness."

Silence stretched. "I'll never be happy again," he said.

"That isn't true." The flat resignation in his voice brought tears to her eyes, and she dashed them away with her fists. "Please say you do not truly believe that."

"Percy, for God's sake, don't cry."

Perhaps the intensity of the past month was catching up to her, for all of a sudden she couldn't hold back sobs. "I c-can't help it," she said between choked breaths. "Even if you are a nodcock, I love you. And to th-think you're throwing away your l-life ..."

A hunted, desperate look came over his face. "I—I am going to stop. I swear it. I just have to pay these debts to O'Brien, and then... I'm done."

"Do you swear it?" she said with a sniffle.

"Yes."

She wanted so badly to believe him. "And you'll stop the drinking as well?"

He raked a hand through his mussed curls. "Devil take it, do you want to make a monk out of me?"

"I just want to have my brother back," she whispered.

"Bloody hell." His arms circled her in a brief, fierce hug, and she clung to the strength that had always anchored her. Then he stepped back, his lips in their familiar wry twist. "What the blazes do you want that sod back for? He's a feckless fool who'll never amount to anything."

"Do not say that," she said, frowning.

"Why not? Papa did often enough."

"He didn't mean it, not really. He loved you. 'Twas merely his way of trying to motivate you—"

"The way he motivated *you* by filling your head with faerie tales of the *ton*?" Snorting, Paul sank back onto the settee. After a moment, he patted the adjacent seat, and Percy joined him with the wholehearted gladness she'd always felt whenever her older brother invited her along. "So tell me," he drawled, "how goes things with the object of your undying affection?"

She chewed on her lip. "I suppose you mean Lord Portland?"

"Who else?" Paul cast his eyes heavenward. "You've been extolling the virtues of the valiant viscount for months."

"Well, you see... he and I..." Flushing, she looked down at her hands. Yet there wasn't a way of saying it that didn't make her sound like a fickle fool, so she said plainly, "I've gotten over him. He wasn't at all the gentleman I thought he was."

"Not a *gentleman*?" Paul stared at her. "Did he make inappropriate advances toward you?"

Her cheeks burned. "Well, sort of. But it wasn't his fault entirely, you see—"

"*The bloody bastard.*" Paul rose, his hands balling. "I am going to put a bullet through—"

"Oh, no. You are *not* going to call him out." She sprang up in horror. "You'll just draw more attention to the whole thing, and then I'll be disgraced entirely. Besides, nothing happened. I knocked him onto his, um, backside before anything could." When Paul continued to look at her, a muscle ticking in his jaw, she said in a small voice, "The truth is that I led Portland along as much as he did me. It was all just a mistake. One that would only be made bigger by your interference."

"So that's it. You're done with Portland."

"He wasn't what I wanted. Nor was marrying into the *ton*," she said. "Well intentioned as Papa was, those were his dreams, not mine."

Her brother scrutinized her in an uncomfortably keen manner. Though he might be tap-shackled and worse for the wear, he was still one of the cleverest men she knew. Her shoulders tensed. He hadn't guessed about Gavin... had he? The hothead would never listen to her explanations about the wager. He'd like as not challenge Gavin to a duel—and that was the very last thing she needed.

"You *have* grown up some, haven't you?" Paul arched a brow. "I wonder at the source of this newfound maturity."

She shrugged, hoping to convey an air of nonchalance. "Every miss has to grow up sometime. I am no exception. By the by," she said innocently, "I've heard from Nicholas."

This piece of information distracted Paul, as she'd known it would. "And what did he say... about my situation?"

"I believe Nicholas' precise words were, *I am returning immediately to take care of the matter. For God's sake, tell Paul to keep his damned hide out of trouble until then.*"

Her brother grimaced. "Never a man to mince words, our Nicholas."

"Honestly, Paul, what do you expect him to say? You should be glad that he will salvage the situation."

If I haven't already fixed it first. She wondered how she would explain her wager to Nick and everyone else. And who knew how matters would be settled between her and Gavin?

Whilst she'd grown more and more certain of her own feelings, she did not know how he felt about her. Oh, she knew he wanted her, was possessive of her. But did he love her? Would he want a future with her even after she won her brother's freedom? She bit her lip.

"Nicholas fishing me out of the suds," Paul said bitterly. "Now there's a first."

Uneasy with her brother's shifting mood, she said, "You will do as Nick says, won't you? Stay out of trouble until he returns? This O'Brien you mentioned, you won't—"

"Careful, sis, you're starting to sound like mater. Nothing puts a fellow off more than nagging." Her brother cut off further conversation by rising unsteadily to his feet. "Now if you don't mind, I'll take you up on your offer of a loan and be on my way."

"Oh." She drew a breath. "Yes, of course."

As they left their mother's bedchamber, Percy recognized she was not helping her brother and did not know *how* to. But perhaps she knew someone who did.

Chapter Twenty-Four

GAVIN GLOWERED AT the pair of men sprawled and bleeding in the street before including the rest of the audience in his gaze. The crowd of passers-by ringed the front steps of The Underworld, eager for the sight of more bloodshed.

"Anyone else want a go?" he said.

Gazes averted, feet shuffled.

"Begone then," he growled. "The club doesn't open until noon."

He turned and headed inside, Stewart behind him.

"You alright, lad?" his mentor asked as they entered the empty foyer.

"Fine." He flexed his hands, wincing at the sore knuckles. "Lyon's men are all bark and no bite—just like the dead bastard himself."

"That's three times this week they've challenged you. How long are you goin' to let this go on?" Stewart's voice was an irritated rumble. "We ought to go in and take down Lyon's club."

"Everyone already thinks we did Lyon in. I don't want to add fuel to the rumors. There's enough carnage going on," Gavin said grimly.

Though Lyon had been a bastard through and through, news of his death had roared through the stews like a lit match thrown to kindling. The men loyal to him had issued a warrant for blood. Since Gavin and Stewart had been the ones to discover Lyon slaughtered at the bawdy house, they'd been fingered as the culprits (like any self-preserving bawd, Antoinette was keeping her lips firmly sealed on the matter). 'Twas a vicious rookery tradition: eye for an eye—kill first, ask questions later.

"Can't 'elp but think the timin' o' the business was convenient. That we 'appened to be the ones to find Lyon an' get pinned for it."

'Twas an echo of Gavin's own thoughts. With Lyon gone, there was new territory for the taking, and Kingsley and the O'Briens were wasting no time jockeying for power. Beatings and opportunistic pillaging occurred daily, escalating the cycle of violence. Meanwhile, Gavin had to focus his energies on preserving his hide.

"Kingsley, Patrick, or Finian could have sent that man to the bookshop. They could have planted Lyon's dagger to rouse suspicion, knowing that I would hunt Lyon down at Antoinette's," Gavin said.

"True enough. We'll get to the bottom o' this." Stewart's eyes thinned. "And speakin' on gettin' to things—thought that old coot Magnus gave you Paul Fines' location."

"He did."

"Then why 'aven't we picked up Fines yet?" Stewart demanded.

Running a hand through his hair—then grimacing as his knuckles stung—Gavin said, "I'm considering my options." Which was true enough. "Don't worry, I know what I'm doing."

"You ain't goin' to give into that chit—"

"I said, leave it to me." As his mentor scowled, clearly wanting to argue further, Gavin said, "Let's focus on more important issues. Lyon's dead, and I can't be far down the list. I want you to arrange for a visit to our rivals."

After a minute, Stewart said in grudging tones, "Get some

ice on those fists, then, since you'll be needin' 'em."

Gavin strode off to the front card salon. Sunshine streamed through the bow window, gleaming off the mahogany bar. Filling a bowl with ice and a glass with whiskey, he sat down at the bar and let the cold numb his skin. Moodily, he nursed his drink. Hell's teeth, would the mayhem never end? He was weary to the bone of all the violence, the need to sleep with one eye open. What he wouldn't give for a moment of peace.

"Sorry to disturb you, sir." The quiet words turned his head. Davey stood in the doorway, holding a tray of glasses. "The butler told me to stock the shelves. But I can come back later—"

"You're not disturbing me," Gavin said impatiently. "Go on and do as you were told."

Davey scurried to the other side of the bar, keeping his eyes lowered as he unloaded the tray. The servants had reported that the boy was a hard worker, with nary a complaint about anything. Yet Gavin had never seen the boy smile—except for that one time. With Percy.

Who could blame Davey? The minx had a way about her. Just the thought of her smiling face warmed Gavin's chest, chasing away some of the chill. The need to see her burned inside him; now, however, it warred with growing concern about her safety. The world was catching fire around him, and he wouldn't let her get singed by the flames. At the same time, he balked at any further delay of their meetings: her family was bound to return soon, and the time to win her was running out.

Which left one option. He had to speed matters along. When she came to him tomorrow night, he would have to renegotiate their terms. He had no choice but to seduce her, take the wager and her heart. And what the hell—if it softened the blow for her, he'd fish her brother out of the hole when it came to O'Brien. Once he had her loyalty secured, he would send her somewhere safe until the business with Lyon died down.

No small order you've set yourself.

He brooded over his whiskey as Davey continued to stow away glasses. Something in the boy's somber, detached demeanor reminded him of himself. *No man is an island*, Percy had said. For so long, he'd prided himself on his self-sufficiency, surrounding himself with a sea of anger. Vengeance had kept him afloat.

For the first time, he wondered if he was also... trapped.

Clink. Clink. Davey stacked the glasses with the soulless efficiency of a soldier. With none of the carefree whimsy of a boy his age.

Gavin's chest tightened. He knew all too well that innocence was the price of survival. Percy's comment about Davey's infatuation leapt into his mind, and for some ungodly reason he heard himself say, "How is your milkmaid?"

The tinkling sound abruptly halted. Brown eyes peered up at him. "Beg your pardon, sir?"

"You were talking to Miss Fines about her," Gavin said. "Nan, was it?"

"Yes, sir."

Drawing conversation from Davey was about as easy as drawing a tooth from another boy. God only knew why he was attempting the task. Rubbing his neck, Gavin said, "How is the matter proceeding?"

"You mean... with Nan?"

For devil's sake. "Yes, her," Gavin said. "Unless you've got others waiting in the wings."

"Oh no, sir. I would ne'er..." Davey turned a bright shade of red. "Nan's the only one fer me. Though I don't reckon she feels the same. What would she want wif an ugly git like me?"

Unfortunately, Gavin could see the other's point. Davey

had not been blessed when it came to matters of appearance. In addition to his lanky frame, the boy had brown hair that stuck up in a habitual cowlick, and his ears occupied an undeniably wide berth. Not the most promising packaging overall.

Gavin recalled the physical awkwardness of his own adolescence. The whores in the hulks had made a game of mocking him. *Jack the Slash, Scarred an' Feathered.* In retrospect, he understood that their pushing him in the dirt had allowed them to avoid the bottom rung; at the time, however, their jeers had only sparked his humiliation and burning need to prove himself.

Jaw tight, Gavin said, "You'll outgrow it."

He had. When he'd finally grown big and strong, ruling those hulks with his fists, the whores' tunes had changed. They'd vied for his attention—and he'd fucked them, coldly, never forgetting that like everything else, sex was about power. A transaction. *Use or be used.*

"A man's worth is measured in more than looks," he said grimly.

"Miss Fines said the same thing. She said,"—Davey reddened further—"'e'vry boy's a prince inside.' And that's 'ow I'm to carry meself if I want to win a princess."

It sounded like something Percy would say. Sweet, idealistic—for an instant, Gavin wondered what his life might have been like if he'd met her earlier. If Morgan hadn't betrayed him, if he hadn't gone through the hulks... if he'd known her love rather than the scorn of slatterns, his mother's rejection...

In other words, if everything was different.

His brows drew together as something raw seeped through the wall of anger. For once, what would it be like to trust someone? To lose himself in Percy's warmth...

"It's Nan's birthday next week. Miss Fines said Nan might

like a present." Once started, Davey couldn't seem to *stop* talking. "She says as 'ow gifts make a girl feel special."

"She said that, did she?"

In his usual dealings with females, Gavin was generous with baubles and the like. His arrangement with Percy, however, had hardly been conventional. He'd been so caught up in the business of the wager (not to mention saving his own neck) that he hadn't thought to buy her anything. He would remedy that oversight. Percy deserved a gift as unique, as breathtakingly beautiful, as she was. Frowning, he wondered what the hell she would like.

He coughed into his fist. "Did she, ahem, give you any suggestions?"

"I asked 'er. She said if it was 'er, she'd want somethin'... personal like." Scratching his head, Davey said, "Somethin' that tells the girl you've been thinkin' bout 'er. A bunch o' vi'lets, if they remind you o' 'er eyes." The boy looked at him glumly. "Problem is, sir, Nan's got *brown* eyes. Only brown flowers I can think o' are dead. An' I don't think she'd like that much."

Gavin's lips quirked. "I'd wager you're wise to skip the dead poesies."

"I did think o' meat pies," Davey said doubtfully.

"Too ordinary."

"Dark treacle?"

"Messy."

"Well... " Davey hesitated. "'Er eyes do remind me a bit o' chocolate."

Gavin thought it over. "A sound choice. Ladies like their dish of chocolate."

"The barrow across the street charges three pence a cup," the boy said, shoulders hunching. "I han't got that much o' the ready."

Gavin fished a shilling from his pocket and pushed it over

the counter. "That should cover it."

For some reason, the coin shattered the camaraderie. Davey backed away, shaking his head vehemently. "No, sir, you've done eno' for me as it is. I can't take your money."

"Take it." When the boy made no move to obey, Gavin scowled. "'Tis a bloody shilling, not an arm and a leg. Consider it my funding of Miss Fines' well-laid plan."

"But sir—"

"I haven't got all day. Take the coin and be off with you. I'm not paying your wages for you to stand around flapping your lips."

"Thank you." A look of misery crossed Davey's face. "I don't deserve it... but thank you."

Odd lad. "One more thing," Gavin said.

"Yes, sir?"

"When you are done with your chores, go see my valet. Have him deal with your hair."

"My 'air?" Davey said in alarm. "But, sir, I don't need—"

"Trust me, you do." The sight of the figure lounging in the doorway cut short Gavin's reply. *Devil take it, just what I need.* "Evangeline," he said in clipped tones. "What are you doing here?"

She sashayed in, clad as usual in a gown that left little to the imagination. "Now, Hunt, is that anyway to greet an old friend?" As Davey scurried out, Evangeline smirked at his departing figure. "New boy? Not much to look at, is 'e?"

Gavin ignored her prattle. "I thought I made it clear the last time that things are done between us."

Her smile slipped for only an instant. "A man can change his mind, can't he?" Her pale eyes slanted as she came closer, sliding onto the stool next to where he stood. She tossed a cloth bag upon the polished counter and ran a hand up his thigh.

He grabbed her wrist and removed her hand. "I told

you—it's over."

"Why?" Her lips drew into a pout.

His jaw tightened. "Because I said so. Now be off."

"Is it someone else? You've found some tart, is that it? You think any light-skirt can give you the kind o' sport you need?"

"You'd better watch yourself," he warned her. "What I do is none of your business."

Abruptly, she switched tactics. "Come on, Hunt. Give us another try. No doxy can fuck you the way I do."

His patience came to an end. He opened his mouth to order her out... but a flash of genuine emotion lit her eyes. Anxiety, the kind that even her practiced sultriness could not mask.

"What's this really about, Evangeline?" he said.

It wasn't jealousy—he knew that much. In the months they'd been bed partners, she hadn't given a damn whom he fucked and vice versa. No ties came with fornication. His unemotional dealings with Evangeline and others before her had never bothered him; yet now, with Percy in his life, he experienced a stab of regret. For the tawdriness that had gone on before her.

God help him, he wished he'd been a better man.

Evangeline's darkened lashes lowered. When she raised them, her eyes were as hard and cold as jade. "I need blunt, lover, an' I'll do whate'er it takes to get it." Reaching to the bar, she picked up her bag and untied the strings. "Anything you want, Hunt. For old time's sake."

Chapter Twenty-Five

HOLDING UP THE veil that covered her bonnet, Percy made a polite curtsy and said, "'Tis a pleasure to see you again, Mr. Stewart."

"Back again, are you?" Hunt's partner, a giant of a man, looked her up and down and grunted. She'd met him in passing at her previous visits to the club, and he hadn't been any friendlier then. "What are you wantin' this time?"

So much for niceties. "I'd like to see Mr. Hunt, if I may," she said. "I shan't bother him long. My chaperone thinks I'm on an errand at the apothecary's."

"As a matter o' fact, now *is* a good time to see Hunt," the man said suddenly. "I'll show you the way myself."

She smiled at him. Perhaps she'd misread his reaction to her—Gavin had said that his mentor tended toward surliness. "I'd appreciate that ever so much, sir."

He led her through the club. When they reached a closed door at the end of the hall, something close to a smile curved his lips. "Seein' as you're old friends, there's no need to knock. Go ahead an' show yourself in."

"Thank you, Mr. Stewart—" she began.

But his long strides had taken him halfway down the hall. *What an odd man.* Pursing her lips, she reached for the brass knob and pushed the door open.

She saw Gavin standing by the bar. He was casually dressed in shirtsleeves, without a cravat... and he was not alone. A woman in a scandalous red gown sat on a stool next to him. The two were so absorbed in conversation that they did not notice her standing there. As Percy watched, blood rushing in her ears, the doxy upended a bag, raining an assortment of objects onto the polished wood. Chains, rope... a pair of cuffs?

"I've brought your favorite toys, lover," the woman said, running her bare fingertips over his chest. "What say we 'ave ourselves a l'il game?"

Gavin took the hand—and removed it. A look of distaste crossed his features. "If it's money you need, Evangeline, say so," he said curtly.

The woman—Evangeline—tossed her brassy curls. "I won't be indebted to you or any man. 'Tis an exchange I'm after... and you want what I 'ave to offer." Leaning forward, she reached between his thighs.

"*Get your hands off of him.*"

The words exploded from Percy. Both Gavin and the other woman jerked in surprise as she marched toward them. Unfamiliar fury boiled in her veins, and she could scarcely think.

"Who the bloody 'ell are you?" Evangeline said with narrowed eyes.

"I. Am. With. Him." Percy stabbed a gloved finger in Gavin's direction. He was staring at her, wariness edging his blunt features.

"You and 'im?" Snorting, the tart had the temerity to eye her up and down. "Hunt needs more than a milk-faced miss to satisfy 'is particular appetites."

"That's enough," Gavin said in a taut voice. "Get out, Evangeline."

Percy glowered at him. "What appetites?"

With a superior smile, the trollop waved toward the counter. "See for yourself." She slid from her stool, sauntering toward the door. "Oh, and a word o' advice, luvie,"—she flung the words over her shoulder—"give 'im a struggle before 'e ties you up. The gent likes 'is wenches with a bit o' sauce."

The door slammed behind Evangeline, and Percy rounded on Gavin. Her breath rushed in and out of her lungs, unaccustomed rage pounding in her heart. All her life, she'd been known for her sunny nature; at the moment, she felt like thunderclouds ripe for a storm.

Hunt eyed her, rubbing the back of his neck. "That wasn't what it looked like."

Of all the *asinine* things to say. "So that *wasn't* a strumpet hanging all over you?" she said through clenched teeth. *Who is she? You're supposed to be mine.*

He took a step toward her, but she moved out of his reach. "She is no one to concern yourself over," he said in stark tones. "Percy, come here."

"I will *not*. Not until you tell me what is going on." Her throat tight, she said, "Don't lie to me—are you... involved with her?"

He cursed. In the next moment, he moved quick as lightning and snatched her up. A squeak left her as he hauled her onto the bar, his hands planting on either side of her hips. Face-to-face, his gaze bored into hers.

"Evangeline and I had an arrangement at one time. But that is over," he said. "It has been over ever since I met you."

Some of the tightness in her chest eased. Whatever Gavin was, he was no liar; she could see the truth in the molten ore of his eyes. "You haven't... been with her since we met?"

He shook his head.

Another thought assailed her. "Or anyone else?"

"No. Nor have I thought to." He looked at her steadily. "'Tis you I want, Percy."

Even as relief seeped through her, her gaze wandered to the assortment of objects next to her on the counter. Her belly fluttered at the coil of silken, tasseled rope. Swallowing, she waved her hand at the paraphernalia. "And what about this?"

His scar whitened. She saw the flexing of his strong, bare throat and had a revelation. Gavin Hunt was nervous. Hah. He *ought* to be. And she supposed she ought to be shocked by Hunt's proclivities; instead, she felt... intrigued. But mostly *hurt* by the fact that he would share his desires with a light-skirt, but not with her.

Does he think I'm too missish to handle his needs? Is that why he hasn't spoken of marriage? I'm... I'm not enough for him?

All of a sudden, she saw herself waiting by the window. Small and insignificant. Not important enough for anyone to return home for.

Though her heart squeezed, she lifted her chin. "I deserve to know," she said.

He straightened, ran a hand over his mouth. "This isn't the sort of thing one talks about with a well-bred miss," he said, dumping salt onto her wounds. "I don't want to shock you, Percy."

"Tell me the truth," she snapped. "Tell me, or I will go. And I won't bloody come back."

Perhaps an ultimatum wasn't the wisest approach. But she was too hurt and angry to care.

His hands dropped to his lean hips. "Have it your way, then." A challenging flare lit his gaze. "What do you know about the prison hulks?"

The non sequitur took her aback. A chill of premonition passed over her. "They're old battle ships. They're used to house prisoners when the jails are overcrowded," she said slowly. "The conditions aboard are said to be deplorable."

"There was one moored not far from here, up on the Thames Estuary." Heartbeats passed. "I spent ten years of my life in that stinking hellhole."

Gavin had been a *convict*? Shock percolated through her.

"For... for what crime?"

"A house burned down, and I was blamed for it," he said in terse tones. "I was innocent, but it didn't matter."

Her chest clenched. "How old were you? What about your family?"

"I was ten." His jaw ticked. "My mother had abandoned me months earlier. She got tired of supporting a bastard. I never knew my father."

Just a boy, with no one to protect him. Eyes welling, she said, "Gavin, I—"

"You asked me once how I got this." He touched his scar, his lips twisting. "'Twas Stewart who gave it to me my first day in that hell. Do you know why?"

She shook her head, a wooden movement.

"Because being pretty gets you buggered. Because if you don't beat the hell out of them first, they'll do worse to you." Gavin's hands fisted at his sides, his eyes burning pitch. "I became a man in that place, and I survived by learning that power is everything."

"You did what you had to," she whispered.

"I lived like a beast," he said darkly. "When another convict tried to steal my food, I cut out his tongue. When a guard flogged me, I took the pain, knowing the scars would toughen my skin. When a whore ridiculed me,"—his knuckles whitened—"I showed her I was a man."

Though she trembled at the savage confession, Percy saw the hidden torment of the man in front of her. For the first time, she began to understand Gavin's complexity. Pieces fell into place... his ferocity and primal need for parity. His compassion for children who'd had to endure too much. And her heart wept a little.

"I'm so sorry," she said, "so sorry that you had to go through—"

"*I do not want your pity.*"

The checked rage in his words broke through her numbness. Instinctively, she knew that this was the first time he'd told his story. He was looking at her with a savage expression: as if he expected her to bolt or scream in fear. Oh, her Hades, her scarred hero—did he not know her better by now?

"It's *not* pity. Gavin, I—"

"I am telling you this because you wanted to know about my appetites. For me, control is everything,"—his gaze shot to the rope—"and sex is no different."

She blinked. *Um, that's your revelation?* She might be a virgin, but she wasn't a fool. In the times they'd been together, Gavin had always been masterful. Dominant... and deliciously so. Her insides grew hot at the notion of what he might do with the objects beside her. She'd always known he wanted her surrender, but she hadn't yielded, not completely, because of the wager. And because she hadn't understood his need the way she did now.

Clarity struck her. He might call it control, but what he truly needed was... love. Someone to trust. She'd sensed his loneliness from the start, and it had drawn her, his intense need for what *she* could offer. Because she did have something to offer: her heart. In that instant, she knew beyond a doubt that she was fully and completely in love with Gavin Hunt.

"Shocked you into silence, have I? There's a first," he said in stark tones.

With a tremulous smile, she said, "Thank you for sharing this with me. For trusting me."

He stared at her. "You're... thanking me."

Hopping down from the bar, she crossed to him. Placed her palm against his hard jaw. "I have feelings for you, Gavin. I know how foolish it sounds coming on the heels of my infatuation with Portland; if I were you, I wouldn't believe me either. But there it is."

His hands closed roughly on her shoulders. "You have feelings... for me?"

Knowing his mistrust of love (and the fiasco with Portland did not help her case), she told herself to ease him into the idea with patience and tact. To try to explain herself in a way Gavin could understand. And believe.

"When I am with you, I feel truly myself—truly *free* as I have never been before. You don't judge me or try to make me into someone I am not. And," she said, flushing yet determined to be as honest as possible, "I desire you. Being in your arms is the best place I've ever been."

"*Percy.*" He sounded stunned.

"Wait, I'm not finished." She put a hand against his chest, his power thrumming beneath her palm. "It pains me beyond bearing to think of the hurt you must have endured. Yet your past has made you the strong, fearless fighter that you are. A man I admire and accept,"—she tipped her head toward the items on the bar—"in all ways."

Flames of need rose in his dark eyes. How badly he wanted to believe her.

"How can you say that when I control your family's future?" he bit out.

She'd asked herself the same question so many times; now, her heart gave the answer. "With Paul—it's about justice, isn't it? You want what's owed to you, and I cannot fault you for that. 'Tis the way of your world."

Expression shuttered, Gavin gave a slow nod. "Aye, justice."

"You've never lied to me, and I won't lie to you: I won't betray my family. If you will not release my brother, then you leave me no choice but to win the wager." Trying to keep her voice from trembling, she said, "And in that case... would you still want me?"

Her breath held.

"I will always want you."

His arms surrounded her, crushing her to his chest. Her eyelids closed as he took her lips in a hot, demanding kiss. She clung to him, opening herself completely to his passion. His hands gripped her bottom, pulling her tight against him. She sighed at the contact with his muscular form, his erect member so strong and fierce between her thighs.

"I've missed you." The admission sounded ragged, torn from a place deep inside him. "I've never wanted anyone like I want you, Percy."

"I'm glad," she said, linking her arms around his neck. "Because if you did, I'd have to scratch her eyes out. And that doesn't sound very pleasant."

At that, his brows raised. "Possessive, are you?"

"*Mine* goes both ways," she informed him.

He kissed her again, this time with a tenderness that made her heart sing. "You have nothing to worry about," he murmured.

Actually... she did. Recalling the purpose of her visit, she felt her belly flutter. Gavin had entrusted her with so much today; could she show the same faith in him?

"There's something I need to tell you. It's about my brother." She faltered and forced herself to say, "He's... he's in trouble again."

Gavin released her. "What sort of trouble?"

"Cards. This time he lost money to a man named O'Brien—do you know him?"

"Aye."

Biting her lip, she said, "I gave Paul all I had, and it still wasn't enough to cover the debt. And I'm afraid he'll only lose more. I don't know what else to do, Gavin. So I thought I'd ask for your advice." She gave him a hopeful look. "Surely you've encountered men with the same affliction?"

Expression neutral, he said, "You trust me when it comes

to your brother's welfare?"

"You gave your word that you wouldn't harm him."

His knuckles grazed her cheek. "And my word is enough?"

She nodded. *Please prove me right.*

He sighed. "I have seen this many times, Percy. Once a man starts down the path to ruin, no one can turn him back but himself. And that usually doesn't happen until the ground falls from beneath his feet."

"That can't be." Her insides turned to ice. "I won't let that happen to Paul."

"It's not your choice, buttercup." Gavin rubbed his neck. "If it puts you at ease, however, I will pay off your brother's debts and request that O'Brien bar him from the premises."

"You'd do that for me?" she breathed.

He does love me as much as I love him…

"For you—and also to protect my own investment. Fines won't be of much use to me if O'Brien gets to him first," he said in wry tones.

Um… or maybe not.

Sighing, she told herself the reason did not matter; for now, the fact that Gavin would intervene on Paul's behalf filled her with gratitude and relief. Until another thought occurred to her. "But what about the threats on your life? You said other proprietors might be involved. Is it *safe* for you to go to O'Brien?"

"I'll be fine. As I said, I can take care of myself." When she made to argue, he placed a finger against her lips. "I was planning on paying O'Brien a visit anyway."

Was he just saying that to make her feel better? "For what purpose?" she said.

He hesitated. "Robbie Lyon was murdered last week."

"*Murdered?*" she gasped. "By whom?"

"That is what I aim to find out," Gavin said.

Her stomach roiled with apprehension. "Do you think

Mr. Lyon's death is related to the threats on your life?"

"He is the second club owner to perish in six months. More than mere coincidence."

"Then you must have a care! You cannot go traipsing about as if you're invincible." When he raised a brow that clearly said *I'm not?*, she said in exasperation, "Can't the magistrates look into the matter?"

"Charleys don't know their arses from their elbows," he said derisively.

"A private investigator, then. Bow Street Runners or..."— she hit upon an inspiration—"I know a member of the Thames River Police. A Mr. Kent. He is a friend of Nick's and ever so clever. I could contact him—"

"Over my dead body." The sharpness of Gavin's tone took her aback. "No policeman is getting involved in this. Nor are you to interfere with my affairs, Percy."

"How can you expect me not to concern myself over this? I love you, you stubborn lout!"

He grew still. His eyes hooded.

So much for patience and tact. "I know your opinion on love," she said, straightening her shoulders, "and that you take no stock in it. But it means something to me, and I cannot allow you to take unnecessary risks. Even for my brother."

"You're worried for me—over your brother?"

She frowned; it wasn't an either-or situation. "I'm worried about you both. But there's no danger to Paul's life at the moment. Whereas with you there's more afoot than you've led on."

"I've told you more than I've shared with anyone." His voice grew hoarse, and he seemed to struggle to get the words out. "You are... important to me, Percy."

'Twas the closest he'd come to declaring his feelings for her. Hope blossomed within her. He *was* capable of love; surely with time he would come to return her feelings.

"As you are to me," she said. Then, looking to the clock, she sighed with frustration. "Dash it all, I *have* to go, but can we talk more about this tomorrow night?"

He hesitated. "For your safety, perhaps it would be better to postpone—"

"Oh no. You're not getting rid of me that easily. I took great pains to convince Lisbett to let me stay over at my friend Charity's tomorrow night." Rising on tiptoe, she pressed her lips to his scarred cheek, and the large, ferocious lord of The Underworld actually *trembled* at her touch.

He rasped, "*All* night?"

"Yes," she said. "And who knows when I'll have another opportunity like this one?"

His answer was a slow, wicked smile. "Then we will have to make the most of it."

Chapter Twenty-Six

THE NEXT MORNING, Gavin faced Finian O'Brien in the sumptuous office of The Emerald Club. A pair of armed men flanked either side of O'Brien's ornately carved chair, and Gavin had his own men outside, ready to act at a moment's notice. Tension crackled as palpably as the logs in the fireplace.

"'Twas horrible what happened to Lyon," Finian said in his high, nasal tone. "Such an unfortunate way to go, with one's vices exposed for all the world to see."

The hair rose on Gavin's nape at the hint of smugness. "'Twas a cowardly act to kill a man who could not fight back."

Finian stroked his thin moustache. "Cowardly? Yes, I suppose. But effective." His teeth flashed. "Though one oughtn't speak ill of the dead, Lyon will not be missed, will he? The fellow pissed on just about everyone—yourself included, Mr. Hunt."

"I didn't kill him," Gavin said evenly.

"I would never suggest such a thing. We are friends, after all." Finian fingered the emerald stick pin in his fussy cravat. "Friends do not accuse friends of murder."

Water was easier to pin down than the slippery bastard. Gavin decided to switch tactics.

"With Lyon gone, there's more for the rest of us, eh?" he said lightly.

Finian grinned and tipped his glass. "I'll drink to that."

"Speaking of business, there's a matter I want to speak to you about. Concerns a fellow by the name of Paul Fines. I think you know him."

"Might ring a bell."

Lying bastard. Finian's memory was legendary. He could recite the name, address, and background story of every cove who owed him money. Gavin didn't buy for an instant that the other man didn't recall Fines.

Gavin still could not believe what he was about to do. He'd told himself that bailing Fines out of trouble was part of his plan for revenge, yet who was he fooling? The truth was he'd been swayed by Percy's distress. By the need to soothe and protect her.

I love you. 'Twas the first time he'd heard those words. They'd hit him like pellets of sunshine, dissolving the dank chill in his soul. At moments, he could almost let himself believe that she'd meant what she said... Well, he'd have his proof soon. If Percy truly had such strong feelings for him, she'd surrender to him tonight. He would make her his, get the bloody wager over with... and perhaps even tell her about Morgan.

If she loved him, wouldn't she take his side? For his part, he wouldn't give her cause to regret him and was proving it that very moment by bargaining with a damned cutthroat for her brother's life.

He kept his tone casual. "The thing of it is, Fines owes me a load of blunt. I aim to collect it, and I don't intend to wait in line to get my due."

"Ah, now I have it. Blond fellow with an appetite for hazard." Finian's smile had a razor's edge. "Owes me a hundred quid."

Gavin reached into his pockets, causing Finian's men to twitch. He withdrew his wallet and counted out banknotes on the desk. "Two hundred pounds," he said, "and my thanks for barring Fines from further play."

"I pride myself on running a hospitable establishment," Finian said mournfully. "Who am I to cut a cove off?"

Narrowing his eyes, Gavin added another note to the pile. "I am certain you can make an exception in this case."

"The cull must owe you quite a sum." With a satisfied smile, Finian reached for the money. "Ah well, there's no getting blood from a stone, is there? I will leave you to get what you can from the gent."

"My thanks," Gavin said.

"Cooperation does have its benefits." Finian stroked a finger across his mustache. "In that vein, I've a proposition for you, Mr. Hunt."

"What is it?"

"My brother and I have an eye on Lyon's club. The business won't last long under Lyon's second-in-command. With a third partner, Patrick and I could take it over."

In other words, the O'Briens didn't have enough coin or manpower to take it over between the two of them. "I work alone," Gavin said.

"Do you? From what I hear, Kingsley paid you a visit not long ago."

Nosy bastard. "I said the same to him as I'm saying to you. My business is my own."

"Are you certain you aren't in league with Kingsley? Planning to divvy up Lyon's territory between the two of you?" Finian had an odd smirk on his face. "From what I can tell, you and Kingsley share a lot in common."

"I have nothing in common with Kingsley. And I don't take on partners because I don't like being double-crossed," Gavin snapped.

Finian studied him for a long moment. "If you're not working with Kingsley, then you had better watch your back with the rest of us. He's hired on an army of brutes. Early this morning, one of them bloodied a pair of my best customers and warned them to stay away from my club." Eyes glittering, he said, "I believe you're familiar with that experience."

Bloody hell. If Finian was speaking the truth, then had Kingsley been behind the attacks on Gavin's patrons as well? Gavin's hands curled into fists. "These cutthroats—you have proof that they work for Kingsley?"

"They *boasted* of the fact. Kingsley has grown fearless." Lines of tension bracketed Finian's mouth. "My guess? Kingsley's found someone to back him. Someone who prefers to remain in the shadows."

The news sent a chill down Gavin's spine. "Black?" With the support of his father-in-law, Kingsley could become more than a nuisance.

"A likely possibility." Genuine fear flashed in Finian's eyes. "You see, Hunt? We must band together or Kingsley will bring us all down."

"I want no part in the scuffle over Lyon's club," Gavin said.

Yet he found himself pausing as Percy's words played in his head. *No man is an island.* Though he didn't trust the O'Briens farther than he could toss them, mayhap it wouldn't hurt to try building bridges instead of burning them.

"I do, however, have an offer for you and your brother. We put the past behind us and agree to no further violence between our men. Negotiation instead of bloodshed," Gavin said evenly. "What say you?"

Finian looked relieved. "I say that sounds like we have an understanding, Hunt."

He reached out a hand, and Gavin took it.

Back in the carriage, Gavin filled Stewart in on the

proceedings.

"You trust Finian?" His mentor's bushy brows came together.

"No, but I trust Kingsley less. Any news from Will?" Gavin's head guard was monitoring the comings and goings of Kingsley's club.

"Not yet."

"We'll wait to hear his report before interrogating Kingsley," Gavin said.

As the carriage slowed, Stewart frowned. "We can't be back at the club as yet." He lifted the curtain and at the sight of the dilapidated building that housed the second-rate Temple Bar Theatre, he said with a knowing leer, "Oh, it's like that, is it?"

"I'm not here for a tumble," Gavin said curtly.

"No need to play coy with me, lad. You take as long as you need. Better Evangeline 'Arper than that other one."

"What do you have against Percy exactly?" Gavin heard himself say.

"No need to get testy with me. And *Percy*, is it?" Stewart glowered at him. "I *knew* this would 'appen. Tried to warn you, didn't I, but you wouldn't listen. You've gone arsey varsey o'er the chit."

Gavin's face heated like that of a child being taken to task. Which was ridiculous, seeing as how he was a grown man who hadn't asked permission for anything in as long as he could remember.

"It's none of your bloody business what goes on between her and me," he said, his jaw tightening. "And you best get used to the idea of her being around. I mean to have her."

Stewart's eyes widened. A pang struck Gavin for he'd never seen that look on his mentor's face before. The man looked... hurt?

"So that's how it's to be, eh? Fifteen years we've known

each other, an' you'd toss my advice aside for a slip o' a wench."

"Devil take it, that's not what I meant." Guilt needled Gavin as he contemplated the scowling man who had, for all intents and purposes, fathered him. A man he had always trusted. In a gruff voice, he said, "Is it such a bad thing to want companionship?"

"That's what the likes o' Evangeline 'Arper is for," Stewart burst out. "Or some other fancy piece if 'er tricks 'ave grown tiresome. Don't shackle yourself to the ball and chain, lad—weren't the 'ulks enough? 'Ang onto to your freedom; that's a man's true companion."

"You cannot be comparing marriage to imprisonment," Gavin said with a frown.

"Can't I, lad? I thought I wanted the one an' ended up with the other."

"Percy is not like Marissa."

"How do you know that, son? 'Twixt 'er own family an' you, a bastard from the stews she's known but a month or two, who do you think she'll choose? Will she even believe your story when Morgan 'as 'is own tale to convince 'er?"

She'll take my side. She won't betray me.

Yet the doubt crept in, widening the cracks in Gavin's earlier confidence. The idea of Percy siding with Morgan made his muscles tense in denial.

What if she leaves me, turns her back?

"Don't make any 'asty decisions you'll regret. That's all I'm sayin'."

"I will think on it." An awkward silence filled the carriage; as ever, unspoken words hovered between them. His hand on the door handle, Gavin struggled to express the sentiment within him... and gave up. "I'll be back shortly," he said instead. "Keep an eye out for me, will you?"

"Always 'ave and always will, lad. *That* you can count on,"

Stewart said.

Gavin entered the rickety building. He didn't know what possessed him to search out Evangeline. It wasn't pity precisely, but he couldn't forget the desperation he'd seen in her eyes—the most genuine emotion he'd ever seen from her. She'd needed that money. He'd give it to her, as a parting gift and as a small thank you; for though Evangeline had meant to stir the pot with Percy, she'd instead opened up a world of possibility.

Percy hadn't been afraid of his darker desires. He'd seen her peeking at those tools of pleasure, and her cheeks had gone rosy with curiosity, not disgust. His innocent yet seductive goddess would accept him as he was... with all his flaws, the darkness in his soul. By God, he *craved* her. Luckily, he had only to wait for tonight.

Passing by the unattended ticketing counter, he made his way into the small auditorium. Several women stood on the cramped stage, bickering with a beleaguered looking fellow with ink stains on his shirtsleeves.

"I ain't arsin' 'round wif this scene no more, Johnny." This came from the skimpily clad brunette standing in the middle of the stage. She had one hand on her hip, her lips held in a pout. "I'm tired an' me feet 'urt from standin' round."

"Just one more time," the director pleaded as he pushed up his spectacles. "Please, darling, you've got to get your lines right. Think of your adoring crowds."

"Gor, t'isn't 'er lines they're 'ere for, is it?" said another of the females.

"I reckon there's more 'an one kind o' talent." The brunette wiggled her shoulders to show off her obvious twin assets, and the rest of the cast roared with laughter.

"Pardon," Gavin said.

All eyes turned to him.

"I am looking for Miss Harper," he said. "Where can I

find her?"

The brunette strolled over toward him. "She ain't 'ere, luvie." She winked at him. "I'm Tilly, and I han't see you 'ere before. Would remember a fine lookin' gent like yourself."

"Do you know when Miss Harper will be back?" he said.

"She won't be." This came from the director. Shooing the actors away, he took Gavin aside and said suspiciously, "Why are you looking for her?"

"I'm an old friend, and I have something for her." Gavin frowned. "Do you mean to say she has left the theatre?"

The other man nodded. Pushed his spectacles up again—clearly a nervous habit.

"Do you know where I can find her?"

"She didn't leave a forwarding address," the other man said in guarded tones.

"Look, I *am* a friend. This is what I meant to leave for her." Removing the envelope from his jacket pocket, Gavin showed the contents to the director, whose eyes grew large at the sight of the money.

"'Tis a fortune," he breathed.

Gavin withdrew a single note, held it up between two fingers. "This is for you, if you'll tell me what you know."

The man licked his lips. "You really don't intend Evangeline harm? Not like that other man?"

"What man?" Hairs rose on Gavin's neck.

"The one who came looking for her earlier. Didn't leave his card, but he was a right nasty looking brute. I think he meant to hurt her."

"What sort of trouble is she in?"

"I don't know exactly." The man's eyes darted from the money to Gavin's face. "She was a bit of a clam. Which was why she never made it past the bit parts—didn't emote enough, you know. But there was this one time..."

Gavin handed him the money. "Go on."

"Several weeks ago after everyone had left, I found her in the changing room. She was drinking and more than half seas over, I suspect. From what I could gather from her rambling, she'd been seeing a fellow. Some rich toff she was head over heels for. He'd promised her the moon and stars..." The fellow shrugged. "You'd think she'd have known better."

"Did Evangeline tell you his name?" Gavin asked.

The director shook his head. "She wasn't speaking too clearly by that point. She kept crying and saying as how he'd ended the affair and was threatening to hurt her if she didn't leave town."

"And you have no idea where she went?"

The other man shook his head again.

Gavin handed him another banknote. "If you happen to hear from her, tell her the rest of the money is waiting for her at The Underworld."

"Yes, sir. Will you leave your name?"

"She'll know who I am," Gavin said.

Chapter Twenty-Seven

ENSCONCED IN A chair in Charity's snug parlor, Percy looked at the clock on the mantel. Eight o' clock in the evening. Butterflies swarmed in her belly at the thought of seeing Gavin soon. She needed something to keep her busy until then or she might go mad with impatience.

"Are you certain I can't help with those display case cloths?" she asked.

Charity looked up from the elaborate silver "S" she was embroidering onto dark blue velvet. "No, thank you," she said. "The last time you helped it took me twice as long to finish."

So Percy wasn't the most facile with needle and thread.

"Why don't you have a bite to eat? You haven't touched the collation," her friend added.

"I can't stomach anything at the moment. I'm too excited."

"Heavens, now you're making *me* nervous." Charity set down the hoop. Seeing the notch between the other's straight brows, Percy forecasted what her friend would say next; after all, Charity had been uttering the refrain for weeks. "Are you certain I can't dissuade you from this, Percy? I feel very strongly that this is a bad idea."

"I know you do," Percy said, "which makes you twice the dear for helping me tonight. Even when you disapprove."

"*Worry* is more accurate. Oh, Percy, are you certain this is the future you want? I cannot fault you for being disillusioned with the *ton*, but surely there are options less extreme than this. Within our own circle there are plenty of eligible bachelors—"

"I love Mr. Hunt. He's the one that I want," Percy said.

"And does he want you?"

You're important to me. Her chest warmed; the time for self-doubt was over. "I rather think he does," she said.

"I mean in a respectable way. Has he proposed?"

"Not yet. But I have a feeling the topic may come up this evening." If Gavin didn't bring it up, Percy told herself she would. She was no longer a powerless girl to wait for what she wanted. Gavin had given her the confidence to reach for the stars—even if it meant a shift in her universe. "Charity, if I'm to become the wife of a gambling hell owner," she said in a tremulous tone, "would you still be my friend?"

"Of course. We're to be bosom companions for the rest of our lives, remember?" Charity came to sit beside her. "You told me so that first day at Mrs. Southbridge's when I was standing there, frightened and alone. I don't know what I would have done without you all those years."

"Nor I you," Percy said.

"And now you are about to embark on the grandest adventure of all."

Hearing the wistful edge to her friend's voice, Percy said, "You could have an adventure too. If you wanted, you could search out your own destiny—"

"Papa needs me. And you know I've never been a dreamer like you."

"You *do* have dreams, Charity," Percy said. "You used to talk of opening your own shop, remember? And of getting married and having your own household."

"You know I can't leave Papa. Not when he is so alone." Charity picked up her embroidery again. Her gaze focused on the fine cloth, she said, "Have you seen Mr. Fines since earlier this week?"

Percy studied her friend a moment longer before sighing. "I haven't. And I hope I did the right thing in giving him more money."

"What else could you do, dear?" her friend murmured.

"Well, Mr. Hunt has a better idea. He is getting Paul barred from some of the clubs—doing this at no small risk to himself, I might add." Craftily, Percy said, "Even you have to admit that is noble."

"Perhaps. Or perhaps Mr. Hunt has given you the skirmish with the intention of winning the war." Charity put in another stitch. "If he loves you, why doesn't he simply set your brother free?"

Though she now knew Gavin's true history, Percy did not feel free to divulge it.

"He has his reasons," she said softly. "Suffice it to say, I understand why it must be difficult for him to trust his feelings."

I wouldn't either if my mother abandoned me, if I was imprisoned for a crime I did not commit. Yet why did she feel a niggle of doubt? A shadow of fear, as if there was something more that Gavin hadn't told her...

"Have you prepared what you'll tell your family when they return?"

Percy bit her lip. She'd received a letter from Mama; it had been sent over a week ago from the port in France. Which meant her family would be back any day now.

"I'll think of something," she said.

Charity's smile did not quite hide the worry in her eyes. "You always do, Percy."

To lighten her friend's heart, Percy said, "By the by, I am making excellent progress on my novel. Miss Priscilla is getting into all sorts of scrapes these days."

"Not stuck anymore?"

"No. In fact, I have a new beginning." Lowering her voice to a dramatic whisper, Percy began, "Once upon a time in the dark, shadowy catacomb beneath a haunted castle..."

Her thin cheeks curving, Charity continued to sew as the story unfolded.

"Goodness, you do know how to sweep a girl off her feet," Percy said breathlessly.

Her windedness was due in part to the way Gavin had insisted on carrying her over the threshold into his apartments. The other part had to do with what they had been doing during the carriage ride over.

"I try," he said.

His eyes gleamed with the raw passion she loved. At the same time, there was a playfulness in him that she'd not seen before. 'Twas as if they both sensed the shifting winds and had decided to throw themselves fully into this present moment. In tacit agreement, they'd put aside their troubles and worries. To spend this one night together with nothing but desire and joy swirling between them.

As he let her slide down to her toes, she pressed herself fully against him. Her blood thickened when she encountered the protruding evidence of his desire. *Goodness*, he was red-blooded. With great daring, she shimmied against that hard bulge, smiling when he groaned against her lips.

"'Tis nice to know you missed me," she said.

"Bold as brass." His lips quirked. "Good thing for you I like that in a woman."

"Not just any woman," she reminded him.

"No," he agreed huskily. "*My* woman."

Melting like an ice from Gunter's, she tipped her head

back for his kiss... and blinked when his lips brushed her nose.

"Lusty chit. There's plenty of time for that." When she flushed, he laughed aloud and kissed her hard on the mouth. Then he removed a velvet box from his jacket pocket. "I have something for you."

"For me?" She *loved* surprises. Opening the lid, she lost all power of speech. Ran a reverent finger over the exquisite piece of jewelry. Fashioned in gold, the brooch took the graceful form of a feather. Yet it was no ordinary feather—a tiny sapphire dripped from its tip. A drop of ink from a quill.

"I had it specially made. Gifts for the aspiring female novelist are difficult to come by."

His thoughtfulness made her eyes swim. "Oh, Gavin. It's the most *beautiful* thing I've ever seen." She threw her arms around his neck. "I shall wear it with pride."

After another long, smoldering kiss, he murmured, "God Almighty, you whet a man's appetite. But I have another surprise planned. Shall we eat first so we can keep up our energy?"

Following his gaze, she saw the magnificent feast laid out upon the Aubusson rug. Everything from roasted meats to vegetables in aspic and tiered plates piled with dessert.

"A picnic by candlelight," she sighed. "How *romantic*."

"Just don't tell anyone. I have a reputation to uphold."

"I know. The dark, terrifying Lord of the Underworld." She settled happily on the carpet, patting the space next to her. "Well, even he has to eat."

"What about you, buttercup?" He arched his brow as he got down beside her. "No slimming plan this time?"

Percy grinned. "No. This time I intend to indulge myself."

His eyes gleamed. "Allow me the pleasure, then." Reaching over, he plucked a rich, purple grape off the stem. He bit into it, eating half and placing the other at her lips.

"Open for me, Percy," he murmured.

She did, and as the tart sweetness filled her mouth, she saw the way his eyes went heavy-lidded. An answering warmth curled in her tummy. Oh my. Who knew eating could be such a stimulating exercise?

Next came a tidbit of chicken. The fragrant smell of rosemary and garlic made her mouth water. When she made to take the succulent morsel from his fingertips, he pulled it out of reach.

"There are rules, sweet," he said.

Her stomach growled. She'd been too excited to eat at Charity's and now she was hungrier than she realized. Eyeing the piece of meat, she said, "What do you mean rules?"

"You recall what I told you last time. About the nature of my desires."

As *if* she'd forget. Heat crept into her cheeks. "Oh. You mean... this is part of it?"

"If you will allow it." The golden flames of the fire reflected in his dark eyes. "I want you in all ways, Persephone. To make love to you, take care of you... even to feed you."

His possessiveness caused a pulse to thrum in her throat. Somehow, his proposition seemed more shocking even than the instruments that had littered the bar. A binding more permanent and deeper than a piece of rope could provide.

Tingles of desire and anxiety ran up her spine. She licked her lips. "Our truce, it still holds, doesn't it?"

His gaze hooded. "I won't force you into anything." Eating the piece of chicken, he wiped his fingers on a napkin before filling a wine glass. "But I will win this bloody wager, and you will marry me," he said with calm arrogance. "You know you want to."

There it was: the proposal she'd yearned for.

Though not exactly under those terms.

Elation blazed within her; caution dampened the flames.

"And if I win the wager," she said, "does your proposal still stand? Because I'm not giving up on my brother, you know."

"One way or another, you're going to be my wife," he said firmly.

Take that as a yes, her heart sang. Her brain—irritating organ—issued another warning, however. *His imperiousness might be exciting now, but do you really want to be ordered about for the rest of your life? You've never been good at following commands. Best begin the way you mean to go on...*

"Um, doesn't an offer of marriage usually involve a question?" she asked. "Preferably asked upon bended knee, perhaps accompanied by a declaration of undying devotion?" She thought a moment. "Violins wouldn't hurt, either."

"Bended knee is not my style. And there's no blasted orchestra right now." Jaw tight, he said, "Persephone Fines, will you marry me or not?"

She peeked at his scowling visage from beneath her lashes. "I might *consider* wedding you. But you might as well know now: I shan't be a brow-beaten wife."

"You? Brow-beaten?" he said in a strangled voice.

"I won't do everything you tell me to." Thinking on it, she felt compelled to add, "The truth is, I'm not likely to do even half of it."

He frowned. "What makes you think I'd want blind obedience from you?"

"Um, perhaps the way you've decided I belong to you? Or the way you like to be in control of things and people around you? And there is the small matter of your sexual predilections, though I've only heard about those second hand..."

"No need to pour on the paint—I get the picture," he said dryly. "I admit I am dominant by nature. But that does not mean I want you to submit to me in all things."

"It doesn't?" she said skeptically.

"If what I wanted was a submissive female, why the devil would I find you the most desirable chit I've ever met? You've many fine qualities, buttercup; being biddable isn't one of them."

She digested that, even as his compliment glowed in her chest. *The most desirable.* "So you are saying you *like* the fact that I am... "

"A hoyden? A saucy little romp?" In a sudden movement that knocked the breath from her lungs, he had her beneath him. "Percy," he said, his eyes dark with hunger, "I *love* it."

His kiss proved that beyond a doubt. Caught between the lush carpet and his tough, masculine form, she gave herself up to the joy of the moment. To the wonder of being desired for who she was. Heat flared instantly between them. She drank in the hot, wine-spiced taste of him as their tongues twined, mated. When he managed to get her gown off her shoulders, she reached for his waistcoat. He caught her hands, pinned them above her head.

"Did you mean what you said," he rasped, "about accepting me as I am?"

A deep flush heated her skin as she realized what he was asking. Curiosity and craving mingled, and she sighed, "Yes."

His nostrils flared. "Good." Slowly, he untied his cravat and folded it to form a neat oblong. "Stand up, sweeting."

Hesitant, but growing more aroused by the moment, she did as he asked. What did he intend to do with his neck cloth—bind her hands? Shivering at the notion, she waited, the insides of her wrists tingling with expectation. Her breath hitched when instead warm linen slid over her eyes, turning her world into a muted, shapeless glow.

She couldn't *see*; she felt utterly powerless. With each rapid breath, worries entered her head. At the same time, the sublime, masculine scent of him wafted from the blindfold, making her tremble with desire.

"Give into me, sweet." His voice rippled hotly over her nape. "I'd never hurt you. Trust me to take care of you."

The guttural yearning in his words undid her. She understood what he needed. Perhaps more than he did. Control, yes, but at a deeper level wasn't this about *trust*? From what she knew of his past, he'd little experience with it. If she wanted him to trust her, she'd have to show him how it was done.

All her life, she'd longed for a heroine's adventure—and a true journey did not come without risk. Releasing a shaky exhale, she bucked up her courage and did what she'd never done before: she surrendered, letting herself tumble into the darkness.

Chapter Twenty-Eight

EVERY EROTIC DREAM he'd ever had, she surpassed in a single heartbeat.

Gavin's hands shook slightly as he fastened the knot behind her head. Tight enough to hold, loose enough not to cause her discomfort. He'd never hurt his brave girl, never. What she was giving him... a shudder of arousal passed through him. His cock had already gone harder than a pike. *Everything I've ever wanted.*

He planned to take her virginity tonight. He wouldn't force her, however—he wouldn't have to. By the time the night was done, she would be begging him to make her fully his.

For this first go around, he wouldn't rush things. They had all night, and he was going to savor his goddess, pleasure her beyond her wildest imaginings. He circled her; her pale blue gown parted like wings in the back where he'd unfastened the tiny pearl buttons. In the firelight, her shoulders gleamed with the translucence of the finest porcelain. He pressed his lips to one shoulder blade and felt her tremor from head to toe.

"It feels strange not being able to see," she said breathlessly.

"You don't need to see. I'll take care of you, love."

He made short work of the remaining buttons. Her gown pooled at her feet, followed shortly by her petticoats and other hindrances. He pulled the final barrier, her chemise, over her head, careful not to disturb the blindfold. His breath stuttered at the sight of her.

"By God, you are perfection," he said hoarsely. He watched in fascination as a flush travelled across her nubile form. When her hands moved automatically to cover herself, he stopped them, returning them to her sides. "No hiding, sweet. Let me see all of you."

Her lips parted, yet she acquiesced.

Circling her, he took in her loveliness with a rapacious gaze. She was a flower of a goddess, with her hair a bloom of gold and the rest of her graceful as a stem. His mouth pooled at the high, firm thrust of her breasts and their saucy, budded tips. She was slim of waist and hip, the sleek line of her legs accentuated by white, striped silk stockings. Then and there he decided to leave the stockings on—he had to swallow, lust gripping his balls at the sight of the sky blue garters framing her sunny nest of curls.

Without a doubt, she had the sweetest, most delectable pussy he'd ever seen.

"Are you done... looking yet?" she said, biting her lip.

He'd never be done. Not in a million years. "You steal my breath, buttercup."

Standing behind her, he grasped her supple waist and pulled her back against him. Shuddered at the contact with the smooth firmness of her ass. He cupped her breasts, thumbing the stiff peaks as she sighed and wriggled against him. The friction made his blood burn, his erect prick threatening to burst through the thin layer of wool.

"You have the most gorgeous tits," he growled against her ear.

"Um, thank you?"

He grinned at her impish response. Only Percy could amuse and arouse him at once. His grin turned into a chuckle when in the midst of the love play her stomach gave an unladylike growl.

"Pardon," she said in an abashed voice. "I haven't eaten much today."

Still smiling, he went to fill a plate and led her to the sofa. He pulled her onto his lap, and choosing a ripe strawberry, held it to her lips. "Take a bite."

Red juice dribbled down her chin as she did so. He leaned over and licked up the sweet trail. Sighing, she said, "More please?"

He selected a chicken leg, pulling off bite-sized chunks. She ate it greedily, and when she was done, he murmured to her, "Now be a good girl and lick my fingers clean."

Lust bolted through him as she obeyed. Her small tongue lapped at him, sucking one long digit between her pink lips. An image flashed of her taking his cock this way, of pushing his shaft all the way into her sweet mouth... Just as quickly, he shook the notion away. That was a paid pleasure, and he was done with those. Breathing heavily, he pulled his fingers out. He had to stay in control, or this game would not last much longer.

"Very good," he said. "And now for dessert."

Beneath the strip of linen, her lips curved. "I love dessert—What are you doing?"

He'd eased from under her, pressing her into a reclining position on the sofa. "I'm preparing it." He knelt on the floor next to her and reached for the dish of trifle. A house specialty, Cook's version was a closely guarded recipe of ratafia cakes, custard, and whipped cream.

When he spooned a dollop onto Percy's navel, she yelped. "What on earth—"

He licked the trifle off her smooth skin, savoring the creamy sweetness. "As I said, I'm having my dessert. You. No, hush,"—when she opened her mouth to protest, he inserted a spoonful of trifle—"and let a man enjoy his sweets in peace."

He decorated her breasts next, piling on the confection and drawing the back of the spoon against the taut peaks. She arched her back, gasping, "That is so wicked. Oh, do it again..."

Smiling, he bent to sample his handiwork. He tongued the cream off her nipples, then suckled them deep into his mouth. Her fingers slid against his scalp, holding him to her sweet mounds. He cleaned off every inch of her bosom until she was quaking, sighing his name. And then he picked up the spoon and deposited a dollop where he wanted it most.

"Oh no, you can't possibly—" she squeaked. Her head fell back against the arm of the sofa as he proceeded to do exactly that.

The flavor was indescribable. Whipped cream and Percy, his own personal confection.

"I love the way you taste," he growled.

Spreading her thighs, he feasted on her luscious cunny, his senses exploding with the sweetness of her. His tongue traced her slit upward and found the shy hooded bud. When he lashed her pearl with wet flicks, she began to writhe against the cushions. The sight of her passion was too much. With one hand, he unfastened his trousers to free his painfully swollen shaft.

Let off some steam first. There's plenty of time tonight... when you're finally inside this beautiful quim, you have to last...

He fisted his rod slowly as he gamahauched her. Her moans grew breathier, more desperate. Her eyes—he had to see them when she went over.

"Take off the blind," he commanded roughly.

Delicate fingers grasped the linen, yanked it up. She blinked, her desire-hazed gaze meeting his. "Gavin, oh God, what you do to me."

"That's right, love," he breathed against her dewy flesh. "Do you like watching me eat your pussy? Will you come for me this way?"

She moaned something unintelligible. He eased a finger into her, groaning as her unused muscles softened to let him in. He added another, began to thrust firmly in and out as he frigged himself. He watched her eyes all the while. The blue blurred to midnight as she chanted his name. At the exact moment, he curled his fingers, tickling a spot high inside her.

She cried out as she climaxed. The delicious clench of her passage brought him to the edge as he continued to lick the orgasm from her. When she lay back, panting, he got to his feet. He kicked away his trousers and went to stand before her. He loved the way her eyes widened, the sultry sweep of her lashes as she regarded his jutting manhood.

"Sweeting," he rasped, running his fist up the proud, curving length, "do you want to help me spend?"

"Oh, yes, I'd love to." He almost came then and there at her enthusiastic reply. Sitting up, she was eye level with his thrusting member. She batted his hand away and took the veined shaft between her soft palms. "Just tell me how."

"You're doing just fine." His neck arched as he savored her firm yet gentle stroke. By God, her hands were perfect for the job.

"But I'd like to do better than fine," she said. "For instance, what do you think of this?"

A groan tore from his chest as hot, wet fire clamped around his cockhead. His fingers grasped instinctively in her sunny curls. He couldn't believe what she was doing, that she would pleasure him in this way. With whores, this act cost extra, and the fact that his own sweet Percy would willingly do this for him... he felt himself spurt a little. He wrenched away immediately.

Panting, he said, "Buttercup, you don't have to..."

Beneath his disbelieving gaze, she *licked* the glistening drop that welled at the tip of his cock. A shudder racked him as she caressed his length with her blushing cheek. "I know I don't *have* to. But it felt so good when you kissed me this way." Her eyes, bluer than a dream, gazed up at him. "Don't you like it too?"

"*Like* it? It's bloody amazing." His neck arched as she lapped at the bulging crimson crown, her tongue investigating the slit. "Take me inside your mouth," he bit out, "open wider... hell, *yes...*"

Bliss punched him in the gut as he looked down to see his thick rod disappear within her lips. She couldn't fit him all the way inside, but, devil and damn, this was enough. Too much. The slick pressure, the softness of her hands as they milked the base of his prick... he wanted to hold on, wanted to watch her sucking him forever. But his bollocks tightened, and he felt the warning heat gathering in his groin.

It took all his willpower to wrench from her generous kiss. "Percy, I'm going to—"

"Do it. Spend for me like I did for you," she whispered. Her fist tightened around him. Her breasts quivered as she stroked him faster, harder, giving him everything he needed. His carnal innocent, his adorable love—his vision blurred. He yelled out as his seed shot up his shaft. The climax erupted from him, taking everything he had.

When he regained his senses, he gazed upon her. Satisfaction hummed in his veins, and yet his pulse took a wayward leap. He had marked her, his essence splattered on her flawless bosom. Her golden hair tumbled where he'd dislodged the pins. Not only did she not look put out by the disarray, she was smiling. With a sensual cheekiness that warmed him inside and out.

And that had merely been the appetizer. Just thinking of the main course made his groin stir with renewed interest and his chest expand with something like wonder. Collapsing next to her on the sofa, he slung an arm around her shoulders and pulled her close. When he heard her snicker, he asked, "What is so amusing, buttercup?"

Her eyes held an incorrigible sparkle. "'Tis just that I finally understand the meaning of..."—another gurgle escaped her—"*just deserts*."

His laughter joined hers.

Chapter Twenty-Nine

"GAVIN, OH GOD, don't stop..."

Cuddled in front of Gavin in his oversized tub, Percy moaned as he continued to tease her without mercy. Under the guise of washing her, he drew the wet cloth over her aching nipples, rousing them to taut peaks. His other hand did sinful things beneath the warm, silky water. When he drew a teasing circle over the most sensitive part of her, she arched her back against him. She could feel the sizeable evidence of his desire prodding her bottom and yet he stopped.

Again.

He'd been doing this for the past half-hour... *at least*. As a result, she felt like a firecracker on the verge of exploding. Panting with frustration, she turned her head to look at him. Her pulse quickened at the controlled hunger in his expression, the intent way he was watching her.

"Do stop teasing." To her chagrin, her tone bordered on pleading. "I can't stand any more of this."

His eyes gleamed. "You can. And you will."

"But why can't we—"

"You're too impatient, love. We're going to take this slow." He petted her between her thighs again, causing her to shudder. "Waiting builds the pleasure."

"I *hate* waiting."

His finger worked a little deeper, and she writhed helplessly against him. "What do you want then, love?" he murmured against her ear.

"You know." His hard, slick muscles bunched against her back, titillating her further. Everything about him felt *so good*. "What we did before."

She gasped as he spun her to fully face him. Her knees spread to bracket his hips beneath the water, and she had to steady herself against his shoulders.

"Do you want me to make you come again, love?"

Did she. She nodded eagerly.

"This time, you'll have to work for it." He leaned back, his sinewy arms draped along the tub's edge. Raising a brow in challenge, he said, "Show me you want me. That I am the only one for you."

His sexual command filled her with a blend of excitement... and uncertainty. Though not timid, she still had limited experience when it came to carnal matters. In fact, everything she knew she'd learned from him. This time, could *she* take the lead? Her fingers flexed against his shoulder; instantly, the iron muscles leapt beneath the smooth skin, sending a pulse of confidence through her.

She could do this. She could prove to him just how much she wanted him, loved him. And to herself the power and resolution of her own desire.

She moved her hands upward, spearing her fingers into his thick, damp hair. Though his eyes did not leave hers, she felt his shudder travel through her own limbs. The power was heady, thrilling beyond anything. Leaning closer, she kissed his forehead, his cheek. The raised line of his scar trembled beneath her lips. She nuzzled his ear and could hear the raggedness of his breath as she licked the sensitive organ, sucking the lobe as he'd done to her.

"There's my girl," he rasped.

In answer, she kissed the scratchy plane of his jaw, moving toward his mouth. She loved the sensual yet hard line of his lips. When she ran her tongue along the firm seam, he let her in. She kissed into his open mouth, poured all her desire for him into the mating of lips and tongues. His hands clamped her bottom, pulling her closer.

She stopped him with palms against his chest. "No, wait. You said I get to do this."

Her assertion seemed to surprise him as much as it did her. Slowly, he released her. Driven to please him and herself, she continued to explore him, the first true opportunity she'd had to do so. His body was so different from hers. Dark where she was pale, hard where she was soft. The mementos of old battles marked his skin. She pressed her lips to the jagged star upon his shoulder. Beneath her fingertips, his paved chest quivered with power, and a breath hissed from him when her investigations took her below the line of water.

"You're so magnificent." The flat ridges of his abdomen jumped at her touch. "So large and solid,"—her hand lightly passed over his manhood as she murmured—"all over."

"What are you going to do about it?" he dared her. The fire in his eyes turned her blood to honey, the thickening heat gathering between her thighs.

All thought receded as she climbed further atop him, hitching herself against his huge, burgeoned shaft. They groaned in unison as her sensitive flesh slid slowly against his. Slick and sinful, the exquisite rub of two bodies made to pleasure one another. Her head fell back as she gyrated against him. Rising and falling, each pass a tumult of delight. His fingers gripped her posterior as he grated out his praise of her.

"*Good girl.* You're so hot against my cock. Do you like this?"

He thrust upward, and she gasped as the crown of his member bunted upward against her sensitive nub. "*Gavin, oh my God.*"

Pleasure jolted through every fiber of her being, too

powerful, too overwhelming to deny. Control spun from her, and she clutched at his shoulders. It was too much, not enough. *Heaven and hell.* Moans broke from her as water sloshed over the edge of the tub. She couldn't get enough purchase, couldn't get all that she needed. All of a sudden, his arm clamped her around the waist. Trapped her so that she couldn't move.

She struggled against him. "Oh Gavin, don't stop, I'm close. I need to..."

"I know what you need." His eyes had gone black, burning up at her with mesmerizing power. "You ache here, don't you, love?"

A moan left her as his finger traced her opening. Circled it, reminding her trembling muscles of the emptiness that lay inside. Lungs burning, she managed, "Y-yes. I ache so much. I need you."

His finger left her, replaced by a broader, thicker presence. The head of his cock notched against her, setting off shocking waves of pleasure. Every instinct in her knew that bliss lay inches away. Hard, thick inches, as it were: the last mystery between her and true womanhood.

His dark voice filled her senses. "Feel how your pussy quivers, how badly it wants me to fill it. You need my cock inside you. Let me in where I belong."

Her back bowed as his engorged tip burrowed against her entrance. Delicious stretching. What would it be like to be filled so completely...? Eyes sliding shut, she felt temptation sizzle in her blood. So desperately did she want to say yes, to give herself to him irrevocably and forever.

Need him.

"No, wait—you promised," she gasped.

The powerful muscles beneath her flexed. Gavin's hold on her tightened, and her senses scattered to the wind as his dome nudged deeper against her, sending streaks of heat down her legs. If he meant to take her, she could not stop him.

God help her, she did not *want* to.

"Give yourself to me, Percy," he said in a guttural voice. "*Choose me.*"

She stilled. "I… *can't.*" Looking down into his glittering eyes, shaking with need, she whispered, "I want you Gavin, but I cannot betray my brother. I won't."

Silence stretched between them, broken only by their panting breaths. Neither moved, and it took every shred of her resolve not to shimmy back against his hard, jutting presence. Not to seek relief from the fires burning inside her.

The next instant, she found herself deposited unceremoniously at the other end of the tub. Water sluiced from Gavin's magnificently aroused physique as he rose and stepped onto the tiles. He reached for a towel and began to dry off.

"If you loved me, the choice would be simple," he said flatly.

Her frustration boiled over. "That is so deuced unfair!" she burst out. "If you cared a whit about me, you wouldn't *ask* me to choose."

He faced her, hands on his hips. He made no effort to hide his erection, which only fueled her aggravation as her body quaked with longing at the sight of the rampant instrument. So large and thrillingly masculine… so ready to please. If only the rest of the blasted man could be as accommodating.

Hastily, she lifted her gaze, only to realize he'd caught her ogling him.

"We could both be enjoying this," he said with calm arrogance, "if you weren't so bull-headed. I am going to win this wager one way or another, Persephone. You're only delaying the inevitable."

"If that's the case, why are you pressuring me?" Snatching a towel, she wrapped it around her and left the tub. She faced him with her arms crossed over her chest. "Why won't you tell me what is really going on?"

His eyes hooded, he said, "You know what is going on. I've given you ample time to come to a decision about the wager. You said you love me—now prove it."

"You're not telling me everything." She narrowed her eyes at him. "I know you by now, Gavin Hunt, and you *are* capable of compassion. You protect urchins, you've even protected my brother from that character O'Brien... why can't you at least *consider* relinquishing Paul's vowels? Unless..." A dreadful thought occurred to her. "Why do the shares of Fines & Company mean so much to you?"

He regarded her with a stony expression.

With trembling fear, she asked, "Did... did Paul wrong you in some way? Does he owe you more than money—"

"This has nothing to do with your brother."

"Well, that's a relief." *Thank goodness. We can overcome anything but that.* She took a deep breath. "It's the money, then? I know you don't wish to deal with Nick, but there is another option." Cheeks warming, she said, "I have a dowry. It's not worth as much as the shares of the company, but it's quite substantial."

"I don't want your bleeding money."

Her patience snapped. "For goodness' sake, what *do* you want?"

"Justice." In that instant, Gavin transformed from her playful lover to Lord Hades himself. His eyes blazed with crystalline fire, and his arms bunched, veins prominent against the taut sinew. "Tell me, Percy: if a wrong was done to me, a grave injustice, what would you do?"

She blinked. She hadn't been expecting that. "Well," she said cautiously, "I'd support you, be there for you, no matter what. What injustice are you talking about, Gavin?"

"If it came down to making a choice," he said, ignoring

her question, his eyes pinning hers, "between me and your family, who would you choose?"

"Why would I have to choose?" she asked, bewildered. "I don't understand."

"Answer my question."

"But that's ridiculous. How could I possibly say..."

"It's a simple enough answer. Me or them?"

She chewed on her lip, her head whirling with questions, possibilities. "Is this about whether or not my family will accept our marriage? Because you don't have to worry about that. They may be a bit shocked at first,"—*there's the understatement of the century*—"but they'll come around, trust me. Once Mama gets to know you, I am sure she will adore you. As for Nicholas and Helena—"

"I don't give a damn about them," he roared. "I want to know where your loyalties lie. *Me or them?*"

"You're not giving me enough information. Without knowing the circumstances, I cannot make a choice," she said, lifting her chin.

"You want circumstances? Fine. When I take over Fines & Company and tear it to pieces, will you be standing by my side or theirs?"

Her lips parted in shock. "You mean to *destroy* Papa's company? But why?"

"Tell me this first: will you still *love* me then? Can I still trust you?"

Hope began to slip away. Numbly, she shook her head. "I couldn't allow you to demolish my father's legacy, no matter the reason. You couldn't expect me to."

"So there it is." Though his features were as rigid as a mask, anguished rage flashed through his eyes. "All your talk of love, of trust... in the end, it amounts to nothing. You're no different than the rest."

"Now wait one minute—"

"You thought you could manipulate me. Thought you could wind me round your finger and convince me to release your brother." His hands braced his lean hips. "When were you planning on giving me the ultimatum?"

Enough was enough. Despair gave way to anger.

"I am not planning on giving you an ultimatum, you bloody ass," she said between her teeth, "because I am going to win the wager. The trouble is I fell in love with you—although at the moment I am seriously questioning my judgment."

"Just like a woman to change her mind," he sneered.

"I am *not* your mother. I'm not going to abandon you," she shot back.

Perhaps she'd gone too far. The dark flare in his eyes made her take a wary step back. He stalked toward her, backing her against the bathing room wall.

"Words, Persephone. They mean nothing if they're not backed by action." His gaze flicked deliberately to her towel. "Will you commit yourself to me?"

Her mind spun even as her traitorous body thrummed in response. Questions battled with feelings. "Trust goes both ways," she managed to say. "You cannot expect me to trust you if you do not return the favor."

"I have shared more with you than I have anyone." His jaw looked harder than basalt. "Yet it still isn't enough for you."

Forcing herself to take a breath, she said, "You haven't told me why you want to destroy Fines & Co. If I understood, we could work together toward an alternative solution." She gave him a beseeching look. "If you could just trust me."

When he didn't answer, a sinking feeling entered her midsection. She'd told herself that his intensity, his possessiveness was his way of showing his love for her. That his behavior spoke of the words he'd never been taught to say—that she would eventually reach him. But what if she'd been wrong? What if his past had irreparably damaged his ability to love and trust?

Meet me halfway, she begged silently. *Love me as I love you.*

His scar tautened. "You cannot handle the truth."

Her temper snapped. "For the last bloody time, I am not some insipid miss! If you think so little of me, I might as well leave right now." She shoved at his chest.

She gasped when he took her wrists, pinning them at her sides. A dark storm flashed in his eyes, the charge running through the sliver of air separating their bodies. Quivering, Percy waited.

"It has to do with... Morgan," Gavin bit out. "This is between him and me."

"You mean *Nicholas*?" she said, bewildered. "You know him?"

Before he could answer, a shot tore through the night.

Gavin's head snapped up. "What the devil was that?"

Unintelligible shouting sounded through the walls. Another shot fired.

Releasing her, he yanked on his clothes. He strode to the doorway. Stopped. "We'll finish this later," he said. "For now, you stay put, do you hear me?"

Questions and worry warred within her. "Be careful," she said, her voice trembling.

He looked as though he might say more, but he gave a curt nod and exited.

Chapter Thirty

STEWART MET GAVIN at the door to his apartments.
"'Tis Fines. He's out in the alleyway—drunk and with pistols
drawn."

Hell's teeth. Just what I need. "Did he say what he wants?"

"I'll warrant it's your neck, lad." Stewart's eyes thinned as
Gavin jammed on his boots. "You're not plannin' on going
out there?"

"What bloody choice do I have? He's like as not to shoot
a customer if this keeps up."

"I 'ave a better solution. I've a clear shot from behind the
gate," his mentor said. "Won't aim to kill, just stop the fool
from carryin' on."

He wished the solution was that easy. But Percy would not
want her idiot brother shot or hurt at all. Gavin wrenched
open the door. "No one's shooting anyone."

Grumbling, Stewart followed him out into the rear
courtyard. Several of Gavin's men were already outside,
armed and lining the gate that separated the property from
the alleyway. Shadowed by tall buildings on both sides, the
narrow thoroughfare had become a place for whores to do
their business and a sobering place for customers too
inebriated to find their way home.

One of his men shouted through the bars, "Go home, you
jug-bitten fool!"

Well-bred yet slurred accents replied from beyond the

gate. "Not goin' anywhere 'til I see Hunt. I've a debt to settle with him." The tones rang with rising rage. "Are you in there, you bloody coward? Seduce an innocent girl, will you, but can't face me like a man?"

As he approached the barrier, Gavin could see it was Percy's brother—there was no mistaking the classical Fines features, the glint of golden hair in the darkness. He had to give the man credit: downtrodden fool though he was, Fines stood amidst the filthy peaks of the night's refuse like some virtuous prince.

Out of habit, Gavin scanned the alleyway. He detected no activity in the dark, gravel-lined lane except for a couple of homeless wretches picking through the rubbish heaps and the flicker of an abandoned grate. Fines had probably scared the rest off with his blustering.

"Open the gate," Gavin said to his men.

"Think twice, lad," Stewart growled. "No sayin' what this sot is capable of."

"You don't mean any harm do you, Fines?" Gavin said evenly.

On the other side of the bars, Fines stepped forward, swaying a little. Several leagues beyond drunk. The moon caught the glint of the pistol in his hand. "I mean to kill you, you bastard," he said hoarsely.

Stewart's finger twitched on the trigger.

Gavin shook his head at his mentor. Addressing Percy's brother, he said in a calm voice, "Come now, Fines, you do not mean that. Let us talk this over like gentlemen." The gate opened, and he stepped out, with Stewart following behind. "If this is about your debt—"

"Damn the bloody debt! Do you think I give a donkey's arse about the company? My father and all he worked for can sink to the bottom of the Thames for all I care." Fines stumbled closer, his eyes wild. "But what you have done... to my *sister...*"

Gavin felt the hairs rise on his nape. Fines had found out about the wager? "What do you mean?" he said in neutral tones.

"Don't play the fool with me." Raising a shaking arm, Fines pointed his weapon at Gavin. "I know what you've done. *I know.*"

Suddenly, a voice rang out from behind Gavin.

"For goodness' sake, Paul, put down that pistol at once!"

Despite the seriousness of the situation, Gavin's eyes twitched upward in their sockets. *Hell's teeth, can she not follow instructions just* once?

Percy came dashing toward them, pushing her way through to the alley. Gavin glowered at the guard at the gate, who shrugged as if to say, *How am I supposed to stop her?*

"Are you alright?" she said when she reached him.

"I'm fine," Gavin said shortly. "I thought I told you to stay put."

"Percy?" Fines uttered.

"Yes, dear."

She started toward her brother; Gavin clamped a hand around her wrist. "He's drunk and holding a gun," he said in terse tones.

"It's perfectly alright," she assured him. "Paul would never hurt me."

"Of course I wouldn't," Fines said in tones of bewildered frustration. "Percy, what in blazes is going on? Why are you here with that blackguard?"

Percy tugged at her hand. Gritting his teeth, Gavin forced himself to release her. It took everything in him to watch on as she flew the remaining paces toward Fines. The sight of her in another man's arms—even if that man was her kin—made him want to punch something. The other man, for starters.

"Are you alright, sis?" Fines murmured to her. But he kept

one eye on Gavin, his knuckles white against the pistol.

"Yes, yes, I am fine." She lifted her head from Fines' chest, dashing the back of her hands against her cheeks. The pressure rose in Gavin's veins. Devil take it, her bacon-brained brother did not deserve tears. "Put that away, will you," she sniffled, "before someone gets hurt."

"What is going on here? Percy, did Hunt... did he force..." Fines' eyes widened as he took in Percy's damp, loose curls, her unbuttoned pelisse. His features twisted with tormented rage. For the first time, Gavin commiserated with the cove. If anyone had hurt Percy, he, too, would be fit for murder.

"Oh no, 'tis nothing like that," Percy said quickly. "Mr. Hunt and I are, um, friends."

Gavin's eyebrows lifted in unison with her brother's.

"Friends. With him." As if he failed to comprehend the simple statement, Fines gestured at Gavin with the pistol. "The blackguard standing over there who's holding my vowels ransom?"

"It's a long story," Percy said, "and I'll explain once you put that ridiculous weapon away."

Fines did not budge.

"This show of male bravado isn't helping anything," Percy said in exasperated tones. "How did you come to find me here?"

"I was down at the Red Lion nursing a drink because your *friend* here"—Fines spat the word—"saw to it that my credit's worth less than ashes at O'Brien's. And anywhere else, for that matter. He's destroyed my good name and for that alone I should call the rotter out."

Percy lifted her chin. "That was my doing, so don't blame Mr. Hunt."

"*Your* doing?"

"I hadn't any other means of stopping you. So I asked Mr. Hunt to put an end to your gaming because clearly you cannot stop on your own."

"You asked..." In a sudden movement, Fines grabbed Percy by the arm. A growl emerged from Gavin's throat.

"Stay back, Gavin. I'm fine." Percy glared at her brother, shaking free. "I can take care of this."

"*Gavin.* What they said was true, then." Fines whirled on him, eyes blazing in a bloodless face. "You've ruined my sister, Hunt, and I am going to put a bullet through you."

Gavin tensed, ready to spring. Stewart's pistol cocked with a deadly click.

"For heaven's sake!" Before Gavin could react, Percy flung herself in front of him. "If you're going to shoot him, you will have to go through me first. I love him, you nodcock! And I'll probably end up marrying him, once he gets it through his thick skull that he loves me back."

Her words blazed to the knotted, tangled morass within Gavin's soul. A breath that he hadn't realized he'd been holding left him, replaced by an almost overwhelming sense of... relief. Despite their earlier row, *she still loved him.*

"What the devil are you talking about?" Fines shouted. "Get out of the way."

Percy shook her head. Though her gesture would warm his heart for the rest of his days, Gavin could not let this continue. She squeaked in surprise when he lifted her by the waist and set her gently aside.

"I can fight my own battles, love," he said.

"It isn't your battle," she insisted. "The numbskull over there is *my* brother. And as usual he's not listening to me."

"For once, do as you're told. I'm not going to hide behind your skirts."

She crossed her arms. "Are trousers any more bulletproof? Because I'm not letting you get hurt."

"Oh, for crying aloud, have I interrupted a lover's quarrel?" They both looked over at Fines, who lowered his pistol in disgust. "Are you going to explain what is going on, Percy, or should I take myself off to Bedlam and call it a night?"

"As I said, it's rather a complicated—"

Gavin cut her off. "First tell me, Fines, how did you come to show up tonight?"

The man gave him a sullen look. "I was drinking at the Red Lion, like I said. Met a pair of toffs and we got to talking. Happened that they're former employees of yours and none too happy about it."

Gavin traded quick looks with Stewart, who shrugged. Apparently the other man couldn't recall any recent disgruntled workers either.

"And?" Gavin prompted.

Fines scrubbed a hand over his face. "And they said you'd been keeping company with a pretty miss who could be my twin. Said her name was Persephone—how many of those could there be? So I put two and two and figured you had somehow gotten to her." His face darkened. "The culls at the Red Lion said this would be the best place to nab you, so that's why I'm here in this filthy armpit of a place. To defend my sister's honor."

"Oh, Paul," Percy said in a tremulous voice.

"Those men—what did they look like?"

No sooner had the words left his mouth, then Gavin heard a shuffle. The hairs rose on his nape. He heard his name—a warning cry from Stewart. He spun to see the two homeless wretches approaching, cloaks thrown off to reveal the pistols in their hands. Shots flashed, and he was knocked bodily to the ground. For an instant he lay there, stunned, blood pounding in his ears. Through the roar in his head, he heard more shots being fired.

Percy. Must protect her.

He struggled to sit up—couldn't. A dead weight held him

down. His blood froze at the sight of Stewart's body collapsed atop his own, the dark pool spreading beneath the grizzled head.

Chapter Thirty-One

"DAMNIT, PERCY, STOP squirming about and stay down!"

When the first shots had gone off, Paul had shoved her behind a rubbish heap and covered her body with his own. Paralyzed, she'd watched as the two brutes advanced, loaded pistols swinging from their belts. Blast after blast had gone off as Gavin's men returned the fire. And now Gavin lay in the dirt...

"*Let me go.*" She resisted with all her might. "I have to get to him."

"You're not going anywhere," her brother panted, keeping her pinned.

To her relief, Gavin moved. He struggled to sit up—no wonder, as Mr. Stewart had fallen atop him. Her eyes widened as Gavin rolled the other man over, lifting the grizzled head into his lap.

Blood... there's so much blood.

Gavin's gaze whirled around the alley, found hers. Seeing the flare in his eyes, the trembling tension in his shoulders, she shouted, "I'm unhurt."

He gave a dazed nod, his gaze dropping once more to his mentor.

His guards swarmed the alley now. A pair went to prod at the fallen bodies of the attackers. From her vantage point, Percy could see the unblinking gazes of the brutes, their weapons scattered in the dirt around them.

"All clear, sir," one of the guards shouted. When Gavin did not respond, the other man took charge, saying, "Boys, let's block off the alley. A pair at each end and be quick about it."

"It's safe now, Paul. Let me go," Percy said urgently.

Her brother grunted as she threw him off, scrambled toward Gavin. He had his hand pressed against his mentor's temple, and she shivered to see the blood seeping through his fingers. Reaching to her petticoats, she tore off a strip and passed it to him. He took it mutely, pressing it to the wound.

Percy's throat clenched as the cloth turned red. "Should we take him inside?" she whispered.

"Can't move him. He's... bleeding too much," Gavin said tonelessly.

"Doctor's on 'is way," one of the guards said.

Yet even Percy could tell it was too late. The pallor of Stewart's face shone in the darkness, each of his breaths fainter than the last. Not knowing what else to do, she knelt beside Gavin and put her hand on his shoulder.

Stewart's eyelashes lifted. "That you, lad?"

"It's me. I've got you," Gavin said hoarsely. "You hold on, Stewart—help is coming."

"Ain't no 'elp for me this time," the other man said, coughing.

"We've been through worse." Gavin's stark voice made Percy's eyes well. "I'm not letting you go this easy."

"Not up to you, lad." Steward took a long, rasping breath. "'Ave to... 'ave to... say my peace before I go."

Gavin shook his head in denial, his eyes wet.

"Never been... good with words. Should've said... long time ago..."—Stewart reached a large hand to Gavin's scarred cheek—"... sorry."

"You did it to protect me. You've always protected me."

Moisture streaked Gavin's face. "*Don't go.*"

A faint smile showed through Stewart's beard. "You're the son... I ne'er..."

And his hand fell.

Through a veil of tears, Percy watched as Gavin closed his mentor's eyes.

"Mr. Hunt, someone's coming! We can't slow 'em down!"

Shots blasted through the night. Gavin jerked upright. Before Percy knew what was happening, he shoved her behind him and drew his pistols. Paul ran to stand next to her just as an enormous black carriage came hurtling down the lane. It came to a sudden stop, the door flying open. Percy's jaw slackened at the sight of the familiar golden crest.

"No, Gavin! Don't shoot!" She pushed in front of him. "It's Nicholas!"

A group of large men in dark coats descended from the carriage. The leader headed straight for her, his gloved hands closing on her shoulders.

"Are you hurt, Percy?" His grey eyes assessed her, and above the pristine folds of his cravat, his mouth formed a tight, imperious line. He'd never looked more like the powerful and foreboding marquess that he was.

"I'm fine," she said quickly. She addressed the tall, lanky man standing next to Nicholas, who held a gun pointed at Gavin. "Mr. Kent, please put your weapon away. This is Mr. Hunt, and he is a friend—"

The Thames River policeman's aim did not waver. "I'd be more careful in my choice of friends, Miss Fines. This man is a known scoundrel."

"Rather a dramatic entrance, wouldn't you say, Morgan?" This came from Paul. "Not your usual understated style. But rest assured, Percy is fine. I have been with her this entire time—"

"As for you, Fines," Nicholas said in even tones, "we have

much to discuss. You have caused your mama no small amount of worry. Go wait in the carriage,"—his tones booked no refusal—"and we will go see her directly."

Shoulders hunching, Paul did as he was told.

Percy looked anxiously at Gavin... and all breath left her in a rush. His scar was a violent slash across his hard features, and his eyes raged with hellfire. His words before the mayhem returned to her: *It has to do with Morgan. This is between him and me.*

"Percy, we must leave now," Nicholas said. "As for you Hunt, rest assured I will deal with you later."

"Will you indeed, my lord?" 'Twas the first time Gavin had spoken, and the lethal quality of his voice sent a warning shiver up Percy's spine.

Nicholas' eyes turned to silver-grey slits. "You wish to settle this now? Fine." He removed a wallet from inside his jacket. "How much?"

"How much," Gavin repeated softly.

"Yes, man, how much is owed to you?"

"Are you referring to Fines' debt to me... or your own?"

"Mine?" A look of distaste crossed Nicholas' handsome features. "I do not frequent establishments such as yours, Hunt."

"What about an establishment owned by one Benjamin Grimes?"

Nicholas paled. "Who... who are you?"

Gavin's teeth flashed, his look that of a predator cornering his prey at last.

Chapter Thirty-Two

COLD SATISFACTION WASHED over Gavin to see the uppity whoreson turn whiter than a ghost. Indeed, he had raised one straight in Morgan's smug face. Rage numbed the rawness of his insides, blanked his mind of things he couldn't think about, not now. His instincts kicked in.

Whatever happens, show no fear. Be brave. Look strong.

"Who are you?" Morgan's voice had lost its authority now, was no more than a whisper.

Power surged through Gavin. "I think you know."

"My lord." This came from the River Charley still holding a gun at him. "Perhaps you wish for privacy?"

Morgan blinked, as if he'd forgotten that they had an audience.

"You may take this inside, sir." The Charley gave Gavin a hard stare. "Know that The Thames River Police have surrounded your premises. We will ensure Lord Harteford and Miss Fines safe passage from here. One false move, and I will have you thrown in Newgate."

"'Twould hardly be the first time Morgan put an innocent man behind bars, would it?" Gavin sneered.

"Will someone *please* tell me what is going on?" Percy said.

"Wait in the carriage, Percy," Morgan said.

"I will *not* wait," she said, her chin at a mutinous angle. "I'm not a child, and I want to know what is going on."

"Come along, Percy." Gavin held out his arm, felt a heady sense of triumph when she took it. "I think you should hear this. Unless you have something to hide, Morgan?"

A muscle ticked along Morgan's jaw. But he said nothing, following behind.

Once inside the sitting room, Percy said, "Nicholas, do you *know* Gavin?"

"I'm not certain." Morgan's hands curled in their fine leather gloves, white lines bracketing his mouth. "Unless... you can't be... the boy?"

"Can't even remember my name, can you?" The familiar hatred bubbled like acid through Gavin. All these years he'd fed upon it, building his world around this day: the moment of his retribution. "I'm just the nameless, faceless boy you beat and left to die in Grimes' room."

"You escaped," Morgan said in a low voice.

"With no help from you, obviously."

"Nicholas. What is he talking about?" Percy pleaded.

Morgan shifted his gaze to her, said tonelessly, "'Twas the time before I met your father. Those were... dark days." He removed his hat, raking a hand through black hair silvering at the temples. "At thirteen, I was making my living as an apprentice to a sweep named Ben Grimes."

"Only he wasn't just a sweep, was he?" Though his own stomach gave an uneasy quiver, Gavin went on in a sneering tone, "And the duties you performed—more than just cleaning the stacks, eh? You and all the young boys the master fancied."

Percy's gasp of shock faded into the background. As did everything else. His gaze honed in on Morgan. *So long have I waited for this moment, my reckoning...*

A tremor crossed the other man's shoulders. "You know as well as I what went on at that house. But it is not fit for a lady's ears." Exhaling, Morgan said, "We will set another time to discuss—"

"*We will discuss this now.*" Gavin no longer had to think; the words rushed out of their own accord. "You are in my territory, and you will not leave until I am satisfied. You will admit what you did that night—*say it.*"

A shuddering breath left Morgan. His fist crushed the brim of his hat. His head bowed, and he was silent for so long that Gavin thought that he would not admit his crime.

"I killed him." The words broke over the hush like china hitting a stone floor. "I stabbed Grimes in the heart because I could not bear for him to... touch me. Not ever again."

"Nick." To Gavin's stupefaction, Percy crossed over to Morgan. She put her arms around him—*around Gavin's enemy.* Tears were rolling down her face. "Oh, Nick. Did Papa know?"

Morgan shook his head. "For years, I told no one and hid my shame. Not until Helena..." Though the other man's eyes held a sheen of moisture, his gaze softened. "She would not allow any secrets between us."

Percy nodded, still crying. When she swayed, Gavin started toward her—but Morgan was already leading her over to a chair. With furious bewilderment, Gavin watched the tender scene. Did she not understand that her so-called brother had been buggered repeatedly—and that he'd killed the man who'd done the deed? That he'd left Gavin *to die*? She should be recoiling in disgust, should be...

Over here. With me.

Steadying herself against the arm of the chair, Percy looked up at him. Her eyes brimmed with tears. "Gavin," she whispered "were you...?"

"Grimes didn't touch me," he snapped. He could scarcely think as the vortex whipped inside him. He found rage, letting it anchor him. He had yet to bare all of Morgan's sins; surely then Percy would side with him. "I'd been there a week. But it changed the course of my life nonetheless—because of what *he* did." He pointed a finger at Morgan. "Because after he murdered that bastard, he beat me senseless and left me to burn."

Color drained from Percy's face. "Nick wouldn't do that," she whispered. "Nick, say you didn't."

Morgan did not flinch at the accusation. Instead, he stood very straight and said, "I have done you an insurmountable wrong, Mr. Hunt. I turned my back on you, beat you, when instead I should have offered my hand." His voice broke as he said, "I have no excuse for my actions save that I... panicked. I thought only to get away from what I had done. In truth, I cannot recall thinking at all." He swallowed audibly. "I know words mean little, but know that every day since I have thought of my cowardly actions and despised myself. And I have hoped against hope that you might have survived, that I might find some way to make amends."

"*Make amends? For the ten years I spent rotting in the hulks because of the crime you committed?*" Gavin yelled.

Morgan turned ashen. "But Grimes' murder... I heard it was ruled an accident, because of a fire..."

"The fire that later got blamed on *me*. A decade I spent in prison for arson—because of the fire *you* started."

So consumed was he that he hadn't noticed Percy coming to stand beside him. She touched him on the arm. "Gavin, darling, please calm yourself—"

"*I will not calm.*"

His last vestige of control snapped. He did not even know that he had shaken her off until she staggered backward, losing her balance. Before he could grab her, Morgan caught her first. Set her behind him in a protective gesture that made Gavin want to howl with rage.

"I set no fire that night," Morgan said.

"Don't lie to me. I came to and the place was in flames.

Who set it, if not you?" Gavin snarled. "Who else had evidence to burn?"

Silence stretched. Frowning, Morgan said, "Anyone might have come into that room. Anyone who hated Grimes might have seen him lying there and decided to destroy the place." The compassion that came into Morgan's eyes made Gavin recoil. "I am sorry, Mr. Hunt, for everything you have suffered. More sorry than I could possibly say for the part that I played in it. But the fire—that was not me."

Chaos broke through the rage. Threatened to swallow Gavin alive.

"You stinking liar. Of course it was you," he spat. "And I will have my revenge. You ruined my life—and now I will ruin yours. Thanks to Fines, I have the majority shares in your company, Morgan, and I will tear down every brick and mortar of the empire you spent your life building."

Morgan's lips trembled, but he pressed them together. "And that will give you the satisfaction you seek?"

"Aye, and that is not all." He made a beckoning movement at Percy, who was staring at him with wide eyes. "Come here, Percy, and tell him what you've told me. That you love me. That you are going to marry me."

"Gavin." She whispered his name, but made no move to cross over to his side.

"Tell him." *Don't you dare betray me. Not now.*

"Was this all about... revenge?" she said, her voice hitching. "Our wager, would you have honored it, had I won?"

"You never would have won. I could have seduced you at any time. You love me." The words were coming out harshly, wrong, but he had no means of controlling them. Of controlling anything. Even fury began to abandon him, leaving fear and anarchy in its wake.

"Come here," he said again.

Morgan put a protective arm in front of Percy. "Go

outside," he said to her quietly. "Let me finish this."

Percy stood, unmoving.

"If you step foot outside, do not ever come back." Gavin's heart palpitated with desperation, but he could not show weakness, not in front of the enemy. *Not you, Percy. Don't you leave me, too.*

She looked at him with bright eyes. "Did you ever love me, Gavin? See me as a person—as more than a pawn?"

From the corner of his eye, he saw Morgan's expression— the raised brow, the haughty disbelief. *Show no weakness.*

"You're mine. You belong to me," he said between clenched teeth.

In a voice that wobbled, she said, "Give up your revenge, then, and I will stay. I will marry you. We can be happy, I know we can."

"Percy," Morgan said sharply.

"Prove that you love *me*," she said with sudden fierceness, "as much as I love you."

Even as the words beat in Gavin's weakest organ, chaos ruled the rest of him. *You can't trust a woman, lad, and that's a fact.* Stewart's voice... but Stewart was gone—*No, focus.* Was Percy trying to manipulate him, make him weak? He needed to clear his head. Needed to think through the storms of past and present. Yet another voice rang in his ears. *You worthless guttersnipe. Who could love you? Who would choose to be saddled with a filthy git?*

"I don't have to prove a bloody thing," he shouted.

He heard her sharp intake of breath. Then she turned and walked in rapid steps away from him. The closing of the door punctuated the silence. He stared at the place where she'd been. Couldn't believe she was... gone.

Morgan remained, his eyes cold. "You and I have unfinished business, Mr. Hunt, and I will do what is in my power to atone for the suffering I have caused you." Then a thread of anger entered his voice. "But hear me well: you will leave Miss Fines out of this. She is a young, innocent girl, and when I think of what—" His fists curled at his side, and he said tightly, "If it is satisfaction you want, then come for it like a gentleman. Good night, sir."

The door shut behind him, and Gavin was alone. Trapped in hell, with no escape.

As he'd always been.

Chapter Thirty-Three

Back in her own snug breakfast parlor, Miss Priscilla Farnham ought to have felt safe at last. She'd escaped the villain; the pristine windows offered views of an unclouded sky. Around the table, her family members ate their toast and marmalade in contented silence.

"Priscilla, dear, why aren't you eating?" her mother said.

Miss Farnham bit her lip. "The truth is, Mama," she burst out, "I've always hated marmalade."

—from *The Perils of Priscilla*, a nearly completed manuscript by P. R. Fines

"I'M DONE CRYING," Percy announced from the doorway of her mother's sitting room.

Mama looked up from her reading. Her brows lifted above her rounded spectacles.

"Well, there's a relief," she said mildly. "I thought you meant to carry on for days yet. As you are recovered, have a seat."

Percy sighed. She had been expecting this—in truth, had been putting it off for as long as possible. But a person could only shut herself in her chambers and sustain hysterics for so long.

She dropped into the adjacent chair. Curled on Mama's lap, Fitzwell lifted his head. His snort seemed to say, *You're in for it now.*

"Before you lecture me, I want to say... I am sorry, Mama," Percy muttered. "I know how disappointed you are in me."

"I haven't moved beyond shock yet. I still don't understand how you could do such a thing." Lace fluttered against Mama's graying curls as she shook her head and put down her book. "You've always been headstrong, but this... Have you lost your mind *completely*?"

"I wanted to help Paul," Percy said in a small voice.

"I have dealt with Paul," her parent said in tones that made Percy wince in empathy for her sibling, "so you will leave him out of this. What I want to know is why *you* would willingly throw yourself at ruin."

"But I am not ruined. Ga—I mean to say, Mr. Hunt, promised to keep our wager secret. And he's kept his word. There hasn't been a whiff of scandal about me. Well, other than the fact that I threw Lord Portland over." Hastily, she added, "Not that that was my fault."

To her surprise, her mother said grimly, "That was the one thing you did *right*. Lady Helena filled me in on the latest *on-dit* surrounding his lordship. Apparently, it's all over Town that the man is buried in debt. Thank heavens you escaped the clutches of that fortune hunter."

Percy lifted her brows. *I actually did something right?* Wanting to maintain the direction the ship was sailing, she said, "When did you see Lady Helena, Mama?"

"She came by yesterday. You were taking a nap, and she did not wish to disturb you. Now do not try to change the topic," her parent said. "Though by some miracle you seemed to have slipped beneath society's notice, the fact remains that *you* know what you did. And do not think for a moment that I believe you have told me everything, young lady."

Percy gulped. When Nicholas had brought her back to the townhouse two nights ago, she'd given a summary of events to Mama. A rather *edited* version. Even then, her mother had stared at her in mute astonishment; she'd counted herself lucky when, instead of being interrogated further, she'd been sent up to bed.

Apparently, Mama had recovered from the shock.

"I must ask you this, Percy. And know that this is the last question any mother wishes to ask of her unwed daughter." A pause. "Have you done anything..."—her parent's chin trembled—"... irrevocable?"

Heat flooded Percy's cheeks. "No, Mama, I have not," she mumbled.

Her parent's sigh rushed into the silence. "Well, thank goodness for that at least."

Percy understood her mother's relief, of course. At the same time, misery flooded her. Because despite everything that had passed and her frustration at Gavin's intransigence, she still yearned to be in his arms. The tears she'd shed these past two days had mostly been for his suffering—his and Nicholas'. To think of what they had both endured... and with the loss of Stewart, Gavin's pain must be double-fold.

Having had time to reflect, she could understand why Gavin had felt that he needed his revenge; why, in the horrifying wake of losing his mentor, he might have chosen it over her. Yet his choice *hurt*. Why was she so easy to set aside? Why couldn't she for once be important enough to come first? Why couldn't the man she loved love her back?

If she was wise, she would abandon any hope of a relationship with Gavin Hunt.

Unfortunately, prudence was still not one of her virtues.

"Well, the Season's not over yet," her mother continued. "Lady Helena mentioned an eligible young earl—"

"No, Mama." *No more skulking around and hiding who you are.* Gavin might not return her love, but she knew the truth of her own feelings—and they remained steadfast. Something to fight for. Taking a breath for courage, she said, "I'm not interested in any other gentleman. I... I'm already in love."

"You cannot mean with this Hunt character," Mama said sharply.

She gave a small yet firm nod.

"From what Nicholas has said, the man is a dangerous scoundrel. He'll do anything to get his revenge and hurt anyone standing in his way. How could you believe yourself in love with such a heartless blackguard?"

"He's *not* a blackguard. If you only knew what he has gone through. His own mother abandoned him, he lived in a flash house with that terrible Grimes, and he spent a decade in the hulks for a crime he did not commit—"

Mama's hand stilled atop Fitzwell's head. "He's a *convict* on top of it all?"

Dash it. "Well, not a *true* convict. I mean, he was convicted of burning down the flash house, but he didn't do it. Anyway," Percy said hastily, "he has a good heart. If you met him, you'd see it's true. He takes in orphans—"

"Persephone Fines, you listen to me." Mama pinned her with a steely gaze. "This man plans to destroy the company your dear Papa built with his own hands. He plans to hurt Nicholas. And you, my foolish girl, are merely a means to those ends."

Percy straightened her shoulders. "I'm not a girl any longer. And I'm not as foolish as you think. If I could just speak to Mr. Hunt again, perhaps I could persuade him to—"

Mama cursed. Percy's jaw dropped; she'd never heard her mother utter such words before. "I *knew* I would come to regret all that novel reading I permitted." Mama set Fitzwell aside, causing the pug to glare accusingly at Percy. Leaning forward, her parent said, "Listen to me: the reformation of rakes is the stuff of *fiction*. In real life, a pretty girl can no more change a man's heart than a leopard can its own spots."

"Does that mean there is no hope for Paul?" Percy shot back.

Mama frowned. "Your brother may act like a rake, but he isn't one by nature. After this disaster, I am sure he will find his way. He merely needs to grow up and take his responsibilities more seriously."

"And what if Gavin isn't a villain by nature either? What if circumstances have prevented him from showing his true, noble character? What if he is at heart a kind and decent man?"

Mama's brows shot up. "Who lied to you about his true intentions? Who threw you over in favor of his retribution?"

A direct hit to her bruised heart. "I didn't say he was perfect," she muttered.

"Lord above, I'm not going to argue with you about this. You stay away from that man, do you hear me? If necessary, I will keep you locked in your room for your own safety."

Trembling, Percy rose. "I understand you will not hear me on this, Mama. And I'm sorry I've never been the proper, sensible daughter you wanted. I'm sorry I'm such a disappointment." She blinked back the tears that threatened to spill over. "But I will not yield on this: I love Mr. Hunt."

"Blasted novels." Shaking her head, Mama sighed and went on, "You're misguided, but I never said you were a disappointment."

"You don't have to. I *know* I am. I'm prone to disaster and free of accomplishments." The crack in Percy's heart widened. "And you went on vacation to get away from me."

Mama's brow furrowed. "I wanted to have a break from my routine. Not from you."

"You're ashamed of me."

"That's not true, Persephone."

"Don't deny it," Percy said, her throat swelling. "We've been locking horns for ages, and I don't blame you for it one bit. Nor Papa for being too busy for me."

"What has your father to do with this?"

The dam within Percy burst open, releasing a flood of words that seemed to come from nowhere. "I'm not the daughter the two of you wanted. If I was, Papa would have wanted to spend time with me. And you would not be upset with me all the time."

Sudden, racking sobs took over. Arms enfolded her, holding her tight. She clung to her mother's embrace as the storm raged through her.

"How could think such nonsense, Percy?" Mama's voice chided her gently. "You know I love you, you silly girl."

"Because you have to," Percy wailed. "You haven't any choice in the matter. You're saddled with me."

"You were the apple of your father's eye as well. Don't you remember the nights when he did come home early and the first thing he asked for was his little poppet?"

Sniffling, Percy said, "Perhaps if I had been good at something, had something worthwhile to show him..."

"Oh, Percy. You're old enough to understand that while Papa loved you—loved us all—he had another love as well."

"You can't mean Papa... had a mistress?" Percy's moorings shook loose again. It couldn't be true. He'd adored Mama.

"Heavens, no. Not a human one at any rate. I'm talking about his work, which indeed was more demanding than any lady of the night." Hearing the pain in Mama's voice, Percy snuggled closer, this time offering as well as taking comfort. "It took me many years to recognize that no matter what I did, I would always play second fiddle to the company. Your father could not tame his ambition." She took Percy firmly by the shoulders and looked her in the eye. "But that was not my failing—and most definitely not yours."

Until that moment, Percy had not recognized how much she needed to hear these words. "I'm sorry you had to come second, Mama," she whispered, "and I wish I might have been more of a comfort. More like the proper daughter you deserved."

"Goodness, to hear you talk. You haven't any idea do you?"

"Any idea of what?" Percy said.

Her mother snorted. "Do you know what your Grandmama said to me after her visit with us last summer?"

Percy shook her head.

"*Well, Anna, you have finally gotten what you deserved. How I enjoy seeing that gel of yours give you a taste of your own medicine. She's just like you were at her age.*'"

"You mean... you were like *me*?" Percy said, stunned.

"I'd say it is the opposite way around," Mama replied dryly. "Either way, we are much alike you and I. Why do you think I've kept such a close eye on you all these years? It takes a hoyden to know one."

Mama... a hoyden!

"But you're so perfect," Percy blurted. "You do everything right."

"No one does *everything* right, my dear. I daresay I did grow up during my marriage," her mother said with a twinkle in her eye, "and you will, too, once you find the right husband."

With the newfound intimacy between them, Percy said, "Oh, Mama, I think I already *have*."

Mama gave her a stern look. "There's to be no more of that Mr. Hunt nonsense. Trust me, with time your feelings will fade. Until you come to your senses, however, you will not go anywhere without my permission. I shall have that window of yours bolted from the outside if necessary."

"Yes, Mama." Deciding not to stir the pot further for now, Percy said, "May I at least call upon Nick and Helena? I should dearly like to see them and the twins."

"As a matter of fact, the Hartefords are coming over this afternoon." Mama's expression softened. "Lisbett has been bustling about all morning preparing a special collation."

Perfect. Percy would take the opportunity to talk privately with Nick. If she could figure out how to free Gavin from the past, perhaps there might be hope for the future. Because she wouldn't give up on him—on them—without a fight.

Chapter Thirty-Four

THE HARTEFORDS ARRIVED at half-past three. Mama ushered them into the parlor where Lisbett had laid out a scrumptious side board. Given his lack of table manners, Fitzwell had been banned from the occasion.

"Helena and Nick, 'tis so good to see you," Percy exclaimed as soon as they were all seated. "Where are the twins?"

The marchioness smiled ruefully. "We thought we'd spare you the holy terrors this afternoon. Nurse has taken them to the park instead." With concern glowing in her lovely hazel eyes, she asked, "How are you, dear?"

"I'm well," Percy said. More truthfully, she added, "But clearly not as well as you. Why, you've got a glow about you, Helena. Time away from London must have agreed with you."

Though the other lady was always fashionable, today Helena looked especially splendid in a flounced carriage dress of deep green, which complimented her glossy russet curls and porcelain skin. Pink entered the marchioness' smooth cheeks, and she exchanged a glance with her husband. A silent message passed between them; Nicholas gave her a faint nod, his large hand covering her small one.

"The vacation was lovely, but the truth is"—Helena's blush deepened—"we are expecting a new addition to our family. Next spring."

"Oh my dears, how wonderful!" Mama beamed at the couple. "A full nursery is a blessed thing indeed. The twins must be so excited."

"We haven't told Jeremiah and Thomas as yet," Nicholas said.

"You saw how they were during our travels, Anna. With the questions." Helena sighed.

Mama chuckled as she passed around the tea cups. "I don't believe I've heard the word *why* used so many times in a single sentence." She slid a look at Percy. "At least, not since this one was in her leading strings. She was the most inquisitive poppet."

Percy rolled her eyes.

"You do encourage the boys, my love," Nicholas reminded his wife. Picking up his cup, he said, "Helena claims curiosity is a hallmark of intelligence."

"They are such clever little fellows, and I should hate to dampen their natural interest in the world," Helena admitted. "Well, I shan't worry about it. When the boys want to know where babies come from,"—she aimed a sweet smile at her husband—"Harteford will handle it brilliantly, I'm sure."

Nicholas choked on his tea. "Why me?"

"Because you are such a wonderful papa. The boys believe everything you say." Helena's eyelashes lowered demurely. "Besides, I'd say the matter falls under your expertise."

A flush crept over Nicholas' jaw at his wife's teasing. Percy exchanged amused glances with her mama. In truth, marriage had done wonders for Nicholas. He'd gone from a stoic, somber sort to one who showed his emotions more freely. He smiled and laughed more often, and there was no doubting his devotion toward his marchioness and their brood.

Of course, this made Percy think of Gavin. It fueled her hope: love *could* change a man for the better. If Nicholas could overcome the horrors of his past, then why couldn't Gavin?

"Nick, could I speak to you? In the garden?" Percy blurted.

The laughter fled his eyes. His grey gaze grew wary, and his shoulders stiffened, as if he had been expecting this. "Of course," he said.

"Now, Percy, do not go pestering Nicholas—" Mama began.

"'Tis fine, Anna." This came from Helena, who gave Percy an encouraging nod. "We came so that Harteford might speak with Percy. And while they are busy, I was hoping you might help me with selecting colors for the new nursery..."

Percy led the way out into the garden. The sun was out, showcasing her mother's prized rose bushes in their rainbow glory. Beside her, Nick walked silently, hands clasped behind his back.

Plucking up her courage, Percy said, "I have questions I want to ask you, Nick. I am afraid they are personal."

"After the events of two nights ago, I don't have many secrets left," he said.

"I know how you value your privacy, and I am so sorry to pry into your past." She bit her lip. "But the thing of it is, Gavin is not as wicked as he seems. He believes he was wronged, and I think if he understood the true circumstances of that night, he would relinquish his desire for revenge." *And give our love a chance.*

"Hunt *was* wronged. I left him there. Left him, when I should have taken him with me from that hell hole," Nicholas said in stark tones.

Poor Nick. How long has he carried the weight of that guilt?

"You were just a boy. You could hardly fend for yourself let alone another," Percy said.

Though his gaze remained bleak, he replied, "Helena said you would think that."

"'Tis what anyone would think," Percy insisted. "The true

villain was not you, but Grimes. Grimes and whoever set the house on fire. And that is the question I have been mulling over. If you didn't start the fire, who did?"

Nicholas ran a hand through his dark hair. "I have been asking myself the same question. 'Twas nearly twenty years ago, Percy, and for so long I have tried to block it all out."

"Can you recall who else was in the house that night?" she asked.

"There were a dozen boys at least. Nameless, broken wretches Grimes kept chained like slaves." Nick's jaw looked harder than granite. "Pathetic as it sounds, I doubt any of them would have set their only home aflame."

"Did Grimes have any enemies? Perhaps one of them seized the opportunity to destroy his place once and for all," Percy mused.

"Any number of men wanted Grimes dead." His brows drawn, Nicholas hesitated before saying, "When I was discussing this with Helena, I did recall one man in particular. A rival cutthroat whose feud with Grimes had caused bloodshed on both sides."

"What was his name?" Percy said eagerly.

The sun glinted off the silver at Nick's temples as he shook his head in frustration. "I never knew his name. He went by Jack Spades."

"That's not his real name?" Percy asked.

"'Twas a common moniker used in the stews to describe a one-eyed man." At her puzzled look, Nicholas explained, "In a deck of cards, the Jack of Spades has a side profile, so only one of his eyes is seen."

"So it's possible this man would want to burn down the flash house?"

Nick gave a terse nod. "Especially with Grimes' body in it. You see, Grimes was the one who'd cut out Spades' eye. In a street brawl... I witnessed it." Swallowing, he added,

"Grimes always vowed to get the other one, too."

Percy couldn't suppress a shudder.

"None of this is fit for your ears," Nicholas said suddenly, "nor will the past change the present situation. Heed me on this, Percy: Gavin Hunt is a dangerous man. You must stay away from him."

"Gavin wouldn't hurt me," she protested.

"He meant to ruin you and to destroy Paul. Simply to get to me."

"He wanted to marry me. And he protected Paul from falling deeper into debt. He can be tender and kind and... I *know* he isn't a bad man," Percy pleaded. "If we can sort out together what really happened the night of the fire, perhaps he can let go—"

"Hunt has built his life on rage and a need for revenge. I can understand why; I also know that such a man will not change. The rookery and the hulks have made him who he is," Nicholas said flatly.

"But look at you! You've changed. You've risen above your origins."

"I got out earlier than Hunt did. And I had a helping hand from your father." Nicholas took her by the shoulders. "Percy, I owe my life to your family, and I will not stand by and watch you get hurt because of my past. Promise me you'll steer clear of Hunt."

Percy shook free. "First Mama, now you. Why won't anyone treat me like a grown woman capable of making her own decisions? I don't want to lie to you, Nicholas—I... I have feelings for Gavin. Real ones. And I will not give up on him so easily."

"Then you leave me no choice. Until I've settled this business with Hunt, you will be under the watch of Mr. Kent and his men. You will go nowhere without them."

"You might as well toss me in Newgate and throw away

the key!"

"Trust me, I considered a similar option," Nicholas said. "Helena dissuaded me."

"From what?" With a hand shading her eyes from the sun, Helena ambled toward them, an inquisitive smile upon her face. "Apologies for interrupting, but Lisbett's rolls are ready, and you know how she likes to serve them hot."

Percy ran toward her. "You must take my side," she pleaded. "Tell Nicholas I am not to be treated like a prisoner."

"Oh." Helena cleared her throat. "This is about Mr. Kent's protection, I take?"

Percy gave a vigorous nod.

"The thing is, dear, the state of affairs is precarious, and Harteford simply wishes for your well-being," the marchioness said. "Besides, having Mr. Kent and his men for company is surely better than being locked up on our country estate."

"You were *serious* about that?" Percy turned disbelieving eyes upon Nicholas.

"It is my responsibility to keep you safe," he said, his jaw taut.

"Helena," Percy begged, "say something."

"I already did. That is why you're not being banished to Hertfordshire. I know you will hate hearing this, but Percy," Helena said apologetically, "'tis for your own good."

The Hartefords stood side by side: Nicholas large and unyielding, Helena petite and concerned. And Percy knew any further argument would prove futile. When it came to unraveling the secrets of Gavin's past, she would have no further help from this corner; she would have to venture forth on her own.

"Nick, if I agree to this, will you promise me one thing?" she asked.

"What is it?"

"Please don't hurt Gavin," she said.

"If Mr. Hunt attacks, my husband has no choice but to defend himself," Helena said, an edge to her tone. "Surely you don't want to see Harteford hurt."

"Of course not." Percy bit her lip. "But I don't want to see *anyone* hurt."

"I have no desire to harm Hunt. I've done him enough wrong already," Nicholas said quietly. "My hope is to find some way to make amends—if he will accept."

That was something, at least.

"Thank you." Hearing the summons of Lisbett's supper bell, Percy sighed. "We best go in before she comes after us with the rolling pin."

She headed back to the house. At the edge of the garden, she paused; the other two had not followed. They were still standing there, surrounded by roses and sunshine. As she watched, Nicholas pulled his lady close, and a moment later buried his face in her hair. Helena appeared to be murmuring to him, her arms wrapping around his waist.

Percy swallowed, feeling a pang of guilt for Nicholas' pain. Yet she knew Gavin was suffering, too, and she longed to be a comfort to him the way Helena was to Nick. So much was at stake—the lives of everyone she loved. She had to find a way to put an end to this. She had to... but how?

Chapter Thirty-Five

"BLOODY CHRIST!" GAVIN choked out curses as an icy wave towed him into wakefulness. He bolted upright, frigid water dripping down his face; his mind struggled to surface from a sea of spirits. He was sitting on a settee in his office. Two small faces peered down at him. Davey, Alfie… and the latter had an empty bucket in hand.

"What the hell did you do that for?" Gavin growled, swiping water off his face.

"We 'ad to talk to you, and there weren't no other way to get you up," Alfie said. "You've been drunker than a sailor on 'is first leave."

Snatching the towel Davey held out, Gavin mopped irritably at his face. "I said I wasn't to be disturbed." Memories returned, and his gut clenched in pain.

Stewart's… gone. Percy, too.

"Trust me, you'll want to 'ear this. But you'll need this first." Alfie passed him a cup. "'Tis my ma's old recipe—made it e'vry mornin' for 'er 'til the day she cocked 'er toes up."

Gavin eyed the greenish sludge. What did he have to lose? He gulped it down, and the most potent hair of the dog he'd ever had blasted through him.

He coughed. "What news do you have, Alfie?"

"First off, they fished Finian O'Brien from the Thames this mornin'. Soon thereafter, 'is brother went runnin' for the hills."

Christ. The news was as sobering as Alfie's concoction. "Do they know who did it?"

Alfie gave him a wry look. "There ain't many culprits left, I reckon."

The urchin reckoned right. "Kingsley," Gavin said grimly.

Alfie looked at Davey. For some reason, the latter shook his head, his face pulling taut with fear. Alfie nudged him none too gently with an elbow. "Go on, Davey. Tell 'im what you told me." When Davey continued to stand there mutely, Alfie snarled, "Tell the man or I will."

A tremor passed over the boy's narrow shoulders. "I... I'm sorry, Mr. Hunt," he blurted. "I han't been straight with you. And you've been good to me."

"What is it, Davey?" Gavin said.

"I wanted to tell you sooner, but I was afraid. After what 'appened to Mr. Stewart..." As Gavin's insides twisted, the boy lowered his unruly head, his voice emerging as a whisper. "I can't 'ide any longer. 'Tis my fault. I was sent 'ere to spy on you."

A chill gripped Gavin's nape. "By who?"

Fear dilated Davey's pupils. "The gent 'as information on my brother, Mr. Hunt. 'E said 'e'd 'ave Eddie tossed in Newgate if I didn't do what 'e said."

"Who, Davey?" Gavin rose.

The boy let out a shuddery breath. "Mr. Magnus."

Magnus. With a fresh stab of grief, Gavin recalled Stewart's distrust of the old man. "What have you reported to Magnus thus far?"

Davey's face flamed, and even his oversized ears turned scarlet. "I've told 'im bits an' pieces that I overheard. I—I figured out your secret corridor, an' I've been usin' it..."

"To eavesdrop," Gavin said brusquely. "I get it. Now tell me exactly what you've told Magnus."

"I told 'im about Mr. Kingsley's visit and 'ow you turned 'im down. And once I 'eard you and Mr. Stewart..." The boy trailed off, his lip wobbling.

"Go on," Gavin said.

"I 'eard you and 'im talkin' 'bout your past. 'Bout the hulks and the flash house owned by some fellow named Grimes. And 'ow you planned to get your revenge on Nicholas Morgan..."

Gavin's head throbbed as the boy continued to mumble out details. Bloody hell, Davey's ears were clearly more than just for show. The question was why Magnus wanted all this information... and how the bastard planned to use it against Gavin.

"... and I also told 'im about Miss Fines," Davey said, his eyes filled with misery.

Gavin's pulse thudded faster. "What did you say about her?"

"Magnus asked me all sorts o' questions. And I answered 'em." Tears spilled down the boy's cheeks, and he dashed them away with his knuckles. "I didn't want to. She was nice to me, but he said my brother would swing from the gallows if I didn't tell 'im everything."

"*What did you say about her?*" Before he realized what he was doing, he had Davey by the arms; the boy's frail muscles trembled in his grasp.

"I told him..." The boy shut his eyes. "I said you was in love with 'er. I said you'd do anything for 'er, only you tried to 'ide it."

The boy's words held a mirror up to Gavin's soul. The reflection dazzled him. Of course he loved her. Loved her more than anything. Her soft pleas rang in his head. *We can be happy, I know we can... Prove that you love me as much as I love you.* Even with the truth of his revenge revealed, she'd been willing to give him a chance.

And like a fool, he'd run her off. He'd been so torn up that night... so confused... he hadn't been able to sort past from present. To act as he should have.

Another realization hit Gavin. Something Fines had said about the assailants. *Said you'd been keeping company with a pretty miss who could be my twin... said her name was Persephone.* Had Magnus been behind that attack? If Magnus had identified Percy as the weak link in Gavin's armor, then the old whoreson would not hesitate to strike out again—at *her*.

"Please sir, don't 'urt me."

Davey's whimper reached through Gavin's panic. He released his grip, shoving the boy aside. He ran for the door.

"Where are you off to, Hunt?" Alfie called. "What should I do wif Davey?"

He didn't stop to look back. "Keep him here. We'll figure out the business with his brother later. Right now, I've got to find Percy."

Percy studied Mr. Kent from across the carriage. Dressed in dark, well-worn garments that hung from his rangy frame, the investigator looked a bit like a scarecrow. Yet his pale eyes had an intelligent gleam and his thin features an air of sadness that made her wonder about his life's journey. At any rate, she couldn't blame Mr. Kent for following her around like a terrier; he was merely doing his job.

"I am sorry to inconvenience you for naught, sir," she said.

Somber eyes studied her. She was certain she'd never seen Ambrose Kent crack a smile. "'Tis no inconvenience, Miss Fines," he said.

"You must have better things to do. Criminals to apprehend, ships to search, that sort of thing." She wrinkled her nose. "I can't imagine that the Thames River Police typically concerns itself with the errands of a middling class miss."

"The Thames River Police owes much to the patronage of the Marquess of Harteford," Kent said simply.

Ergo, Nick's orders were to be followed. Which meant she had better get used to having an escort. Sighing, she brushed her fingers against the brooch Gavin had given her; she'd pinned it next to her heart, wanting to keep him close as she fought for their future. She cast the policeman a considering glance; perhaps she could turn the situation to her advantage.

"Mr. Kent, might I solicit your advice on a matter?"

Though he looked surprised at her request, the policeman nodded.

"I'm wondering how one might locate the whereabouts of a criminal," she said.

Mr. Kent's brows climbed. "Are you indeed?"

"It's for my novel," she improvised. "One of the characters is, um, a detective. And he needs to search out a villain from the past."

"Ah," Mr. Kent said.

"Now the detective doesn't know the villain's name, and he is working from a single clue." Percy paused. "The man he is looking for has a missing eye."

"Physical characteristics are helpful in a search. How long ago was the suspect last seen?"

She hazarded a guess. "Fifteen years, perhaps twenty?"

"Hmm. Then I'd suggest..."

"Yes?" She bent forward.

"That your character leave the job to the professionals." Mr. Kent aimed a stern look at her. "His lordship is having the matter of Jack Spades investigated, and the last thing he needs is your interference."

Percy heaved a sigh. "If you knew all along, why did you

let me go on?"

For the first time, she saw the policeman smile. The crooked grin transformed his worn features, giving him a raffish charm. "Because your tale was quite entertaining. You really should write a novel, you know."

Soon thereafter, they arrived at Hatchard's. Mr. Kent entered the premises first, signaling a pair of his men to flank the door. He surveyed the bookstore with the same vigilance he might use at the docks or in the stews.

"I am going to browse around, and there's no use following me through the stacks as they're quite narrow," Percy said. "Perhaps you'd care to wait for me at an assigned place?"

His alert gaze scanned the environs. Finally, he nodded to the fireplace, the central point of the store. "I'll be here if you need me, Miss Fines."

Feeling like a bird freed from its cage, Percy escaped into the shelves. She perused her way through sections of history and poetry before winding her way to the back of the store where the novels were housed. She caught Mr. Kent glancing her way and waved at him before wandering off the main aisle into a row of shelves. Selecting a new volume by one of her favorite authors, she was flipping through the pages when she felt a tug on her arm.

Looking down, she saw an urchin, no more than five or six, peering up at her.

"Are you Miss Fines?"

Her pulse sped up. "Yes, I am."

"I've somethin' for you, then." He shoved a note at her; before she could ask him a question or even hand him a coin, he scampered off down the row.

She broke the wax seal.

My dearest love, I must see you again. There is much I need to say to you and know that I will do whatever is required to make things right. I am waiting for you outside the back entrance—please don't make me wait in vain, my darling.

-H

Her heart flip-flopped in her chest. *Whatever is required to make things right.* Could Gavin be saying that he meant to give up his revenge for her? Was he capable of changing after all? More to the point: after all she'd been through, was she willing to risk her pride and heart again for a man like Gavin Hunt?

A thousand times, yes.

Peering down the main aisle, she saw that Mr. Kent remained in position. He nodded at her, and she fluttered her fingers back before returning behind the shelves. She looked to the opposite end of her row: the back door, less than a dozen yards away. She could see Gavin in moments, possibly without Mr. Kent finding out. And if Gavin was proposing what she hoped, they wouldn't need to meet in secret any longer.

Giddy with excitement, she made her decision and walked steadily toward the door. She brushed by another patron who gave her an annoyed look, but she continued on. She saw that the door had a lock on it, but the knob turned easily in her hand. She opened it and slipped through.

Despite the early time of day, the alleyway wavered with shadows from the tall abutting buildings. Her heart leapt as she saw the dark-clothed figure standing a few feet away. His broad shoulders were turned away from her, his head obscured by his hat.

Softly, she said, "Gavin?"

He turned.

"Oh, I—I'm sorry," she stammered. "I thought you were someone else."

Though the stranger was handsome, his smile raised the

hairs on her nape. "You're prettier than I thought you'd be, Miss Fines. No wonder Hunt's been in a constant state of rut. You'll come in handy, I'm sure."

She backed away, only to bump against a solid, burly form. A cloth covered her mouth, muffling her scream. A sweet, pungent smell filled her nostrils, and she knew no more.

Chapter Thirty-Six

GAVIN KICKED THE door open. "Where the hell is she, Morgan?"

The group of men sitting around the long table stared at him. Behind him, the bespectacled idiot who'd tried to bar his way into Morgan's office yapped like an irate dog. "My apologies, my lord. I tried to stop this person, but he would not listen. Shall I have him removed from the premises?"

"I'd like to see you try," Gavin said, baring his teeth.

"Never mind, Jibotts." Morgan rose to his feet. Turning to the group at the table, he said curtly, "The meeting is adjourned for now. I'll expect the shipping reports on my desk tomorrow morning."

After a chorus of *Yes, m'lord*, the toadying fools took off.

Old four-eyes, however, hovered protectively at the doorway. "My lord, I can have the magistrate summoned—"

"Leave us, Jibotts," Morgan said. "And close the door behind you."

With one last suspicious glare, the man departed. Morgan picked up the coffeepot and poured himself a cup of steaming brew. He cocked a dark brow.

"I don't want any bloody coffee," Gavin snarled. "Where the hell is Percy?"

"It's none of your damn business, Hunt. I told you to stay away from her." Morgan studied him with cold, grey eyes. "I'm the one who wronged you and if you're willing to discuss restitution—"

"*She's in danger, goddamnit.*" Fear made Gavin's words boom against the walls. He was known to be coolheaded under any circumstances, yet now his thoughts raced. "I've been by her house and got run off by the old hen who runs the place. Bribed one of the neighbor's grooms—he said he saw her carriage leave two hours ago. *Tell me where she went.*"

Morgan stared at him. "What sort of danger are you referring to?"

Gavin raked his hands through his hair. He'd left in such a rush that he'd forgotten his hat. "Cutthroats, Morgan," he grated out. "There's no time to get into it. If you know where she is, we have to find her."

His words seemed to finally galvanize the marquess into action. "They're after her?" he said, grabbing his jacket.

Self-loathing burned in Gavin's chest. "They're after me," he said, "and they have no qualms about using her to get what they want."

"Come with me," Morgan said.

Such was his fear for Percy's life that Gavin did not balk at the autocratic command. They descended the steps of the warehouse, Morgan barking to have the carriage brought round. Matched grays met them at the entrance.

"Home and be quick about it," Morgan told the driver as they boarded the well-sprung vehicle. They'd barely found their seats before the equipage leaped forward.

"Percy is at your home?" Gavin said tersely.

"Mrs. Fines is having tea with my wife this afternoon," Morgan corrected. "I am not certain if Percy planned to come. If she is not there, her mother will know where she went."

Gavin's fists tightened in his lap. He looked out the window. Though the streets blurred past, the carriage could not move fast enough to suit him. Sweat slickened his brow. *Goddamnit, if anything happens to her…*

"Why are you worried about her, Hunt? I thought she was a pawn in your game," Morgan said. "A means to an end."

"I never said that," Gavin bit out.

"You certainly let her believe it."

Guilt wrenched his gut—if it wasn't already so knotted, he might have felt something. "I should kill you," Gavin snarled. "It would make me feel a damn sight better."

"Perhaps. Before you tear my head off, however, you might like to know that I've put Percy under protection. Wherever she is, Mr. Kent is with her."

Never in his life did Gavin think he'd welcome a Charley's involvement. Some of the tightness in his gut eased, but he muttered, "He better know what he is doing. These aren't petty thieves he's dealing with. These are powerful, ruthless men who'd do anything to keep it that way."

Morgan studied him with an unfathomable gaze. "Tell me who is after Percy—or you, rather."

Gavin weighed his options. Confiding in his nemesis had not figured into his plot for revenge. For Percy's sake, however, he saw no better alternative. "A man named John Magnus. Likely in partnership with another bastard, Warren Kingsley. They're cutthroats who've killed three men already."

"Why?"

Gavin made a scoffing sound. "For power and money, of course. Forgotten what life was like in the rookery, your lordship?"

"I remember," Morgan said, "every bleeding second of it. No title can make a man forget where he came from. I was born in the gutters, no different from you."

A queer pang tightened Gavin's throat. To cover it, he sneered, "Then you'll know that where I come from murder doesn't warrant much of a reason. 'Tis as senseless as abandoning a boy and thrashing him within an inch of his life."

A muscle ticked in Morgan's jaw. A moment later, he said, "You want to know why I did it? Why I not only refused to help you, but beat you and left you in that cesspit?"

Yes. "I don't give a damn."

"I did it because I was scared." Morgan looked at him, and despite the rage burning in Gavin, he knew pain when he saw it. "Three years I lived with Grimes. Days in the stacks, nights in a hell worse than that." The other man passed a hand over his mouth. "As time passed, I forgot to hope. Forgot... myself. I was just another one of the miserable, worthless mongrels willing to do anything to survive."

Gavin had been with Grimes less than a fortnight, yet he could still see the small, pale faces, lifeless eyes. His jaw tightened as he recalled his own fear. His own foolish vow: *I'll never be like them.*

"But a mongrel pushed too far can bite back." Morgan's smile held no humor, only bitterness. "I have no regret for my actions that night, save for what I did to you. I was terrified. All I could think to do was run. And you were crying, begging..."—his voice broke low—"and I saw myself. Saw my own stinking, helpless self, and I couldn't get away fast enough."

The other man looked away. Gavin did the same as alarming heat pushed against the back of his eyes. He heard himself say, "And the fire... ?"

"That is the one sin I cannot claim. I swear it on my life, on everything I hold dear," Morgan said in a gravelly voice.

Slowly, Gavin's anger receded. For the first time, he was able to look quietly into the pool of his past. The surface was... calm. In its reflection, he glimpsed the boy he'd been and another boy—one with a lost look in his grey eyes. They had both been powerless, undeserving of what fate had meted out to them. And somehow they had both survived. Studying the man he'd hated for so long, he was struck by a bewildering feeling of... was it kinship?

As the drive continued in silence, Gavin became aware of the clip-clop of the horses echoing the rhythm of his own heart. An organ that wasn't dead, that *could* feel love. For Stewart, the man who'd fathered him. For Percy, the only woman he'd ever loved. He'd lost one, but he would not give up the other without a fight.

"How... how did you move past it all?" Gavin said gruffly.

The marquess glanced swiftly in his direction, and Gavin saw that the man's lashes were spiked with moisture. Morgan seemed to mull over his response, before saying, "At first, I thought working my arse off was the answer. It kept me focused on the future, on making something of myself." He shrugged. "And then the title came. More money and power. I thought I'd risen above my past at last."

"Control," Gavin said with a nod. "A man can't have too much of that."

"I thought so too—and I was wrong. What I needed was the opposite. To learn to trust, open myself to another." Morgan's austere features softened. "In the end, 'twas my marriage that put the past behind me."

Gavin's throat clenched. Once he had Percy safe and sound, would she give him another chance? She was everything he needed—and blind fool that he was, he hadn't recognized it. How could he, when he had never known love before? But he'd make it up to her. He'd find a way, even if it meant tearing his heart open and showing her what was inside.

"You care about Percy, don't you?"

Under Morgan's scrutiny, Gavin's cheekbones heated. 'Twas one thing to consider falling upon bended knee in front of one's beloved and another entirely to admit such a thing to another man. Especially Morgan.

"What goes on between Percy and me is none of your

business. I don't care if you're a marquess or her adopted brother or the sodding Archbishop of Canterbury," he muttered. "She's mine. And the minute I get the minx back, I'm going to marry her and to hell with what anyone has to say about it—and that includes Percy herself."

He crossed his arms. There was a pause.

"I'll take that as a yes," Morgan said dryly.

The Harteford residence was a Georgian mansion on Upper Brook Street. Gavin took scant notice of the luxurious surroundings, hadn't even a hat to toss to the crotchety old stick who opened the door. He scanned the marble foyer and the grand curving staircase, impatient for any sign of Percy.

"Are the Fineses here, Crikstaff?" Morgan said.

"Yes, my lord," the butler intoned. "The marchioness is entertaining them in the drawing room."

The *Fineses*. Both Percy and her mother were here, then. Relief flooded Gavin. He had to restrain himself from shoving his way past Morgan to get to Percy. It wasn't that he gave a damn about being impolite to his host: he had no bleeding idea where the drawing room was in the sprawling abode. So he was forced to follow Morgan's brisk lead down the hallway to the right.

He heard the laughter first. Then the sounds of a pianoforte... *Christ*. He cringed as notes splintered the air with ear-splitting discordance.

Morgan looked over his shoulder. A faint smile reached his eyes as he opened a pair of French-style doors. "Welcome to Mayhem, Hunt."

The mêlée was worthy of the market at Covent Garden. Two identical, tow-headed boys chased one another round the piano, pounding out notes as they passed and shouting cheerfully all the while. A brunette with a vexed expression was scolding them to stop whilst another lady—middle-aged and with a heart-shaped countenance and blue eyes that identified her as Percy's mother—tried to lure them to the sitting area with a plate of cakes. Meanwhile, Paul Fines sat flirting with a cool blonde who looked amused by the entire situation.

But no Percy.

"Where the hell is she?" Gavin said.

All heads turned in his direction.

Beside him, Morgan cleared his throat. "Everyone, this is Mr. Hunt. He came to the office looking for Percy. Where has she gone today?"

Paul Fines broke the silence. "Are you mad, Morgan? Why did you bring the bastard here?" Rising, he glared at Gavin. "Even if I knew where my sister was, I would not tell you."

Gavin's hands grew clammy. "You mean to say you do not know where she is?"

"What business is it of yours? Haven't you done enough damage already?" Fines said.

Gavin started forward; Morgan stayed him with a hand on the arm. "Whatever the past, Hunt is here to help today," he said calmly to the room at large. "Percy may be in danger. We must locate her—where is she?"

"Hatchard's. Mr. Kent went with her and planned to bring her here afterward. They should have arrived by now." This came from Percy's mother, the lace on her ash-blond curls trembling. She turned an accusing gaze to Gavin. "What have you got her mixed up in now, sir?"

Heat crept up Gavin's neck. "Mrs. Fines, I—"

"There'll be time for explanations later, Anna," Morgan cut in. "Hunt and I must go to Hatchard's immediately."

"I'll come too," Fines said.

"You'll stay here and look after the family," the marquess said. "Kent and Percy may yet show up. If they do, send word to us."

As Fines gave a subdued nod, the brunette came up to Morgan. Her eyes were wide with worry. "You will be careful, won't you?"

Morgan cupped her cheek. "Of course, my love."

Gavin turned impatiently to the door just as a long-limbed figure came striding into the room. He recognized the Charley from the other night.

Kent's face was pale, his posture stiff. His gaze honed on Gavin. "What are you doing here?"

"Where is Percy?" Gavin said as a dull thud started in his ears.

Kent spared him another glance before announcing in a flat voice, "She's been taken."

Chapter Thirty-Seven

PERCY OPENED HER eyes. The lids felt heavy, weighted. She blinked as the world came into focus. She was lying upon a straw pallet, her hands bound behind her back. Maneuvering to a sitting position, she gazed around her. Some sort of storage room, with empty pots stacked against the wall and a strong chemical odor in the air. The door opened, and the stranger from the alleyway strode in. Behind him, she glimpsed stairs leading up, the flash of sunlight on water. She was in a basement... next to the Thames?

"Ah," her kidnapper said. "Awake at last."

"Who are you?" She managed to keep her voice steady. "What do you want?"

"The name's Kingsley." He had the gall to sweep her a bow while flashing white teeth. "I am your host. We'll be having a party this evening, and you, my dear, will be the main attraction."

She was no fool. The cad planned to use her to lure Gavin. "Mr. Hunt knows better than to waltz into your trap," she said, lifting her chin.

"A man in love tends to lose his head. No pun intended." Kingsley came toward her. She edged backward, her shoulders hitting the wall. "You are a pretty thing, aren't you?" he mused. "No wonder you've got the bastard tied up in knots."

When he reached a hand to her hair, she spat, "Stay away from me!"

"Little hellion, eh? Hunt always liked his women full of sauce." Kingsley's smile drew chills down her spine. "And I should know—I've fucked all of his women."

Percy screamed as he yanked her head back, his lips descending upon hers.

"Goddamnit, Kingsley, keep your cock in your pants."

At the sound of the new voice, Kingsley's grip eased, and Percy tore free, scrambling away. She turned to see the newcomer... and her heart skipped a beat at the sight of the black patch covering one eye.

"Jack Spades," she breathed.

"The name is John Magnus, Miss Fines." The scruffy old man stared at her with his good eye. One of his hands gripped a cane; the other aimed a pistol at her chest. "And I prefer to keep it that way."

"What's the chit talking about, Magnus?" Kingsley demanded.

"Nothing of consequence."

Magnus gave her a warning look, and Percy realized that his partner in crime knew nothing of the past. Recalling what Gavin had told her about the betrayal and back-biting that went on amongst the club owners, she hit upon an idea.

Bucking up her courage, she said, "I wouldn't call your motive for killing Mr. Hunt inconsequential, Mr. Magnus."

"What motive? What does she mean?" Kingsley demanded.

Magnus clucked his tongue as he turned to his colleague. "She's just a foolish miss with a wild imagination. Why didn't you gag her like I told you to?"

"Had other uses for her mouth." Kingsley's smirk made Percy want to retch. "Your flag may not fly, old man, but others of us still run a high mast."

"You and your prick," Magnus said in disgust. "I'm still cleaning up your mess with O'Brien. Had everything going according to schedule and you turned it a shambles. And for what? A stupid wench."

Percy's ears pricked. O'Brien—the man Paul had owed money to? What had happened to him?

Kingsley's eyes narrowed. "It wasn't my fault. I had Evangeline taken care of; the bitch wouldn't dare breathe word of our affair. If Finian hadn't stuck his nose where it didn't belong and tried to blackmail me over fucking her—"

"Enough." Magnus' gaze returned to Percy, who tried to keep her expression neutral. Inside, her heart thudded. "Little pitchers have big ears, don't you know. Hand me your cravat, Kingsley, and be quick about it."

"Did Mr. Magnus tell you he knew Mr. Hunt years ago?" Percy said in a rush. "That he wants to kill Mr. Hunt to keep his crime a secret?"

Kingsley paused, his neck cloth stretched between his hands. "What secret? What haven't you told me, Magnus?"

"I said shut the wench up. Give me that bloody cloth." Letting go of his cane, Magnus tried to snatch the material from the other man. He clawed futilely at the air.

Kingsley held it out of reach. "Oh no, you don't. Not until I hear the truth."

Just as Percy was scouting escape routes, Magnus regained himself. He took a breath, ran a hand over his wild grey locks. "It's not important. But, yes, I knew Hunt when he was a boy. He worked for an old enemy of mine."

"Benjamin Grimes," Percy said, her pulse quickening.

Magnus shot her a murderous look. "Aye. Bastard took my eye. And I took something back of his."

The answer popped into her head. "'Twas *you*. You burned down the flash house that night," she said. "You set it afire and left Gavin to take the blame."

A crafty smile spread over the old man's face. "Aye. That I did."

At last, the truth of what had happened that night. And proof of Nick's innocence. Now if only she had a way to escape, to get back to Gavin...

"That's quite a skeleton you've got rattling in your closet," Kingsley mused. "Hunt would slit your throat if he knew the facts."

"Which is why I'm going to slit his first. Make no mistake, Kingsley: you may know something about me, but I have far more filth on you." As his partner scowled, Magnus said, "We're in this together, and there's only one way out. We kill Hunt tonight. Now are you going to gag this wench, or do I have to do it?"

Percy's hope dwindled as Kingsley approached her.

If someone had told Gavin he would be working together with a marquess, a policeman, and a baroness, he would have asked for the premise of the joke. Yet at present Morgan, Kent, and Lady Marianne Draven clustered around the coffee table in his office. They'd followed him from the Harteford residence, insisting to be part of Percy's rescue plan. Paul Fines had been left the task of guarding his mother and the other Hartefords.

Now Gavin shared grim glances with the three. The brooch he'd given Percy lay on the table between them; it had come wrapped up in a ransom note. The instructions were simple:

Midnight. Watson's Blacking Factory. Come alone or the girl dies.

The clock struck nine. With three hours left, there was little time to prepare an offensive.

"You cannot go in by yourself," Morgan said. "'Tis too dangerous."

"If I don't, they'll kill Percy," Gavin said flatly. "These men mean what they say."

"If you go in alone, they'll kill you. And Percy will be no better off," Lady Draven drawled.

Gavin could not argue with those facts. Yet he had no other alternative. "I'm not taking any chances with Percy's life," he said.

Kent spoke up. "How many men do the villains have between them?"

"Twice or more than I have at my disposal. It's all over the stews that Magnus has called in his favors. He means this to be a bloodbath," Gavin said darkly.

Kent and Harteford traded looks. "The Thames River Police is at your service, Mr. Hunt," Kent said. "However, we will still be at a disadvantage in terms of numbers."

"Not just numbers." Brows arched, Lady Draven said, "I doubt, Mr. Kent, that your band of merry investigators will last long in a rookery brawl."

Gavin thought her observation was spot on. Kent, however, stiffened, his pale eyes flashing with anger. "My men are capable of taking care of themselves in any circumstance. Besides, what would you know of such things, my lady?" His emphasis on the last word conveyed his doubt as to whether she, in fact, belonged in that category.

"I am no lady. I should think that obvious." Her tone had a mocking edge. "For a detective, you are remarkably obtuse, Mr. Kent."

The policeman flushed.

Gavin had no idea what was going on between the pair, but animosity crackled between them. Morgan must have sensed it too, for he said impatiently, "Enough you two. Let us focus on the task at hand and review the reconnaissance."

Earlier, Gavin had sent Alfie to scout out the old factory situated on the Thames. The urchin had drawn a rough map of the abandoned building based on what he'd been able to see from the outside.

"According to Alfie's report, there are four entryways," Gavin said, pointing to the places on the diagram. "All of them will be heavily guarded."

"Approach can be by road or water. Water will have the advantage of stealth," Kent said. "I can have my men patrol the area disguised as watermen."

Gavin had to admit that was a sound idea. "My men can take the streets near the factory. If the exchange goes awry, we can give the bastards a fight." Thinking of the numbers they'd be up against, he added grimly, "Though odds will be against us."

"We'll work with what we have," Morgan said.

"We'll need a signal from you so we know when to attack," Kent put in.

Gavin thought it over. No doubt the villains would confiscate his weapons. "I'll come up with something," he said. "Wait for it."

A knock sounded, and he bade entry to Will. Since Stewart's death, the head guard had taken on the position of overseeing the club. "Sorry to disturb you, Mr. Hunt. Thought you'd want to hear this." Will paused, his gaze wary upon the visitors.

"Speak freely," Gavin said.

"One of the footmen informed me that while you were out Miss Harper stopped by. Took that envelope you left for her and said to give you this."

Gavin took the packet and dismissed Will with a nod. Frowning, he untied the string and paper and found himself holding a bundle of letters. He unfolded the slip of parchment sitting atop the stack, scanning the untidy lettering.

Fair is fair. Thought you might use this and have better luck

*than that sod O'Brien who tried to take down our mutual
acquaintance with an empty pistol. For your health and mine, I hope
you do better. Have a care, lover—this shot could take your head off.
–E.*

Gavin spread the papers on the coffee table. With
disbelieving eyes, he read the three incriminating letters, all
inked in Kingsley's unmistakable hand. The bastard's conceit
was stunning: not only had he dared to spell out his licentious
desires for his mistress, he'd contrasted them with his apathy
and disdain for his *wife*.

"What is that?" Morgan said.

"Ammunition," Gavin said softly. He briefed the group on
Kingsley, Mavis, and Mavis' father, Bartholomew Black. "If
Black learns of his son-in-law's betrayal, he may intervene,"
Gavin concluded. "But to contact him will be to stir up a
hornet's nest. The man is dangerous, unpredictable—and he's
as like as not to shoot the messenger."

"I'll deliver the letters," Kent said.

"Black smells a Charley, and you'll be dead before you
reach twenty paces of his place," Gavin said bluntly. "It has to
be me."

"Risky. If you get detained, then Percy…" Morgan did not
have to finish the sentence.

"I'll do it." Before Gavin knew what she intended, Lady
Draven stood and collected the letters.

"The hell you will." Kent rose and glowered at her.

"I don't require your permission, Mr. Kent," she said,
tucking the letters in her reticule.

Morgan frowned. "This is far too dangerous—"

"Black may be dangerous, but he is just a man. We all have
our expertise, and mine happens to be the opposite sex. Do
you doubt that I am well equipped to deal with Black—or any
male for that matter?"

A derisive smile edged the blonde's lips, as if challenging them to deny her attractions. With her classical beauty, Lady Draven was no doubt accounted as an out and out stunner by most men—though, to Gavin's mind, she couldn't hold a candle to Percy. Then again, every woman paled next to his goddess... his fists curled. If Magnus and Kingsley harmed even a hair on Percy's head, he would tear their heads off.

"Lady Draven has a point," he said. "She has a better chance of getting an audience with Black than any of us. If nothing else, he'll see her out of curiosity."

"Out of the question," Kent snapped.

"I ask you to reconsider, my lady. Helena would have my head if anything happened to you," Morgan said.

"You do your part, I'll do mine," she said, sounding amused. "See you at midnight."

Lady Draven headed to the door, only to be blocked by Kent. He grabbed hold of her arm. "This has gone far enough," he said.

"No man touches me without my permission." Color flooded Lady Draven's high cheekbones, her emerald eyes flashing. "Release me this instant."

"Not until you give up this asinine plan."

"I said *release me*." In a swift movement, the baroness withdrew a delicate pistol from her skirts. She pointed it at Kent's heart.

The policeman did not budge. The baroness' eyes narrowed, her finger upon the trigger.

"Stand down, Kent. You cannot stop her, and obviously she can take care of herself," Morgan said wryly. "Perhaps Lady Draven would agree to take a few men as escorts?"

Lady Draven continued to glare at Kent, who released her with obvious reluctance.

"Men are the last thing I need," she said icily. "I can take care of myself." With that, she vanished out the door in a swish of silver skirts.

In the tense silence that followed, Gavin said, "That covers it. I'll ready my men. Morgan, I suppose you'll take the water route with Kent?"

"No." The marquess regarded him with a steady gaze. "I'm going in with you."

Chapter Thirty-Eight

UNDER THE CLOUDED midnight sky, Watson's Blacking Factory rose three stories, a crooked narrow building that bore an eerie resemblance to Grimes' flash house. The memory of that cesspit had branded Gavin though he'd lived there but a handful of days. He slid a look at his companion, who'd survived years in that place. From the stark lines on Morgan's face to his guarded posture, the man looked prepared to battle the demons of hell.

"You ready?" Gavin said in a low voice.

Morgan gave a terse nod. "Let's go in."

They entered through a creaking door. Long tables and benches lined the rectangular room. A single lamp sat upon one of the tables, releasing ghostly forms across the rotting pillars and beams and the wooden steps that led upward into darkness. Dim shapes piled high against the walls—equipment once used to make the blacking. The corrosive scent of sulfur and linseed oil permeated the air, glass from broken jars crunching beneath their boots. Something scampered across the floorboard, and Morgan flinched.

"Gentlemen, welcome." A few feet away, Kingsley parted from the shadows, his pistol glinting in the lamplight. When Gavin reached instinctively for his weapon, the bastard cocked the trigger. "Slowly now. Unless you want to get that pretty piece of yours killed."

Gavin froze as the rasp of matches came from above.

Lamps flared to life, revealing the men lining the first floor banister; all aimed pistols at him and Morgan. His pulse leapt at the sight of Percy. Despite her disheveled hair and the cloth gag wrapped around her mouth, she appeared otherwise unharmed, Praise God. Her gaze met his, and she began to struggle with the brute holding her by the arm.

"*Let her go.*" Gavin started for the stairs.

"Not so fast, Hunt." The click of Kingsley's pistol halted him. "You may not care if you die—but do you want to see her throat slit?"

On the floor above, Percy's captor raised a blade to her neck.

Breathing hard, Gavin felt a restraining grip on his arm.

"Have a care," Morgan said quietly. "Percy's life is at stake."

"Indeed," Kingsley drawled. "Your weapons, gentlemen."

With no other choice, Gavin and Morgan allowed Kingsley's men to take their guns. They were shoved to their knees, their hands trussed behind their backs. Guards surrounded them as Kingsley pulled up a chair and sat, smirking. "You were told to come alone, Hunt. Who is your friend here?"

"I am the Marquess of Harteford." Gavin had to give Morgan credit. Though bound like a pig for the spit, the fellow's voice rang with authority. "I demand that you release Miss Fines immediately."

Kingsley laughed. "A nob, eh? Well, your demands are no good here, dear fellow."

"What about my coin?"

Kingsley's eyes narrowed, and Gavin could practically see the wheels of greed spinning in the bastard's head. "Go on."

"A thousand pounds," Morgan said evenly, "for setting us free."

"Not a bad offer." Kingsley signaled to the brute holding

Percy.

Gavin grit his teeth as the guard dragged Percy down the steps none too gently. Smiling, Kingsley gestured for her to be brought over. When the bastard pulled her into his lap, Gavin roared, jumping to his feet. The guard's fist slammed into his jaw and knocked him to the ground. Blood gushed in his mouth, lights dancing behind his eyes. Then Percy's muffled cries broke through, and he struggled to get up. The guard held him down with a boot to the chest, crushing him against the floor. An object stabbed through the back of his jacket.

Glass. Though his wrists were bound, he edged his fingers upward beneath his back, trying to get at the shard. He encountered grit, useless bits. Then he grasped it. The sharp edges cut into his fingers as he began to saw it back and forth against the ropes, careful to keep his movements slight. Not that he need have worried—the guard was focused on the negotiations.

"Let her go." Morgan's voice had a lethal edge. "I'll give you the money."

"Surely this spitfire is worth more than a thousand pounds," Kingsley mused, running a finger down Percy's arm.

One of the ropes gave a little. *Almost there.* Gavin could almost feel his hands wrapping around Kingsley's neck.

"How much do you want?" Morgan said.

"Ten thousand pounds," Kingsley said.

Morgan didn't blink. "Done. You release Miss Fines and Mr. Hunt. When I have proof of their safety, I will go with you to get the money."

"I'm afraid that won't be possible." Gavin stilled as Magnus' voice came from above. The old man hobbled down the stairs. "This wasn't part of the plan, Kingsley."

"For ten thousand pounds, I'll consider an amendment," his partner replied.

"Give Hunt and Morgan to me," Magnus said. "Keep the girl. You can ransom her from her family or keep her as your whore. 'Tis up to you."

The ropes slid from Gavin's wrists. Grasping the glass shard, he forced himself to remain still. To watch and wait for the moment to attack. From his position, he counted more than a dozen armed men. Too many to take on—he'd have to go straight for their leader. Grab Kingsley and signal Kent to attack. Yet how could he get Percy to safety before all hell broke loose? Perhaps the large cauldron in the corner would shield her from the gunfire...

"You're... Jack Spades, aren't you?" Morgan's haunted voice cut into his planning. The marquess' face had drained of color, a quiver crossing his wide shoulders. "I... I remember you."

For some reason, Percy nodded emphatically, her words muffled by the cloth.

Who the hell is Jack Spades? Why does Morgan look like he's seen the devil himself?

An icy hand gripped Gavin's gut as Magnus laughed—a menacing sound that was at odds with the old man's decrepit shell.

"And as I recall, you were one of Grimes' pets, my lord," Magnus purred. "Perhaps even his favorite?"

The marquess flinched. Anger roiled in Gavin's veins, his grip tightening on the glass. *Morgan had no choice, you bastard. He didn't deserve his fate—any more than I did.*

"What do you want?" Morgan said in a low voice.

"I've been keeping an eye on you for some time. From the gutter to the *ton*—not many could pull it off. To top that, three years ago you survived my associate's attempt at blackmail." Magnus shook his head. "You're a tough bastard, your lordship, make no mistake about that."

"You... you were behind the extortion? That was how that

villain knew about my past with Grimes—you gave him the information," Morgan said slowly.

Harteford... powerful man. Wouldn't want to tangle with him myself. Recalling Magnus' words, Gavin felt chilled to the core. How long had the old conniver been weaving this malevolent web?

"Aye, but fat lot of good that did my partner, eh? Behind bars and not a shilling to show for it." Magnus gave a philosophical shrug. "This time around, I won't let greed cloud my judgment. I want the past buried once and for all." Withdrawing a blade from his pocket, he advanced toward the marquess. "And the way for that to happen is for you and Hunt to die."

Thinking quickly, Gavin twisted his head toward Kingsley. "You're going to let Magnus rob you of ten thousand pounds?" he said.

Frowning, Kingsley shoved Percy aside. Though the gag slipped from her, one of the guards grabbed her by the arm. "Think this through, old man," Kingsley said, blocking his partner's path. "With this fat purse, we'll take over the stews. No one will be able to challenge us—not even my sodding father-in-law."

"We'll have enough power as it is. A deal's a deal." Magnus' gaze narrowed. "Out of my way."

"Even if you kill Lord Harteford and Mr. Hunt, the past won't die."

Percy's voice drew everyone's attention. A perfect distraction. Gavin tensed, his muscles readied to spring.

"Mr. Kingsley and I both know that 'twas you who torched the flash house that night," she continued in a clear voice. "'Twas you who left Mr. Hunt to take the blame."

Magnus set the fire? Shock paralyzed Gavin.

"It was *you*? How... how did you know to be there that night?" Morgan said.

Magnus's gaze turned sly. "I suppose there's no harm in you knowing the truth before you die. I'd been watching the house for some time. Waiting for the opportunity to get Grimes—*eye for an eye*, as the saying goes." He laughed mirthlessly. "Then one night I caught an unusual sight: Grimes' favorite boy escaping out of his master's window."

Grooves of tension bracketed Morgan's mouth.

"Knowing how much Grimes enjoyed his nightly entertainments, I guessed one of two things had happened: either Grimes had fallen down dead drunk... or the boy had somehow incapacitated his master. Either way, my golden chance had arrived. I entered through the back entrance, went up to Grimes' quarters, and there I found my nemesis..."—Magnus paused—"*alive.*"

Gavin's breath came faster.

Morgan rasped, "That's not possible. I stabbed Grimes in the chest."

"Aye, and after all these years, I get to thank you for your assistance. You'd missed the bastard's heart, but injured him enough so that he couldn't put up a fight. So that he had to watch, to suffer"—a maddened glow lit Magnus' eyes—"while I carved his heart out."

"I... I didn't kill him?" Morgan said hoarsely.

"That pleasure was mine." Satisfaction oozed from the old man's voice. "When I finished with him, I wanted no trace left of Grimes or my deeds that night. So I set the place aflame. Imagine my delight when a boy was later apprehended and jailed in my stead."

Gavin was shaking now. *Hold on. Don't lose control—*

"I had the perfect alibi: a boy who thought he'd killed Grimes, and another blamed for the fire. Fate does enjoy herself at our expense, however. I nearly fell off my chair when I learned from my spy that *Hunt* was the boy who'd served for arson. For years, I'd been doing business with the man whose life I had ruined." Shaking his head in wonderment, Magnus said, "I knew that if you and Hunt ever got together, the truth would come out. I realized then that I had loose ends to tie."

"The attack at Vauxhall... that was you?" Gavin managed.

"That bungled attempt was Kingsley's own doing. I approached him afterward, helped him to get rid of Lyon and O'Brien." Magnus gave his partner a meaningful look. "Kingsley, you need my help to take over Covent Garden, so get out of my way."

"Your past is your problem." Kingsley raised his pistol at Magnus. "Drop the blade. I'm not losing ten thousand pounds over your stupidity."

The knife clattered to the ground. Magnus said calmly, "You'll be sorry for double-crossing me Kingsley."

"Tie him up," Kingsley ordered.

In a quick movement, Magnus grabbed the lamp off the table. Held it above his head. "Anyone comes near me, and you'll all die. For years, linseed has soaked into the walls and floors of this place, and I added more for good measure... combined with gunpowder." A devious smile crossed his face. "I drop this,"—the fire shook in his hand—"and the place explodes."

"You're insane." Looking pale, Kingsley held out a hand. "Give me that."

"Shoot me, and I'll drop it," Magnus said.

Seeing his opportunity, Gavin sprang and caught Kingsley by surprise, wrenching back the other man's weapon arm. Kingsley yelped in pain, dropping the pistol. Gavin pressed the lethal edge of glass against the man's throat.

"Tell your men to drop their weapons," he snarled. "Those on the second floor—toss your arms down the steps." To show he meant business, he let the glass slice deeper, releasing blood.

"For God's sake, do as he says!" Kingsley cried.

Weapons rained to the floor. Morgan rolled to Magnus' fallen knife, freeing himself in an instant. He grabbed a pair of pistols. "On the floor, hands behind your back," he ordered. Once he had the guards subdued, he strode to Percy and cut through her bonds. Without a word, she scooped up weapons and ran over to Gavin.

"Here you go," she said.

Their gazes held. *So much I want to say to you. Soon, love.*

He took the pistol from her, kept it trained on Kingsley as he addressed the man responsible for his suffering. "Game's finished, Magnus," he said. "We have the place surrounded. Put down that lamp, and I'll let you live."

A crazed look came into Magnus' eyes. "I'll take the other option." And he threw the lamp toward Gavin's feet.

Glass smashed. A roar filled the room, sucking the air from it. Gavin yelled out Percy's name the instant an explosion rocked the room. The force hurtled him backward into the air. The ground fell free beneath him, and he slammed into darkness.

Chapter Thirty-Nine

PULSE RACING, PERCY stumbled through the black haze, coughing as thick smoke choked her lungs. The whole place was ablaze—she couldn't see past the wall of flames rising higher and higher. "Gavin, where are you?" she shouted.

"Percy?"

Her head whipped around at the faint sound of her name. Where had it come from? Then she saw it: a crater in the floor. Rushing over, she peered over the smoldering edge. "Thank goodness," she cried, spying Gavin sprawled on the floor below. "I'll be right there."

"No! Don't come down—"

Ignoring him, she lowered herself over the edge, a pile of splintered wood breaking her landing. She scrambled to him. "We've got to get out of here."

He shook his head. "Can't. I'm trapped."

'Twas then that she saw the toppled pillar pinning his left leg. Dashing over, she pushed at the wood beam. It didn't budge. Cursing, she tried harder, shoving with all her might.

"Percy, there's no time. Look at me." The urgency in his voice made her obey. His eyes glittered in his soot-streaked face. "I want you to go. *Now*."

"I'm not leaving you." Perspiration bloomed on her forehead as she shouted, "Help! Can anyone hear me? We're down here in the basement!"

"It's no use. The building could blow at any minute," he bit out. "You have to run."

"Not without you." She scanned the room for anything she could use as a lever. Perhaps the fire iron...

"I love you, Percy," he said in guttural tones.

The stark certainty in his eyes made her heart beat faster, if possible. The man had dashed bad timing. "I love you, too," she said. "Now we have to find a way—"

His hand cupped her cheek. "If you love me, do as I say. I've never begged anyone for anything, but I'm begging you— leave me," he rasped. "Let me die in peace, knowing you are safe."

"No," she said, tears clouding her eyes.

"Percy! Where are you?"

She jumped up in relief. "Nick!" she shouted. "Over here by the stairs! Be careful—there's a hole in the floor."

Seconds later, Nick's soot-covered face appeared over the edge. "Hold on, I'm coming down." He landed on his feet and swiftly assessed the situation. "I'm going to lift the pillar as much as I can. Percy, you pull Hunt free. On the count of three."

Percy positioned herself next to Gavin's trapped leg as Nick gripped the wood beam on the opposite side.

"One... two... *three.*" Nick's powerful shoulders flexed. Sweat dripped down his face as he strained to move the heavy wood. The beam inched upward... Gavin used his good leg to shove away, Percy helping to drag his injured limb free. An instant later, the pillar crashed to the ground again.

Percy threw her arms around Gavin's neck. "Are you alright?" she cried.

His hand tangled in her hair. "Shh, love, I'm fine." His voice hoarsened. "Morgan... my thanks."

"Time for that later," Nicholas said. "Can you walk?"

Gavin grimaced as he tried to move his left leg. "Don't

think so."

"I'll help you," Nick said decisively. "First we'll have to figure out how to hoist you up." They all looked upward into floor above, a hellish inferno of swirling fire and smoke.

Then Percy remembered. "They kept me here in the basement earlier. There was a door, leading outside. I think I saw The Thames."

"Back of the building," Nick said. "Let's go."

Between the three of them, they managed to get Gavin on his feet. With one arm around Nick's shoulders and Nick's arm around his waist, Gavin limped along. Percy led the way, clearing the fallen debris and navigating around the growing flames. At last, they came to the familiar room at the end of the corridor.

"Over there." Racing over to the door, Percy wrenched it open. The three of them struggled up the steps... and into chaos.

The battle outside raged as fiercely as the fire within. Gavin's men and The Thames River Police were fighting valiantly against Kingsley's brutes, but they were far outnumbered. Percy called out a warning as villains surrounded Mr. Kent, knives flashing.

Setting Gavin onto the gravel, Nicholas ordered, "Stay with Hunt, Percy. I've got to help Kent."

"You'll stay right where you are, my lord." Kingsley appeared from behind them, his hair singed and a pistol in each hand. "I've got Hunt and Harteford," he shouted. "Throw down your weapons, or I'll put holes in them both."

The fighting slowly came to a halt. Kingsley's men corralled the others, who stood back to back, their glances wary.

"Now that that's settled," Kingsley said, "I believe the price for your freedom has just gone up. Fifteen thousand, Harteford."

Nicholas gave a terse nod. "Whatever you say."

"Forget it, Morgan," Gavin said. "He's going to kill us anyway."

Kingsley cocked his pistol. "Shut your mouth, Hunt. I've a mind to dispense with you for all the trouble you've caused."

Just as Percy moved to shield Gavin, the thunderous sound of horses broke through the night. A procession of carriages sped in their direction and formed a circle around them. Enormous ebony steeds pawed at the ground; from the windows of the vehicles, men in greatcoats aimed pistols at all of them. A liveried footman scurried to let down the steps of the main carriage, a monstrously elegant equipage of gleaming black and inlaid mother-of-pearl.

A man wearing a grey wig and the fashion of the last century descended. Barrel-chested and short, he nonetheless had an incontrovertible air of command. He pointed the jeweled knob of his walking stick at Kingsley.

"Wh-what are you doing here?" Kingsley stammered. All bravado had fled him, and his voice shook with fear.

Who is this man? Percy wondered.

"Is that any way to greet your own father-in-law?" The newcomer approached Kingsley, his tone deep and menacing. "Then again, it appears you're lackin' in respect for my family in general."

"I—I don't know what you mean, sir. If you're referring to this incursion," Kingsley said, his eyes darting side to side, "I meant to surprise you with my prowess. I've a fortune coming from tonight, one which I'll of course be splitting with—"

"Ain't talkin' 'bout money. Talkin' about my Mavis. The treasure I entrusted you with."

Kingsley paled. "I've made her happy. Ask her yourself. When she returns from Bath—"

"That's the one blessing in all o' this, I suppose. What my

baby doesn't know won't hurt 'er." The stranger sighed. "She'll mourn, poor dove, but she'll find true love the next time. I'll see to that."

"You crazy old bastard. You're not getting rid of me," Kingsley snarled, raising his pistol.

A shot rang through the night. Kingsley fell to the ground, screaming as blood gushed from his arm. Smoke rose from the pistol of the guard atop the main carriage. Two other men came forward and dragged Kingsley, struggling and cursing, into one of the other conveyances. The door closed, and he was heard no more.

Mr. Kent spoke first. "We must attend to the fire."

Black waved his walking stick, and his men dashed to help the others gather buckets and water from the river. Mr. Kent started to follow, but stopped. He turned with his shoulders hunched.

"Mr. Black, if I may ask," he said, "where is Lady Draven?"

Black glowered at him. "Dropped 'er off at 'ome, o' course. Don't think I'd bring a fine lady as that to a place like this?"

"No, of course not," Kent said in a tight voice. "Obliged, sir."

With a stiff nod, the investigator loped off to assist with the fire.

Nicholas stepped forward and bowed. "Thank you, Mr. Black. I am in your debt."

The man looked him up and down. A grin broke across his face. "A marquess, bowing to me. Ain't that priceless." Chuckling, he peered down at Gavin, who remained sitting on the ground. "What about you, Hunt? Ain't you going to make a leg for me, too?"

"It'd be half a leg and a bloody one at that," Gavin said.

Black laughed until he wiped at his eyes. "I've 'eard about

you, Hunt. Liked most o' what I 'eard, too. Don't suppose you'd be browsin' the marriage mart?"

"Oh no, sir," Percy blurted. As all eyes turned to her, her cheeks warmed. "That is, Mr. Hunt is otherwise engaged. Um, to me."

"That so, Hunt?" Black's brows nearly reached his wig.

"Not quite," Gavin said. Percy's breath stopped, found a hitched rhythm when he continued in a grave voice, "Miss Fines, would you have a seat next to me, please?"

Mesmerized by the burnished intensity in his eyes, she did as he asked.

He took her hand in his own. "I said once I wouldn't go down on bended knee. But I want you to know I would for you, if it wasn't for this leg." Though ruddy color spread over his cheekbones, he shot a defiant look at their audience and added, "And I don't give a damn who knows it."

She nodded, joy welling in her eyes.

"I want to do this right this time. I don't have a poet's tongue or fancy words to declare myself," he said, "and there's still no violins. All I can do is beg your forgiveness for my mistakes. For not trusting you when I should have. For being so bloody stupid and letting you go."

"I understand, Gavin," she said. "Truly, I do."

"I don't deserve you, Percy." When she tried to protest, he cupped her cheek, pressing his thumb against her lips. "You're too good for me, love, there's no denying it. You're brave and loyal, so damnably sweet—you light all the dark corners of my soul." Emotion glittered in his eyes. "In return, you'd be taking on a scoundrel, scarred inside and out, who didn't even know he had a heart until he met you."

"You have a heart, Gavin. You always have," she sniffled.

"It beats only for you. And I swear that if you will have me, Percy, I will never give you cause to regret that decision. I will love and protect you until the day I die," he said fiercely.

Her tears overflowed.

Gripping her hand, he said, "Will you marry me, Persephone Fines? Will you accept me as I am now? Knowing that I will strive to be a better man, to one day be the husband you deserve?"

"Oh, Gavin," she whispered, "I love you exactly as you are."

"Then... you'll have me?"

She adored the note of wonder in his tone. "Yes," she said, smiling through her tears, "a thousand times, *yes*."

He gathered her in his arms, and the kiss they shared shot fireworks across the sky. An orchestra played, the world rocked on its axis... though perhaps that last part was due to Mr. Black's impatient thumping of his walking stick against the ground.

"Chit's got pluck, I'll give 'er that." With a grunt, Black warned, "You'll 'ave your 'ands full, Hunt."

"I wouldn't have it any other way," Gavin said, giving her a squeeze.

"Well, my Mavis might need a bit o' female companionship when she returns. Ain't much genteel company in the stews. Maybe you'll 'ave 'er for tea one o' these days?"

Percy sensed it wasn't a question. She was filled with too much gratitude to care. "Of course, Mr. Black," she said sincerely. "I should love to meet your daughter."

He nodded. "I'll go see about Magnus."

Gavin stilled. "You have him?"

"Caught him alongside the road. Old goat caused quite a bit o' trouble for me, and I planned to teach 'im a lesson." Black shrugged. "But if you want 'im, 'e's yours."

Percy felt the quivering tension pass through Gavin. She didn't fool herself about the world her husband-to-be came from and wouldn't blame him for whatever choice he made.

He had suffered so much because of Magnus.

Yet would more bloodshed bring him peace?

Gavin exhaled slowly. "I'll take him. Over to the magistrates."

"Charleys, eh? Well, 'tis your business." Snorting, Black started back toward his carriage, his voice drifting back. "Off we go, boys—an' to all a good night."

"What about your revenge, Hunt?" Nicholas asked.

"The past has been laid to rest—all of it." Clearing his throat, Gavin looked up at Nick and extended his hand. Nick took it. Percy thought her heart couldn't get any fuller, yet it did to see two of the men she loved most find peace with their past... and one another.

The moment passed, and both men coughed and looked away.

"Well, I suppose that's for the best," Nicholas said, "as it appears we are to be family."

"I have your permission, then?" Percy said brightly.

Nick gave her a wry look. "Would it matter?"

"Not at all. But I was hoping you might help persuade Mama," she admitted.

"Don't worry about your mother, love," Gavin said, pulling her close. "I'll speak for myself. In fact, I already have a speech planned."

"You do? Whatever will you say?"

His tender smile sent joy skipping through her. "I'll tell her that I don't begrudge a moment of my past because all of it led me to you. That I thought I wanted revenge, but all I've ever needed is your love." He paused, and that wicked gleam she loved entered his eyes. "And I'll thank her for giving me permission to wed you in a proper ceremony. To spare me the inconvenience of having to cart you off like your namesake."

Percy choked back a laugh at the none-too-subtle threat. "You wouldn't really do that, would you?"

"I'll do anything to have you, buttercup," he said solemnly. "Mine, remember?"

"Mine, too," she said and, still smiling, pulled him close for a kiss.

Chapter Forty

THE NEXT THREE months passed in a blur—though to Gavin's accounting, still not fast enough. To him, waiting twelve weeks to have Percy was nothing short of torture. Yet according to Mrs. Fines and Lady Harteford, that was the absolute minimum time necessary to prepare for a wedding, and given their tenuous acceptance of him, he'd grudgingly acquiesced. In truth, he needed the time for his leg to heal— a fracture, as it turned out—for he'd be damned if he hobbled down the aisle toward his bride-to-be.

There were other matters to attend to as well.

John Magnus had been sentenced to life imprisonment. From the looks of him at the trial—which both Gavin and Morgan had attended—the old bastard wasn't for long anyway. It nonetheless brought Gavin a measure of peace to see justice finally served. Afterward, he and Morgan had gone to a coffeehouse and discussed the future.

To Gavin's shock, Morgan had offered him a partnership in Fines & Co. *You can't stay in the gaming business forever*, the marquess had said. *Think of Percy and the children you may have one day. Do you want them exposed to that sort of life?*

He... didn't.

He hadn't given Morgan an answer as of yet, but the fact that he was now considering joining forces with the man he'd once hated spoke to how much his life had changed. Freed from the past, from his own anger, he was beginning to feel like a different man. More like the one he'd promised Percy he'd one day be. At times, 'twas disconcerting, but mostly it felt... right.

Though every moment he spent with Percy was under his future mama-in-law's eagle eye, Gavin relished their cozy talks in the Fines' parlor or garden. Percy wanted to know everything about his past, and he told her, holding nothing back. One Sunday afternoon, she accompanied him to the cemetery where he'd buried Stewart. She held his hand as he said his final farewell to his old friend.

The love shining in Percy's eyes had made their long engagement bearable. Almost.

Now, on the night of his wedding, Gavin paced the length of his suite in his dressing gown. Determined to give Percy the kind of life she deserved, he'd purchased a fashionable townhouse close to the Harteford residence. They'd come here after the wedding brunch hosted by the marquess and marchioness; after meeting the line of servants, Percy had excused herself to get ready for bed.

Bed. His eyes shot to the door of the adjoining bedchamber. The only barrier that separated him from his new bride. Even as elation and lust rushed through him, he felt unaccountably... nervous. 'Twas the damnedest thing. For so long he'd been intent upon seducing her; now that she finally belonged to him, a twinge of apprehension mingled with his desire.

He scowled, thinking that he had Paul Fines to thank for the bridegroom jitters. His new relation had thrown him a party last week, a silly tribute to Gavin's last moments of freedom. As if Gavin could give a damn about his bachelorhood—given the choice, he'd have thrown it over for Percy in a heartbeat. But he knew a white flag when it was being flown. And now that Fines was staying away from the cards and appeared sober most of the time, Gavin didn't mind the cull so much. So he'd gone.

He'd spent the night being plied with drink and bawdy stories told by well-bred gents. Though Gavin was no stranger to depravity, all the talk of wedding night deflowering had unsettled him. He'd never been with a virgin before. Apparently, they bled. Some even screamed.

A lot.

His hands went clammy at the thought of causing Percy pain. Of her turning away from him in fear or revulsion. Going to the liquor cabinet, he downed a shot of liquid courage. *Don't be an idiot, Hunt. She wants you—she loves you.* Shaking his head at his own foolishness, he went to the door and knocked. When no response came, he drew back his shoulders and opened the door.

The shriek made him jump from his skin.

"*Pardon, monsieur!* Mrs. Hunt is not ready—" A prune-faced maid barred the way to the room like a soldier on his last stand. From the expression on her face, she clearly thought she was protecting her new mistress from a fate worse than death. Weren't the French supposed to be blasé when it came to sexual matters? Perhaps the maid knew something about wedding nights that Gavin didn't. He swallowed.

"Is that you, Mr. Hunt?"

Following the direction of Percy's sweet voice, he spied her silhouette behind the silk screen in the far corner. The candlelight outlined her nubile figure as she dressed. The sight of her entranced him and brought him back to reality. This was his Percy, now his *wife*. He'd never hurt her. Then the shadow of her hands began smoothing along her body, and lust bolted through him, momentarily scattering his wits.

For God's sake, man, rein it in.

"Er, do you need more time?" he said.

"*Absolutment.*" The maid nodded vigorously.

"Not really," Percy called out at the same time. "I'm

almost done. Thank you for your help, Yvette—you can run along now."

With a last suspicious look at Gavin, the maid departed.

Gavin sat in one of the armchairs by the fire. Silence stretched as he racked his brain for conversation. Unfortunately, his ability to think was severely compromised by Percy's seductive movements behind the screen. God, he hadn't been alone with her for months. Now to see her this way... He felt randier than a sailor on leave.

A minute later Percy emerged, and the sight of her unbalanced him utterly. He'd seen her in every kind of get-up, from breeches to turbans, but never in the simplicity of her night clothes. She was a bleeding *goddess*. In a white flannel wrapper dotted with pink flowers, her golden hair falling in shining waves to her waist, she'd never looked more vibrant and pure.

More virginal.

He stood, his chest tangled with want and the desire to do this right.

"Hello, Mr. Hunt," she said.

Her smile loosened some of the knots. "Hello, Mrs. Hunt." He cleared his throat. "May I say you look ravishing?"

"You may." Her eyes sparkled as she approached him. "You look rather ravishing yourself, sir."

His rod twitched at her compliment, eager to prove just how ravishing he found her. *Stay in control and go slow*, he told himself firmly.

"There's champagne and food," he said, gesturing to the table by the fire. "Would you care to have some?"

"Not really. I'm still full from the brunch." Curling onto the settee, she patted the cushion next to her. "Won't you sit with me?"

He lowered himself next to her, careful to keep his distance lest he pounce on her. Her fresh, citrusy scent made his mouth water. His shaft swelled.

"It's a bit strange to be alone, isn't it?" Percy said into the awkward moment.

"There's no need to rush things. We have all night," he said. To show her he meant it, he added in conversational tones, "I thought the wedding went well, don't you?"

She gave him a look from beneath her lashes. "Very well. To be honest, I wasn't sure how the guests would rub together."

The guest list had represented a hodgepodge of society. Peers of the realm had sat side by side with men from the rookery and middling class folk. For the most part, everyone had behaved themselves—even Alfie, who'd performed the duty of ring bearer with surprising dignity. A near mishap had occurred when the Harteford twins ran into the table holding the wedding cake, but Davey and his brother had managed to save the masterpiece from toppling to the ground. For Gavin, the only sad moment had been Stewart's marked absence; he wished his mentor could have seen Percy, the most radiant bride ever—

Gavin jerked as said bride slid onto his lap. "Percy?" Her name came out as more of a groan for her bottom wriggled enticingly against his member.

"Keep talking if you'd like," she said cheerfully. "I understand 'tis normal to be a trifle anxious on one's wedding night. Or so everyone keeps telling me."

"You little minx," he said, his eyes narrowing. "Are you laughing at me?"

"Only a little." Her hands snuck past the lapels of his robe, and he sucked in his breath when her nails scored lightly against his taut muscles. "I thought I was the virgin here."

He caught her hands. "Aren't you nervous, buttercup?" he said seriously.

She tipped her head to one side. "Not really. No. I'd

describe my feelings more as..."

He waited, the epitome of husbandly virtue.

"... impatient? Ready and willing?"

That did it. He took her laughing mouth in a hungry kiss, and all thought of restraint fled at the taste of her, his Percy, sweeter than any nectar. How had he gone weeks without touching her this way? She kissed him back with a passionate urgency that told him she'd missed him just as much.

Lifting her into his arms, he strode toward the bed. He set her down on her feet, his hands fumbling with the tie on her robe as she planted hot kisses along his jaw. God in heaven, she set him afire. He pushed the flannel off her shoulders... and his breath stuttered.

"What have you got on there?" he rasped.

Percy peered up at him with laughing eyes. "Do you like it?"

"*Like* is not the word I would use." He ran reverent hands over her white shoulders, fingering the thin cherry straps. "Where the devil did you get this?"

"From Helena's modiste. Helena advised against night-rails, especially the big, frilly ones. She said husbands don't prefer them—what do you think?"

"I think the marchioness has an eye for fashion. I think you should let her dress you from now on." His blood throbbing with anticipation, he murmured, "Give us a turn, love."

Looking a bit bashful, his bride did a slow pirouette. The red silk clung to her form like a second skin, and the slits at the side offered delicious views of her sleek legs. In the front, the neckline plunged nearly to her navel, the deep V filled with peek-a-boo lace of a matching shade. As for the back... there was none.

He pulled her close, his hand on the smooth, bare dip of her spine. "Do you know how irresistible you are?" he breathed against her neck.

"I'm glad you think so." She sighed as he kissed her shoulder. "Hopefully that means we can get on with things?"

Chuckling at her impatience, he lay her back on the mattress, filling his gaze with the luscious sight of her. His treasure. Covetous as Hades, he ran his hands through her silken tresses. Tonight, he was determined to pleasure his Persephone so that she'd want to stay with him forever. Lowering his head to one firm breast, he suckled the nipple through the silk. He adored her response to him, the way she gasped his name, gripped his hair. He flicked his tongue, teasing the bud into full pertness before moving on to lavish the same attention on the other.

"Oh, Gavin, don't stop," she moaned.

He blew softly against the wet silk, and she trembled. "Not until you come for me, love," he promised. "Again and again..."

Kneeling between her thighs, he drew the red silk upward to her waist. His shaft throbbed as his gaze followed the shapely line of her legs all the way up to the crown of fluffy blond curls. He swallowed, seeing the dew gathered upon her soft little puss and remembering the sweetness of her honey.

"If you don't touch me, Gavin, I'll go mad," she said.

His blood heated further at her beseeching tone. He *wanted* her mad for him. Wanted her as mad for him as he was for her. "Touch you... where?"

"Stop teasing. You know," she said.

"Show me, my love. Touch yourself so I'll have no doubt where you want me."

She bit her lip, her passion-flushed cheeks growing even pinker. He wondered if he'd pushed her too far. But then her delicate fingers crept downward. He watched, his cock hard as granite, as she shyly petted herself.

"There. Are you satisfied?" she said in a breathless voice.

He covered her hand with his, encouraging her movement. "Not until you are," he said huskily. She moaned as he guided their joined fingers to her pearl, rubbing her sensitive bud with insistent pressure. His chest heaved as her moisture coated their fingers. Suddenly, her hips bucked off the mattress as she gave a sharp gasp.

With a growl, he buried his mouth in her pussy, needing to taste her pleasure. He devoured her like a man starved. Her womanly ambrosia intoxicated him; he couldn't get enough of her. As he feasted on her honeyed flesh, he eased a finger inside her. Tight. Unbelievably lush and hot. He began to move his digit, slowly at first, then fucking her steadily as he ate her. Tremors took his wife anew, her sweet cries filling his ears as another orgasm shook her.

Surfacing from an ocean of bliss, Percy gazed up at her husband. With his eyes wild and his tawny hair disheveled, he looked like a man driven to the edge of arousal. Scraps of her negligee were scattered across the bed. He'd brought her to the peak of ecstasy three times already... yet for some reason he hadn't made the move to take his own pleasure. Then she remembered his earlier nervousness.

Silly man, did he truly fear to hurt her?

"Ready for more, my love?" he said.

Clearly, it was time to take matters into her own hands. She found the tie on his robe, tugged away the knot. His sharp intake of breath filled her ear at the same time that his rampant manhood overflowed her palms. She stroked his deliciously hard flesh, adoring the feel of him, his desperate groans as she pumped him the way he'd once shown her.

"I'm ready for you," she whispered, kissing his quivering jaw. "Ready to be yours in every way."

"Percy... " His eyes shut as she explored a bit further. Nestled against crisp, dark hair, his sac felt heavy, intriguingly supple. She gave an experimental squeeze. "Christ, woman, I'm not going to last if you do that," he gasped.

"I don't want you to last. I just want you inside me." She smiled at him. "Now, please?"

A crazed look came over him. He tore off his robe, and she gloried in the feel of his hard muscled length pressing her into the mattress, his stiff manhood prodding between her thighs. He smoothed a strand of hair off her forehead.

"I love you, Percy. I'd give anything not to hurt you." His scar taut, he said hoarsely, "I want this to be perfect for you."

"It will be perfect. Because we are together." She cupped his hard jaw in her hands. "You're the man I love, now and forever."

A shudder crossed his heavy shoulders. The intent, adoring look he gave her curled her toes. Her name left his lips in a ragged whisper as he pressed forward. She felt a stinging stretch, a hot, thick glide ... and then he was inside her, filling her so completely. A part of her. Tears spilled from her eyes.

"Am I hurting you? Should I stop?" The cords of his neck stood out in stark relief as he held himself still above her, clearly battling for control.

"Don't ever stop," she whispered, wrapping her legs around his lean hips. "Love me, Gavin. Love me as I love you."

"Always," he vowed.

He began to move inside her. Slow, steady thrusts that took away her innocence and replaced it with something far more wondrous. The feeling of belonging she'd yearned for all her life. His eyes never left her face, even as a pleasure flush spread across his lean cheeks and the force and pace of his lovemaking intensified. Her discomfort faded, his deep surges calling forth a new excitement. She moaned as the sensations built, different and more intense than before. Seeking relief from the tension, she instinctively raised her hips to meet his rhythm.

"That's it, love, move with me." Pleasure slurred his words. "I knew it would be this way for us. So hot, so perfect."

"Yes, yes." She clutched his bulging forearms as he drove even deeper, pushing out her breath. The coil in her belly tautened unbearably.

"Can't last much longer. You're milking me... like a *fist*." His eyes shut. "Feels too bloody good…"

"Then let go. Come for me, Gavin," she whispered.

"*God, yes.*" His eyes rolled back in his head as he yelled out.

His big body shuddered again and again as he climaxed. His fierce heat shot deep inside her, and the forceful jets propelled her over the edge once more. She tumbled freely, moorings lost to the wild joy of being in her husband's arms.

Later, they lay on their sides, facing each other. Their bodies remained joined, and she saw her own sense of wonderment reflected in his ore-flecked eyes. He skimmed his knuckles against her jaw.

"I'd say that was worth the wait, buttercup," he murmured.

She sighed dreamily. "It was worth *anything*."

"Spoken like a gracious loser, my love."

"Wait a minute." Frowning at his smug expression, she said, "Who are you calling a loser?"

"Strictly speaking, this was our fifth meeting. Therefore, you just lost the wager." He patted her rump with satisfaction. "Don't worry, sweetheart, I won't rub your nose in the fact... too often."

"Why you... *cheat*! I assumed the bet was off when you gave Paul back his vowels. This isn't fair," she said indignantly.

"Would you like a re-match then?" Before she could reply, he rolled on top of her. His renewed vigor made her breath catch. "I believe I could be *up* for it."

"It won't make for much of a wager now that we're in love and married. There's no reason why we shouldn't go to bed together whenever we want," she grumbled.

"Truer words were never spoken." Smiling, he touched his nose to hers. "If it's any consolation, Percy, I might have taken the wager... but you have won my heart and soul."

Dash the man—how could she argue with that?

With a happy sigh, she gave herself up to his kiss.

Epilogue

GAVIN AWAKENED TO the rocking motion of ocean waves. For a moment, he felt disoriented, then the warm body curled against his righted his world. His lips curved as he ran a possessive hand over his wife's bare hip, burying his face in her fragrant hair. Last night, he'd inaugurated their wedding trip by teaching her to ride astride; with her pretty tits bouncing and her hips gyrating wantonly atop him, she'd driven them both mad with pleasure.

She sighed, her bottom snuggling against his rapidly hardening groin. Yet she slept on. Apparently, he'd worn his insatiable little hoyden out.

Not wanting to disturb her rest, he gently extricated himself and tucked the blankets around her. Donning his clothes, he made his way to the cabin door, pausing at the small desk. A familiar leather-bound volume lay open, and he couldn't resist reading the last paragraph again:

As Miss Priscilla Farnham looked up into the face that had haunted her dreams, she was no longer afraid. The villain had shed his disguise; before her was a prince amongst men. Taking a deep breath, she said the words that would change her life.

"I do," she said.

Her new husband bent to kiss her, and her heart sang with joy and the certainty that she'd found her own happily ever after at last.

Lips curved, Gavin headed up to the deck. Several sleepy-eyed sailors, employees of Fines & Co., bowed respectfully as he passed. He nodded back; as the newly joined partner of the company, he wanted to start things off on the right foot.

He went to stand by the railing, the cool wind ruffling his hair. Dawn had not yet broken. When once the vast darkness of ocean meeting sky might have triggered feelings of fear and loneliness, now he felt only peace. Much had changed. He'd sold his club last month to Black's new son-in-law; though Percy had protested about his giving up his life's work, he himself had experienced no regret. As he'd told her, handing over the keys to The Underworld had brought a feeling of freedom. Hope. With love as his compass, he knew his life was headed in the right direction.

"Why didn't you wake me?" Percy's voice reached him from behind, making his lips curl. "We're supposed to watch the first sunrise together."

He pulled her close. "You were sleeping so soundly, love. I didn't want to wake you. Not to worry—you haven't missed a thing."

"That's good because I want to get every detail down. A romantic view of daybreak over the ocean is just what I need for my next novel," she said.

"Greedy chit," he teased. "Isn't it enough that *The Perils of Priscilla* is flying off the shelves? Already onto the next book, are you?"

"I can't help it," she said ruefully. "I have so much inspiration these days that the words seem to write themselves. It seems that though Priscilla is *Miss* Farnham no more, she has plenty of adventure to come." She gave him a flirtatious look from her beneath her lashes. "'Tis one of the benefits of being the wife of a scoundrel."

He chuckled. "I'll keep that in mind, buttercup."

"Speaking of adventures," she said, fiddling with a button on his jacket, "I think we're due for another one soon."

"I hope Greece lives up to your expectations," he said. They'd postponed their wedding trip until after the sale of his club and the publication of Percy's novel. Now they would finally have six uninterrupted weeks together… alone. Unable to help himself, he leaned down and kissed her ear.

"I'm sure our vacation will be lovely. But that's not the adventure I'm referring to." She wriggled away to look at him. "When we get back to London, we'll be having a visitor."

"Your mama? Not to worry," he said confidently. "She's getting used to me."

"Mama adores you, and you know it. Ever since you recruited her to help with your school for foundlings, she practically sings your praises. She's got her sewing circle working on the uniforms already."

With the club gone, he'd had to decide what to do with the urchins. Training them in a trade had seemed the best investment. Construction would soon be completed on the large property he'd purchased just outside Covent Garden. Within those walls, children of the rookery would find a safe haven, a place to learn and to flourish.

"Mama says you're a steadying influence on me," Percy continued, and he hid a grin at the way she wrinkled her nose. "But she's not the visitor I'm referring to."

Unable to resist, he kissed his wife's pert little appendage. "Who, then?" God Almighty, she smelled fine. He figured that after the sunrise, he would steer her back to their cabin…

"Well, I can't be sure. Other than to say he or she will be arriving in… seven months, give or take?"

It took a moment for her words to sink in. He stared at her blushing cheeks, the vivid sparkle in her eyes. "You mean… you and I… we're going to…?"

She nodded. When he continued to gawk at her, speechless, she said a bit nervously, "Are you alright? I know there's already a lot of change ahead, what with you selling the club and coming aboard with Nick and—"

"Love, I'm more than *alright*." Gazing down at her, he felt emotion clog his throat. "You've already brought me more happiness than any man has a right to. Because of you, I'm no longer alone. And now this, to share more together..." He cupped her precious face in his palms. "Don't you know, Percy? You are everything to me."

"And you're my hero, Gavin. The adventure I've waited for all my life," his wife said with glowing eyes. "Every moment with you is my happy ending."

They missed the sunrise. Dazzled by love's glorious rays, they didn't even notice.

**Please enjoy a peek at
Grace's other books...**

The *Mayhem in Mayfair* series

Book 1: *Her Husband's Harlot*
How far will a wallflower go to win her husband's love? When her disguise as a courtesan backfires, Lady Helena finds herself entangled in a game of deception and desire with her husband Nicholas, the Marquess of Harteford... and discovers that he has dark secrets of his own.

Book 2: *Her Wanton Wager*
To what lengths will a feisty miss go to save her family from ruin? Miss Persephone Fines takes on a wager of seduction with notorious gaming hell owner Gavin Hunt and discovers that love is the most dangerous risk of all.

Book 3: *Her Protector's Pleasure*
Wealthy widow Lady Marianne Draven will stop at nothing to find her kidnapped daughter. Having suffered betrayal in the past, she trusts no man—and especially not Thames River Policeman Ambrose Kent, who has a few secrets of his own. Yet fiery passion ignites between the unlikely pair as they battle a shadowy foe. Can they work together to save Marianne's daughter? And will nights of pleasure turn into a love for all time?

Book 4: *Her Prodigal Passion*
Sensible Miss Charity Sparkler has been in love with Paul Fines, her best friend's brother, for years. When he accidentally compromises her, they find themselves wed in haste. Can an ugly duckling recognize her own beauty and a reformed rake his own value? As secrets of the past lead to present dangers, will this marriage of convenience transform into one of love?

The *Heart of Enquiry* series

Prequel Novella: ***The Widow Vanishes***
Fate throws beautiful widow Annabel Foster into the arms of William McLeod, her enemy's most ruthless soldier. When an unexpected and explosive night of passion ensues, she must decide: should she run for her life—or stay for her heart?

Book 1: ***The Duke Who Knew Too Much***
When Miss Emma Kent witnesses a depraved encounter involving the wicked Duke of Strathaven, her honor compels her to do the right thing. But steamy desire challenges her quest for justice, and she and Strathaven must work together to unravel a dangerous mystery ... before it's too late.

Book 2: ***M is for Marquess***
With her frail constitution improving, Miss Dorothea Kent yearns to live a full and passionate life. Desire blooms between her and Gabriel Ridgley, the Marquess of Tremont, an enigmatic widower with a disabled son. But the road to love proves treacherous as Gabriel's past as a spy emerges to threaten them both... and they must defeat a dangerous enemy lying in wait.

Book 3: ***The Lady Who Came in from the Cold***
Former spy Pandora Hudson gave up espionage for love. Twelve years later, her dark secret rises to threaten her blissful marriage to Marcus, Marquess of Blackwood, and she must face her most challenging mission yet: winning back the heart of the only man she's ever loved.

Book 4: ***The Viscount Always Knocks Twice***
Sparks fly when feisty hoyden Violet Kent and proper

gentleman Richard Murray, Viscount Carlisle, meet at a house party. Yet their forbidden passion and blossoming romance are not the only adventures afoot. For a guest is soon discovered dead—and Violet and Richard must join forces to solve the mystery and protect their loved ones... before the murderer strikes again.

Book 5: *Never Say to an Earl*
Wallflower Polly Kent and Sinjin Pelham, the wild Earl of Revelstoke, believe they have naught in common, yet both have secrets to hide. Tempestuous passion and a dangerous enemy bring the two together; will their secrets keep them apart?

The *Chronicles of Abigail Jones* series

Book 1: *Abigail Jones*
When destiny brings shy Victorian maid Abigail Jones into the home of the brooding and enigmatic Earl of Huxton, she discovers forbidden passion ... and a dangerous world of supernatural forces.

About the Author

Grace Callaway's debut novel, *Her Husband's Harlot*, was a Romance Writers of America® Golden Heart® Finalist and went on to become a National #1 Bestselling Regency Romance. Since then, the books in her *Mayhem in Mayfair* and *Heart of Enquiry* series have landed on multiple national and international bestselling lists. She's received top-starred reviews from *Love Romance Passion*, *Bitten by Paranormal Romance*, and *Nightowl Reviews*, amongst others.

Grace grew up on the Canadian prairies battling mosquitoes and freezing temperatures. She made her way south to earn a Ph.D. in Psychology at the University of Michigan. She thought writing a dissertation was difficult until she started writing a book; she thought writing a book was challenging until she became a mom. She's learned that the greater the effort, the sweeter the rewards. Currently, she and her family live in California, where their adventures include remodeling a ramshackle house, exploring the great outdoors, and sampling local artisanal goodies.

Grace loves to hear from her readers and can be reached at grace@gracecallaway.com

Other ways to connect:
Newsletter: www.gracecallaway.com/newsleter
Facebook: www.facebook.com/GraceCallawayBooks
Website: www.gracecallaway.com

Made in the USA
San Bernardino, CA
29 January 2019